RISE

of

ORION

Also by Rachel O'Laughlin

———

SERENGARD SERIES

Coldness of Marek

Knights of Rilch

Rise of Orion

Blood of Ashlin

RACHEL O'LAUGHLIN

RISE

of

ORION

the T H I R D in the
SERENGARD SERIES

DUBLIN MIST PRESS

MAINE

This book is a work of fiction. Names, characters, places, and incidents are either products of the author's imagination or are used fictitiously. Any resemblance to actual persons, living or dead, events, or locales is entirely coincidental.

First Edition. December 2014.
Published by Dublin Mist Press, Newport, Maine.
Printed in the United States of America and the United Kingdom.

www.rachelolaughlin.com

ISBN: 978-0-9849194-5-1
e-Book ISBN: 978-0-9849194-6-8

Rise of orion : Serengard, book three / by Rachel O'Laughlin

1. Fiction—Fantasy—Epic

Library of Congress Control Number: 2014955819

Edited by Rebecca A. Weston.
Original Watercolor and Pencil Artwork Copyright © 2014 by Dan Tare. All Rights Reserved.

FOR MY ONE —

if I had a genie in a bottle...

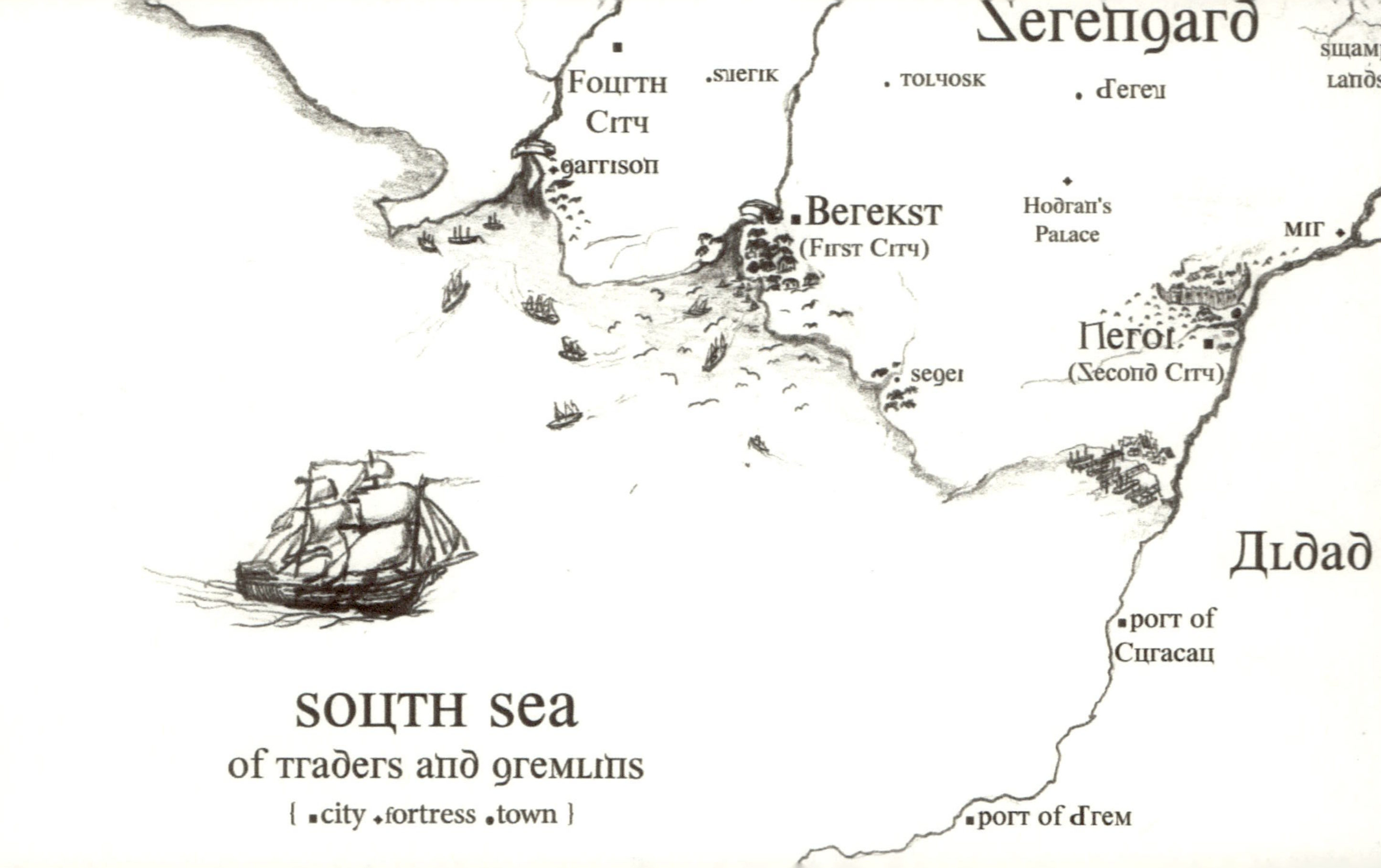
Xerengard
swamp lands
Fourth City
garrison
snerik
tolvosk
deren
Berekst
(First City)
Hodran's Palace
Mir
Neror
(Second City)
segei
Drdad
port of Curacau
port of drem
SOUTH sea
of traders and gremlins
{ city fortress town }

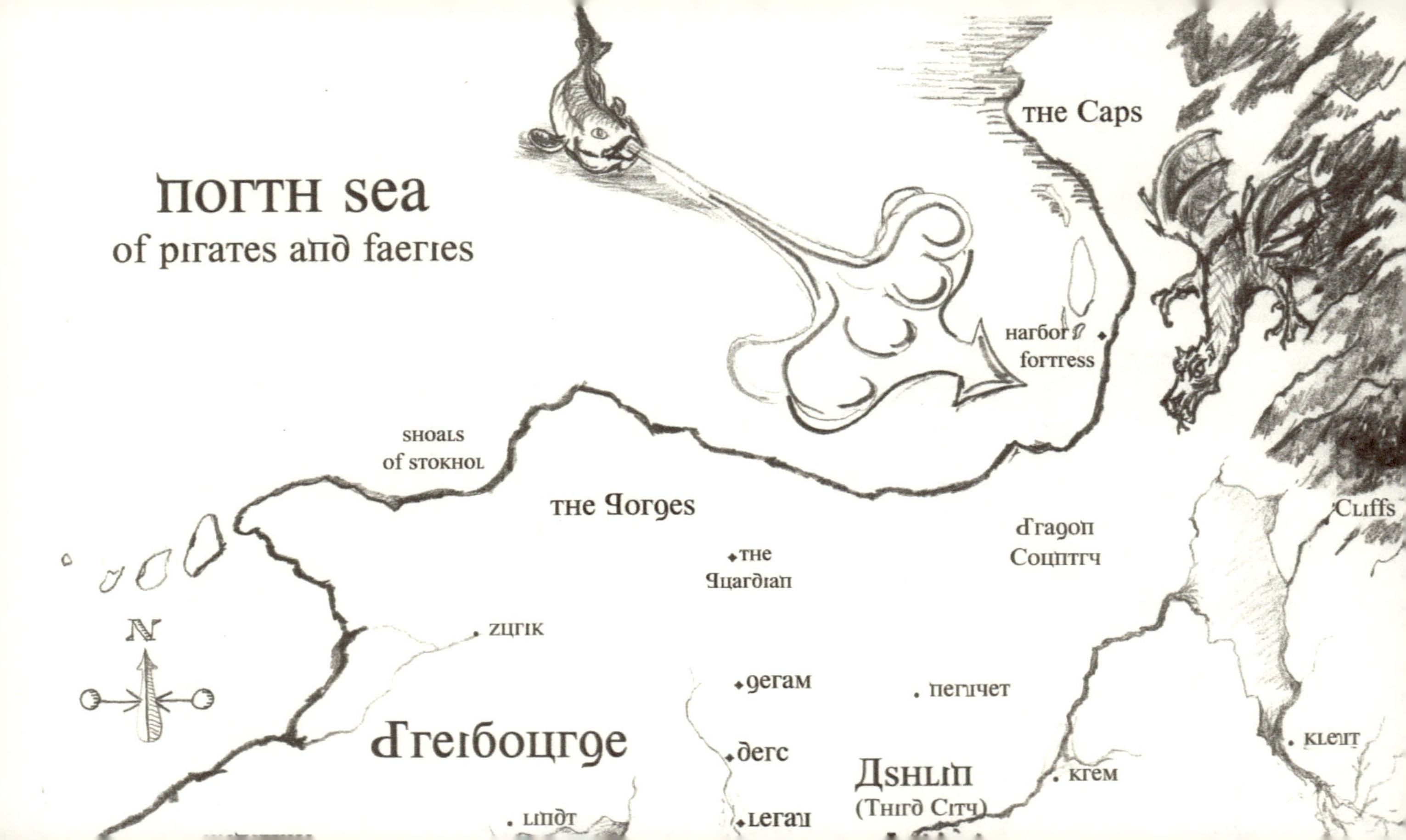

north sea
of pirates and faeries
the Caps
shoals of stokhol
the Gorges
the Guardian
dragon Country
harbor fortress
Cliffs
zurik
geram
derc
leran
lindt
penchet
krem
klen
Dshlin (Third City)
dreibourge
N

Tнε Recεпt Kiпgs

the past two hundred years as measured by the Serengard Orions

---

Ⅲαгεκ

Ruled for 7 years

Καгαмоι

Ruled for 21 years

♂εгει ɪɪɪ

Ruled for 36 years

Таме

Ruled for 34 years

Cαιцм

Ruled for 19 years

Дιтгιπ

Ruled for 42 years

Ιzαппαн

Ruled for 36 years

Ρεтгоιαι

Ruled for 24 years

The Emperors

enstated at the rise of The Four Cities

Kovim

an advisor from King Petrolai's council

ruled for 9 years and killed by Lord Marek

Uekst

one of Hodran's force during the Border Wars

and trusted military advisor to Kovim

{1}
Нощ

In the Fourth City of the Seren Empire.
In the 4th year of Emperor Vekst.

MIKEL KNEW THE SOUND OF each set of footsteps outside his cell—the speed, the heaviness, the footwear gave them away. This set of feet he didn't know. Light footfalls on soft leather soles. Behind them came the clack of the guards' metal shoes and, finally, Trzl's silk boots.

They stopped at the entrance to the cell on his right. The lock lifted, the body with the leather soles was thrown in, and then the door closed. There was mumbling, the sound of the guards conferring, the flicker of light outside the grate. He didn't hear Trzl's voice.

Mikel had candles in his cell, but he rarely lit them. He preferred the irksome inkiness. It reminded him of the ship he'd been on, reminded him he was a prisoner—something the chains on his ankles could make him forget.

The latch to his own door lifted, and the light became obnoxiously bright.

He had two rooms. The front room held a small bench; the other, where he was now, had a bed with a full mammoth skin on it. There was no furniture in the two cells next to him, and mammoth skin was rare and expensive, fit for a prince. It bothered him whenever he thought of it.

Trzl's footsteps came around the corner, and then her face was there—sharp, vivid features accented by heavy eye paint and a new combination of braids that pulled the hair up and away. Severe, if ever she was.

"Avoiding my presence?" Her mouth twitched. The light at her back made her shadow against the wall rather foreboding.

Mikel shook his head, but he hadn't a decent reply.

"I am not as frightful as all that, am I?"

"The last time I saw you, Colstadt was taken to another building for questioning. It's been a month, and he hasn't returned." He looked up at her through hair that fell into his eyes. "Tell me, are you frightful?"

Trzl took three steps toward him. He leaned back until his head hit the wall above his bed, and she stopped moving. "I only kept him near you because you were worried about him. Once his wound was healed, it was indulgent to spoil you with his company. You should understand the pressure I am under."

Mikel bit the inside of his mouth, his eyes down.

"No need to be sullen, Mikel. I didn't hurt him."

"I'll believe that when I see him."

Trzl tossed her head and sat down on his bed. "Your food is here. I'm sorry, but you can't have a knife today."

"Why should anything change today?" He smiled slightly, but she made no explanation. "Is it pheasant again?"

She slid her hand across the mammoth fur, and her fingers grazed his elbow. He winced. Trzl was the only person who'd touched him since they came here four months ago. As much as he pretended to hate her company, he looked forward to it as he would a strong cup of arabica. Only she never thought to bring him one.

He stood abruptly, slid out from under her arm.

Her gaze followed him until he had left the room, then she took a few steps and leaned against the doorway. "Do I make you nervous?"

Mikel shrugged, took the food from the guard without lingering, and walked back to the wall. He perched on the bench with one leg sprawled in front and the other half-bent beside him. "I do find myself wondering what you're doing here."

"I came to bring a new prisoner and thought I'd see how you were getting on."

Mikel set his plate of food down. "You should have brought ale if you wanted to reminisce."

She walked to him, picked up his leg, and moved it out of her way so that she could sit next to him. "My apologies. I did forget the ale."

There was a quirk to her mouth, as if she knew a secret that made her laugh. Whatever it was, she certainly should not share it. They were, after all, deep in the belly of the Fourth City—a modern atrocity on the ancient soil of Serengard. He'd been brought here with a mask over his eyes, guarded by twelve men, and kept under sporadic watch.

Trzl was the granddaughter of one of the most powerful men in the world, second only to the Emperor; Mikel was the son of the dead king she'd helped overthrow. They were supposed to be enemies.

"Did you give Colstadt pheasant today as well?"

Trzl let out her breath in a huff. "Must you speak of him? I'm tired of hearing his name."

"Then free him. He presents no danger to you. Keep Pier if you must."

"I cannot free political prisoners unless they give me something that warrants it, and nothing Colstadt has told me has meant enough to tempt the Emperor."

Mikel knew she was playing him. Colstadt wouldn't tell her anything at all.

"Oh, come now," she said. "You cannot induce me to move him back here. I won't have you consorting with my imprisoned Drei, Orion, not since I've begun questioning. The three of you might prop up each other's lies."

She leaned a shoulder against his, and he didn't move away. Her eyes were dreamy, and while that was better than distant, he was never sure what to do with her in this state. She twirled a finger around a strand of hair and looked at him with a slight pout.

"You haven't touched your bread," she scolded him.

Mikel stared at the wall. "I'll eat it later."

"The mice may claim it if you leave it unguarded."

He lifted the bread between two fingers. "If I return this to you, will you give a double ration to my knights?"

She let out a half-laugh. "Mikel, they are not your knights anymore. They are my prisoners, the same as you are. I give them favors, and someone may begin to think I am in love with one of them." She laughed, but he didn't think it was funny. "Mikel, you... You should eat the bread. I swear they are looked after."

"I saw fresh bruises on Pier."

"I never meant for you to pass him in the hall." Her brow furrowed. "But I am sure the Drei can handle pain far better than you."

"But I am the one who has been chained in cages before."

"For true?" Her jaw went slack, and her eyes grew suspicious. "You must tell."

Mikel leaned his head back and looked at the rough, unpolished marble of the floor above him. "Forget I spoke of it."

"No, please, I am intrigued." Trzl put a hand to his cheek. "Did someone lock you up and hurt you? Is that why you don't trust me? You should know I would never do that. I would never hurt you."

Mikel flinched away from her. "Don't make false promises, faerie."

She perked up. "Is that why you locked me up in the Castle of Marek? Some kind of lesson to teach me?"

He set his half-empty plate on the floor and stood, just to get away from her. "You should know me a damn sight better than that by now."

She ignored him and tipped her head invitingly. "Well?"

"Is knowing this truly going to aid you in your cause? Because I feel as if I am on trial for a position in your wretched kingdom."

She laughed gently, the dark blue makeup around her eyes crinkling and almost looking soft. "Oh, no need to fear for the stability of your prison stay. I won't read your thoughts, Mikel."

"You always tried to."

"I never succeeded. You're a mystery to me, as always."

"That is a Dermed lie. I was a simple mark to you from the first moment we met in the Derev Theatre. At last you have me quite truly eating out of your hand."

Trzl recoiled, but her eyes snapped with victory. She must have wanted him to say it—to admit defeat. *Treacher.* She stood and walked to him, sliding her fingers up his chest and into his hair. "I've heard there's only one woman who's succeeded in bringing you to this state before."

He let out a bitter laugh. "I know how desperate you are to make me trust you. Believe me, talking about her will not help."

"What do you want, then? Mead? Wine? Something to drown it all out? I'll give you whatever you want to unhinge your tongue."

"Would Otreya pursue this line of questioning? Somehow, I feel it would conflict with his interests. Perhaps that is why you must corner me in my cell."

"No, he wouldn't care that you've made a regular gremlin of yourself down here. You aren't even sleeping. If I can help—"

"I haven't slept well in years. Don't flatter yourself by thinking you can do a thing about it." He stared into nothing for a moment, and she was surprisingly quiet. He let out a heavy breath and whispered, "There are some things I will never tell you for fear your mind touching them would taint them forever."

"Soon enough you'll realize I am your only friend, Mikel Orion. Even those Drei of yours merely follow you because you are the tallest and mightiest Seren they've ever seen."

That rankled him so deeply that, for a moment, he wanted to strangle her. He blinked, banished that desire with a fist pressed into the wall. "You'd best leave."

Trzl laughed, sounding slightly mad. "You'll call for me soon enough."

The door clanged shut, the tumblers of the locks fell in place, and the footsteps echoed back down the passageway. Mikel kept his hand against the wall. Scars from the Border Wars merged with scars from taking Romianz's ship for Trzl. If she was the one constant in his life, she was the bane that chased him, tortured him, seduced him with earthly pleasure. He couldn't name the number of times he'd wanted her. It wasn't her body; it was the sheer power she portrayed, the dazzling, endless confidence. It made her as attractive as cool water on a hot day or a warm fire on a cold one. And right now, he was lonely enough to want to touch that power, feel it through and through.

"I thought Mikel Orion was dead."

Mikel jumped, nearly running into the wall. At first, it felt as if the voice was inside his head, but he knew it wasn't.

"Are you some secret she's been keeping?" The voice was coming from the other cell through the grate at his feet.

Mikel didn't bother to kneel next to it; he was loud enough, thanks to the mood he was in. "Whoever you are, I'm sure she meant for you to hear that."

"No doubt." The voice betrayed its owner to be a woman, probably young. "Is it always so dark here?"

Mikel shrugged, but of course she couldn't see him. He felt slightly repentant for using a rough tone with her when it was Trzl he was angry with. "Do you want my candles? I don't use them."

There was a scuffle, and then came the soft sound of fingers scraping against the iron bars between their cells.

He tipped his head toward her in the dark. "Send me word when you decide."

"Orion. You're not really him. You couldn't be him. He wouldn't have left Ashlin and all of us alone at the border. Unless they kept you locked up all this time? Why would they do that?"

Perhaps that would have been better. "Just what do you think you know about it?"

"More than you, it would seem. My father fought in the wars."

"Of course," Mikel said with a ragged laugh. "Why else would you be a prisoner now?"

There was silence on the other side of the grate between cells, and then the sound of a tankard being drained and bread cracking as it was torn.

"I'd go easy on that food," he said. "No promises she will feed you as well as she feeds me."

"Oh? It does sound as if she has a weakness for you. I'll simply make you share." There was mischief in the words, but behind it was a tremor of fear. "Your accent is that of a Drei."

"For true? If you could see me, you would know I've not a trace of Drei in my blood."

"I *could* see you if you would light a candle. These grates are as long as my body."

"I offered to share the candles, not to show you my face."

She let out a breath that sounded annoyed. "Well enough." He heard her bite her bread again. "Does she think you know where her son is?"

Mikel cleared his throat. It went further than that. Her son was his son—not in blood, but in spirit. The boy was more his than he would ever be hers again. *She doesn't* think *I know. She* knows *I know.*

He knelt next to the grate, shoulder against the wall. He slid a candle through, felt her fingers grasp it in the darkness, and then scratched a flint against the stone floor, holding a piece of straw close to it.

"She wants me for much more than locating a boy."

The girl inhaled sharply. "Well, that is all I am here for."

A spark hopped to the dry straw and set it smoldering. Mikel blew gently on it until it became a flame, and then he handed it to her through the bars. A few moments, and there was a steady flicker in her cell.

"I'm grateful."

He almost winced at the simple words. "You needn't be. I would have shared with a mouse."

She replied in a quiet, timid voice. "Do her claws drag in your skin so much that you must drag yours in mine?"

Mikel ground his teeth. The back of his neck hurt.

"How long have you been here?" she asked.

"Four months."

"Four months is nothing. Where were you before that?"

He couldn't tell her. "Under rocks."

"Hiding?"

Keeping others hidden. "Staying alive."

"You know why these cages have grates between them? So we'll share, 'feel human.' Speak and trust each other. And then, when next they torture you, you'll tell them everything they want to know about me and I'll tell them everything they want to know about you."

Mikel smiled. "Fortunately, my lips are sealed as tight as a crypt and you needn't worry."

"Good because I don't want to be beaten for your secrets, especially if you have as many as you imply."

Something hard caught in his throat. "Has she beaten you?"

There was silence. He could hear her breathing, the sound echoing off of the walls. "Yes."

"How?"

"Water, on my face. She said next time she would..."

"Would what?"

"I don't want to talk about it."

"What did she want to know?"

The girl let out a half-laugh. "See, this is what I meant when I said we should not share secrets."

"I didn't ask for your answer. I asked for her request."

The girl slid her candle right next to the grate and brought her face down where he could see it. "She wants to know where my brother is. She told me he is a spy for her, and he disappeared around the time my father died in battle. Four months ago."

He was transfixed for a moment by her features in the flickering candlelight. There was nothing notable about them—classic Seren skin the color of dead grass, deep brown hair and eyes nearly golden—but she looked familiar somehow. His heart started to race. "Why does she want your brother?"

"I've shown you my face. The least you could do is show me yours."

"I have to know why she wants him. There is more than your brother's life at stake."

"Because of her son? You are quite obvious, using such a tactic. You didn't even give me a moment to trust you before you as much as asked me for a drop of my heart's blood. If I've learned anything in the years I've been in and out of these halls, it's to always pretend to know more than I do. It makes you more valuable. Value is everything."

Her jaw. Her jaw and her nose and that widow's peak. Romianz. "Your father didn't die in battle. Otreya had him killed for aiding me. I was in the room when they did it."

Her mouth opened and closed several times before words formed. "You...you would claim such a thing—that he was helping you—so that I would want to do the same. You don't even know my name."

"I know he had two daughters. Is that why you've been here before? Because your father was the haven knight..." He closed his eyes for a moment. "I've seen your face once before." When she didn't answer, he reached into the grate and pulled her candle back through, letting the light fall on his scars and half-beard and shoulders far too muscular to be Drei. "You won't recognize me no matter how hard you try."

"How do you... You know me? You pretend to. I never..." Her brow pulled together in a tight bunch, and her neck flinched. "Your armor was covered in blood. You were tall, and you frightened me just a little."

"Not as much as you frightened me."

Her head started to shake, and her eyes clouded. "Then which are you? Are you Lomius? Or are you..."

"I'm shadows of both of them, I imagine, but right now I am neither of them. Call me whichever you choose."

"Julian banished you." She reached through the bars and ran a hand along his rough cheek. "Where *were* you?"

part one
Дıдад

Oh, that the desert were my dwelling place,

With one fair spirit for my minister,

That I might all forget the human race,

And, hating no one, love but only her.

— Lord Byron

{2}
Theπ

At the port of Cherov, west of Berekst.

Fourteen years ago, in the 2nd year of Emperor Kovim.

MIKEL DIDN'T FLINCH WHEN THE Elloyan slave trader slapped him in irons. If anything, he was relieved to be finally free of the heavy fetters that had kept him shackled to his sword this past year.

Kierstaz was tossed in next to him, her anklets chained to the floor beside his. Fury was still all over her face. It hadn't waned in the two weeks it had taken them to slip down to the coast, avoiding roads and towns and any set of eyes that might recognize the marks of a soldier.

Mikel leaned toward his sister, unable to keep the sarcasm from dripping from his miserable words. "This what you wanted?"

The creaking of the hull masked his whisper, but it hardly mattered. They were the only people in the hold. Slave traders picked up most of their cargo on islands and in remote villages, not at crowded ports where they were likely to be boarded and searched by the Border Guard. Slave trade was supposed to be illegal. Although, that must have changed, mustn't it? The slave trade could be flourishing in broad daylight for all he knew.

Kierstaz hissed back at him, "Does it look like it?"

He raised a hand, and his chain clanked. "I would have gone to the Caps or the far east. Don't complain to me because you wanted to be a slave."

"Ric said the Desert was a good place."

"I've always trusted Desert folk, but you? As princess of the realm, you found them senseless and ill-bred. Those were your exact words."

Kierstaz colored up to the roots of her hair. Well, at least she still knew how to be embarrassed. "I don't... I meant in matters of rule. They have no king, no authority. It drives me mad."

"Still... Ill-bred?"

Kierstaz shrugged. "Well..."

"And now you want them to own you? Beat you when you misbehave?"

"You are the reason we are here, Mikel. I would never have given up my sword. You made me."

Mikel knew he should feel sorry for what he'd done, but he didn't. Neither one of them would still be breathing if he hadn't surrendered to the Drei. Hodran wasn't going to stand for an uprising at the border. "Pier will keep your sword."

Kierstaz lifted her nose. "Pier. He doesn't care about us."

"I beg to differ."

"How?"

Mikel shifted. He didn't really want to tell her that Pier had sworn to be at the northern border of Aldad a year from their parting with a force of warriors. She would be angry that he'd shared their destination or, worse, get ideas in her head about striking at the interior when they clearly had no grip there.

"No one cares for us, Mikel, not even you. I saw you the morning we gave Derc over to Julian's son. You *smiled.* With Ric not cold in his grave."

"I'm sure *he* would be pleased with your stubbornness."

Kierstaz ground her teeth. "Much good it does me. I can't even command my own captains. Can't save my own men."

Mikel swallowed. He couldn't handle the hurt that pulsed into him at her words, so he ignored them. He already didn't sleep at night—couldn't feel anything in his chest—because of the things he'd done and the knights he'd lost to preserve her kingdom. She was all he had in the world. Could she blame him for protecting her the only way he knew how? Trying to hold the Border another summer would have been suicide.

In the back of his head was the nagging knowledge that her death would mean the birthright fell solely to him. A birthright he might be suited to but could never desire.

"To the Derm with all of it," he growled softly.

"Forgive me if I do not share the sentiment."

"We are going to be on this ship for nearly a moon, I wager. You'll probably see things as I do by the time we are drowned by our unhappy multans."

Kierstaz rolled her eyes. "You would rather be a soulless minion for a Drei general? Or fodder for Hodran's new dungeons?"

"I would rather be left alone in a hovel, not sold to the highest bidder."

She glared at him. "You could have said."

"No, it was your choice. You're the one, Kiers. You always were." He scuffed at the worn oak beneath them. "I often wish I was born without the blood of our parents."

Kierstaz shuddered. "Don't say that."

"It's the truth."

"What could you possibly want enough to be so selfish?"

If he said it out loud, it would sound shallow and childish, but he wanted it. So badly he'd burned with the need for it every moment since he'd left Ashlin. "I wanted a family."

Kierstaz didn't laugh, but that was probably because she was still furious with him. "You wanted to marry some deluded little village woman and make spawn?"

"No." She didn't know the half of it. That he'd almost run away and made love to the very breath of the rebellion because she was intoxicating and beautiful and he'd thought she loved him. The very name *Trzl* haunted his brain. Every moment, in the back of his head, a taunting, twisted word of hers would tug at his memory and pull on him. Even now, in the hold of a slave ship, shackled to the floor, the revenge she'd inflicted made his skin simmer and his eyes smart. He couldn't shake her. "It doesn't matter. I'm not that kind of man anymore."

♆

MIKEL GOT HIS FIRST FACEFUL of Desert sand the instant they stepped off the dock. Arms as strong as his pulled him down into the salty granules and removed the iron cuffs on his wrists, only to replace them with heavy cord. The sky was so bright with sun it could hardly be called blue.

A heavyset Elloyan dragged him toward an awning with a fire beneath it, a metal worker kneeling beside the flames. His back was bronze, his shoulders were covered in ink, and his hair was long and tousled, but his skin was Seren.

Mikel tossed his head to try to find Kierstaz, but he couldn't see her. Not before his face was shoved onto a brick and a steel awl pierced his ear. It surprised him, but he didn't flinch, not even when a hot, gold ring was strung through it and he could smell his own burning flesh.

He was pushed to the ground again, right next to his sister. Her ear was bloody, but she was smiling slightly. More Elloyans came toward them, their varied garb colorful and snapping in the breeze. He hadn't seen a Desert man yet. Maybe they hadn't even landed in Aldad. Could be they made shore at an encampment of Elloyans, although their people weren't known to stay in one place much longer than they had to.

The Elloyan trader had a crew of strong, fit lackeys who herded them up the beach and into the outskirts of some sort of city. All at once, they were surrounded with dark-skinned folk of every shade, clad in intense, deep, vibrant hues Seren dyes were incapable of capturing—yellows and oranges and sapphires mixed with browns and scarlets. Nothing was orderly. Traders set up their wares in haphazard fashion, seemingly wherever they pleased.

Mikel didn't realize he was being bid for until a bearded Desert man grabbed his mouth roughly to check his teeth.

"Fighter," one of the Elloyan crew told the man in Aldadi.

The man smacked Mikel's chest with the back of his hand a few times. "Hmph. My father doesn't need another fighter. His are the best in the port." He looked to his left, down the line...at Kierstaz. "This one. I could use another boy to carry water."

The Elloyan replied in a singsong, guttural tone that Mikel knew well but hadn't heard in a while. "A woman, but strong. She can carry water with the best of them."

"A woman?" He raised an eyebrow and grabbed Kierstaz roughly by the arm. His other hand reached for her breasts, slid over them more than once, then inside her clothes, running the length of her body. Mikel saw her bite her lip. He dug his fingernails into his palms to control the blood that pulsed hotly in his neck.

The Desert man flicked his hand flippantly. "What an ugly girl. Just having her around would make me vomit."

Mikel let a breath out. He waited until the man moved on before he stole a glance at his sister. Her brow was puzzled and nervous. She didn't understand their language. Mikel nodded once, but he wasn't certain what he was reassuring her of. The next purchaser did the same— pressed on Mikel's chest and ran his hands over Kierstaz's body—but at least he was brief.

"She's solid. I'll pay. But I don't need a fighter. You should try the lands to the south."

The Elloyan shrugged. "They are brother and sister."

"But what can they do? If they are both fighters, you should take them south."

Kierstaz looked over at Mikel with a petition in her eyes. So she wanted to be owned by this one, did she? Could be the best they got.

"I'm not a fighter. I'm a metal worker," Mikel said. Truth be told, he had never more than shod a horse and tempered a sword, but he had done it a million times.

Without hesitation, the Desert man backslapped Mikel with a strip of leather. It hurt but just barely. "You speak our language? Does she?" He grabbed Kierstaz's wrist and twisted it.

Damn. Not an hour here and they already knew they could control him by hurting her. *A fine plan, Kierstaz.* "No."

"Good. I would claw my eyeballs out with two insolent bastards. I'll take them both, at least for the day. Could use them in the mines. Five hundred in silver."

They were tossed onto an oxcart that was already jammed with seven other half-clad Seren bodies. Kierstaz brought her knees up to her face and peered out between her legs with wide eyes. It was not lost on Mikel that not one of the other slaves was female. The cart started to move and jostle.

Once there was enough noise, Kierstaz leaned toward Mikel and whispered, "How did he know we were siblings?"

"I told him when we boarded."

"If Hodran searches for us together..."

"No one will look here. That's why you chose it."

"But—"

"The sacred bond of a sibling is held in high esteem. Families equal tribes to them, and anyone who has not married out of their tribe or started their own is bound to the others by blood covenant." *Blood* and *covenant* together made his spine ripple. It sounded ominous. He lowered his voice still more. "If they split us up, I may never find you again. At least together we have a chance of escaping if we ever need to."

"You think they will keep us together? For true?"

"I hope."

Kierstaz shifted her shoulders and raised her voice so that the others in the cart could hear her. "They won't try to rape me, will they? Because that would be bloody." She was smirking, but Mikel didn't think it was funny.

He cleared his throat and ignored the confused looks she had attracted. "I know they think it is shameful and beneath them to lie with a white woman. That's why that kind of slavery is only common in the far east. Or in the halls of corrupt kings."

The cart stopped abruptly. Mikel was pulled down, but the rest of them left. A rough arm pushed on him at a double pace across a dusty strip of street flanked by stalls and into a dark building. For a moment, he could see nothing aside from a fire in the corner—not a wood fire, but one from crystal ore. Mined in the southeast of Aldad, no trader ever brought it north and no one in Serengard knew how to find or recreate it. Whether it even came out of the mine in such a state or was refined by mad Desert science, the Serens did not know.

Once his eyes adjusted to the dimness, Mikel could see dark faces, some of them almost as black as night. He'd never seen skin that color among the Aldadi field hands and horse traders, and his awe was likely stamped all over his face. There was an especially tall man covered in light fabric—either linen or silk—and draped with jewelry studded with stones at every point. He looked Mikel's body over with a scrutiny that made him shift.

"You are a metal worker?"

Mikel looked down and became aware that his own arms, torso, and middle were built to capacity—likely from the action of using a sword for hours a day while weighted down with steel armor, not to mention swinging on and off of a horse constantly when speed was of utmost importance. He had not noticed any change, partially because he seldom undressed completely and partially because he'd always trained hard.

Mikel met the man's stare with one of equal intensity. "Yes."

The beard rose with his chin. "Show me."

Mikel walked to the fire and picked up the tools. They fit in his hands like they'd been made for him. "You have a flat piece of metal?" He tried to sound nonchalant, but inside he was afraid that Kierstaz was disappearing outside—sold, manhandled, or merely dispersed to a place he wouldn't be able to find. He didn't even know which port they had docked in.

"He speaks Aldadi, Ladin?" A younger voice said the words, but Mikel did not glance up. *Ladin. My owner's name is Ladin. The tall man with the silk and jewelry.*

A rough piece of steel was handed to him. It heated easily and took only a few minutes to turn red. A ghost of a smile played on his face as the hot metal turned light orange. So swift, like boiling a pot of water. As soon as it neared white, he drew it from the fire and placed it on the anvil. He was quite bad at it, yet the men watched him intently, as if he were performing a grandiose play of fire and steel. The rugged, curved blade he produced was dull and chunky.

"It needs sharpening. You have a whetstone?"

Ladin raised his eyebrows, but he turned to the one who'd pushed Mikel inside and said, "Get him what he needs, Tierrof."

Tierrof shrugged and arched a shoulder toward the opposite end of the room. "Sharpen."

Mikel went, but he was sure the sweat on his brow was not from the heat. Everything he did now was for Kierstaz—not for her kingdom, not for the next generation of Orion rule. Those were *her* duties; his was to be her guardian to the end of his days. She had not been gone from his side in three fortnights, and for her to be away longer than a few minutes made the hair prickle on the back of his neck.

Mikel didn't stop grinding until the weapon was sharp. Not as sharp as Seren steel would be but passable. He didn't like the weight of it—it felt too top-heavy for serious use.

"Here." He tossed it to Tierrof.

Ladin reached for it. He didn't seem to care for the weapon in a tactical sense, but he held it up to the light to see it shine. "Can you make finer things? Not only tools, I mean. Gold." He lifted his necklace to make it clear.

Mikel nodded, not sure he should be promising it. He'd overseen more jewelry production than he could name. All of the gold and silver in the kingdom had been slowly sold off, the designs made into molds and forms and recast in nickel, bronze, and copper. "Yes. I can make finer things."

Ladin smacked his hands together and handed the blade back to Mikel. "Ah. We'll take this one."

For a stupid moment, Mikel stared, thinking he meant he would take the blade. It wasn't the worst, but it was hardly suitable as a weapon.

Tierrof nodded approval. "Sell the others before we leave the coast? Serteth wants to make a profit today."

Serteth. Was he the one who had purchased them? "I have a sister outside. Will you take her as well?"

Tierrof snickered. "He says she is his sister. Yet the only girl I saw was different in height and build and chin and forehead."

Mikel grasped at the only likeness that came to mind. "We share a birthmark."

Ladin laughed. "I wonder where. Should Tierrof go check?"

Mikel hesitated. This was something that could be on Hodran's bounty parchments. He had been close enough to notice everything.

"There is a brown fleck in my left eye and in hers."

Tierrof turned back to Mikel with an eyebrow raised. "I believe you. Doesn't mean she is useful for anything, and you are."

"I can work twice as hard and make it worth your trouble."

"You'll work twice as hard, anyway," Tierrof said. "I am in charge of my uncle's slaves, and I will see to it."

Mikel didn't wait to hear more. He pushed past the man and ran out into the street, but the cart full of slaves was gone already. *Treacher.* He turned and grabbed Tierrof, only to be thrown into the dirt by more than one set of hands. He swung wide, hitting someone in the ribs and bringing him down into the dirt next to him. Then he was smacked across the face with something iron.

{3}
Slaves

MIKEL WOKE TO HOT SAND tearing at his shins. The sun baked his skin. He couldn't tell how long he'd been out in it, but he thought he could feel blisters forming. His hands were constrained with something—leather cord. He was being dragged. That's why his legs stung.

Well, that had been singularly foolish of him. Now they wouldn't trust him worth the Derm—if indeed they trusted any white man.

It took a moment to get his legs underneath him, but once he did, the pace was easy. A donkey dragged the travois-like contraption he was tied to, and no one in the huge caravan around him seemed to be in any kind of hurry.

The Desert rippled like water. Mikel could see so far into the distance that the sunset turned into a colorful maze, a zigzag that was confusing to look at. He couldn't see the port anywhere, although the south horizon had a heavy banner of blue across it that must have been the sea.

Tierrof rode up next to him atop a horse that made Mikel's eyes wander. Flanks that were as sleek as they were muscular, a neck that was toned in all the right places, and large, brown eyes that flickered with spirit. He couldn't help but lust after the beauty of the animal.

"You're awake." Tierrof sounded rather jovial.

"I am."

"You understand not to run, now, don't you?"

Mikel would have liked to laugh. Did he? Were Serens so easily beaten? "I had no intention of running."

"No?"

"I want to see my sister."

Tierrof took a flask from his saddle and drank deeply. "You'll see her. Soon enough."

Mikel's forearms tensed against the leather restraint. His temper told him to threaten the man, but he swallowed instead, diverting his eyes. "Are you hurting her?"

Tierrof leaned toward him and nearly growled. "I didn't hear you."

"I said, are you hurting her?"

He tossed his head back and laughed. "Why would you think that? We do not harm our slaves the way you useless, God-hating Serens do. Such savages." He clucked to his horse and disappeared to the back of the line.

Mikel didn't see him again until night when they camped. Tierrof tied him to a stake buried in the hard ground. Behind him was the camp—rather lavish and involved for one night's stay. It was a veritable palace in the middle of the dry, barren desert. Although, this close to the coast, they must only have skimmed the surface of the meaning of "dry."

"You'll stay here for the night. Forgive the bonds—not all of my metal workers have attempted to wrestle me to the ground."

"I am not a rebellious sort, I assure you."

Tierrof's eyes quirked up at the corners. "Oh, all of you are. Running from the heavy hand of fathers or landlords in your sediment-laden hovels, or maybe even filthy, spoiled landowners yourselves, kidnapped and sold for a high price. Always proud until you reach our desert and realize you are incapable of surviving, that the Aldadi are far more strong and lovely and intelligent than your kind." He flashed a grin and left Mikel there.

Fires were lit as the light waned, and more slaves were brought over to the edge of the camp and tied to stakes for the night. No one brought Kierstaz or any women at all. Maybe Tierrof had been skirting the truth when he implied she was with them. All the more reason why he could not waste a moment. He had to find her.

Mikel waited until it was fully dark and then kicked one of the slave owners in the shins as he walked right past him. The nameless Aldadi fell on his back, the breath knocked out of him, and Mikel grabbed him about the neck with his legs, dragging him up close to grip him with an arm.

"Hand me your knife and be quick about it."

The man's hands were occupied trying to release himself from Mikel's grip, but he nodded and wheezed until Mikel eased up. "What do you want with freedom, slave? Your skin is too white for you to find anything but servitude here." He pulled out a knife but did not hand it to him.

"I only want freedom for a moment. For a drink of water." Mikel kept a grip on the man's throat with one arm and reached for the knife with his other hand, then turned it to the inside of the knot. He nicked himself more than once as he sawed on the thick leather. Shadows ran across the fires, but no one seemed concerned about what the slaves might be doing. Mikel released the half-breathing man and rolled away from the stakes and other slaves into the shadows of a tall tent.

All of the dwellings were richly decorated. No way to tell where she might be. If she truly was purchased to water goats, she could be with the animals, but he doubted anyone looking at Kierstaz would think she could haul much water. They'd put her to something like carrying fruit— although, he wagered that Kierstaz would be terrible at that, too.

Perhaps slaves were just an indulgence for richer people. Judging by the fine show of muscle he'd already observed, Desert People did a lot of their own heavy lifting. It was best, of course. Serens used to be that strong, back when they'd farmed all of their own food, before they became lazy and entitled, but progression seemed to have done that on its own. Once there was bounty, artists and tradesmen could sell their brilliance in exchange for it, and someone somewhere got it into their heads that all that was required was to have a tradesman in one's pocket and food would magically appear.

And that was the end. Of food, of bounty, of brilliance. Nothing left at all but tinkerers who were sure to get hungry at some point. Trzl and her folk would have nothing to rebuild on, not unless they started where they should: with their fingers and toes curled in the sopping earth. He already knew Trzl would have none of that. She didn't feel useful unless she was destroying something.

He glanced back once to see how far he'd gone out into the blanket of night. Behind the last row of tents, a few torches bobbed. They moved slowly, as if the men who carried them were half-drunk. Maybe they were. Maybe they weren't even looking for him yet. He started at the closest tent, one made of something rough-spun and hung with tapestries of colors he couldn't see in the dark. There was no breeze to mask his voice, only the raucous laughter of some heavily wine-laden groups of women by the closest campfire.

"Tev," he said softly. It sounded loud. Too loud. He used the name she'd taken for herself as a knight since *Kierstaz* was as uncommon as mammoth skin. He waited a moment, then moved on to the next, crept right up against the wall, and whispered, "Tev."

A few seconds, and he moved on.

Then she was there, skidding softly into the sand beside him, whispering in Seren. "Mikel, you've the whole west end of camp in a scramble."

He breathed better than he had all day. "You're here?"

"Yes."

"Not hurt?"

"No."

"What do they have you doing?"

She wore a robe that looked crimson in the dark. It flowed about her like silk or muslin. Almost queenly. *Poor, dear queen.*

"They're still deciding what I'm good for. Mikel, you shouldn't have come over here. The woman who owns me is as sour as a goblin's tooth and she—"

"Does she beat you?"

Kierstaz shrugged.

"Tev, we can leave."

"No! I want to stay."

"If you are in any kind of trouble, light something on fire. Something that will catch and burn fast. Or anything violent that will attract attention. I'll come find you."

"Mikel, I have to go." She stood and disappeared into the night.

Mikel felt stupid for a moment and then moved back in the direction he'd come until he reached the edge of camp and ran up against a herd of cattle. There was a trough of water that must have been drawn recently. He dunked his sunburned face in and drank. He would have thought the water here would be stale and rank, but it was cool and vibrant as he ran it through his fingertips.

He drew back just as a knife came across his throat and a husky voice said, "Back to your place, slave."

Mikel suppressed his instinct to grab the knife and slam the body into the sand. He turned around, his hands spread. "I sought only a drink of water."

The Desert man grunted. "You Seren lot are all such weaklings." He pulled a whip from his belt and dealt him a quick stripe across his bare shoulder. Mikel had always wondered what that felt like. It stung much like the bite of a shallow scratch, and he almost laughed. That was no wound.

Two more men appeared and dragged Mikel by his heels until they reached an open space. The tents were arranged in a half-moon around a cluster of fires in the middle. Up close, he could see groupings—young women giggling together, older men boring each other, the middle-aged mixing, and the children running about. If they had classes, he couldn't see them.

"Tierrof, isn't this one of your uncle's new lot?" the one who'd dragged him said.

Tierrof spat out a breath, and a mouthful of wine came with it. "He's the one who escaped? I thought for sure it would be that shameful merchant."

"No, thanks to the stars. He's yours."

Tierrof tossed his head back. He must have been quite drunk, yet his eyes were not even glassy. "You want to learn this lesson on your first day?"

Mikel shrugged. He had seen Kierstaz. He was satisfied. "I'd like to sleep, same as you."

Tierrof ordered twenty stripes and rolled over, his clay jug cradled under his arm.

Mikel did not care. They bound his wrists to tent stakes and used a whip of smooth goatskin. It still felt like shallow scratches. Twenty shallow scratches.

ℐ

DUST KICKED UP BY TWO dozen horses billowed across the heated dunes and made Tev choke. She brought her head around to the other side of her water skein and tried to see who made for camp with such speed, but there were no faces. Just a blur of horseflesh and painted skin.

She didn't give them a second glance.

Ladin's tribe was camped outside of a small, spiraling city, one built of sticky clay and rising high above a sparkling aqua oasis. Either there were no inns or no one saw a need to frequent them. Tev felt smug. If she were a multan—the head of a tribe—she would sleep under a roof, at least for herself.

The dust settled as the men dismounted. Everything had grown quiet. Tev glanced around her, realizing suddenly that she was alone, that none of the other slaves were out in the open at all. She froze and wondered if she should slip away as well. Was this visitor a slave trader? Why was everyone hiding?

Tev tucked herself against the edge of a tent and dropped her water skein, but she was too curious not to watch the open space in the center of the camp.

The flesh of the riders was not painted, she noticed. It was tattooed, like her arm, all the way down the neck on the right sides of their intimidating faces. Men came out of the tents in a rush, brandishing spears and daggers and machetes. There were about a hundred of them, and they crouched against the sand, eyes on the lead rider.

Maybe Mikel is right and Desert People do *know how to be fierce.* She hadn't thought so, at first. Drei had always been far more frightful to her.

"Behret, you mock Norani's word by coming here," someone yelled—or something like that. Tev's Aldadi was still quite rough.

The lead rider swung down from his horse with the command of a battle captain and sauntered a few feet. "Serteth, I come in peace." But the rider had many weapons on the cord about his waist, and he did not look happy.

Serteth, one of the older men in the tribe and somehow related to Tierrof (she wasn't sure how), wore a heavy scowl. He spurted out some words Tev couldn't catch, but she gathered that the invading rider, Behret, wanted something that Serteth didn't have.

Behret was as tall as his horse's shoulder and almost as muscled. He wore no shirt in the Desert sun. His chest was dark and well-shaped, the tattoos on his face a deep green color. He would have been a handsome man if his skin was not covered in so much ink that it looked like ivy claws climbing him, trying to drag him under.

Ric's face flashed in her mind. *Treachers such as these...* She jumped. Ric was barely cold in his grave and she didn't want to forget him swiftly, but why those words—that avenging rage—should haunt her now, she couldn't say. She shuddered and tried to listen to what Serteth was saying, but he spoke so rapidly and angrily that she could not understand. At long last, Behret broke in again—something about someone called Norani and Serteth not sharing knowledge of his whereabouts.

More defensive words were shouted.

Behret started to pace around Serteth in semicircles. She caught a phrase that sounded like, "*You know where he is.*"

A flap lifted, and a tall, broad-shouldered man came out. Ladin, the multan. Tev found his stature and rectangular face madly attractive for a man her father's age. Or was he that old? Hard to tell.

Ladin put a hand on Serteth's shoulder. "Anything you wish to say to my face, Behret?"

Behret bowed halfway, and Tev gathered that it was half-hearted. "Ladin. I am looking for Norani, and Serteth refuses to tell me where he has seasoned."

"How could you lose a caravan that large?" Ladin asked.

"How could *you*?" Behret spat in the sand. "You are Norani's cousin, and Serteth, his uncle. Do you not associate with your kin? Ever?"

"Very distant cousin. By marriage." Ladin smiled slightly, but Tev could see the tension. Behret was scary and frightful to him, too.

"Yet it is you I am watching, Ladin," Behret said.

Serteth spit on the ground. "Norani comes and goes as he pleases, and

I know not where."

"Yet he must see you before the seasons have circled." Behret stepped up close to Serteth and spoke in a voice too quiet for Tev to hear, but she saw Serteth go ashen.

"No more," Ladin broke in. "I am multan of this tribe. You speak to me."

"Serteth knows where he is," Behret said.

"Norani has always been a brazen one. His tribe is strong—they go where they please."

Behret turned on his heel, yelling a word that must have been an insult. He mounted his horse and rode back out the way he had come. His tattooed men followed.

ꝫ

MIKEL CAUGHT ANOTHER GLIMPSE OF Kierstaz the day the new slaves received tattoos. They had been moving camp constantly for nearly a fortnight, he thought, though it was hard to keep track. There was nowhere to keep a tally of days and he hadn't learned the stars as well as he should have.

She was on the other side of the tent, sitting with her legs crossed and her arm laid out. Her face was composed of a wide-eyed curiosity, almost girlish, and she wore a loose robe of dark maroon. A part of it wrapped around her head and made her look quite womanly, even with her scarred face and short hair. She smiled across the tent at him in some kind of relief.

Mikel was tempted to try to speak to her. He already missed conversation. Speaking without being spoken to was a whipping offense whenever a whim made it so. If they ever truly wished to punish him, they would only have to drag Kierstaz out to the beating stakes and he would be instantly repentant, and Tierrof knew it. Her skin was far softer than his.

His own arm was engraved with the same design, the artistry delicate and precise. The tiny pinpricks in his skin gave him a thrill. The sign of their multan, Ladin, was a jackal's paw with a snake coiled at its toes. They liked their snakes, these Desert folk. As soon as the tattoo was finished, he was escorted back toward a rough awning by the tent stakes where he stayed with the slaves who hadn't been assigned a task yet.

Tierrof came toward him, a short length of heavy rope coiled in his hand. He flashed a grin. "Think this will hold you, Seren?"

Mikel frowned. "From what?"

"Running. You are to have your own forge—Ladin has ordered it—but because you have run before, you must be bound to your work."

Mikel laughed. "You do not think my leather tether is what has kept me here thus far, do you?"

Tierrof did not smile in return. "This is different. You will be handling jewels without price and metal that can be used to make knives. There must be something to slow you down." He tipped his face up to the sun and closed his eyes as if in prayer. "A man does what he wills. Nothing stops him if God does not intervene."

Mikel would have agreed, but his wrists were still bound, so he raised his eyebrows. "I told you. I have a sister here. I wouldn't steal or use weapons within my reach and jeopardize her." *Unless you hurt her.*

Tierrof laughed. "Ah, yes, your sister." He untied the leather. "In this desert, we know that our strength comes not from our skill, but from our traditions. Weapons have been the same in our country for a thousand years, but every day, an Aldadi child is born who sees a new face for our story and is able to paint it with their lives in some way."

Was he saying that they were not a people who made war? But Mikel knew better than that. Desert People feuded…or so he had always heard.

Tierrof led Mikel across to the tents. Built of fabrics so large they covered poles that were nearly twenty feet high at the peak, it was strange to think that they picked up and carried these monstrous dwellings. His knights had made camps with branches, stones, and small strips of canvas.

Tierrof lifted a tent flap, shoved Mikel inside, and let it fall. The space was not especially large, but the firing pits were decently sized, with venting in the sides of the tent far less generous than he would have liked.

"I'm not sure this will draft properly," he told Tierrof.

Tierrof waved a hand. "It will. You have never used our ore."

True. "But the air…"

"Our air here is thin and clean, not heavy with the breath of trees."

Mikel narrowed his eyes. "You have been to Serengard?"

Tierrof smirked. "A few moons ago. A very famous priest of ours went to design tumblers for a priest of yours and was paid the sum of a city for it. Many Aldadi went with him to protect his payment and himself." He shrugged. "I went because I was curious."

The tent flap stirred, and Ladin entered with a small entourage. Mikel hadn't seen the multan since the day he'd been purchased. Mikel bowed at the waist, unsure what the custom was.

Ladin laughed. "This is the one who is good with metals, yes? He looks bony, nephew. Fatten him up if you can."

Tierrof bit the inside of his cheek and nodded.

A breeze blew through the tent. Ladin turned around spoke to the others as he left. "Hasn't had his mettle tested yet," he drawled.

Out in the sunlight, a caravan was pulling in, their camels moaning and grunting and settling down in the sand.

"He likes you, bony Seren." Tierrof hitched his chin. "Come with me. Choose materials."

So this was a caravan of traders? Mikel studied the faces and the clothing, curious. They actually *did* resemble the gypsies of eastern Serengard. Unkempt beards. Bright colors. Ladin's people poured out of their tents and swarmed the newcomers. Tierrof had to lean in close to Mikel to be heard.

"You will need metals?" he shouted.

"Metals, colored stones, chunks of this fuel you gave me, the powder that comes from the mines—"

"Slow down." Tierrof frowned. "The slaves and bodyguards will be gone first, then the cattle and goats. I can buy you all the materials you require, but you must be specific."

Mikel thought he *had* been specific. "Gold, silver, nickel."

"What is nickel?"

Never mind. "They have copper?"

Tierrof furrowed his brow. "For tools? But you are not being paid to make tools."

"For jewelry. And I need more braziers because I can create more if I have several at a time. And Drei steel, if your weapons are ever to improve."

Tierrof laughed. "We have finer weapons than you can imagine, made from powders and substances you know nothing of. But what is Drei steel?"

"It is dark blue in color, almost gray. The only blue metal you will ever see." Mikel had never owned any himself. Part of the Orion treaty with the Drei was never to steal or duplicate their weaponry. He had always wanted to handle it, and maybe Tierrof could find some.

"Why not brown steel? The brown steel of your people?"

Mikel shrugged. "Drei steel is lighter. Your people like their weapons light."

Tierrof smiled slowly. He smacked Mikel across the shoulders with his whole arm. "I like you. You are the best slave I have owned."

Hard to say where all his wealth came from, but Tierrof spent so much of it that day even Mikel was embarrassed for him.

{4}
Дцга

AURA WASN'T SURPRISED THAT LADIN had trouble with traders over the dry season. The smaller tribes were outright failures at asserting themselves, yet Ladin was insistent upon being alone and Serteth's family was insistent upon being with Ladin, although their relation was slight.

In comparison, Aura's tribe was as tight-knit as they came. Her father, three of his brothers, and ten of his cousins (both distant and close), all of their wives and children, and no one else straggling along to muddy the pot or dilute their great cache of goods and riches. They brought a veritable city with them and camped right next to Ladin. Serteth's people disliked her father, Norani—the multan of the tribe— and griped constantly, claiming they could not wait until he left them, but they were never above trading their days away for another glimpse of something pretty.

Especially if it was Aura.

She felt their eyes flicker over her, rest on her, stay. These days, she wasn't above encouraging it, even if their glances were all she would get for now. The idle chatter of the less-favored girls never ceased to give her a pang of jealousy. They cooed over the young men in Ladin's camp as if they were fresh pups to be cuddled and traded for.

"Did you see? Tierrof has grown strong and handsome. I would like him for a husband."

"You and every other girl."

"Serteth does not have many sons."

"Eight, to be precise."

"As I say, not many."

There was loud laughter. Aura added, "Ladin's sons have darker skin. I think they are more handsome."

One of her friends grumbled. "Of course, but what makes you think any of us could snare one of them?"

Aura tossed her hair. "I could."

"I'd like to see you try."

She swallowed a lump in her throat. "Would you?"

"Have you seen this jewelry? The art is strange." One of the girls held up a necklace that belonged to one of Ladin's tribe. "There are wings and hind legs on this snake."

"Truly?"

"Is it a dragon?"

They clustered about, and the girl took it off of her neck for a moment and let it dangle in her hand.

"I have never seen a dragon."

"No one has," Aura breathed. The detail on the piece was elaborate.

"Are they really snakes with wings?"

"Who gave it to you? Did someone buy it?"

The girl who owned it pulled it back and held onto it. "Serteth gave it to my father. He said—"

Suddenly a short, white slave dashed into their midst and grabbed at the trinket. A score of arms reached for her, smacked her fingers, scraped at her arm.

"Slave, get back."

"Ew, she touched me."

One elbow jabbed the slave in a manner that must have hurt, but still she managed to grasp the necklace. Aura caught the slave's wrist. It was strong for how tiny it was. After staring at the piece for a minute, the slave let go of it. Aura stumbled back, the necklace in her fingers, and the slave fell onto the linens that lined the floor of the tent.

Aura tossed the necklace back to the girl who owned it, stood up, and looked at the slave. She appeared quite Seren, chunky enough to be a boy but young enough to be a child. "What is your name, little girl?"

The girl frowned. "Tev."

Aura studied her eyes—cloudy gray, as if in an eternal storm. "Why did you take this, Tev? You could be beaten for such a thing."

Tev shook her head.

"Do you know our language?"

Tev held up two fingers a hair's breadth apart.

"Not much? But you should learn or you'll be thought a thief."

"She is a thief, Aura," another interjected.

Aura held the Seren girl's gaze, not sure why she trusted her, yet certain the slave had meant no harm. "Why did you take this?" she asked again.

"My brother," Tev stuttered. "He formed this."

Aura raised an eyebrow. That seemed as foolish as anything. If indeed there was such a Seren, he was probably being indulged on Ladin's dinner pillows this very moment.

"A slave would not make this."

Tev shrugged. "He did."

The girls laughed. "Is he white like you?"

"You should have her beaten, Aura."

"I do not beat my slaves and certainly not someone else's." Aura looked down at Tev, then raised her chin pointedly. A very demeaning gesture, though she meant it kindly.

One of Serteth's tribe spoke up. "There is a Seren slave here who knows what dragons look like. He says they are stronger than snakes, and he makes art with them."

Another girl said, "If he has seen a dragon and lived, he may be a Creeper himself."

Tev rolled her eyes and snickered.

Aura put a hand on the girl's arm. "You understood what was said just now?"

Tev blinked for a moment, as if not sure she should speak. "My brother has never seen a dragon save for a young one. Crippled and malnourished, kept in a cage by a gypsy." The words were half-Seren, half-Aldadi, but Aura understood them.

Aura shrugged. "I like his work," she proclaimed.

The girls were quiet for a moment and then chimed in.

"Yes, it is lovely."

"I wonder if I can get one, too."

"As long as no one knows a Seren made it."

"We will pretend we do not know," Aura giggled. She flung her hair back at Tev as if to say, *And I will pretend I don't know you, either.*

Tev left quickly—a wise choice, in Aura's estimation.

Aura opened her trunk of hand paint and started to mix some pigments, but she couldn't shake the girl from her mind. Most of the slaves her tribe owned were either cowardly or brazen; they had nothing to lose when they came to the Desert and no hope at all if they returned to their country. It worked in the Aldadi's favor because their slaves were easily convinced that their way was the best. But Tev had been neither. She'd been something else.

The girls chattered behind her. Aura's closest friend, Perel, leaned over her shoulder and said, "They have new colors. Ladin has been trading much."

"What colors?" Before Perel could answer, a name in the conversation made Aura whirl. "Behret came here?"

The girl who'd mentioned him paused mid-sentence. "Yes."

Aura's chest felt like it might explode. "Why? What did he say?"

"He asked where Norani was. Ladin wouldn't tell him."

Aura clenched her hands into fists to try to keep them from shaking. "What else did he say?"

The girl shrugged. "Not much. He seemed angry. No one said anything about you..."

Aura said nothing. She returned to unpacking the colors in her trunk, but she couldn't think straight. She wished they had kept talking about dragons and strange Serens.

♋

AURA NEARLY SCREAMED WHEN SHE heard the horses a moon later. She knew the sound; it had marked every season of her life for the past four years. There weren't many who rode in with such drama. Behret would stay for days, as he always did whenever he managed to track down their camp. There was no way Norani could hide his banners and the size of his tribe, and where Norani was, his favorite daughter was also.

Aura stepped to the edge of the tent and pulled back the heavy tapestry that covered the entrance, leaving only the thin brown linen to see through.

Behret rode in and dismounted. He wore his full regalia, all manner of blades crisscrossing the colorful tattoos on his bare brown chest. The latest ink was gold, a coiled rope design starting just below his ribs and ending at the lowest muscles in his stomach. It would have been handsome on most any other man, but on him, it made Aura's skin crawl.

His face was already stamped with a smug grin before he swung down from his horse. His eyes wandered over the tents to his left and then to his right, and she felt the slippery gaze travel over her. He couldn't see her through the linen, but it felt like he could.

He shouted, "Norani. Where is Norani?"

"Here." Norani strode out from the tent next to Aura's at nearly a run. Though his beard was sprinkled with white, he moved with a powerful presence. He was richer and stronger than Behret. By all rights, he should have been far more respected, but Behret was the son of one of the most revered priests in Perena. He had endless clout in his dealings with traders and tribes alike and a reputation for dancing and drinking that inspired a reckless following. Many a girl of Aura's crowd wanted more to do with him than dance and feast.

"Your caravan has been avoiding mine. Admit it is so." Behret spit on the ground at Norani's feet in challenge.

"If you sought me, I did not know it," Norani evaded. "Certainly I do not know to what purpose." He spit at the ground as well, and Aura hung on his next words. "You could have come and spoken to me on peaceful terms and been guests in my camp. Instead, you ride in like eastern raiders. What need is there for this unpleasantness?"

A steely grin split Behret's face for an instant, then disappeared. Aura wished she was farther away. It felt like he could see her.

"When am I ever unpleasant? I will be all kinds of pleasant once you hand me my wife. We can dine and dance as brothers."

Norani flashed an equally brief grin and walked up to Behret, close enough to touch him. His words were whispered—or hissed—and Aura couldn't hear them. Her stomach was a tangle of crooked knots; they never actually went away. If she could only be rid of them, cough them up or untangle them. She couldn't see Norani's face, but she watched the back of his head with bated breath as Behret's features grew more and more angry.

At last Norani raised his voice again. "Aura."

Her stomach flopped. Twisted. She couldn't move, but she had to. She lifted the dark linen and stepped outside, not sure whether it was by her own power or her father's will. Her bare toes touched the sand; she hadn't time to put sandals on. Her footfalls were like walking on water—she couldn't feel the surface beneath. Behret's eyes gorged on her. She could feel them, drawing her toward him with that silky smoothness desired by so many. She hated that he did this in front of everyone. It would make her envied among her sisters and cousins, and she never liked that. She kept her gaze riveted to her father's face, but his jaw was tightly closed and she couldn't read his features.

Smile. Seduce. Keep him interested.

Behret stopped her with a hand clamping down around her arm. His fingers loosened just enough to slide up to her shoulder, and he grunted softly when he reached the incurving of her throat. She was breathing now, every breath a gasp. His fingers were heavy. They slid down the inside of her collar with as much gravity as a comet falling from the sky— or so it felt. His palm dug into her right breast. He stepped close to her, and his breath brushed her cheek.

"Delicious," was all he said.

Norani smacked his arm away with a strike that was almost a blow. "You see," he growled. "She is not yet mature. Too young to be wed."

Behret let out a tolerant sigh. "I fear you are lying to me, Norani. Your lies are endless."

"Why should I lie to you about a girl? I have plenty of children."

"I know you want to keep her. She polishes your vanity, like a boy polishing a pitcher of pure silver. Nothing you can't live without, old man. I'm sure she will shine brighter in my hands and in my bed."

It was good that Behret did not know her father well. The look in his eyes was one of deadly disdain, one that preceded the drawing of a blade and the slicing of skin.

Behret raised an eyebrow and smiled at her. "I would speak to Aura alone."

Norani nodded, though Aura could see his hesitance. She almost wanted to rebuke her father for his protectiveness. If he scared Behret off, she would never have another opportunity.

Behret raised the edge of her tent with the back of his hand and waited while she brushed past him. As soon as the flap fell, he caught her hair and pulled her body up against his. "My sweet."

"My love," she mumbled into his bare chest, keeping her forehead pressed against it so he couldn't see her eyes.

"Is it true you wish to wait? I do not trust your father. I never have."

Aura gritted her teeth. "You should. He is revered in all the lands. No one doubts his word."

"I doubt it. Why would he keep you from me when I desire you so?"

"Maybe because you have been married before. He frowns on you. He thinks you have already taken much from this tribe. From Serteth, as well."

The hand in her hair tensed. "He says these things?"

"Not in so many words."

"I will take you away from him as soon as I can."

"I am not ready."

"You believe this?"

"I love you, Behret, but I want to learn more first. I am only just old enough to begin training for what marriage requires. I should like to be more experienced before I share your bed."

He slid his hands down to her hips and pulled her thighs tight against his. "I could teach you."

Aura slipped her hand up and dug her fingernails into his chest. "No. I want to come to you as an equal, not a student." She met his eyes with a steely glare. Behret was not a man easily defied. He must think that she meant it sincerely.

His eyes narrowed, and then he let out a ragged breath. "You do tease most heavily, my sweet, but I relinquish my claim until you wish."

"Thank you," she whispered.

As they emerged from the tent, Aura blushed slightly, knowing all eyes were on her in sheer jealousy. Alone with Behret in a tent? She must play this hand carefully, else Behret may get tired of waiting and succumb to the charms of one of the many girls who conspired to thwart her. No one understood the tight rope she walked, and there was no one she could tell about it.

Behret crossed his arms over his chest and leveled his gaze at Norani. "You wish to delay, and so does Aura."

"In a year's time, Behret," Norani said. "As we have agreed."

"In two seasons. After the storms."

"In a year."

"Bah." Behret spat at the ground, shrugged, and let his fingers dig into her soft skin once more. "If I must be tempted and toyed with, at least it will be by a beauty such as she, hmm?" He withdrew his hand from her clothing but kept a hold of her arm. "In a year, Norani. I must have her."

Norani bowed his head once. "And you shall."

"Do not go marrying her off to some fat old cattle herder before I can have my spoils. You know I will treat her with great esteem, shower upon her whatever lavishness her heart desires." He flashed a white-toothed grin at her and turned on his heel, back to his horse. They rode out, but Aura knew it would not be a year. He would return.

As she ducked away, she caught a glimpse of her father's face. Puzzlement. Surprise. Did he think she was a fool for allowing a man to treat her that way?

Well. There was no help for it.

{5}
Chances

MIKEL WAS ALLOWED OFF OF his rope for the evening. Seemed to be a special occasion, as no one was watching the slaves with much dedication and some of them were even allowed to eat of the fresh goat meat and partake of the wine.

There was wine every night, only it was nothing like Seren wine by the smell of it. It was fruity and mild, and they drank it as if it were water, even during the morning hours. Their major goal seemed to be to enjoy the heat and the sand with as much food—and as little clothing—as humanly possible. This season would end, followed by the season of dust and oppressive winds, and Mikel wondered if they would party as heavily then. He would rather deal with a snowstorm any day.

Tonight, there was a wedding. With it came a sharing of blood with sharp daggers and a simple festival that consisted of little food and much dancing.

Mikel sat at the edge of the firelight, just between the mayhem and the dark. Kierstaz found him, slid down next to him in the sand. She looked out at the shadows moving in the firelight for a while without speaking. Mikel didn't mind. Her company alone was comforting.

At last she drew in a breath and said, "I work for a woman named Fialli. She is very old and grouchy, but she is nice to me. I believe she thinks of me as her pet."

"They have me making medallions and rings and bracelets of every kind. The men want toe rings and belly rings and tongue rings for their wives. Seems they already have so much jewelry they have to come up with something new to woo them with." An element of disgust colored his voice. "Apparently, they want me to make enough to sell to other tribes. I'm some new kind of commodity."

Kierstaz laughed, a sound that jarred Mikel back to the echoing halls of Ashlin stone. "I heard a girl—Ladin's daughter, I think—fighting with the multan. She says she does not want to marry a trader who has to work for his goats. Yet the match was made long ago, back when he gave her jewelry he can no longer afford."

"She should be grateful that he is poor. I fear the richer they are, the less polite. Quite different from Seren ways."

Kierstaz laughed again. He looked at her curiously, trying to remember the last time she had laughed at anything.

"Does Ladin make a lot of coin selling your work?" she asked.

"I don't know. If he does, I do not see much of it." Mikel lifted a large hunk of graphite from around his neck. It was set into a copper casing that curved back on itself numerous times. "They have always worked with gold and silver alone. Copper is plentiful, but they use it for tent clasps and the hilts of steel blades. They have everything a Seren would pay endless coin for, begging to be used."

"Fialli gave me a piercing. Is it your work?" Kierstaz turned her head. Her left ear had a second jagged stud in it, a twisted silver design.

"No, not mine."

She smirked. "You are not the only metal worker."

"I am the better one."

"We'll see about that." She looked over at him and said, "You've changed already."

He frowned. "What do you mean?"

She shrugged. "I thought you would be…unhappy here."

"Why?"

"There's little honor among them. So long as they can find water and skewer some goat meat, they kill for sport and make love the rest of the time. Desert People do as they feel."

Mikel frowned. "I'm not sure that's true. I think they seek to justify their wants with their traditions instead of using law to curb them. They believe Allel's wishes are a changing thing, that the Creator can be bargained with."

"Who is to say He cannot be?"

Mikel coughed loudly. "What would Pem say if he heard you?"

Kierstaz shifted, looked up at him in the firelight, and he could tell she was debating whether to say something or not. In the end she didn't, so he did.

"I don't know if we should stay here. I cannot help wondering if we should have kept closer. If our blood being gone from the soil of Serengard will cause…" He shrugged. "What if the land sickens without us? What if it is our fault for being gone? I can find us another place to hide, somewhere on Seren soil. I swear it."

Kierstaz shook her head. "No."

"You have to be willing to trust me. Stop acting like my older sister and realize I am taller and stronger than most everyone. Well, except them." He gestured toward the fire—Tierrof, his family, all of the Desert men.

She giggled. "Are you feeling outnumbered, Mikel?"

That wasn't like her. She had always cared about Serengard more than he did. Truth be told, he hadn't expected them to last long here.

Now it seemed like she wanted to stay. "I am serious."

Kierstaz started to shake her head. She let out a hot, heavy breath. "Pem made me promise not to tell you. Not to tell you ever. No matter what happened, he said it would ruin you to know."

"Know what?"

"This is why I finally let you take me away from Serengard—something you found easy, Mikel. In truth we have no right to be there, no right to fight for rule. We are not the Orion family."

He felt his throat tighten. "Of course we are."

"No. It was a ruse to hold Serengard together."

"Pem was Orion. His mother was Orion. Mem would never... She loved him."

"No, no. It wasn't like that. It wasn't Mem or Pem. It was Izannah."

"Izannah was not Pem's mother?"

Kierstaz put a hand to her forehead. "Mikel, stop. You are confusing yourself. I've told you enough. I should not have." She refused to look at him. Her voice was sad, lonely. "Only know that our blood on the throne accomplishes nothing. Nothing at all."

Mikel refused to believe it. "That can't be. We were always the indomitable force for generations. Everything you fought for, every scrap of land I held onto, we did that for a reason. It was our responsibility as the only..."

Kierstaz let out a choked laugh, running her hands over her arms as if she was cold. "I should not have said anything."

"Whoever told you that lied. They didn't want you to believe in your own power."

She gave him a blank look, one that said she was not convinced.

"Kierstaz, why else would you have held to the people with such tenacity? You wouldn't let me hide you. You fought until we had nothing left merely to hold onto a scrap of Seren soil. You believe you had no reason for that? Dermed if you actually believe such filth."

She dropped her voice very low. "You misread my fervor."

No, he hadn't. He had known that molten look in her eyes after Pem was killed. He had known exactly what it meant. "You know why I put armor on? The same reason I surrendered to the Drei. I knew that if I didn't, you would have done anything to keep your toes in our dirt. You would have sold your soul to Hodran and your body, too. Forgive me for finding that too sick to stomach. I did *not* misread your fervor."

Kierstaz froze, looked down at the sand again. "You needn't have feared such a thing."

"I did fear it. If I had not been there, if Hodran had taken Ciar or turned Romianz, if someone had flat-out betrayed you, if the new Council had offered—"

"Offered what?"

Mikel shrugged. "A place of power. Some way to keep Serengard alive, breathing. I know he wanted you badly. They all did. Some wanted your head, and some wanted your living, breathing self. I couldn't let you run headlong into that."

She was shaking her head. "No. You do not know the half of it, Mikel. Hodran already offered that to my face—before the bloodshed, before Ashlin fell—and I turned him down."

Mikel furrowed his brow, his heart starting to pound angrily. "You never told me."

"Yes, I did."

"We had an entirely different conversation about Hodran."

She swallowed. "You don't remember."

"He was... He tried to rape you, didn't he? More than once. You said so, as smoothly as if he'd asked to dance at a party in front of everyone. I remember."

"Because, in truth, it had no bearing."

"No bearing that he may have meant to..." For true, that was all he remembered. As soon as she said he'd touched her, Mikel had seen red.

She had come into his rooms, all quiet and sober, and talked to him, which she never did back then. She never even glanced at her brother in the hall. "You asked me to kill him in cold blood. I imagined that he…tried to hurt you."

"He tried to. But you have the basest memory, brother." Kierstaz let out a bitter laugh. "I *said*, if you've ever the provocation to duel Hodran, please do it and fight dirty. For me. You invented your own story."

"What else was I to conclude when you asked me to stay home during planting and harvest but that you were in bodily danger and wanted me about the castle as a witness, in case you had to stab him to death? I'd only just been blooded. Captain of the Guard for—what, two months? I wasn't skilled enough to take him down. Yet you could slaughter him any day at that age. I'd thought if you truly wanted me to do it, it would be because it would be righteous for the Guard to kill him, even if I had to do it in an alley."

Sarcasm worked into her voice. "It wouldn't have hurt you to be present with your own Guard once in a while instead of lurking about the countryside, sending Pier back and forth doing things you should have done yourself."

Did they have to talk about this, too? "Pem trusted me with the Kymsai—the one task he couldn't imagine you would have the patience to endure—and you are angry forever?"

"Pem kept no other secrets from me."

Mikel scoffed. "And you kept none from him?"

Kierstaz ground her teeth. "I told you that Hodran cornered me. I told *you* because I couldn't tell Pem. He already felt too much pressure from the Council as it was, and he needed to be free to marry me to Hodran if he must in order to save Serengard."

"Pem would never have done that. He wouldn't have married you to anyone you didn't want."

She looked as if he'd struck her. "Pem told him no. Then Hodran informed me that he had blackmail on the crown and that he would use it if I didn't accept his offer or at least fornicate with him once or twice."

"What offer? To marry you?"

"He was willing to turn in his friends, those who were orchestrating the rebellion, in exchange for my hand. An excellent opportunity, except that Pem had no wish to execute half the inhabitants of Ashlin."

"He wanted to marry you? You damn well should have said. I've always been your brother, Kierstaz. Treacher."

"It didn't concern you. I only told you that he came after me with threats because I was selfish and I wanted someone to know what I was fighting. Hodran had more ambition than you ever knew. He wanted to be king. He wanted to force the kingdom into progressive thought, return to the freedom of Altrun, and turn over power to the Council, all while keeping Orion blood on the throne."

"What freedom? I know my history, and Altrun never brought—"

She interrupted him. "The Orion line passes from eldest child to eldest child, with only one mate allowed. Any other children are not considered heirs. Because Altrun had four wives, he was going to choose the child. That's the only reason the story of Izannah being chosen was not met with rioting. The people were ready for the youngest, and she was able to stem the tide for eighty more years."

Mikel saw his world start to crumble. Was she making this up? To convince him to stay in her precious desert now that she'd decided she liked it?

"Izannah was chosen because she was the only one left alive," he said.

Kierstaz ran her fingertips up into her hair and held her head. "No, she wasn't even an Orion. Izannah changed the records. She changed everything."

Mikel wanted to shake her, but all he could do was bury his hands deep into the soft sand. This was starting to sound like truth. The dark, clawing sound of unwanted, nasty truth. "Doesn't matter. It's a lie, Kiers.

It's a lie they have told you to try to—"

"Pem? Pem lied to me?" She gave him a smile of pity.

Oh no, you don't, Kierstaz, I'll not take that from you. "Pem is dead."

She diverted him. "You are one to talk of secrets. When I found Kold hurt at Ciar—"

"There was no secret. You know you couldn't be there. Someone could have seen you and asked."

"You never told me what happened. I never got to speak to you alone, not ever."

"What do you want to know? Kold had been drugged. He lost a lot of blood. When he woke, he didn't remember anything. There was nothing to tell, Kierstaz."

"Stop calling me that."

"It is your name."

"There may be bounty hunters, even here." She shivered. "I am Tev still."

Mikel snorted, stared out into the night. "If Hodran could not search you out in his own camp, do you really think a huntsman could find us here?"

"You always enjoyed life too much to understand its cold soberness."

"You never enjoyed it at all. One of us had to."

Kierstaz stood and brushed off her plain Desert robe. "I will find you again. Next time someone is married, I suppose."

{6}
Σecrets

MIKEL LIKED THE ADMIRERS DROPPING in on him, although they ignored him completely and cooed over his work as if it had been done by gremlins in the night. Most of them assumed he knew nothing of their language, and he learned far more than they must have intended. It was rather nice, actually, to be ignored instead of expected to have an opinion on everything and lead and strategize and sacrifice.

That morning, he heard one voice above the others, through the giggles and sass that were the norm for those who slipped into his tent; one voice that arrested him and tugged at him. There was something behind it—a mature pain, older than her years. He spared one glance for the elderly Desert man who watched him and the tall, young one who guarded the door. Neither of them noticed. Neither seemed to care that there was a voice outside the tent that was full of heavenly complexity.

"I want to see your Seren slave," the voice said. Young and confident.

The man at the entrance grunted and frowned. "Are you here to buy anything? Best ask Ladin yourself."

"He belongs to my father's cousin, and I can see him if I wish."

She walked past the guard in a sweep of loud jewelry and yards of light, silky fabric, into the dark canvas room dank with smoke. Three other girls followed. A little younger than her, they whispered under their breath, barely sparing him a glance as if they were bored with this excursion.

Mikel wasn't bored. Not in the slightest.

"I have been wanting to meet you," the first girl said in Aldadi with a bossy tip to her head. Her friends glanced up at him at last, and alarm crossed their features.

"He really is white!"

"What will my mother say?"

"Quick, let us flee. This is frightful."

"Now I will have nightmares whenever I wear his handiwork."

Mikel kept his eyes down, waiting for them to finish. It didn't end, so he stooped to check something in the clay pit that didn't need to be checked. Maybe if he looked less menacing...

Once his back was turned, the torrent of words slowed to more coy examinations.

"Look at his muscles."

"I did not know Seren men were this tall."

"How many slaves does your cousin own? I didn't know he was *this* rich."

"This is his handsomest," the bold girl said.

Mikel could not help glancing up through his hair. She wasn't as young as he'd thought; she must be at least eighteen. Paint circled her face in delicate, curled petals that begged to be touched. He didn't dare look at her for more than an instant. A girl dressed as richly as that was sure to be seen as someone's treasure in one form or another.

She tossed her head, and some black hair escaped her shawl. "What did I tell you? My father taught me how to shop." Her audience laughed, and at last she acknowledged him with a slight tilt of her chin.

Mikel glanced back up, into her eyes, then away quickly. He could not tell their color. In the dimness, with the light of the fire flickering in them, all he could think was, *Golden. She's pure gold.*

"Aura, do not flatter him."

"He is dangerous. See? They have him bound and guarded."

"And look at the scars on him. Maybe he has tried to escape."

Golden-Eyed Girl—*Aura*—ignored them. She flashed a daring, mischievous grin and stepped toward him, into the area where the cord about his ankles had play. Mikel stood frozen, wondering if he should turn away and ignore her. It was not pleasant to be played with like a dog on a leash.

"Come, Aura, before someone sees we are in here."

"I'm not afraid of him." She brought her eyes up until they pierced his, reached out and touched his arm, then withdrew it instantly as if he had burned her.

"You didn't," one of the other girls groaned.

"We are leaving," another said.

Aura ran after them, her silky cloth swirling behind her. She turned and looked at him again and said, "I know what you are."

And then she was gone.

Mikel suppressed a shiver. What he was? What *was* he? And how could she know?

♏

TEV WAITED ON THE OUTSKIRTS of the firelight until it was very late. She hadn't seen Mikel in over a month. She'd heard much about him through the other slaves and the Desert girls who asked her to do their hair for them, but all of it was about what work he did and how he was shut up and never saw the sun.

Tev saw the sun all she wanted and then some. It burned her skin until she had to wrap herself in cloth. And tonight, though no one would tell her what the celebration was in simple enough terms for her to understand, all of the slaves were allowed to eat with the rest of them and even indulge in a little wine. Tev wasn't sure she wanted to touch the stuff. It had been too long since she'd had liquor, and she might start thinking about things better left in the darker recesses of her mind. She might think about Ric, downing a jug of ale the night of her mother's death, carrying dozens of unspoken stories that she would never know.

Mikel appeared at last. His stride was stiff, as if he had spent too much time on a horse. He slid down next to her and said, "If we are not the blood we thought we were, what are we?"

Tev pretended not to hear him. "I've not seen you since the caravan arrived."

"I've been kept busy since. Ladin wanted new wares to trade. Nothing like a new fashion to increase his status in the eyes of his rich cousin. They've had me tied to my tools and constantly watched. I think Ladin is afraid Norani will steal me."

His tone was flat, impatient. No doubt he was thinking of the truths she desperately wished had never slipped from her lips. Dispensing with secrets could only be a dreadful mistake when it came to their family; secrets kept them safe. Pem had been right: the truth would ruin what Mikel believed, would tear the very fabric of who he was. Without it... Well, she shuddered to think what kind of shell she would carve out by spilling this into his ears.

Mikel inched closer to her, as close as he could without looking conspicuous. She drew in a breath and tried not to look at him.

"It is better that I know," Mikel said, his voice low. "Look where we are. We are at the end of the world. We sell trinkets. We are gypsies. We have no home and no hope for one. If there is anything I must know, it is how I came to be nothing but a gypsy." He looked at her fervently, and she saw the strong chin of the Castle Guard clench with stubbornness. "I need to know who our parents were."

Tev hated to say no to him. Ever since he was a little boy asking for half of her dessert, those green eyes were pitiful.

I am sorry, Pem.

She swallowed hard. "In the time of Altrun, when his children fought for the throne, it was told to the people—and it is still told to this day—that they fought to the death in willing duels, that Izannah was the only one left alive because she was too young to fight. The truth of it is that most were stabbed in their sleep, others poisoned in ways no one was truly able to sort out. It was all the Castle Guard could do to try to keep any of them alive. In the end, it was Altrun the Second who was left—probably because he had contrived to have all of his siblings killed, but that could not be proved."

"But Izannah lived."

"No, Izannah died."

Mikel shifted. He wanted to insist. "Izannah is our grandmother, Kierstaz. She died only a few years before you were born—"

"Izannah Orion was murdered. She was killed at a mere thirteen years of age. The rest of the family was gone as well. Uncles, cousins... They don't know who did it, or if they did, no one told Pem."

"But Pem's mother?"

"No one knows who she was. They wanted to keep her bloodline a secret, so no one has any knowledge of who she was or where she came from. But she looked enough like the real Izannah to replace her." Tev grew quiet. Mikel looked angry, protective of their grandmother who was dead and gone, which was something she loved about him. He would always be a protector, Orion or not.

"How old was she?"

"She told Pem she was fifteen."

Mikel's jaw clenched, and she saw his arms flex. "By the Derm."

Tev looked at him for a moment. "These are secrets Izannah told her oldest son, so closely held that Pem would not even tell Mem. King Rendl ordered them forgotten for eternity. Pem only told me because I am the heir and I needed to know."

"Then her marriage was a means of controlling her, of forging her into the new savior of Serengard." Mikel let out a heavy breath. "Did she *want* to marry Rendl?"

Tev looked off into the distance. "The Captains sentenced Altrun the Second to death and dictated that Izannah had to choose a husband from among them so that the Guard would have access to the throne. They did it for Serengard, Mikel, else it would have fallen apart sixty years ago. They thought they were saving the kingdom from a worse fate. Probably not. Matters little now."

Mikel cleared his throat. "They staved it off long enough for her to have two sons and two daughters, for her eldest to father us, and for us to make a royal mess at a border that should have been left alone."

His words stung her. The only thing Tev had ever wanted was to hold her country together for one more reign, to hold it together long enough for her to find out what it needed and heal it, as Izannah had in her time. He needn't flaunt her failure in her face. "It shouldn't have been left alone. You kept people from undeserved death at the hands of the lawless, Mikel. What you did was selfless and right."

"Fine difference it made. It wouldn't have even mattered if I'd saved you and put you back on the throne. Wouldn't have mattered at all."

Tev clenched her jaw. "You don't understand, Mikel."

"What? That Pem knew this his entire life and never told his only son? Haven't I given my every drop of blood to you? The least you could have done was be honest with me. The very least." He turned away, as if too disgusted to look at her.

"Pem said you needed to be an Orion, and he was right. You couldn't have led the Guard with any strength at all if you hadn't thought yourself born a royal. Not unless you were the brother of their rightful queen. I know you."

"You think I couldn't have? You underestimate the power of my mind, Kierstaz."

"I've made that mistake before," she said quietly. She didn't want to fight about this anymore. She wanted him to understand and not have to speak about it. But Mikel had never been like that. He dwelt on the things that hurt him, felt them too deeply—precisely the reason Pem had tried to protect him from this.

ჟ

MIKEL CHEWED ON THE INSIDE of his cheek. He couldn't look at her just now. He didn't want to be jealous of the trust Pem had had for her, yet he felt it pushing at him, ready to pounce. Surely a father should be able to trust his son as well as his daughter.

The Castle Guard had been an honorary force who came and went as their conscience dictated. They were a type of slave in and of themselves, bound to protect the Orion monarchy, even if that meant coming back to the burning city of Ashlin to fight an angry mob and kill your queen with your own knife. If that was all Mikel had been, that made him the equal of Pier and Seref, of Ric and Romianz. That made him nothing but a sword.

"Did Hodran know this?" he asked quietly. Kierstaz seemed almost selfish in this new light. What made her so different from him? Was she, truly? "Was this the blackmail he tried to use against you?"

"Some of it. Allel alone knows where he found out. There was no record ever written. Only the Captains of the Guard knew and King Rendl and maybe some of his family. Even Pem's sisters and brother did not know."

Mikel was silent again, thinking of his twin aunts, killed in the rebellion like most other loyalists. They'd had families. Children. Dead as well. "You should have told someone. Maybe Miana and Miraz would have lived. If the rebellion leaders had known they were not Orion blood, they could have—"

"No, there was nothing to be done, else you know Pem would have done it. They were as safe as they could be, kept as far away from Ashlin as possible. He would not have let the lie continue unless it had to."

That burned. "Did he know what was about to happen? Did he truly think there was somewhere safe enough to lock them away, that everyone would just forget that there were more with our blood? He should have told the people of Ashlin that it was all a farce. Before the last, he should have." He let righteous rage fill him for a moment. "If I'd known, I could have saved them. If I can lead a few hundred knights inside bad country to drag out a few loyalists, I could have done the same for—"

Kierstaz put a hand on his arm. "Mikel, you couldn't have. You can't do everything. You have to stop thinking that you must."

He coughed bitterly. "You are the one who told me to. You and Pem. I was the Captain of the Guard." There was no more explanation needed. It was the highest rank of the Guard, the highest attainable rank in the kingdom. Of course he was responsible. For everything.

"And it was all you should have been. You wouldn't have escaped that responsibility no matter what blood you thought you were."

"The Captain of the Guard is a contended role. I could have begged off. I could have been a farmer."

She shrugged almost lamely. "Orions were for ruling, not fighting, and they never mixed blood with the Guard because their strengths were different. Strength in battle and training. But you're the grandson of King Rendl, and he was the greatest warrior of Izannah's day. You had to be the Captain of the Guard, Mikel, since the moment of your birth."

Mikel shook his head. "Don't talk to me about blood anymore, Kiers." He stared off into the mix of Desert People as they moved in time to some wild, repetitive music. It was gorgeous and terrifying all at once.

To the Derm with all of it.

It held a note of irony that he and the rightful queen ended here, as slaves, without family or loyalty. As he watched the dancers move in and out of the light of the fire, he let his last shred of respect for his people slip away. A fading dizziness took over, and his mind melded into it with a relaxed pleasure. He didn't need the endless pressure anymore. He didn't have to be the voice of truth and the ambassador of reason to a generation gone mad. He could be nothing. He could be one person in a long line of foolish gremlins who lived, died, had children, and left only a name on a plaque. He could be mortal.

"You're only my sister. Nothing more," he mumbled.

Kierstaz didn't reply. Whatever her thoughts were, they were probably far different from his. For the first time in his life, he let go of everything that held him. Even her, sitting right next to him. She could go her own way and never come back if she chose. They could have things they'd never dreamed of. Choices.

The dancers had turned into a square to make a space around one long, dark creature. They followed her actions in a worshipful state, built a structure around her with the arcs of their bodies. She moved her arms above her head in the gestures of a weaver, brought the motion down to her breasts, her belly, her hips, her knees. Mikel narrowed his eyes. He'd never noticed any intentional structure about these folk. Any hints of order among them seemed to be purely accidental or force of habit, such as setting up camp in a semicircle. They didn't like conformity. They liked to move with the wind. But this was different.

The yells and calls and moans came in a pattern that turned to song. The tempo quickened. While the younger, more idealistic Mikel would have turned his eyes away, now he drank this in, freely followed every curve, every arch of her back and roll of her head. One leg was brought up high, almost vertical to the rest of her body, and then curled and slid back down, entwined with her other leg.

The rest faded, and he was watching only her. She danced like a wild bird—dipping, diving, bending into strange shapes, curling back out of them with the grace of a water swan. Onto her hands for a moment, balanced, bringing her body slowly down to the dusty Desert floor. He couldn't tell if everyone watched her the way he did or if he was alone in his reverie. He couldn't imagine any of them *not* watching her. How could they avoid it?

Mikel caught a look in her eyes—a free, wild pleasure—and thought for a second she had seen him, but her gaze danced across the top of his head and around to the others. He glanced slowly back up again. Her eyes were black in the night, but every time she turned toward the fire, they glowed bright orange. They must have been brown by day. She wore a piece of red fabric wrapped tightly in a design across her chest, and her belly was bare, the color of heavily toasted arabica beans. About her hips was a swath of fabric that matched the wrap for her top. It flowed down to her ankles, but the cloth didn't meet all the way, instead allowing her legs the freedom to move outside of it. He fixated on them like a boy barely of age. Her calves were smooth and shapely, almost glowing in the firelight. He wanted to touch them, and the desire made a fiery heat pulse in his fingertips.

The amount of times his eyes dragged over her body became countless. He was tired of looking at corpses and torn flesh and burned countryside. He'd been starved for beauty, and he hadn't realized how much until this moment. He was in some sort of trance in which he hardly cared.

He glanced at her face for moments at a time, hoping she didn't see him staring, revisiting it every few seconds. It was a round, symmetrical face of smooth, womanly skin, cheekbones at precisely the midpoint between her chin and her brow, full lips. Her eyes were large ovals with lashes too long to measure. Black hair swirled about her as she moved, making a dance of its own across the bare skin of her belly. The heat in his fingertips spread to his arms, his chest. In a moment, he'd burn up.

The music stopped. The drums started again, slower this time. The girl walked away languidly, abandoning the fire and the dancers and coming...toward him.

Derm. Did she see him?

No. She kept walking, right past his nose. He caught a whiff of her scent, and the image in his mind turned to tugging her gently down in the sand, her hair around him, curling into the ground. He looked away as quickly as he could, but he couldn't stop his imagination. Running a finger down the bare skin at her waist, causing a deep murmur of pleasure. What would a murmur sound like from those lips?

Damn. Damn. Damn. Damn.

There was no sound of footsteps, but suddenly she was there. "My sandal strap came off. Can you fix it?" Her voice was a little slurred, as if she'd had too much wine.

Mikel reached out tentatively, afraid she would notice that his skin was white and retract her request, but she wasn't even looking at him. Her eyes wandered out toward the dark, the moonlight draped over hills covered with slight, dry grass.

His fingers touched her skin and started to tremble. It took him a second to recall that the last time he'd touched a woman was nearly a year ago. A golden-haired Seren girl, trapped beneath a burning beam on a ransacked farm near Nervyet. Before that, it had been Romianz's wife, clutching his hand and asking him not to let her son's death be in vain. Before that...

He couldn't remember a touch that had been simple, free—instead of desperate and wracked with pain.

It took him far too long to fix her laces. Kierstaz, to her credit, was silent. Good thing she couldn't read his mind, couldn't see the nearly desperate need he had to run the tip of his finger down this girl's ankle, to see if he could evoke any feeling besides violence.

He lingered a second, just long enough to grip her heel with his palm while he checked to be sure the straps on the sole were in the right place.

"Is that better?" He only whispered it, but he saw her brow furrow. She must have thought he was someone else until she heard the voice of a foreigner.

"Much." Her leg recoiled toward her, and her mouth twisted into a perplexed smile that was almost a pout. He imagined her lips trailing down his neck, and the want paralyzed him. "I thank you."

She stood and wrapped her silk shoulder drape across her neck. She still hadn't looked at him. If she knew he was a Seren, she showed no sign of it. She stood shakily, and then she was gone, flitting off into the shadows, still dancing.

"Mikel." Kierstaz finally spoke again. Or maybe she had spoken minutes ago and he had not noticed. He was sweating, his entire body weak.

"Hmm." Mikel blocked her out. Whoever that girl was, he wanted her. Shallow, pungent want. Something he hadn't indulged in...ever. He was damned sick of all of this. Of strength and honor and never giving in to a selfish lust. He wanted to have her bodily. Make her curl her legs about him in tempestuous contentment.

"You are drooling," she said in Seren.

"Go to the Treacher," he snapped.

"You're staring like a saber tooth at prey. Only *you'd* be the prey as soon as someone caught wind of it. Didn't you say that if you even look at a—"

"I'd be out of my mind if I thought I could." He turned as sarcastic as he could manage. "But then, when have I had any girl at all?"

"You'd get yourself mutilated at best." Her voice was back to that worried, eldest-sister tone. "Do I have to chain you up myself?"

"I told you to go to the Treacher."

"I don't think I should abandon you like this." She laughed. "You cannot even move. You appear like dead meat already, roasted and chopped and served."

"I've never seen...the like of her," he finished lamely.

"It is a dance, Mikel. And Seren women wear more clothing due to the cold. You are not used to this. You'll wake up and be better. Did you have any wine, by chance?"

"They do not allow me any wine. What is her name?"

Kierstaz shrugged. "I don't know her name." He suspected she was lying. "She must be one of Norani's tribe."

"Then she's leaving with them in a week." He knew he couldn't even speak to her. He wouldn't. He just had to know her name. Had to know whom he was tangling with in dark daydreams.

Kierstaz rolled her eyes. "Thank Allel. You say a word to her and—"

"I'd rather kiss her," Mikel corrected rebelliously. "It'd be a fine way to die."

Kierstaz mumbled to herself as she stood up. "Better if they left tomorrow. You are no brother to me if you are dead." She whirled around as she walked away. "Don't think that I won't warn Tierrof that you're a fool for this girl."

Mikel laughed quietly, tried to make light of it. "He keeps me guarded, anyway."

{7}
Blood Keeper

AURA WOKE WITH A POUNDING headache the morning they were to make Perena, the finest city in the east of Aldad. Many called it the City of God because it was where the prophets had their greatest revelations and teachers filled the heads of the faithful with new ideas.

Aura rolled over and dug her elbows into her silk bedding and her fingertips into her eyelids. As good as it felt to stay up every night, drink wine and flirt with the boys across the fire, it was starting to wear on her. She couldn't do this for the next three seasons before Behret finally claimed her, and if anything, things were likely to become far worse once she was swept into the busy rotating wheel of Perena. Early morning prayers, market shopping all day, feasting at night. There would be no stopping and no sleep. She wasn't sure she could take it.

The curtain to her quarter of the tent lifted, and her mother slipped in. "Aura, you must get up. The slaves are ready to pack your rooms and garments."

Aura groaned and rolled her back to her mother. "I'm not prepared."

"You'd best be. Your cousin Gavriel is here already with a new herd of horses from the south. They have much to arrange upon our arrival, and I am certain he will give you one of the young ones as he always does. Best be dressed and out there to choose."

Aura didn't even want a horse this year. She was certain she would have to use Behret's once they were married, so it hardly mattered anymore. "I don't want to see Gavriel."

"Child, what is it?" Her mother was always quite sympathetic. Too much so, at times. "Have you been out too late? Is someone making you ill with devices you'd best be resting from?"

That phrase hurt her head. "What do you mean?"

"I mean that Nerri has been trying to convince me to let you come on the snake hunts with her and the children, and when I told her you were a betrothed woman with things to prepare for, she said you had been acting like a spoiled child and playing with boys."

"Nerri is jealous."

"She may want Behret as you do, but—"

Aura ground her teeth. "Mother, everyone wants Behret. Even Father respects him."

"Your father has great respect for any man who can win his daughter's heart, but Behret is the spoiled son of a priest. He makes Norani sick with his confidence at times—myself, as well."

"Glad to hear you think highly of my betrothed." Aura didn't want to talk about him. "Did you question Nerri on how much time she spends with the slaves?"

Mother blinked. "Do you think they are influencing her for ill?"

"No."

"Then I see little wrong with it. Perhaps she will learn how to fill her own flute of water from them."

"Perhaps she will also learn how to keep her mouth shut."

Mother folded her hands and placed them on the mat next to Aura. "I am not talking to Nerri. I am talking to you." Her slim hand slipped around Aura's shoulder, caught her chin, and turned her face. "Allel gave you beautiful, smooth skin, darker than any of your sisters. You are admired by many. Norani thinks you are too young to be given to a man twice married already, and maybe he is right. You act as if you would rather play as a child than commit yourself to a multan."

"Behret won't care," Aura mumbled. She tried to turn her face away, but her mother's hold was strong.

"I care. I care because you are hurting others, Aura. Do you not see that you give these boys hope? They think maybe you don't love Behret, maybe you will be seeking new company in a season. You must put a stop to it."

Something flopped over in her stomach. She had never been rebellious or selfish by nature, but right now, she felt like both. Hurting them, was she? She was sorry, but not sorry enough to stop. Somehow, she knew that if Behret was the only man who looked at her in desire, she would suffocate. "I am only a girl, Mother."

"Then perhaps I should tell your father that so he can revoke your engagement and make recompense."

"No! Don't do that."

"Then be a woman, Aura—honest to others and responsible for yourself. It isn't easy, I know."

No, you don't know, Aura thought. *Father is a gentle man, kind and good.* Her mother was now wearing the serene look she got when she'd said her piece. She must think they now understood each other. *Not even close.*

Aura waited until she had gone before she flung herself from bed. The lies she had to tell burned in her chest, but she had to keep her parents pleased. They did not know what it meant to be young, to be confused, to be angry—but then, she had never told them. Maybe she expected too much.

She wrapped herself in a fabric almost as dark as her skin, and the golden paint from yesterday was bright and stark against it. Then, jewelry. As much as she could wear without looking like a northern warlord's prize.

She hadn't the patience to listen to the gossip on the way into the city. She went straight for the men on the outskirts, riding horses about in rings and haggling with each other for good sales. Every time a new tribe came in, they were met by traders who wanted to acquire the best of their goods before the city salesmen talked them down.

People here knew her face. Perena was their home city; they came here at least once a year to pray and drink and trade. They would fill their skins with water from the spring, fill their houses with laughter and feasting, and fill their alleys with endless betting.

Men from Ladin's tribe recognized Aura as she walked by, and they nodded or grinned at her. She responded with a coy smile to those she liked and frowns for those her mother would like her to discourage. Most of them weren't deterred, and she was secretly relieved. She wanted to breathe a few moons more.

Her earrings clinked loudly in the wind that circled the city. She focused on the sound and let the rest of the noise fade into a background. Her eyes closed momentarily, and she drank in the soft smell of grass.

"Aura!"

She opened her eyes just as she smacked lightly into the shoulder of a horse. Tierrof stood next to it, holding the bridle.

"I'm sorry." He appraised her quickly, his eyes glancing over her the way everyone else's did—painfully aware that she was not available. She didn't like that look.

"Selling horses, are you, Tierrof?"

He made a short, little bow. "As always. Trading for what goods there are that I might grace my uncle's family with more wealth."

She smiled thinly. "And well you do so." There was a slave next to him, bent over to check the horse's foreleg, skin barely tan but stature tall enough to make her take a step back. He glanced up, blond hair tangled with his eyelashes, and she recognized him. "Aren't you the metal worker?"

The slave didn't answer and returned his eyes to the horse. His face was concealed beneath the locks of hair that fell over his closely shaven cheekbones. All she could make out was a nose more Seren than any she'd ever seen.

Aura flung her head back and glared at Tierrof, as if it were his fault that his slave ignored her. "I said, aren't you the metal worker?"

"He is," Tierrof answered, taking a step toward her.

"And what is he doing away from his tools? Out with the horses?" She shouldn't care, and Tierrof knew it was none of her concern. But something about the slave irked her, as if he knew something about her with barely a glance.

Tierrof shrugged. "He knows horseflesh." He reached out a slender brown hand and ran his fingertips through the horse's mane. "You? Something particular you'd like?"

He was always kind enough. It made her sorry that she was in such a terrible mood. "I would tell you if there was," she lied.

༄

THE MORNING WAS FILLED WITH strange men who had business or feuds with Norani and Ladin charging into camp. They jumped off their horses and yelled so rapidly in their tongue that Tev could not discern their words, and then matters were ended either with a smile and a spit in the sand or with a sudden brandishing of weapons and exchange of curses.

"Stay away while the men do their business, Seren slave," one of Norani's tribe warned Tev when she stepped outside.

To the Derm with that. The next to ride in was a young man with blades dangling from his saddle, though he came slowly and peaceably. His face could have been Tierrof's, except he looked slightly older. He had liquid brown eyes, trim eyebrows, and a slim nose that Tev couldn't stop staring at. Like Tierrof, he was taller than any Seren and had ink scrolls tattooed on his collarbone.

Tev hunkered down against a tall tent stake. She was supposed to be helping break camp, but this newcomer fascinated her and she was tired of being told what to do by someone who wasn't her captain. She inched as close as she could.

Ladin strode out to meet him. "I owe you much coin, Gavriel."

Gavriel flashed a smile and embraced him. "And I will expect all of it, Father."

Tev started. So he was the multan's son? Why was he not here, inheriting his wealth? She tried to see the resemblance, to piece together the families in her mind. At first, they seemed alike to her: the color of their skin, their tall lankiness, their dark eyes—all so similar. She imagined the artistic way Mikel would look at them and that helped. Massive shoulders on this man. Wide forehead on another. This one always wears purple. That one likes earrings—lots of earrings.

"You have not come for trade, I hope? I would be pleased if you seasoned with us at the City of God, especially as there are some of our tribe who need counsel."

Gavriel tossed his head. "I may stay a fair while, but there are some on the coast who requested I return quickly. I came especially to bring you the blood of a man of our tribe who has died. I hoped I might find the blood keeper here."

"Died? Not of disease, I hope."

"No. He entered a fight with a man of the mines. A foolish thing." Gavriel flicked his arm, and one of his men brought forward a horse laden with a truss that was wrapped in silken cloth.

"You come at an opportune moment. Norani is here, as is the blood keeper of our family."

Gavriel smiled almost sheepishly. "I know of it. I have men to reap the words on the wind, as you do."

Within a few minutes, the blood keeper came forward. He set up small, sharp instruments and tiny vials made of glass in a semicircle on his own fine fabric. Tev was able to gather that he was relieving the dead man of his blood. Some of it or all of it—it was hard to see...

"Tev!" Fialli's voice was shrill.

No. Wait. I have to see this. Her arms ached the way they did before a fight, and she felt herself bristling. Was it Gavriel? His uncle? Or this blood keeper?

Another girl—not a slave—came up behind her and whispered, "You should go now."

Tev did as she said, but she followed the girl instead of going straight to Fialli. "Have you ever seen the blood keeper before?"

"Of course. Gavriel needs him often because he is a keeper of fighters. There is more bloodshed among them than among Ladin's tribe."

"Does every tribe have one?"

"Every bloodline." The girl shrugged and tipped her head. "You're the little one who doesn't know our language yet, aren't you?"

Tev nodded. "My name is Tev."

"I am Nerri. I remember you. Your brother makes dragons."

Tev just nodded again. She didn't want to talk about herself. "Would a blood keeper take the blood of a slave if they died?"

The girl shrugged. "Maybe, but only if he suspected their blood was part-Aldadi."

Tev let out a breath. "Oh." Nothing in hers or Mikel's features looked remotely similar to those of the Desert People—she knew that from the way even their blood relation was doubted. But if their owners should chance to take a sample of blood, they might have a way of determining it to be Castle Guard. And if they did, ransoms and bounties couldn't be above them. They were, after all, slaveholders.

"Nerri!"

Tev gave a start. The Aldadi girl's head turned to Aura, the dark, confident girl Mikel was a fool for. She was striding toward them at a fast pace, a frown etched into her features.

Nerri's eyebrows wiggled with mischief. "What do you want, Aura?"

"Nerri, did you tell mother I—" Aura broke off. Her eyes flickered over Tev, and suddenly she was no longer speaking to her sister. "Your brother is the metal worker."

Tev wasn't sure if she was supposed to speak, but it was silent and both girls were staring at her, so she said, "Yes."

"At least you know how to answer when spoken to. He ignored me this morning."

Nerri rolled her eyes. "He isn't your slave, Aura. Not everyone answers to you."

Aura ground her teeth. "They all *like* you."

"Maybe because I'm interesting and I know a few phrases of Seren. Would you have the slaves flirt with you?"

"Maybe they like you because you spend more time out with the cattle than bathing and taking care of the dust behind your ears. You are filthy. Do you think men will want to look at you ever?"

Nerri laughed. "They like me just fine." She narrowed her eyes smugly. "Because I'm *interesting. And* know a few phrases of *Seren.*"

Aura stepped close to her. "You cannot squander all of your time and think you will have something to show for it. You won't. As Lia would tell you."

Nerri sobered, and tears crept into her eyes. She grabbed Tev's arm and pulled. "Let's go."

Tev tried to squirm out of Nerri's grip, but she wouldn't let go. "Who is Lia?"

"Our older sister. She died. I barely remember her, but Aura does."

"Why does she speak of her like that? Is she angry?"

Nerri wrinkled her nose. "Aura's soul is dark. She is cruel to the living because she misses the dead."

The words sank into Tev a little heavily. Was that what she was? Cruel to Mikel because she missed her parents? Did she make him pay for her own pain?

Nerri held onto her hand as they entered the city. Buildings started near the outskirts at ground level, and then, as the city worked inward, they grew in height. They were built of clay, street after street, level upon level, up and up. There were moments when they came to the top of a new level and she could see the entire city sprawled out like a blanket. A river ran down through the middle of it; it sprang up out of the center of a large temple, turned into a delta on the far eastern side, and then dispersed into marshes.

"Allel made this for us," Nerri said quietly. "He built the city with his bare hands."

Tev doubted that. It was clearly built by men. But how long had it been here, awash with loveliness that must have been brought from the ports along the coast? There were striped horses and lions in cages they passed, and she couldn't decide if they were for sport or for gentling. Everything that met her eyes was lavish and temperate at the same time—simple, yet lovely. She wanted to giggle or sing.

Where are you, brother? I feel giddy for the first time in my life. I must tell someone.

They stopped at last at a large house with a courtyard and three outbuildings. Some of the men had started a fire in a large brazier near the entrance, and impromptu dancing began immediately, encompassing the streets, the passersby, and an occasional half-breed.

For a moment, Tev pondered whether this was all hysterics. Last night, she had been quiet, resigned. This morning, she had felt a strange wish to fight the blood keeper. And tonight? She was giggling with Nerri. None of this was like her. Had she inhaled something in this air? Was it breathed by God or something?

Nerri tapped her arm. "This one is quite drunk already. See how he staggers?"

Tev nodded and laughed, though she felt as if she'd downed wine as well.

"Ah! Tomorrow I must take you to the fighter pits. We'll see some of the best white flesh mangle each other." Nerri giggled again, then coughed self-consciously. "Uh, you won't mind, will you? It is all in sport."

It cannot be worse than anything I've seen. "No."

"Do people fight in your country?"

"Only when someone has wronged another." Although not from lack of wanting. They were not allowed to. "Perhaps you can tell me something. About the blood keeper."

Nerri laughed. "Are you afraid of him? Don't worry. He only takes the blood of dead men."

"No. I am not afraid of anyone."

Nerri's eyebrows raised, and her eyes bulged. "You shouldn't boast such things. Allel might test you for it. I know multans who could make your blood sting in your veins."

Not if I had a sword. Tev smirked. "You should introduce us."

Tierrof rode in through the gate, high and mighty on his own horse. Tev watched him closely, hopeful that Mikel might be near him, but he wasn't. Tierrof frowned down at Tev, and she looked back up at him with an eyebrow cocked.

"So what do you want to know about the blood keeper?" Nerri asked.

"Why does he do it? Where does the blood go?"

Nerri laughed again. Apparently Tev was hilarious. "He does not do anything with it. His work is very important. He records each of the bloodlines of the tribes. Many years from now, a great grandson of

Gavriel may claim to be related to him, to have the right to his symbols, banners, and marriage rights. There must be a way to verify that man's claim to tribe."

Tev felt an icy ripple run up her spine. *Maybe that was how Hodran had known. Maybe he had access to Desert science. Maybe...*

"Oh, here's Aura. I don't want to see her." Nerri pouted. "You talk to her while I dance, won't you? I order you to." She grinned and ran off before Tev could answer.

{8}
Cцstoмeг

MIKEL HAD NOT STOPPED FOR much more than eating and sleeping since he had been moved into the market, a market which comprised an entire half of the city. He slept on the roof above the shop, but still, nights were warm. Tierrof bought a boy of light Desert skin—possibly a half-breed—to kindle Mikel's fires and hold his tools.

"Been making enough coin off of me to afford that?" Mikel asked him.

"More than enough to tile a market square." Tierrof grinned back at Mikel. "You tell me if the boy does not suit?"

"I am sure he will."

"You can use him to run errands for you, so you will not have to wait for me to come and bring what you require." Tierrof gestured to the shackle about Mikel's ankle.

No more rope for him—a heavy iron chain anchored to the stone forge kept him at bay. He'd broken it with a mallet once, just to be sure he could do it, and then forged it back together. He had promised Kierstaz he would come if she were in trouble, and surely he could find a way. But every day more distance and buildings and locks were put between them, and such a moment would no doubt end with an ugly death for both of them. Mikel didn't like to think of how hard it would be to actually meet Pier at the border in less than half a year. If he was still there. If there was a point to meeting Pier at all.

Tierrof stalked about, as he did every morning, checking to be sure Mikel's things were in order and that he wanted for nothing. "You like your place, yes?"

"Yes." The forge was spacious and bright with sunshine. He had four fire pits, all of them well-designed with perfect air flow. There were only half walls on three sides to allow the smoke to escape. Thin fabric hung in the windows and allowed light to enter but kept out inquisitive eyes, so no one had to see that a Seren created these pricey trinkets if they did not care to.

"I've brought you more of that food, the roasted vegetables you had yesterday."

Tierrof may want to visit, but Mikel did not have the time. "I'm grateful," he said as he added fuel to one of three fires.

"Did you even sleep this night past?"

"Not last night. Two necklaces—old man said they must be done first thing this morning, and they were no easy pieces."

"And did you have them done?"

"Certainly."

Tierrof smirked. "You know, you should take an hour in the morning to pray. Go back up to your mat and sleep. The old man who keeps the market stall will not care."

"Pray? I thought a white man could not know God."

Tierrof looked guilty for a moment. He had said it more than once. "Well, you certainly cannot read anything written by him. You would not know the Books of Elohai if you were left alone with them in a bright cell for a year."

"My people also believe in the Creator, Tierrof. Their ignorance, as you say, does not keep them from some measure of faith."

Tierrof shrugged, uncomfortable. "As I say, you can pray all you like."

Any excuse would do to sit on the roof and watch the sun rise and the people fill the market, some of them bowing in the dirt or going to the temple or putting their faces to the floors of their own rooftops. What their prayers consisted of, Mikel hardly dared guess. Those he heard were not reverent or specific. They were languid chants that they spoke with a somber look pulled over their faces, and then, as soon as they were done, they returned to life.

Tierrof stopped eating and made a face that belied he had a hard time controlling his appetite. "Another excellent day before us." He stood, smacked his lips, and clapped Mikel on the shoulder. "Sometimes I forget you are white, but not when it pertains to business."

The boy stayed after Tierrof went, staring at Mikel.

"What is your name?" Mikel asked.

The boy just spit.

"Don't like talking to a white man, is that it? Well, can you fan this fire?"

He shrugged and set to work.

"What did you do that made you a slave?"

The boy shrugged again.

Mikel let him be. The day was opening like any other day, yet it was not. Mikel knew it the instant he heard the girl's voice through the heavy canvas.

"I want to see your Seren slave."

The keeper of the market stall said no.

She'd been inside his tent at Ladin's camp in the Desert, touched his arm as she'd been dared to. He could almost remember her name. Almost. What was it?

She let out a loud sigh. "He's no secret. He belongs to my father's uncle. Out of my way."

The curtain rustled, and he was staring at her. His mouth went dry. He tried to look away but couldn't. The voice belonged to *her*? Every curve and color and sweet taste rushed in and disoriented his senses.

"I need this mended." She held out a huge, chunky necklace, decorative pieces of pure gold woven together without a chain to connect them. The break was substantial: a flower broken into three pieces, leaving the necklace severed and impossible to wear.

"When do you need it?" Mikel thought he spoke, but it came out so quiet he couldn't tell if she could hear him. He cleared his throat and opened his mouth to repeat himself.

"Please fix it now," she said. "As quickly as possible."

He wanted to meet her eyes—they were bright and dazzling—but he knew she wouldn't expect that from a slave. "It will take some time. This is intricate."

She nodded. "I can linger." The broken necklace hung from her fingers. As soon as his hand was outstretched, she dropped the pieces into his palm as if she could not wait to be rid of them.

Mikel brought the necklace over to one of his tables and examined it closely. "How did you break—"

"Please don't ask me questions. I will pay you anything."

The urgency in her voice made him curious. "I'll do it for you. It will take a few hours if you want to leave and come back."

"You needn't tell me what to do with myself. I will wait." She sat down on the edge of the window and wrung her hands. Slim, fluid hands. He looked away, tried to focus on the piece of jewelry. The flower was one he was not familiar with, and that would make his task harder. He set about choosing a color of gold to match.

She must have noticed his nervousness, for she said, "You needn't worry that you'll be in trouble for this. I am the daughter of Norani. Anything you do for me will pardon you from tardiness."

Aura, daughter of Norani. You touched my arm, and I watched you dance. Mikel shook his head, glancing up at her once. "I wasn't afraid for myself. I was curious."

"You needn't be." Her voice was ragged, but it relaxed slowly. "Keep those thoughts to yourself, please."

He tried not to smile. "As you wish. I don't want you to be bored, my lady."

"Who are you calling lady? I'm a girl who broke a priceless necklace."

Mikel raised an eyebrow. "You're no girl."

Her eyes flickered away from his, and her hands went to her own wrists, rubbing back and forth. "I am betrothed, but I stay with my family until I am old enough to be married."

"You are old enough."

"I am my father's favorite."

"So your father lies to your betrothed about your age so he can keep you? Selfish man," Mikel mumbled.

"What?" The question came out flatly, as if she did not care to hear the answer. Then her face grew bright again, as if she'd drawn a mask over it. "You needn't try to understand me, Seren. It will do your head no good."

Mikel grinned. "The first time I saw you, you acted like a curious child, wanting to see if light skin felt the same as dark under your fingertips. The second time, you were dancing around a campfire like an ageless faerie. My head is beyond engaged." He did not glance up at her, but he could feel her eyes on the back of his head. He had her attention. "There are a hundred jewelers in this city. Why step into the shop of the Seren? Curious about my skin again?"

She coughed once and shifted. "I have admired your work since Tierrof first bought you. I tell all my friends to buy from you."

"So you are the one who is making me work so hard."

She laughed, a rippling, confident laugh. "Oh no. It is not my fault that everyone takes my advice, though I do prove myself reliable. But you make jewelry from inexpensive materials. At last I can tell my less fortunate accomplices where to buy beautiful things at market. I am indebted to you, Seren."

"I am yours to command."

Aura looked startled. "Mine? You are impudent."

"If you already think me impudent, I'm sure I cannot injure my reputation by asking if you chose my shop because you thought I would not recognize you."

She swallowed. "I...don't know why you would suggest such a thing."

"You haven't stopped shaking since you sat down."

Her feet curled against the stone floor, then swung up and tucked beneath her. Yes, she was nervous. "Should you not conclude that a Seren is fearful to me?"

"I'm chained to this floor, Aura, daughter of Norani. There is nothing I can do unless you say I may."

"Don't use my name."

"Well enough." Mikel had been looking in her eyes without intending to. Maybe that was what made her uneasy. He focused on his work, determined again to avoid her gaze. But there was something comforting about her scolding—like having a mother again. He wished he could prolong it.

"You make very odd conversation, Seren."

"How so?"

"You ask too many questions. Don't you know it is for customers to question you and not the other way around?"

"Perhaps you should enlighten me."

"So long as it will not slow your work."

Mikel smiled to himself. "It won't."

"You speak our language well."

"I do."

"How did you learn?"

"I studied in Ashlin, where our books are kept."

"You must have studied very hard. Aldadi is a fluid and changing speech."

"I did."

"How were you rich enough to afford the time? Boy like you should be working the fields, I should think. Lazy Serens not working their fields make Allel sad. The land goes to waste. The wild animals have no friends."

How right she was in that. "I spent winters with books."

Aura propped her elbows on her knees and narrowed her eyes. "Where did you get your scars?"

That was a very complicated question. "Battle."

"Whom did you battle?"

"My countrymen."

"You must be a better fighter than they. When my people fought the Serens, they came away mangled beyond these scrapes of yours."

"My side still hurts on bad days." But her observation made him wince. *The legend of the Captain of the Guard is not real,* he reminded himself, but it tugged at him more than it used to. If he truly was descended from a long line of Castle Guard, the tale that he could not die in battle could be as true as the necessity for Orion blood on the throne.

Every drop of blood bears its own strength, the Books of Derev said.

He turned to the side so Aura could see the ugly, puckered scar that ran the length of his ribs and down to his belly, made by something jagged, so it would go deep and inflict damage.

"Got this retrieving…" He trailed off, not sure why he felt he could tell her this at all. "Some children being held hostage."

Her breath caught, and she sat all the way up and looked at him, her eyes wide now, engrossed. "Why were they held hostage? Who would do a thing like that?"

"Their kin were Border Guard. The army was fighting the Border Guard and needed an upper hand." Damn, this necklace was pure gold all the way through. It must feel like a manacle about her neck when she wore it.

"Did you save them?"

"Yes."

"All of them?"

"Yes."

Her stare was frank and unabashed, and their eyes met now without a bit of pretension between them. "You must be a truly skilled soldier."

He let out a half-laugh and answered quietly, "Why do you say that?"

"It was your task to retrieve the children of this Border Guard, so you must be trusted. You are covered in scars made by swords, so you must have done much battle. And yet you are still alive, your chest still quite handsome, so you must defend yourself well."

He wasn't sure what to say to that.

Aura laughed. "I've just gotten you to blush. You don't like me talking of your chest? Why? Would you talk of mine?"

No, he wouldn't, but she'd just made him blush again. "For a girl with a taste for flirting and jewelry, your interest in battle seems misplaced." Not that he hadn't known girls with a taste for all three—he'd known many—but he wanted to distract her.

Aura laughed. "I know nothing of battle or war or your Serengard, but I'd like to. I want to fill my head with everything that is missing." She leaned forward, almost in range of the chain on his ankle. "I can touch you again if I please." Her fingertips moved, tapping her knee in a slight rhythm.

He looked up at her, his brow wrinkled. "I'm sorry if I—"

She let out a half-laugh. "Why are you sorry?" A heavy sigh slipped out, her features serious again. "I should not have teased you. Tierrof would have my hide if he knew I were baiting you as one does a chained lion."

"You are welcome to use me for amusement." *It might kill me, though.*

"If you were to touch me in return, you would be slowly tortured to death. I am entirely too accustomed to having my way with anyone I like."

"Are you?"

She shrugged. "I told you I was my father's favorite."

Mikel narrowed his eyes. "I refuse to believe you are that shallow."

Her gaze flickered up and then back down. She looked suddenly as if she might cry. "Would you know?"

"I know what it is to pretend to be someone you're not." He held up the heavy gold necklace that was still not mended and would not be for another hour. "What is this ugly thing to you?"

Her nose scrunched up. "It *is* horrid, isn't it?"

Mikel grinned. "You have taste after all."

"I told you I sent my friends to your shop."

"Wait right here. Don't...don't leave."

He pulled on the chain about his ankle to get the slack out and then stepped up the stone stairs to the roof. Under his straw mat, he kept things he thought too pretty to sell, made from leftover pieces of metal so they would not be missed. Mixed alloys of copper, gold, silver, and nickel, and a small piece of Drei steel he'd managed to convince Tierrof to buy. He grasped a handful. His legs got tangled in the chain on his way back down the ladder, and he tripped ungracefully back into the room. He half-expected her to be gone, but she was sitting against the wall again, out of his reach, wide-eyed. He took a knee in front of her so he would not be so tall and imposing and opened his palm.

She just stared at him.

He picked out a necklace of copper melted with gold. Vines of the soft, rosy color entwined with leaves of silver, curling into a maze of twigs near the top. It lay flat against the throat and then became more elaborate the farther toward the bosom it ventured. "For you."

Aura didn't reach for it, so Mikel held it out on the tips of his fingers. He wanted to wrap it around her neck, but he waited for her to take it.

Her face turned into a blank, frozen slate. "You cannot... You mustn't give me one of these."

Mikel felt like she'd kicked him in the face. "Why not?"

"I already have one. The one you are mending..."

"You buy lots of jewelry."

"Not for my neck. Not like this. Not heavy and long and made from gold. This..." She stood, walked toward his forge, and reached for the chain he had set on a table. "This belongs to the man I must marry. You cannot give me one."

Mikel backtracked quickly. "I'm only a slave, Aura. You can wear what you please—"

She shook her head violently. "I cannot take it. A man gives this to a woman when he betroths her. I have one already."

"I never meant that." He had made a bracelet of a similar theme, though it had a strand of pure, unmixed copper in it and had been more of an experiment. He hadn't been as pleased with the result. "At least take this. I have no one to give it to."

Her chin rose in the air defensively. "Behret is a powerful man, more powerful than my father. You wouldn't want to step into his arena." But she took the bracelet with her fingertips, turned it around, her look of admiration unhidden. "How much?"

"I told you. A gift."

"Men give gifts to their wives, sisters to sisters, brothers to brothers. Slaves do not give gifts to their masters. A master chooses what he wants."

"Choose, then." He had a few other bracelets and a set of four small rings that were meant to pierce along the length of the ear and lock together. "If anyone asks, tell them you bought it."

She took the bracelet and curled it against her skin. "You may know our language, but you know nothing of what it is to be Aldadi. You mustn't ever speak of this. To anyone. Jewelry is given to exchange promises, friendships, covenants, and secrets."

Something turned over in his stomach. "What kinds of secrets?"

"All kinds."

His eyes flickered over her, taking in the blankness of her face. She'd come in here anxious—not because he was a Seren, but because she must have her necklace mended. "You're afraid of him. Your betrothed. You think he'll hurt you? Or he has?"

Aura's mouth dropped open as if she could not believe his gall. She marched past him in a swirl of fabric that brushed his cheek, a wave of heavy perfume that made him dizzy. Then she swung around, knelt in front of him, reached behind his head, and grabbed him by his hair.

"Don't ever pretend to know me again. You don't know. No one hurts me that I don't allow. No one frightens me unless I let them."

He could not stop the ripple of ice that ran from the back of his neck down his spine. "I won't."

She stood up, went back to the corner of the room, and sat down, her demeanor calm again. "Finish my necklace? Please?"

Mikel nodded. He said nothing to her as he fashioned the broken necklace, recast it, redesigned it. He held it out when it was passable, but it still wasn't very well made. "If you want this perfect, I will have to spend more time..."

Aura took it by her fingertips, avoiding his touch. "Well enough."

{9}
Treading

AURA MEANT TO STAY AWAY. It wasn't as if she needed the trouble. The metal worker asked her questions she didn't want to answer, pried where everyone else simply assumed. It should have frightened her, but after she left, it felt as if a weight had been lifted off of her.

No one in her family and not one of her admirers had noticed how little she slept at night and how hard it was to smile, but this slave had. She didn't mind that he was a Seren, that he had ugly skin and a strange accent and no knowledge of the ways of Allel. He'd noticed.

So she found an excuse. Then two excuses. Then reason after reason to come sit in the corner while he worked. She ordered jewelry she would never wear, gave it to her mother and her friends. She ordered wrong and had to get them changed; he made them wrong and had to start over; she broke them and had to get them replaced. Often she brought girls with her, pretended that she hadn't seen his latest designs yet. Mikel the Seren was no idiot—he had something new every time she came in. Aura overpaid him, and he pretended she was his best customer that he must hustle to impress.

Today, Perel was with her, shopping for new cloth from the southern peninsula. Perel was observant, and Aura wasn't sure she should risk it but stepping past the shop without setting foot in it was hard. Inside that cramped room was a brightness she hadn't yet known under the sun or in the warmth of a bonfire. It was hard to resist, and she had a perfect excuse.

"Oh, let's see if the Seren has made another of that bracelet you admired," she told Perel. Without waiting for a reply, she nodded to the old man outside, slipped in, and leaned confidently against the wall. "We've come to watch you work, slave."

He looked up at her and smiled. It had become an endearing term overnight.

"Watch all you like." Mikel glanced down at the boy who worked in the shop and made a face. Aura knew that face. It meant something about spoiled girls. The boy smiled back.

Perel said, "Just as long as you don't touch him, Aura. I was scared when you did that."

"Nothing scary about him. He stays on a leash." Aura offered a teasing smile in Mikel's direction, one that made him frown. Was she being mean to him? She did not intend to be. "So, Perel, ask him."

Mikel turned and faced them politely. "Ask me what?"

Perel shook her head, suddenly petulant.

Aura almost laughed. "Perel wants a bracelet like mine. Can you make her one?"

"What bracelet?"

Aura held out her arm. "This one."

Mikel looked Aura in the eyes, and it startled her. She read into them a defiance for the way she was treating him—as if he refused to acknowledge the noncommittal friendship she offered.

"No," he said flatly.

"Why not?"

"I cannot make that."

"Yes, you can. I bought it in this shop," she lied. After all, she had told him it was a secret, and he had told her to say she bought it. Everyone saw her jewelry—she couldn't pretend it didn't exist.

"I am certain you did not buy it here. Unless the old man made it." He gave her a hard glare, and she backed off.

Perel spoke up. "Why couldn't—"

"Forget that I asked." Aura waved her hand and shrugged, looking at him with displeasure to try to hide her embarrassment. Did he think the bracelet meant nothing to her? Did he regret having given it?

Perel started talking about the season of rain and what it might do to the city, her eyes going over Mikel as if he weren't there, but still she asked about the weather in Serengard.

He was curt, as if there were something he expected Aura to understand, and she, like an unwilling student, refused to listen or acknowledge it. At first it puzzled her, and then she felt just as surly. Did he think she came here to listen to details about some ugly, faraway country that she had always hated? If he did, he was a fool. She came because she wanted to hear about the places and food and music he loved, cold and stupid wars where thousands of men were tricked into fighting each other for something he called honor. She wanted to hear who *he* was.

"We are not all as blessed as you, Seren," she broke into whatever Perel was saying. "Some of us are not chained to our work. Some of us must keep promises that are not small and ordinary."

Mikel smiled oddly. He seemed pleased that she had chosen to rise to his mood with an overly sullen mood of her own. "Should I tell you how false your words are, or would you prefer I act the inferior?"

"You may keep the act and the honesty today for I haven't the time." She held the bracelet out to him again. "You refuse to make this for my friend? You may find I take my business elsewhere."

His eyes grew stormy. "You have said that before, yet you haven't stayed away more than a week." It was as if she had awakened someone in him that he had attempted to strangle, but not managed to kill. He lifted her wrist, ran the bracelet about on the bone, and a jolt shot up her arm. "No one makes you come here. No one makes you wear your shiny things."

He must have seen the shock in her face because he dropped her hand. Aura stared back at him, her blood pulsing quickly. She couldn't decide whether to answer him in kind, stalk out, tell Tierrof...

"I apologize," he said quickly, glancing behind her at Perel's wide eyes. "A reflex. I've not always been a slave, as you know from my thorough accounts, and I've not always been chained to my work."

Aura swallowed, smiled. "No harm," she whispered, then lifted the fabric to the outer shop and ran smack into Tierrof. Did he come here often? Did he see how often *she* came? For a moment, she was too startled and worried to know what to say.

Tierrof bowed slightly. "Aura. My humble shop is blessed by your presence."

She blushed. For all her popularity, there was never enough to make her entirely immune to flattery. "Your shop is the best."

Tierrof raised an eyebrow. "Is it now?"

She shrugged. "Only, teach your Seren some manners."

"Was he rude to you?"

"No." She wanted to slap herself as soon as she realized she was somehow implicating Mikel. "No, he treats his customers well, as a slave should," she mumbled and pushed past him.

As soon as they were out the door, she whispered to Perel, "You did not see or hear any of this."

"Any of what?"

"I did not argue with a slave nor defend him to Tierrof."

Perel was a loyal follower of Aura. All she said was, "My lips and eyes are woven shut."

ℒ

"YOUR SHOP IS SUDDENLY FREQUENTED by Aura, daughter of Norani?" There was a definite edge to Tierrof's voice, one Mikel could not miss.

"She likes what I make."

Tierrof laughed. "Apparently she is mistaken in what you make."

Had he overheard their exchange? Mikel averted his gaze and shrugged. "She is pleasant enough."

"Pleasant. And beautiful."

"I didn't notice."

Tierrof's voice became suspicious. "Anyone who does not notice Aura is either a liar or a fool. I think you are lying."

Of course he was. His fingers were still tingling from grazing her wrist. "If I did notice her, what of it?"

"Perhaps you would try to steal her."

Mikel tried to laugh, but it came out half-hearted. "And how could a slave of my kind steal her?"

Tierrof's eyes narrowed, and his wrist flicked nervously. "You could try. Like everyone else does. I'd warn heavily against it, though."

Mikel shook his head. He had no illusions that he could be anything of consequence to her. The chain of Aldadi prejudice about him was as real as the manacle around his ankle. That knowledge was, in a way, a relief. "I'm no fool. Even if I were Aldadi, she is betrothed to a multan."

"But she is rather free with herself, isn't she? Especially for a betrothed. Maybe she isn't so sure. Everyone says she isn't."

Mikel was not sure he wanted to discover what might happen if he allowed himself to fully need someone so different from him—again. Or was she? Could be she was bound by loyalty to her family, as he was. Could be their souls were similar. Either way, that he could provide the cool metal that graced her skin was enough. It had to be. "If you're implying that I touched her on purpose just now—"

"I'm sure you did *not* touch her or else I'd have to lop your hand off." Tierrof smiled, albeit shallowly. "You are aware that, if you had, there would be instant death for you? A slave, with his hands on an Aldadi girl... It could look very bad indeed."

"As I said, I'm no fool."

"How often does she come here?"

Mikel wouldn't lie to Tierrof. "Twice a week."

Tierrof let out a stream of words that could only be swears. "By all the snakes," he mumbled at the end of it.

"You care for her?"

Tierrof flung out an arm, his voice kept to a hiss. "Everyone does. This is trouble I don't need. Having her here in this shop, cooing at my slave? I have never wished to be this close to Norani or Gavriel or the powerful kinds they exchange vows and children with. Do you know how many men never dare to stand as close to Aura as you just stood?"

That didn't frighten Mikel as much as he was sure Tierrof intended. "For fear of her betrothed?"

"For fear of her father, at the very least."

Mikel's eyes narrowed. While he'd do bodily harm to anyone who wanted to hurt Kierstaz, he wasn't sure fathers were the best judge of a young man's motives. Actually, he was quite sure they weren't. Petrolai had not even noticed Hodran trying to rape his daughter in his very own castle. A father could assume he knew his daughter inside and out, but in truth, he knew only a little of her. Only the part she chose to show.

"You should be pleased with the business she brings. Soon enough she will tire of my jewelry and my company—"

Tierrof ran a hand through his black hair and fixed steely eyes on

Mikel. "You expect me to believe that she comes to buy jewelry? Hideous lie. Aura marries in two seasons. Every step of hers is ordered. Nothing she does is ever flippant or ill-meant."

Mikel raised an eyebrow. "You worship her as well? Does anyone see her as merely a girl?"

"Do not speak that way." Tierrof turned savagely. "Everyone follows her. Everyone watches her. Do you not notice how she glances about? It's not safe for her to spend so much time in the shop of any one man. If she is suspected of being here often, who will be blamed? I will—after you are executed for good measure."

It was hard to keep up a light banter when Tierrof was this serious. Mikel lowered his voice. "I can scare her away if you wish it."

"No. Behret is powerful and well-liked, and there is already bad blood between him and my uncle. Scare her, and Norani will be even angrier."

Mikel put up his hands. "I'll do whatever pleases you, master."

Tierrof looked at him sharply. "I've not required you to call me that in some time."

"And you've not questioned my loyalty for some time."

They were cut off by the jingle of jewelry and Aura stepping in once more. Mikel dropped his hands, and Tierrof let out an audible breath. Her face was both bright and pale at once, as if she had been running.

Tierrof gripped Mikel's arm, pushed him away. "Can I help you, Aura?"

"Yes. You mustn't say a word to anyone about my accepting gifts from your slave else I'd die of embarrassment." She offered a light smile that looked as fake as any Mikel had ever seen. She was terrified.

Tierrof blinked. "Yes, of course. Whatever you wish, Aura."

She nodded quickly, then added, "And, Tierrof, don't flog him for it, either. I begged him to give it to me because I desired it." Without another word, she ran out. In her wake, Tierrof and Mikel stared at each other.

"Gifts?" Tierrof hissed.

Mikel clenched his jaw, but he had no excuse. She'd warned him. He hadn't understood.

Tierrof groaned. "By all the stars, I am doomed."

♋

FOR WEEKS AFTERWARD, AURA WAS flushed with the feel of him. It started where he'd touched her wrist and spread until every bit of her was on fire. At night—when she used to toss with nightmares—her sleep was deep and heated, haunted by the cool metal against her skin that had been made by his hands. She wondered if it meant something, if indeed the Serens were cursed, if she should stay away from him. Yet still she found her way there.

Life as she knew it was a waning moon that would soon be dark. She might as well burn it down.

When she broke through the canvas entry to the shop, she startled the boy who worked there. There was no one else about; it must be a slow day. Good.

Mikel only looked up once and then became far too intent on his work for her taste. Aura frowned. She walked slowly toward him, giving him time to listen to her steps approach, to feel her gaze boring into him.

"I've been wanting to ask you this for many days. Why won't you sell this colored gold to my friends?"

Mikel flexed his jaw. "I don't know what you mean."

"You know." She stamped a foot in frustration, invaded his work area, and flung the bracelet under his nose. "This. Gold the color of sunset. Every woman I speak to wants something made from it, and some men besides. They have never seen the like."

"Nor should they." He said it almost angrily. His back was turned to her, and she had to stop herself from staring at the scars on it. He walked into the cooler, darker part of the shop. Aura tripped over something—a bushel of raw metal—it hurt her toe, sharp and brittle, like the pain that tugged at her just below her collarbone.

"Give me a reason, you gutless beetle, or I'll tell Tierrof you've disobeyed a buyer and he'll flog you for it." She followed him all the way into the nook behind the forge where there were no windows, tucked around a corner and out of sight of the door.

Mikel kept his back to her, his voice low and mumbling. "You think I am afraid of a flogging?"

"I am not some poor goat farmer's child, Mikel the Seren. I am not a conquest to be toyed with."

"Is that what you think?" He turned suddenly to face her, and his height and build filled the cramped space, made her unable to breathe. Or maybe it was the heat from the forge. "You think I would toy with you? Do I strike you as the kind?"

Aura shivered and glanced behind her. She could hear voices outside. If someone came in, the only thing she could do would be to crouch down and hope they didn't smell her perfume. "I have to go."

Mikel's voice was raspy. "Go then."

"Answer my question or Allel strike you."

"You can strike me yourself."

She did, very hard, right across his face. His cheek was rough—clean-shaven but too scarred to ever be smooth. She wondered how many times he'd been hit by a woman, if doing it again would help her feel better, if touching him again would make her stomach knot too tightly.

"You...want me to have the only one. Why?" She kept her face down, a submissive request. He raised a hand as if he might grasp her chin, make her look up. She wished he would do it, and she hoped he would not at the same time.

He leaned in, his breath touching her face, and there was a pull, like the force of the sun, that tried to get her lift her gaze and look into his eyes. Then the tenseness went out of him, and he ducked into the room again.

"I won't lie to you, but surely it is best if you forget I ever gave it to you. Bury it, destroy it, or return it. Pretend I was never so brazen."

"You're a coward." She spewed the words at him before thinking about how they would sound, before realizing she'd meant to say them to herself.

Mikel's eyes became dark and pained. "I've reason to be afraid."

"Everyone is afraid of me. Everyone thinks if they are near me, they're breaking some unspoken law. I hate them for it, and I hate you, too."

His voice was barely audible. "You're not supposed to think of a white man at all."

"My thoughts are my own and no one else's, damn you."

"And I'll be afraid of your thoughts for my own reasons, Aura."

The way he said her name gave her a heady rush, like the feeling she got when she watched a dust storm pummeling toward her across the sand. She didn't care about the bracelet. She knew there was a deeper reason, and she knew she was selfish to try to make him say it. And yet, words were merely words. They could both deny them in a moment, swear to forget, choose whether or not to be changed by them—couldn't they?

"You are afraid of me, too. How can your reasons be any different?"

Mikel sucked in a breath and ran a hand through his hair.

"And don't say you can't tell me, or Allel help me, I will hit you again."

"I am not afraid of you. I am afraid of being worth something to you." He looked her up and down the way a buyer assesses a fighter. "I am a swordsman, a knight, a soldier. You are not tarnished and ungentle as I. If there was...a friendship between us...I am afraid it would be less than you hope."

That was how she felt: tarnished. Like the very breath she drew would bring pain to everyone she touched. Like she had to bury her true self and her need for the love of others and pretend she was a tower of sandstone.

Aura let out a shallow laugh, but it ended ungracefully from the heavy lump in her throat. "You think you could hurt me? You are misguided."

A muscle in his cheek flexed. "I know I could."

That was ridiculous. "You couldn't begin to know how."

He answered without a pause, without pretense. "I was close to a girl once, a rebel girl. I lied to her about who I was, and she exacted a full revenge for it, one that included the deaths of many innocent people. Not a day goes by I don't wish I'd plunged a knife into her throat when I'd had the chance. You have enemies, Aura, and they are yours to keep if you wish. But if I were your ally..."

Her stomach trembled, and for the first time in months, she felt tears prickle at her eyes. There was a certain freedom to it, as if she were admitting that she were human. She stiffened, determined not to let herself soften. To soften would be to let in the pain, the fear, the turmoil. Anger was a better friend.

"What do you mean?" she asked him.

"I'll hold my tongue like a civil slave before you have me shredded at the rack."

She had no idea what a rack was, but she grabbed his arm with as much strength as her fingers could muster. He jerked away as if he couldn't stand her touch.

"Speak your words," she said, "and I'll not judge you."

"Who is making you marry a man you are afraid of?" The words came out as if torn from him, like he felt what she'd felt just now.

Aura shook her head and backed away. "I don't know what you're talking about."

"Don't play innocent."

"No one makes me do anything."

"Yet your fear is real."

"I am not afraid."

He raised his voice. "Then why do you tremble when you speak of him?"

"I don't."

Mikel flinched and then ran a touch down the side of her cheek. It seemed almost like a reflex. A ripple ran through her, a huge, forceful relief. She wanted to cry with how good it felt—gentle, unassuming. *Do that again.* He was close to her. Very close.

"He is going to kill me." The words tumbled from her, and once they were out, the others came after in a rush. "He killed my cousin, Dehli, and my sister, Lia, and I am next. He wants me. He'll use me, and when he's tired of me, he'll kill me."

Mikel said nothing. He stood there, close, not touching her anymore. Then, at last, he moved his lips near her ear and said in a tiny whisper, "May I kill him first?"

Aura stepped back. The room reeled about her. She felt dazed, like she'd been struck. "No."

She fled through the door without a backward glance.

{10}
Fighters

TEV FINALLY BROKE INTO THE higher ranks of the house slaves when she proved she could wash feet with marked speed, and her talent for wrapping clothing with an expert eye when it came untied or unraveled was another mark in her favor. Not everyone was nice to her, but it was a fair trade for her to be inside a social circle.

The Desert People weren't very physical with each other—at least nowhere approaching the way Serens were and not to mention cliff people, who were renowned for brawls so intense that sometimes people lost an eye. She was kicked and smacked a fair bit, but usually there was a gentleness to it—probably because she looked like a child. Sometimes Tev forgot herself and responded in kind.

The first time she smacked Tierrof back, he stared at her as if he expected her to sprout horns next.

"I can have you beaten for that."

She looked up from where he had tossed her to the floor just to get her out of the way. "You won't beat me."

"Won't I?" A smile tugged at the corners of his mouth. All of Serteth's sons were cocky and overly commanding, Tierrof especially so.

"You would not want my brother to hear of it. He might do shoddy work in return."

Tierrof worked hard to hide the smile, but she saw it. "I would beat you if I thought you needed it. And I'd lock you in a wash house and keep you under constant watch so you couldn't get to your brother."

Tev hid her own smile. She did not like Tierrof, but she stood in a sort of awe of him. She respected his open lack of fear; although sometimes he reminded her of a Drei—headstrong and sure of himself and too good to consort with anyone below him.

Norani and Ladin's families shared enough quarters and enough food that they all came and went in similar fashion, ate and slept in each other's dwellings and about each other's cook fires, so Tev served and consorted with Nerri almost as much as she wished. The houses they stayed in would be known as estates in Serengard and would only exist in the countryside. Perhaps the size of the houses and the amount of people living in them was the reason this city sprawled across the hard, tan dust without walls? It was crowded and utterly unlike the cold, spacious halls of the Castle of Orion.

It was a warm day when Tev slipped into the stables to meet Nerri and her sisters. They were to go to the fighter pits in the lower end of the city. If their mother caught them, it would be "roasting day," in Nerri's words. Tev wasn't sure what that would mean for her. Fialli might consider her ignorant and let her off. Or she might have her flogged bloody.

There were nine girls in the stables, and Aura was among them.

"We'll walk," Nerri said quietly. "No horses because they draw attention. And Tev, not a sound."

Tev hid a sarcastic giggle. *Not make a sound? I'll see if I can manage it.*

"In the season of rain, the river floods and rolls through the streets on the eastern side," Aura told her. "It waters many marshes before it turns again to desert. Some tribes like it and live there during that time. It is not so hot, but that means they live near the fighter pits. It's noisy and smells of sweat and blood."

Sweat and blood? She was already numb to the smell. *I could live right in a fighter pit and not mind.*

"My family does," one of Nerri's friends said.

Tev frowned. "Is the flooding the reason why there are no lower levels? No crypts or cellars? You could keep some of these rooms cooler during the hot months—"

"Shh," one of Nerri's sisters answered, looking frightened. "Do you want to invite the Creepers? They like the dark. That is why there is always light here."

Tev shook her head. "You cannot stay in the light always. Night comes. You have to fight the darkness. Make your own light."

A couple of the girls stared at her openly, and Nerri leaned in close. "Careful what you say. Only Allel gives light."

"Day *and* night."

"Hush. The girls will think I don't control my slaves."

Aura interrupted. "You don't, Nerri. She's not your slave, remember? She's not even Father's." She looked Tev up and down. "I hope you'll excuse my sister for being a child at times. It amuses her."

Nerri's face grew red. "Aura, Tev is my friend. I'll thank you to leave her to me."

"Oh, a moment ago, she was your slave and now she's your friend?" Aura's eyes danced with something like jealousy.

Were these girls fighting over *her*? That was a new experience indeed.

Aura pulled on Tev's arm and drew her close. "I am sorry I was rude to you when last we met. It wasn't something you did. It was...something else."

"You needn't explain to me," Tev said.

"Yes. Yes, I do need to." Aura lowered her voice and glanced behind her. "I...was not ready to come to this city. Not ready to be here in all the usual upheaval."

Tev couldn't help but say, "What upheaval?"

Aura blinked at her. "You know. Enemies are a boast-worthy accessory. There is a fight in the eastern side, in the northern side, in the market. Someone has overturned a number of tables running from someone else. Someone has drawn a dagger. Someone has yelled threats. There is no peace, no calm."

Tev didn't know. It sounded like Aura spoke in riddles. She frowned. "In my country, such things were settled by the Guard."

"The who?"

"The Guard. A group of soldiers who served as judges."

Aura waved a hand. "Oh, we have judges. They are priests."

Nerri jumped in. "I don't like any of the priests."

"Nerri!" Aura snapped. "You mustn't speak such thoughts. Say an extra prayer tonight."

Nerri stuck out her tongue.

Aura rambled on, undeterred. "When an occasional body falls to the dirt in Perena, the family says their prayers and buries their kin and plots their own revenge. It is no one else's affair. Feuds and wrongs are a manner of keeping life interesting in the city, instead of the tranquil life of the Desert."

Tev giggled. "What is tranquil about that Desert?"

Nerri interjected, "All we have are tribal splits."

"And dust storms. And snakes and jackals and lions."

"And rival tribes." Aura frowned. "Often it can go quickly from spitting in each other's water to burning each other's tents in one night."

Tev shook her head. "How do you know they are rivals?"

"Everyone knows. Tribes have been circling each other as long as the sun has circled the earth."

They'd walked quite a ways, deep into the southern side of town, when Tev's ears perked up at the sound of singing steel. Every fiber of her body started to tingle, and she knew she could not rest until she found it. No one looked at her curiously, but she could swear her every muscle was taut, every limb ready to pounce. She dropped one of the wraps she was supposed to be carrying, stopped, and picked it up. None of them even glanced at her.

The sounds grew louder until at last they came around a corner into an open arena, level upon level of tournament grounds inside large rings surrounded by heavy chain. Inside each ring were bronzed men with bare chests and sweat dripping down between their muscles, and as Tev looked closer, she saw there were also some women. They were smaller, covered in so much fabric that only their eyes showed, and they fought in a more flowery manner, flinging their weapons about in wild arcs, catching the light on the shiny blades. It was less battle-like than the blunt force of the men, but then, the entire point was to put on a good show for their owners, wasn't it? Or did some of them train for actual fighting? She didn't know if the Aldadi truly had any enemies or when the last time they had gone to war had been. Did they fight the Elloyans? The Drei? They hadn't fought the Serens in a very long time, though they'd come close to conflict once in Calum's rule and once in Izannah's. Now they just picked up Seren strays and used them for slaves. No one said anything about it.

Tev slipped underneath Nerri's elbow and watched closely. Someone must train them. Someone must invent these stylish arts. But the more she watched, the stranger it became. It looked as if each fighter had his or her own style. In Serengard, only the best of the Guard were given time to develop their own style, and if they did, they became a trainer and had to teach it to others of the Guard. Her own trainer had been an old man, the same who'd taught her father.

The fight closest to her was between two Elloyans—evident because they wore the ragged, inventive garb of the sea and because their skin and features were too mixed to be any one race.

"Are they…owned as well? You have Elloyan slaves?"

Aura laughed, and her eyes grew animated. "Of a sort. Elloyans train against us because they wish to go against our fighters in tournament. Though they used to be as strong as the Aldadi, they now trade what they have for this honor. It is sad. They used to have their own identity, but because of their traveling and mingling with other tribes and peoples, their culture is lost. We are the color of skin that rules the earth. Ours is the only true beauty."

Tev rolled her eyes. Her words sounded rehearsed. Aura confused her—one moment she was free and open, the next distant and guarded.

The ring beyond the Elloyans held an Aldadi man and a half-Seren. Their fight was fierce, seemingly random at first, but Tev found the patterns, the habits, the weaknesses. Theirs was not for show, and the half-breed was getting the worst of it.

"Gavriel is training a new slave," Nerri informed her.

Tev pretended she hadn't been staring too closely. "Gavriel?"

Nerri pointed to the handsome, fine-boned Aldadi man who watched the fight from a brick-made rise. The very same Gavriel who had brought the blood keeper. Hadn't Nerri said he was a keeper of fighters? Tev hadn't cared at the time.

"His new half-breed has nice eyes," Nerri said.

Tev frowned. "What is the difference between an Elloyan and a half-breed?"

"A half-breed is half-Seren and half-Aldadi, but that only happens in your country where there are classes of Aldadi low enough to breed with a Seren."

"What is a half-Drei that is half-Aldadi?"

Nerri blinked. "There aren't any."

The half-breed didn't *look* new. His chest was scarred, and his technique was solid. It seemed as if he had been doing this for a while, but he was young. Couldn't be older than fourteen, if that. "How do you know he is new?"

Nerri giggled. "I come here a lot."

The half-breed turned toward Tev for a moment, and she caught his eyes. Yes, they were nice, though they held a certain darkness. Haunted? Or angry. She could swear she recognized him. "But...Gavriel isn't fighting him. How then is he training him?"

"No, Gavriel doesn't do everything himself. He's too rich for that." Nerri giggled again, and it started to grate on Tev. She didn't want to hear any more giggling—not with the heat flooding her veins right now. She stood stock-still, transfixed by the beauty of it. The power in the men's arms, the competitive nature they displayed, the smoothness of the women doing somersaults in silks and curved blades.

"Why do you have to sneak out to come here?" Tev asked before she could stop herself.

Aura was the one who answered. "Our mother does not approve of fighting. Most of them don't."

"But...if everyone owns them..."

Aura blinked. "Not everyone. Not the priests and their families, nor those who aspire to be priests. Violence is a sin in the eyes of Allel, but some pretend that because it is for sport, it is all right. Even my own father keeps fighters, but he does not use them much."

"But why...why do your people work so hard to make nations fear you if violence is a sin?"

Aura waved her hand. "It isn't a sin when it is just. It is a sin if it is done in anger or without provocation."

Nerri nudged her and rolled her eyes. "Yeah, Tev, try not to be such an idiot."

Fialli told her often that she was an idiot, but it did not bother her.

She didn't care who called her an idiot. Ric had called her many names. He had upbraided her, lectured her, scolded her, and every word had been a cipher for what he meant to say: *you are strong, you are needed, you are loved.* Hearts were what mattered.

"Aura is betrothed to a priest's son. She's very devout." Nerri smirked. "Gavriel has more fighters than anyone, and he is my cousin. He dines with my father often. She is just being a prude about it."

Tev pretended to understand, but she was more confused than ever.

{11}
Refuge

THE STREET WAS QUIET THE day after a feast. Aura threw her wrap over her shoulders and glanced behind her for the twelfth time. She knew it couldn't be, but she felt as if Behret was watching her everywhere. It never let up, no matter how far she was from the coast. Or the spires. Or the snake lands. She saw Behret in her nightmares, in her mind when she walked anywhere.

Sometimes her father sent one of her brothers with her. She was often tempted to ask one of them herself, but she always changed her mind. Not only because she knew Behret was not in the city, but because if he was, a show of force would not faze him. Behret wouldn't touch her—he wouldn't dare risk breaking faith this close to the day they were wed—but he might touch her brothers. Threaten them. He was a cocky man, and he kept unrespectable company. They thought they could get away with anything.

Aura glanced behind her once more. There were two men whose features she didn't recognize, but she wasn't certain they were following her. Maybe she was being paranoid. She closed her eyes and pictured the ink she had glimpsed on their arms: it could have been a Desert snake or a dragon, but her mind made it a seasnake—the sign of Behret's father.

Her stride was almost a run now, and still the men drew closer. She darted down an alley. She was only three blocks from Mikel's shop. A part of her wanted to lead them there and beg him to fulfill his offer after all, but the rest of her nature fought the urge. That wasn't her wish. And even if it was, Mikel had said the word *kill*. She didn't want anyone killed. Ever.

The men caught her around the next corner. One of them grabbed her shoulders and threw her against the wall, and it knocked the wind out of her so she couldn't even scream. *Allel must hate me. He must see the hatred I have in my heart for Behret, and he hates me for it.* She caught the man closest to her and shoved his chin up until his neck made a snapping sound. He cursed loudly and bent over for a moment.

The second man hit her in the ribs. "We heard your father is going to try to marry you off to one of the Rifahi tribe. Is that true?"

"I don't know what you're speaking of." She could barely gasp out the words. The one she'd hit stood up straight and backhanded her across the face, and she choked back a sob.

"Don't, Ashi," the other one said. "She could show a bruise for weeks."

"Bruise me if you like," Aura yelled in his face, as menacing as she could manage. "I'm going to tell my father about this, and I'm going to stab you in the back next time you get near me. Don't think I can't." Her own words startled her. She'd never known herself to be capable of such threats, much less of carrying them out.

A horrid, rippling laugh came from Ashi's belly. "You think Behret cares whether we're hurt? He wants to know if *you* still hold your virtue and whether your father plans to marry you off so we can kill that man and then kill your father for his breach of betrothal."

Aura spat on the ground. "I have done nothing to breach my

betrothal, and neither has my father. Now let me go."

"No."

Aura kicked the one called Ashi in the groin, grabbed the weapon from the hand of the second man and stabbed him in the arm, then ran again, as fast as she could. Sobs shook her, although she couldn't release them with how hard her breath came. She glanced behind her as she neared the jewelry shop, and when she saw no one, she ducked through the window and huddled beneath it. The moments dragged by like hours. She listened for heavy, running footfalls, but there was nothing and that was worse. Where were they? She couldn't breathe unless she knew they had passed her by. She couldn't. She...

And then his arm was around her.

༄

SHE ALMOST SCREAMED, AND MIKEL wrapped his hand around her mouth. "Shh. It's me."

When her body did not relax, he let go, but the instant he moved away, she shrank back into his arms and buried her face in his chest. He knew the look of panic written on her face, all the more evident because she had never displayed it before.

"I am sorry. I had nowhere else to go," she blurted.

"Take a walk, boy," Mikel said. The boy obeyed.

She had not come for months. He had been afraid for her some, but mostly he'd blamed himself for scaring her. For offering to kill someone. "What is it? What happened? What are you—"

"They...someone...hit me...is chasing me." Her voice was a quiet whisper, one so frightened he could feel the anger building inside of him.

He held her face with one hand, the other braced against the stone floor, fingers spread like claws. "How many?"

"Two."

The chain about his ankle was only a momentary delay. He had to leave her side to reach a heavy mallet that he kept beneath a worktable, but before he broke the manacle, he asked, "You want them dead or merely frightened?"

Aura shook her head rapidly. "Don't do anything unless they come in here. I beg you. There's... I will pay for it." She lay against the wall, crumpling up smaller and smaller.

Mikel's back stiffened, and his neck flexed. "Aura, who will make you pay? Your family?"

"No!" She caught a tiny tear with the tip of her finger. "No."

"Do you tell anyone when you're scared? Anyone at all?"

"No. But I am fine."

He hated this. Her body was trembling, her dark face as pale as it could get, and he wanted to kill someone for doing that to her. The same as he wanted to kill the men who'd razed the villages at the border, who'd left little girls alone in burned-out huts with their dead parents. "Where did they hit you?"

"My stomach." She pulled her knees up to her chin and leaned back against the wall. She was still trembling like mad.

"Come away from the window." Mikel reached for her hand, and she gave it. He wanted to wrap his arms around her, nestle her close, tell her he'd protect her. Instead, he led her gently toward the back of the shop, to the other side of the forge fires. They were blazing for a warm day, but the roar would mask their voices. "Do you know whose men they were?"

She nodded but said nothing.

He had to clear his throat because it hurt. "Your betrothed?"

She looked away, but another nod came. Slow. Deliberate.

"Why would he do that?"

"I don't know. Maybe he didn't know they would hurt me. Maybe he just told them to watch and they—"

"How cruel a man is your father if he pledges you to such a man?

Surely being beaten by his cohorts should be enough cause to—"

"No! No. You don't understand."

Mikel felt a surge of anger so ripe he couldn't keep his voice from cracking. "I am trying to, but I'm quite sure you said he was going to kill you."

"My father wants to protect me. If he knew that Behret... If he knew, he would try to find an excuse to kill him, and my family would lose *him* to justice."

He bit the inside of his mouth, his voice low and confused. "Are you certain it would be a worse loss than your death? If your father has a heart at all, he would gladly die in your place."

She shoved herself away from him. "You don't understand." Her breath caught. "I *am* going to marry Behret. I *want* to marry Behret. You cannot stop me, and please don't try. Only...hold me."

He wrapped an arm about her shoulders, tried to hide the ragged desperation inside of him. It didn't matter what hurt her, frightened her, drove her to him for safety. She wasn't going to change her course. Wouldn't let him change it for her. He was an observer, watching in a theatre.

I can do this. I can give her this. I can let her go and not let it destroy me.

It would destroy him. He felt it. Knew it. Just out of sight, only a step away—a plummet down a cliff face, a death on the rocks. Whether it was his death or hers, he didn't care to decipher. He wanted to never see her tremble with such fear again, to stop whatever rushing torrent induced her to run headlong into danger.

"Listen, if you want him dealt with, I can kill him for you. Silently, without a trace, and no one would know."

She leaned in toward him, her face going blank. "You couldn't."

"Yes, I could. I could break this manacle, find the man in the night, and kill him, and you wouldn't have to be tormented by this fate any longer. Just tell me where to find him and how to identify him when he'll be alone, drunk, or asleep. Preferably all three."

She shook her head even harder. "No! I won't tell you. I would never wish a man murdered."

"The Dermed you wouldn't."

Her voice grew sharp. "Stop tempting me, you devil."

"I've told you I am a man of blood."

"Do you think it helps when you offer to kill for me when in truth it will haunt me as if I'd done it myself? I want justice, not vengeance."

Mikel nearly snarled at the air. "They are usually the same thing."

"No, they are not. I know. I have seen and been the cause of vengeance since I was a child. Since a wilderness trader swept in and saved my tribe from some raiders and my father offered any of his livestock in gratitude. The trader told my father he thought I was a beautiful little girl and that he would take me instead. My father told him no, and they fought. Two of my brothers died that day. They killed the entire caravan, though. That was vengeance. I've seen that many times since then, and I know it solves nothing. It only hurts."

"Your brothers died well. The world is better without such pigs in it. I know because there is one I should have killed long ago."

"You know *nothing* of which you speak."

"I know nothing?" The moments of agony and anger and betrayal at the hands of friends rushed back into his head and made it hard to keep his voice gentle. "I fought duels when I was young. Men who wanted someone to fight challenged me because I am—I was—Mikel Orion."

She blinked emptily. "What does that second name mean?"

"I was the Captain of the Guard for four years." She looked grateful for the distraction, so he continued. "The Guard was to hear the cases of the accused and choose whether to kill or maim or release. I never wanted innocent blood on my hands; none of us did. I let most off as easily as I could. But I tell you, when there was a man accused of harming a woman or a child—someone smaller and weaker than him—and I saw that unrepentant emptiness in his eyes, I pinned him to the ground with my sword and let him bleed out."

Aura said nothing, but she drew her arms closer to herself. He hadn't meant to be that honest. If she thought killing was a sin in and of itself, he might have just admitted to being the Treacher in her eyes.

"And then I fought the Border Wars and I didn't know what justice was anymore. You can't kill a man for bearing a sword against you if he doesn't know why he took up the sword in the first place, can you?"

She looked puzzled. Her fingers were picking at something in her lap that her eyes weren't focused on. "I don't know what the Border Wars are."

"They started with riots, went on for nearly a year. Might still be happening for all I know." He couldn't stop talking now. He felt as if he'd been holding this back forever. Things he wanted to tell someone. No, wanted to tell *her*. "There is a man who worked closely with my father, yet when the rebels breached the gates and killed my family, he walked among the dead bodies looking for mine and my sister's...to finish us off. I fought clean and fair against him, refrained from chasing him down even when I was a sword's length away. But some people are vicious enough that no amount of mercy you show them will suffice." Mikel looked straight into Aura's eyes. They flickered, but she didn't blink. "Behret is not worth your mercy. He is not worth anything, not even the dust he touches. Certainly not the dust that you have touched."

Her fingers were tight against her clothing, and her knuckles were white.

"I'm sorry. I shouldn't have said all of those things."

"No," she whispered. "You should have." She leaned toward him, and something warmed in her voice. "Your world is simple. You are the one in my life who wasn't on my set course. You are the one thing that is out of place, and that is why I trust you. No one made you come here. No one put you in my path but Allel."

Mikel drew in a sharp breath, the urge to push a strand of hair out of her face nearly overcoming him. He turned away so he couldn't stare at it.

"When Behret's first wife, Dehli, died, no one from my tribe noticed." Her voice was a mere whisper. "She was a distant cousin we rarely saw, none of us moved in the same tribes as Behret, and there are many common ways for a girl to die. It was said she died of a snake bite, and none of the physicians who tried could save her. We all believed the story. But then he came to our camp, time and again, and he would not leave my sister Lia alone. He followed her everywhere, as if entranced by her. She loved it—perhaps even loved him. He was the richest man any of us had ever seen, let alone been worshiped by. He had a reputation for doing scandalous things, and that fascinated some and horrified others. We are quite devout, my family. Always have been." Aura glanced up at him, then back down. "Still, my father has never had much use for priests or spoiled priests' sons. He made Behret court her for two years. The night he married her was the most lavish feast we'd ever thrown, and it lasted twelve days. Had to impress the bastard." Her voice shook with anger.

There. Let it to the surface. Breathe it out. Own it. Embrace it. Mikel reached toward her shoulder, then drew back. He kept forgetting how offensive a touch could be to an Aldadi. Yet she glanced at his arm with a look that was far from condemning.

"They were married for two years. Lia grew furtive and strange. Behret was cruel to her. I don't know if he beat her or not, but he did something that scared her. And when he killed her, he was stealthy. No one knew but I, and anyone else she might have told."

"Told?"

"A few weeks before, Lia told me that Behret had tired of her and that he had made a habit of following her when she was swimming. He would race her to the pools, claim he could swim faster and better than her, challenge her to beat him, and it had scared her. I don't know if she told anyone else this."

"But how was that—"

"She drowned. A few weeks later. Mikel, my sister was a good swimmer."

Mikel felt a cold ripple run over him. "Aura, you must have told your father this. Someone—anyone?"

"Not my father. His grief was too much as it was. No one could prove her murder, especially against one as powerful as Behret. There were hundreds who mourned her, and not one questioned his story. I saw them. I spoke to them. I tried to make them doubt. None of them would."

"So you are going to do what? Let him kill you, too?"

"Yes. Only this time everyone will know because I will drive him to do it in a rage in front of witnesses. The man has a thirst for blood, and he will do it. Then my family will avenge me in a way that is truly just."

Mikel's tongue stuck to the roof of his mouth because it was so dry. "It may take him years to tire of you."

Her skin seemed to glow. "I don't care."

"He'll hurt you."

"If Lia could suffer his touch, so can I."

To the Derm with not touching her. Mikel reached for both of her shoulders and held her so that she had to look into his eyes. "That will not be justice. They'll punish him for your murder but never for Lia's."

"A man who murders will be tortured for days without rest and then killed by jackals or lions. It will be a fitting end for him."

He finally let himself touch that stray hair. "You are far braver than I, Aura of Norani."

She closed her eyes, but there were no tears slipping down her cheeks. "I don't want to be brave. I want to make him pay."

Make him pay. Yes, but... "First, you'll give him his third young, beautiful wife."

She opened her eyes, heavy, vivid brown flickering under dark lids. "Virgin wife."

That made him feel sick, tore harsh and deep, as if he were a part of her, feeling the awful cruelty of the fate she'd chosen. *Don't tell me these things.* He stood suddenly, looked away from her, raked a hand through his hair. "Have you told me all of your secrets?"

"Have you told me all of yours?"

He leveled his eyes at her and winced. "Yes."

She walked to him and slid her hands beneath his shirt, along the edges of his ribs, up his torso, letting her fingertips dance on his shoulders. His blood pulsed madly in his temples, so hard he could barely think. He wanted to catch her up in his arms and kiss her shoulders, her cheeks, her jaw, her hair... He gripped her wrists, but he couldn't even clamp down on them and push her away. He was too weak.

Aura looked up at him frankly. "I dream of you at night."

God, no. She couldn't do this. He couldn't. "Stop," he whispered.

"What?"

"You can't...you can't." Not unless he could ask her to run with him, to never come back, and he couldn't do that. He had nowhere to take her. He pushed her gently away, though it was like tearing open a wound. "Aura, don't."

She slid her arms up, laced her hands behind his neck, and laid her head on his chest. The thin shirt let her breath through, warm against his skin. Her fingers bunched in the fabric. "Don't?"

"Please."

She pulled back, gracing his ears with her fingertips. "I'm sorry. I didn't mean to..." The backs of her hands touched his arms, bare skin on bare skin.

Mikel caught at her wrists again. He searched her eyes for a moment, a second, a minute. She blinked once, a long heavy drop of her lids, and when they came up again, he leaned toward her, pushed her lightly away from him. She didn't move. The closer he nudged, the deeper and longer and slower her breath eased from her lungs, through her lips, and intoxicatingly close to his mouth. Then his mind blacked out.

He kissed her—a slight, desperate taste that lurched through him, made him want more. She didn't struggle, and he didn't release her. Her lips trembled against his, and his own become heavy, insistent, demanding. A soft murmur escaped her throat. He needed her to stop him, to shove back, to protest, but instead she dipped her tongue inside his mouth and he lost it. He pushed her against the wall. Her body reacted, curled and braced against him. She nipped at his skin until he pressed his stomach hard against hers and moaned through his teeth.

"You can't—" he whispered, just as her fingers slid into his hair and dug into his scalp. He let go of her wrists and reached for the fabric around her throat, pulling it away until her bare collarbone was beneath his lips. Heated and needy, he trailed down until the skin grew soft and curved into breasts.

He drew back, pushed on her shoulders until her fingers disentangled from his hair.

"Did you forget the color of my skin?" he gasped out.

She reached for him, caught the back of his neck. "No."

He held her as far from him as he could. His chest hurt, pounded, so bad he thought he would fall over. "You should go."

Quick, hot tears poured out of her eyes without pause. "Don't be the frightened slave now. Not after what you just—"

"Forget what I did. *Forget.* Any man would have done the same."

Aura looked as if she might slap him. "Don't lie to me."

"Tierrof would protect you if you asked him. Half your tribe will avenge you as soon as they know the truth. And I would kill for you if you'd let me."

"You know I don't want that from you."

Mikel leaned against the wall. "Then why are you still here? Mustn't spoil your own plans."

Aura raised her chin in the air, and her tears stopped instantly. "You are right." She left the same way she came: quickly, by the window.

ॐ

AURA BOUGHT FOUR IDENTICAL DRESSES for her sisters to cover how long she had been at market, but she dropped them on the floor the instant she reached the outer part of her chambers. Norani was there, and he was quiet—far too quiet.

"Do you need something, Father?"

He shook his head. "No."

"Why are you in this part of the house?"

"This is the door you always come in."

Aura shifted. "What is it?"

"You know I sometimes have one of your brothers follow you when you go to market? You've never seemed to mind this, and so I never ask you."

"No, I don't mind."

"Abel followed you today."

Abel? Her littlest brother. Only seven. "Yes?"

"He saw one of Behret's men strike you in the stomach." Norani's voice betrayed nothing, but his eye twitched when he said it.

"What of it? It did not hurt that much."

"He came to tell me because he couldn't fight them himself. If he hadn't told me you fought them off and escaped, I would have feared for you."

"Well, I'm fine, as you can see. I am sure Abel exaggerated." Aura even managed a smile.

Norani stood up and walked to her, raised a hand as if to touch her cheek. "You've been crying."

"It is nothing."

Before she could stop him, he pressed his hand to her stomach. Gently, but enough that she flinched and bit her lip. "I'll send the midwife up to look at it. If she tells me there is a bruise or anything of the sort..."

Aura shook her head. "No, Father."

"I can use this to terminate your marriage to that man."

Aura picked up the dresses from the floor and busied herself arranging them in their packages again. "Please don't do that. It wasn't Behret's fault. His men are merely wild. I thought you liked him."

"Not if he allows his men to touch you as if you belong to them." Norani's voice rose slightly. "He may be gentle to some, pretend to be selfless when he needs to make a friend, but he has made many a multan shiver and step away from him."

"As you have, Father. That is no fault."

"But he is a selfish man, Aura. There is a difference. Your sister Lia was happy with him, but the only reason I have tolerated him depriving me of two daughters is because you care for him so fiercely." He was watching her too closely.

Don't tremble, she told herself. "I do care for him."

"Then I have nothing to object to. His selfishness may work in your favor, as every man knows his wife's happiness is his own happiness."

The sick feeling in her stomach began to ebb. Father was rightly cautious in regard to Behret. He would avenge her. He would. Aura stood on her tiptoes and kissed him on the forehead. "I will go to the midwife, but I assure you, the men were just looking for a little fun." She smiled. "I can take care of myself, Father. I'm not a child anymore."

He grunted and walked out without another word.

{12}
Gabriel

THERE WAS A FEAST ON the morrow. The excitement was so high that even the servants barely slept. Tev was kept up well past what would have been third watch in Ashlin, refreshing paint on the girls' arms and legs, helping the women wash and dress, standing about holding dress material so outfits for the next day could be chosen. She went to sleep sometime past midnight, more sore from holding still than she had ever been from battle.

She woke again sometime in the night. A dream? She rolled over and glanced at the other sleeping girls. Yes, a dream—of a dark, cloaked assassin slipping into the room. She'd stabbed him, dragged his body outside, and buried it in the sand, but even after it was over, she kept seeing his eyes—bright, young, almost gray—losing their life slowly. Halfway through the spiral to death, his chest would turn to dark red armor and his black hood would turn to rumpled black hair and she would watch Tofer or sometimes Ric die at her hand. Then it would happen again and again until she woke.

There was no way she was going to sleep again.

Tev crept out of the house and past the first set of guards. They weren't truly guards as they weren't even armed—more like watchmen. They were sleeping heavily, probably brought on by too much wine and dancing. The main house was still lit from the inside, so she went around back to Nerri's room and stole a few fine wraps to place on top of her own spun twill. She wrapped silk around her face so most of her skin could not be seen, then crept out the front gate.

She wasn't even sure where she was going until she got there: the fighting arena. The smell of sweat hung in the air even in the dusky, unlit dark. The tall, clay building that swept around the entire perimeter had dozens of entrances, and there must be weapons inside. The first door she tried was locked, but the second was held shut only by a bar. She managed to lift it out of place and slip inside.

There were sleeping bodies inside. Probably drunk as well, in preparation for the feast. What was the point of drinking *before* the feast? It didn't make any sense. Likely a new tradition, built upon an old one.

Tev slunk about in the shadows, up and down hallways until she found something she could use—a slim longsword. It looked like it had been stolen from a Drei, as it hadn't the thick tempering of Seren steel, but also lacked the curvature of mountain weaponry.

She walked slowly out into the rings. Her face was perfect for this— scarred and hacked, her skin far from soft and womanly. Anyone who saw her would believe she had always been a fighter. Maybe they would even mistake her for a boy. She knelt in the dirt for a moment and breathed in the thin, hot air. It would be unbearable by daybreak, and yet these dark Desert People would walk about in it without breaking a sweat. One swing of the sword through the silent air and Tev broke into a grin that was so wide it hurt her face.

The sword responded well, though it was far more rickety than anything she would use in combat. She was likely fooling herself into thinking it was passable. The sheer bliss of moving it against an imaginary opponent made her happy...and then terribly unsettled.

There were faces before her: Hodran's. Kovim's. That nasty rebel who'd killed her armor-bearer and chained her to a chair. The bastard she'd stabbed with Ric in a barn. Julian, the Drei general her brother had surrendered to. The cold blue eyes of his son, Sark. The nameless, faceless shadow who'd stabbed Tofer in the back. She slew them all, as cruelly as she could, and then she did it again. The dream she'd had repeated itself to her, and she tried to banish it by imagining her own foes more vividly.

A sound from behind her shattered the scene. She whirled and came face to face with Gavriel, Nerri's cousin. In the dark, his skin looked like midnight, his eyes and machete bright against his dark form.

Gavriel cocked his head to one side. "Best put that knife down before you hurt yourself, Seren." His voice was full and deep, as she remembered it. Something in it was warm and reassuring, too. She didn't fear him at all. His shoulders shifted beneath his robes. "What are you doing here?"

Tev answered in his language. "I'm here to train."

"And whose little cobra are you?"

Her jaw twitched. Little cobra? She'd never been called such a thing, but she liked it. "Tierrof's."

"Tierrof only has a few fighters, and I know them all."

"I'm new."

Gavriel took a stride toward her, and she stepped back accordingly, her gaze down. "Not to worry. I won't judge a house slave for wishing she'd been sold as a fighter. I treat my slaves better than Tierrof does, anyhow. If you like, I could buy you."

Tev looked up at him slowly. It was tempting. Ric had told her once that she could be a fighter if she came here, but Mikel hadn't wanted them to and for good reason: fighters drew attention. "I am happy with my master."

"Ah." Gavriel strode into one of the rings, peeled off a heavy robe, and reached for a weapon. "Well, no need to waste the evening. You came to train, little cobra. I'll be your opponent."

Her palms were sweating. She wanted to badly, but if he recognized her training... "You are twice my weight. We would not be pitted against each other in a duel."

"Bah. No matter. I want to see what you have." A sincere smile broke his face, wide enough to reveal bright white teeth, and Tev felt a ripple run up her spine. Not a frightened ripple, but one of anticipation. She wasn't sure how vicious he would be with a blade, but she didn't care.

He said no more words. He ran at her and met her sword in the air. She told herself this was necessary. She had to refresh her instincts, had to be ready. Truthfully? She felt her heart pulse with wild freedom as Gavriel's body twisted around and above her, as his sword found hers again and again. Her own arms reacted—met, blocked, returned, drove him back to the center of the ring—without thought. It was fluid as music. She hadn't sparred since the night her mother died, and then it had not been joyful but angry, broken, in need of an outlet. She had missed this with a passion, missed the simple acts of graceful movement. No blood, no death, no severing limbs from living bodies. Just the turning of swords through the air.

Gavriel let her swat at him and banter for a time, and then he closed in. His curved machete nicked her arm twice, and she cursed the robes she wore. He was good. Terribly so. Maybe even as good as her. Fine. Tev flew at him, landed a foot squarely in his chest, knocked the wind out of him, and gave him a warning scratch on the edge of his bicep. She felt a little heady, like she had drunk too much fresh air, and it made her giggle as she looked down at his closely trimmed beard and moppy black curls. "You're easy."

Gavriel grinned up at her. He had given her that ripple up her spine ever since she first saw him with the blood keeper, but she hadn't known for sure what that was until now: he shared her passion for swordplay, for the beauty of combat. An ache grew in her throat as he flung her off and toyed with her blade again. She missed Ric so much it hurt at the back of her eyes, and then she thought of Ashlin, of training and sparring with her father, and the dull pain grew sharp. *Pem, I would do anything to see you again.*

Then he had her. Flung her down into the sand with his full weight atop her, his machete against her throat.

"You were saying?"

Tev couldn't move beneath him, but she was too impressed to be angry. How he'd done it, she wasn't sure. She struggled briefly. "I was saying—again."

He gripped her wrist and hauled her up, meeting her parry before she had a moment to breathe. She tried to get used to the weapon in her hand, but it was strangely top-heavy. That was why she'd lost to him, she decided. It was this gangly longsword.

He let her come in close this time, run him up against the rope corner, and then flipped her down again.

"How do you do that?" Tev growled in Aldadi.

"Why do you let me?"

"I...don't." Well, that wasn't entirely true. She wasn't fighting him with everything in her. Still, she wasn't sure how he managed to pin her in one motion. He really was quite good.

Gavriel dragged her upright and dusted off his hands, but she came at him again. It made him laugh. "An Aldadi knows when he is bested."

"I can take more." Tev's body was just getting warm. She knew she would find his flaw if she kept at it long enough. Either that or he would get sloppy.

"You are dead many times over by now, Seren. Be grateful I am not a challenger in the ring." He walked away from her, his dark back shining with sweat. Then he turned and looked at her with a half-smile. "Tell me your name?"

Suddenly, she remembered a certain half-breed fighter and Nerri telling her he belonged to Gavriel. She wanted something in return. "Tell me the name of one of your new fighters and I will."

The smile widened, but he slowly turned away again and kept walking. "If I'm selling anyone, they'll be at the slave market, and that is the only place to make friends. Best forget whomever you wish to know and I will forget you."

He picked up his robe out of the sand and gave her a final nod, his eyes gleaming. Tev got goose bumps. If he'd guessed who she was, she'd just done something unbearably stupid.

{13}
Pause

MIKEL HAD TO PHYSICALLY RESTRAIN himself from running to her.

Aura stayed near the door, as clean and poised and stately as he'd ever seen her, and asked if he could make a set of linking toe rings for her mother. "I want them made from bronze with green stones set in them."

Mikel stood on the far side of the room and leaned on the edge of his fire pit. "I can have them ready in a week."

"And I want a matching wrist bangle for my father."

"A week."

"Two sets of earrings for my sisters, also made from bronze, with five green stones in each earring."

"At least two weeks. I'll need Tierrof to trade for more green."

She nodded briskly. "I'll send a slave for them in two weeks. No later."

Mikel clenched his jaw. "A slave?"

She shrugged at him, and her face was dead, devoid of emotion. "Is something wrong with that?"

"No. Nothing."

"Good."

She stood well out of his reach. He took that as a message and turned his back to her. "Am I to expect this slave to pay for them as well?"

"I will pay you now, so that there is no confusion."

He nodded once, just enough so that she could see it from where she was. He heard her get out the coins, set them on one of the tables. He wouldn't turn to look at her, not unless she said something. *It is better this way*, he told himself, but everything in him fought that it wasn't better.

"You didn't tell me how much," she said.

"Five hundred in coin."

"That price is high."

"Then buy somewhere else." He still had a fierce need to run to her. Hold her. Apologize... His voice strained as he said, "Well, why don't you go?"

"I want to stay a while."

"It is warmer by the fire."

"I am warm enough."

So am I, he thought. The sweat was literally dripping off of his bare chest.

"I'll not come again."

He looked at her. Poised, calm, elegant. Sharp need slammed through him. *Damn.* "You will be married."

"Not yet. But Behret is coming to the city tomorrow, and once we are wed, I will be part of another tribe that does not like my father's or Ladin's. I won't be able to come often, but maybe..."

He stepped toward her, blurted, "You can say it, Aura. You're not coming back. Ever."

She shook her head. "No."

He took the coin from the table, came as close to her as the chain would let him, and reached for her hand. "Tierrof would want them to be a gift." He did not expect her to heed him, but she did. Very slowly, tentatively, her fingertips met his in the middle, slim, soft and long against his rugged, hacked and hard. He tugged gently.

She pulled back even as the coins slipped into her hand. "Do you have nothing more to say, Seren? Not even to me?"

He listened for a moment. The sounds of the market were distant. Not a voice or a footstep near them. He tugged again toward the far corner where they'd be hidden behind tables and crates. She followed him, not a hint of resistance in her grasp. He turned the fingers over in his hand slowly, stared at them, tried to memorize them. He knew he couldn't, that no memory could do her justice. Then he knelt on the hard floor and kissed her knuckles.

Her composure went out of her, and she found the floor next to him, her back against the wall and her knees bumping his. She didn't ask for her fingers back, and he didn't let go. When she spoke, her voice was tired, pained. "The sun does not sleep for long in the Desert, no matter the season. We haven't much night. I've stayed always in the day. I thought I could live these past six seasons, happy and free, and then let go of everything. But I can't." She raised her eyes slowly to meet his.

He pulled her in, the soft silk of her exquisite dress against his calloused ribs. She whimpered, just once. His hands cupped her face, and he started to kiss her cheekbones softly, as if they had time.

"You are no man's wife yet," he said. "You can say no to him, can't you? Find a man who will honor you. Please you. Stay alive, Aura."

"I can." She shook her head, her breath becoming ragged. "But don't tell me I am supposed to meet a poor goat-herding boy and bring him happiness with a smile. Simple. True. You, a Seren—you think I should do what is sensible, what fits in your little square of righteousness, but it is not to be. You are a slave, and I am to marry a multan—a man who could own you or order your death—because he has an unsettled debt with his Creator."

Mikel reached behind her to a cleft in the wall and pulled out a handful of small daggers he'd fashioned. It had been two weeks since she was last in here, time enough for him to make plenty of weapons. "If you must have your own vengeance, settle the debt the way it was made."

She shoved them away. "No! No. I've told you I'll not kill. He must die by the hand of witnesses, the way Allel intended."

"Allel sees what is done in secret and keeps an account of it, Aura." He tried not to let his frustration through, but he couldn't help raising his voice a little. "I don't want you to die. Your soul is the cleanest and purest of any I've known. You, of all people, should live."

Aura smiled. "I have moments when I wish I could, but those are selfish moments when I find life too terribly beautiful to want to leave. What is it that makes you think death is a thing to fear?"

He laughed nervously. "I've too much blood on my hands to not fear death."

Her shoulders squared, and she leaned toward him until her fingers brushed the rough skin on the edge of his jaw. His eyes closed. It felt refreshing, like a touch of coolness on a hot, fevered brow.

"I know you," she whispered. "You have the tattoo of a slave and the voice of a Seren and the body of a warrior, but it matters little. I know who you are. I know your heart, and a heart such as yours is a friend to Allel."

He swallowed, and his eyes opened. "You might say otherwise if you had seen what I did in the war. There's been nothing but blood to color my sky."

Her fingers slipped away, and he wanted to grab them back. "I wish I had time to know." Her own eyes were closed, her gaze down, as if waiting for him to release her.

Mikel stood up, walked a few paces away, and turned to watch her, crossing his arms across his chest. "I may fear death, but I don't fear the means of it. I've grown calloused to pain. If you'd let me die in your place, let me avenge your sister for you... I've no selfish reasons, no game to play. I will do your deed for you and spare you the pain. I trained for killing—I am better at it than you. Let me do this."

A crease formed between her brows, but she did not answer.

He breached her silence again with the most final words he could conjure. "I'd never dream of having you, Aura, if that's what you're waiting to hear."

That made her look at him. Her eyes flashed open. "That was *you* who strapped on my sandal, who watched me dance. I know the rough feel of your hands. Don't tell me you never dreamed of me, Mikel of Orion."

The sound of his full name from her lips—a name he couldn't even claim any more—made him want to weep. He walked back to her in one step and kissed the edge of her face. "I dreamed of you. I wished for you. And knowing you'll never come back will make me feel as if you've torn my heart from my chest and crushed it on a rock. But I never hoped to be yours, and I do not hope now. All I ask is to go to war for you, once. The one time you desperately need a warrior." He nipped at her ear, listened to her tiny sound of protest turn into a pleased whine. "You walk undaunted toward death, and I am nothing at your feet."

A tear ran down her cheek. "You say this, but my only fear is watching them torture you instead of Behret."

He tightened his fingers around hers, and she did the same, just for a moment. "Better me than you."

She drew away sharply and turned toward the door, her skirts trailing behind her. Mikel caught a glimpse of her eyes, wet with tears, and knew he'd hurt her—that knowing him had hurt her. *If I made you want to live, Aura, I'm not sorry.* He grabbed her arm, pulled her back, and kissed her. She gripped the back of his head and drew herself up against him, wrapping her legs around his waist so he had to carry her.

When he let her feet drift to the floor again, she buried her face against his neck and whimpered. "I don't want to leave you."

He slid a dagger into her waistband. "Keep this. In case you must use it."

She shook her head, but she did not throw it away. "I'll say a prayer for you every seventh day. I'll pray Allel gives you faith and peace."

I won't have peace.

The drape at the door blew in the breeze, and she had vanished.

Mikel gripped his own fist, trembling as the muscles flexed. He looked at his skin, turned dark by the sun from hours on the rooftop, hardened from heat and burns, rippling with added strength from the heavy tools he worked with.

He had never felt so helpless.

{14}
Blades

AURA WAS ALMOST READY WHEN Behret and his entourage arrived in the courtyard. Her hair had been combed to a stunning shine, her skin rubbed with scented oils, and her cheeks painted with fresh water birds in gold and red. Behret loved red.

Nerri sat on her bed and watched, picking at her own fingernails. "I am glad we have one season more. Before you're…his."

Aura gulped. Her little sister criticized and gossiped to keep from ever having to be serious. A statement like that was a lot from her. For a moment, Aura had the overwhelming urge to tell Nerri her purpose, but she banished the thought before it could take root. Nerri would tell Father. Father would lock her up and never let her near Behret. She knew this. Why was she thinking about this now?

Aura's dressing girl held out a small chest, an ebony box Mother had given her when she received her first piercing. "Jewelry?"

The coppery metal that Mikel had given her drew her attention immediately, and she flinched away from it. She never took it far from her bosom, but this morning she had placed it in her trunk to keep it out of sight. She didn't even want to look at it.

"Only what I'm wearing," Aura answered her.

Tev came in with a steaming basin of water. The herbs floating in it were rare and sweet and Aura shivered. She had more than a moon of this ahead of her. Bathing, dressing, beautifying herself in order to entice her betrothed and make him more and more excited for their wedding day. Not all girls did this, only those who married into the priesthood. Something told her Behret was not going to take it well. His hands would be on her as soon as her father had turned his face.

Tev slipped off Aura's sandals and started to massage the water into her skin. Her entire body had been bathed not four hours ago, but the dust season was picking up and it coated everything, so she must be washed once more before she went to dine at the home of Behret's parents. They would expect her to be spotless.

"Is that too rough?" Tev asked quietly.

Aura jumped. "No. Why?"

"You were frowning."

Aura did her best to smile. "I did not intend to." Her mind wandered again, this time to the scars on Tev's face. She wondered if Tev had been one of the children Mikel went to rescue. If they'd been through much pain together. How long he'd been protecting her. She was so little. "How old are you?"

Tev looked up sharply, perhaps surprised by the question. "Why do you ask?"

"No matter, it's just... Your hands are very small." It was the best excuse she could give.

Tev's face relaxed. "I am fourteen."

It would be desperately hard to lead a group of knights with a tiny little sister to protect as well. Aura tried to imagine Tev as a spoiled princess and couldn't. She wondered if Seren princesses received the same training on the arts of mating that multan's daughters did. She couldn't imagine that, either.

On impulse, Aura reached for her trunk and pulled out the bracelet from Mikel. "Would you…give this to your brother?"

Tev looked startled. She gulped and took the jewelry from Aura's hand, her forehead wrinkling as she studied it. Aura fidgeted nervously. From today onward, she would be in a whirlwind of company. Who knew when she would have another moment alone with Mikel's baby sister?

Tev turned the jewelry over in her hand several times, then handed it back. "I couldn't. I don't see him at all," she whispered, and Aura was glad she knew to keep quiet. "I'm not permitted to leave the threshold of Ladin's house unless I am with Nerri, and Nerri doesn't shop."

Aura grabbed it back quickly. "I'm sorry. I don't know what I was thinking."

ᢙ

BEHRET'S HOME WAS TWICE AS large as Norani's, and the grounds far more extensive. His father was one of the highest-placed priests and a man of garish taste. Everything was overdone, Aura thought. Behret spent the first hour showing her the house and the second showing her the grounds, and by the time they were to dine, the sun had set and the courtyard was lit by torches. Everything looked still larger in such a light.

Aura hated the way his parents peered condescendingly at hers across the table and how Behret's friends shifted about instead of standing calmly as her family did.

She caught the men leering at her as well, as if she was here to be amusement for them, and one of them winked at Nerri. She wanted to strangle him. *Lia, how did you bear this without screaming?* She was glad none of them came with Behret when he announced he would walk her home. Just her and him, through streets still loud with preparation for the feast. Many torches were lit, the shops staying open late into the night to prepare for the days of gifting that would follow. She half-expected Behret to pull her into a shop and buy her something, but he kept walking, weaving in and out of alleys, whispering words that made even her—highly educated in the arts of mating—color up to the roots of her hair.

Her sisters walked ahead of her, far enough that she eventually lost sight of them in the turns of the crowds. And then the crowds weren't there anymore. It was darker than it had been. There were fewer torches. Or were there? Why was she suddenly dizzy? Had someone put something in her wine?

Behret pushed open a door, and they went down several stairs into a huge, open room that stunk of wine that had not been aged enough. It was full of people. The noise itself made her want to turn and walk back out, but the smell made her actually gag. Behret spoke to someone, and then he guided her through the door again, up a staircase on the outside of the building to a roof. It was lit with candles and torches and draperies hung about in order to cast shadow.

Aura gripped Behret's arm. "What is this place? I thought you were going to walk me home."

"Not tonight." Behret smiled at her and reached for a silver pitcher on a table that was made of a rare, purple wood she didn't know the name of. "More wine, my sweet?"

For some reason, that made her feel like vomiting. "I think I've had enough already."

"Ah. Fine." He grinned at her again. His beard had grown longer since she'd last seen him, and he looked like a stranger for a moment. "Come here." He grabbed her hand and yanked her body toward him. "Your father lied to me. You are a woman grown in every way. I am certain you are quite full of pleasure."

The way he yanked on her arm hurt, and she whined. "What are you doing?"

"I want you tonight. I'm tired of waiting." He grinned again, as if he expected her to be pleased. "Lia liked to come here. We had many a secret night."

Aura tried to make her voice light when she said, "Do you really think you should be talking about what my sister fancied as you try to entice me?"

"I've already enticed you. You're mine. You are a lovely creature. I am eager to see what you have beneath your many robes."

It wasn't tactful of him to put her in the position of denying him what he wanted, but he, a priest's son, should have understood full well that there was to be no soiling of virginity until the words had been said. "I haven't vowed anything to you yet."

He reached inside her dress, found a clasp, and loosed it. "Ah, but you needn't. I know your heart."

Her heart was pounding with confusion. She couldn't decide whether to give him what he wanted or insist he have her on her terms. Her body was afraid of his, but she could tame it. She could force the bile back down her throat and tell herself it was necessary. *The sooner he tires of me, the sooner it will be over.* But something told her that if she didn't have the courage to stop him now, she would never have the courage to drive him to kill her.

"You know they will check me on the eve of our wedding to see if I am still a virgin. To see if what I swear is true."

Behret shrugged and pulled her dress off of her shoulder. "I care nothing for such formalities."

"But if I am not, they will assume I have broken faith with you, and my father will lose his bride price. And his pride."

He unwrapped her dress down to her waist and went to work on the fabric that bound her breasts. "I can see he keeps his price, but why should he be proud of you? He did not make you a luscious flower to be plucked and filled with my seed. Allel did that."

Aura raised her chin, suddenly flush with anger. She didn't want to hear the name of God on his lips again. It made her sick. Even sicker than his fingers twisting against her ribs and the thought of him filling her with anything. She struck him, once, with as much power as she could place in her small hand.

He smacked her back, considerably harder. Her mouth bled, just a little. She had never been struck across the face as a girl, nothing more than the slight smack from a sister or a friend in playful jest. The impact made her jaw throb and her head ring.

"Aw, now, see? You've messed up your perfect face. You shouldn't have distracted me. Even my men know better than to strike you there." He grabbed her wrist and twisted it hard.

"Did you do this to Lia, too? Did you hurt her like this and make her afraid to tell anyone?"

His face darkened. "She wasn't afraid. She understood how someone like me must maintain a certain image in spite of my indulgences. She understood."

Aura tried to rein herself in, to act the pouting betrothed again, but it still came out in a slight hiss, "Would you expect *me* to understand such cruelty?"

Behret laughed, but it was short. He gripped both of her arms and dragged her away from the light, the stone cutting into her heels. "I've heard quite enough of this nonsense, Aura." His beard was so close to her face that it scratched her cheek.

She heard footsteps on the stairs. For a moment, she hoped it was one of her brothers, but Father would not have risked angering Behret himself, would he?

It wasn't. It was a man she didn't recognize. A tall, bulky man with lighter skin and a huge gold earring in his nose. "And how is this one?" he asked by way of introduction.

Behret responded in a voice gratingly pleasant, even as he drove his fingertips into her forearm. "I haven't tried her yet. You are welcome to stay and watch."

The big man just laughed and left. Behret finished undressing her quickly. When the last scrap of fabric hit the floor, the dagger clattered with it, and he picked it up and held it against her stomach.

"Oh, a weapon? Were you afraid of thieves tonight?" He laughed again. He'd never looked so ugly. "Or were you planning to use this on me?"

"I would never..."

"Be honest now." He ran the tip of it up and down her cheek until it drew a thin line of blood.

She winced, bit hard on her lip. There were voices nearby, on the stairs, but none that she recognized.

"Behret has a new one. Richly dressed."

"I don't believe you."

"The gifting feast will be a good one this year."

They were coming up here, weren't they? Aura could see their shadows, moving across the roof, closer to them. She struggled against Behret's body, tried to take her dagger back. She saw the anger rise in his face, and the wildest ray of hope rose in her. Maybe he would kill her tonight. Right now. The other men would see him do it. Her father saw her leave with Behret, and when she never came home, he would look for her and there would be more than one person who saw her...

"She's beautiful."

"Like I said, richly dressed."

"No, I meant her skin. She's from one of the older tribes."

One of them raised his voice to Behret. "Your taste grows more and more difficult to please, Behret. Consider that one day you will grow bored of this."

Yes. She would do it now. Aura sat up as straight as she could with his body pinning her down and spat in his eyes. There was marked approval from those who watched, so she backhanded him hard across the jaw.

"She fights."

Behret wasn't angry enough, though. He turned to one of them and said, "Help me hold her down and you can have her when I'm through."

That wasn't what she'd expected. That wasn't it at all. "No!" Aura yelled in his face. "No."

Someone came and put a hand over her mouth. She bit at his fingers, but it made no difference. They were still laughing. All of them. As much as the thought of giving her body to Behret had made her sick, she had always pictured herself in some measure of control, not pinned in a ring like a fighter. Not laughed at and toyed with and turned into sport.

The hand on her mouth grew slack. He was distracted by something. Aura used the moment to sink her teeth into his hand, but he didn't seem to notice.

There was someone on the roof, their features hidden by a hood. A weapon gleamed in their hand, and Aura had one moment to identify her dagger before the person stabbed one of the men in the side of the neck. He fell instantly. The hooded figure reached down to grab weapons from the dead man's belt before he even hit the floor, blood pooling around him like a puddle. Aura gagged at the sight and turned her head. Behret hadn't noticed and was still trying to kiss her, and that made her gag more.

Another man turned from watching Behret and was dispensed with even faster—half a second of aim, a tight flick of the wrist, and the embedding of sharp steel into his chest. It happened so quickly Aura couldn't look away. She heard the victim grunt, the breath leaving him, not enough life left to yell, and she screamed. As loud as she could.

Behret whirled, finally aware, and yanked her to her feet. "Shut up."

He covered her mouth and pulled her body in front of him. "Do you have a quarrel with me?" he asked the figure. The other three men had weapons out, panting hard, and one of them held a machete.

The fighter didn't answer, just reached for the machete with gloved fingers and wrenched it out of the bearer's grip.

♃

TEV HAD SLIPPED AWAY FROM Nerri as soon as she'd realized Aura was behind them, alone with her betrothed—a man Norani had glared at all night and whose very name made Nerri shiver. She had stolen a hooded robe as the apprehension in her stomach had grown and Ric's voice started to bark in her ear.

It's their instinct. Treachers of this kind drag off their prey to where better men won't interfere.

Tev did not have to pinpoint weak spots. Behret's friends wore no armor. Straight for their most vital portions of flesh.

She ducked beneath the next man to run at her and shoved the dagger into him, but it did not kill him. He came around behind her, even as she dashed for her fourth target—a cow-eyed man who could barely hold his head up. She knelt so his blade went above her and took advantage of his instantaneous loss of balance, slashing her machete into him with a long, wild slice up between his legs and into his gut. She grabbed his machete where it fell, balancing her arms.

You want to do it?

Ric's question, replayed inside her head, didn't make any sense now. Of course she wanted to.

He is not armed.

Neither was she.

It took Behret that long to become aware that she was here to kill him, to drop Aura clumsily. He kicked the girl, sending her sprawling across the room into the body of one of the other men, and her head crashed against something made of stone. Behret was already on edge and reactionary, flushed with wine, but that also made him sloppy. He caught Tev coming up from the floor, kicked her back down, and pressed his heel between her shoulder blades. It gave her a quick moment of searing pain in her shoulder, but that was nothing. She slashed his calf open and sprang up as her third victim staggered toward her with the dagger buried in his ribcage. She slit his throat with a quick, precise cut. It made a singing sound as it split the air and the layers of skin.

When mankind forgets he has a soul...that is when he does not deserve to live anymore.

One who had stood quietly against the rail started to run for the stairs. Tev drew the dagger out of the last man's ribcage and threw it at the retreating form's back. He fell.

Aura was struggling to stand, reaching for clothing. Behret shoved her down on her hands and came at Tev again, hacking at the air. Tev dodged his first few blows, came around him, and carved his chest with a hefty downward draw that cut him all the way open. He crumpled onto his own insides as they fell out of him.

Tev stood in the center of the roof and let it spin around her. Ric's voice in her ear finally eased and calmed, returned to a whisper in her head.

Too good for him.

Aura hadn't moved from where Behret had thrown her. A trickle of blood ran down her face, and her brown eyes stared openly at the weapons in Tev's hands, at the thick dark liquid that pooled on the shiny edges of the blades and formed droplets on the points. Tev lifted them above her, felt the weight of them, the shape and the balance in her arms. They were not familiar, yet she had used them with ease. She looked at the dead bodies around her and waited for the rage in her to ebb, but it stayed, like a warm, kindled fire. Something she would keep.

You did well. Damned well. Your family will be proud of your courage.

Tev went slowly to Aura, but she shrank away, so she flung the hood off of her face. "No need to fear, Aura. It is Tev."

Aura didn't move. Her body shook, her hands holding her dress in front of her. "You killed him."

"Him and his bastard friends."

"You shouldn't have." Aura kept staring past her, through her.

Tev slipped the dress over the girl's head and slid her arms through. Then she grabbed her elbows and said, "Come. You cannot be found in this mess." Neither of them should. Allel alone knew how many friends Behret had in this place.

Aura's eyes settled firmly on Behret's body on the floor. "They're dead. They're dead," she said, her voice gone numb.

"Yes. He and all his friends are dead. They won't hurt you."

Aura did not move.

"Aura, they are *dead*." Tev pulled hard on Aura, but she was heavy. "Move."

She tried to swing the girl up on her shoulder but she could not even heft her, so she just dragged her weight, past Behret and the man with a dagger in his chest and his throat slit.

"You have to walk down these stairs. Aura!" Tev smacked her a few times. Finally Aura's eyes widened with fear, fright, something. She stood up, held the back of her hand against her mouth for one long moment, and then took off down the stairs faster than Tev could follow.

{15}
ꟿUILTY

THEY RAN BLOCK AFTER BLOCK, seemingly in no direction, until Aura stopped against a wall. "I have to go back."

Tev wondered if she should knock her out with something. Perhaps she'd lost her mind this night—it wouldn't surprise her. "You can't go back. Someone will have found those bodies by now."

Aura shook her head about eleven times too many. "I left my dagger there."

"Does anyone else know what it looks like?"

"No, I always keep it hidden."

Tev ground her teeth. "Leave it be."

"But Mikel made it. Anyone with an eye for art will know his styling. They will think he killed those men." She slid against the wall. "I cannot have him blamed. I would rather die myself. I'm going back."

By the Derm, Mikel, what have you done? Tev grabbed Aura's arm. "No, you're not. Likely as not they'll think the dagger belonged to one of those men."

Aura shook her head again. "Mikel doesn't sell weapons, and everyone knows that. If Tierrof sees it, he will know."

"I'll go back for it. I killed them, and I'll take the blame if I have to."

Aura's voice was bitter. "You're only a child. You don't understand what you've done this night."

"I'm not a child, and I know the cost of what I've done." Aura tried to wrench her arm away, but Tev was stronger. She slammed Aura into the wall until she cried out. "Go home. Go home now. If anyone asks, tell them Behret met some friends and forgot about you, that some thieves roughed you up on the way home, and that you're desperately tired and must sleep. Go! I won't go back for the dagger until you are gone."

As soon as Aura turned away, Tev ran as fast as she could back the way they'd come. The streets were twisty, narrow, and confusing, but she didn't have to look hard. There were several dozen torches on that roof now and twice as many men. *By the Derm.*

She ripped off the piece of dark linen she had worn over her face and the thick outer robe she'd stolen and dropped them into the dirt in the alley. Both were surely drenched in blood if one looked closely. And both were higher quality than a slave would wear.

Tev looked for a way onto the roof that wasn't teeming with people, but she saw none. If the dagger was up there, they would have found it already.

ᕤ

MIKEL HEARD THE WINDOW SHUTTER open. Tierrof always latched them both inside and out, and the only person who would try to break in was likely a thief. He slipped down the stairs as quietly as he could with the chain on his ankle clacking softly. He drew a hot poker from the slumbering coals and held it, more to look daunting than anything.

Hands pushed at the window, and then a body shoved against it. He heard her grunt with frustration. *Aura.*

Mikel grabbed a mallet and smashed his manacle at the frailest point. It didn't break off clean, so he applied a hot iron to weaken the remaining steel and smashed it again. It fell away, and he unlatched the window. Her shoulder fell into him. He slid his hands under her arms and lifted her light body into the room. She let out a sound, a soft, quiet whimper, her face instantly pressed hard against his chest.

He didn't ask her questions, didn't force her to speak just yet. Something unspeakable had happened, and that was enough for now. He slipped an arm behind her and reached down for her knees. She curled up instantly and let him carry her, her hands about his neck, her face nestled into the crook below his shoulder.

Mikel took the steps to the roof, set her down on his mat, and leaned back against the railing. He expected her to sit next to him, but she curled back into his arms and clutched his shirt as if afraid he would vanish. She smelled of flowers. He could not say what kind, but it was heavy and drenching, as if the petals were sewn to her skin.

And something else. Fresh, metallic. He looked at her face, turned it gently toward the moonlight.

He couldn't keep the alarm out of his voice. "You are—"

"Not my blood."

"The Derm it isn't. Your face is—"

It bled freely, and she did not reach up to wipe it. "It isn't much."

She said nothing more, so he didn't press her. Holding her, if only for a moment, was a gift he hadn't expected. Her breath was soft and warm against his skin. He was tempted to bury his nose in her hair and drink her in. Instead, he ran a hand down her side to tuck her body closer, tell her she was safe here. Her clothing was arranged haphazardly, torn in places. An odd knot formed in his stomach.

"Who tore up your dress, Aura?"

She shook her head. He heard her sniff, knew she was trying to stop tears. "Don't speak about it," she whispered. "Don't. I've only a few minutes with you before they spoil it."

Behret? He worked his jaw hard to control himself. He wanted to rip flesh, shred the man who did this to her into a thousand pieces. The intensity of the violence in his mind frightened him, and he gripped her body harder. "Aura, if you tell me nothing of it, I will assume Behret hurt you and I *will* kill him for it. If he comes after you, it will make it easy for me."

"You can't." Her voice became thick with a sob. "He's already dead. Your sister did it."

His breath came out full, and it was only then he realized there had been a weight on his chest, as if it were his destiny to kill Behret. But he was dead already. "Where is she?"

"She went back to look for my dagger because I dropped it. It will lead them to you." Aura turned her face up to his and looked in his eyes. "They'll come here, or if they don't, they'll come to my father looking for me because I was seen at that place by a hundred witnesses. I would tell you I want you to run, but I don't know where you should run to, Mikel. They'll find you. Catch you. Kill you." She nestled her face against him again, and he felt her body lurch with sobs. "If she can find the dagger, then they'll think only of me. I'll go home at daybreak, and they can do what they will. But let me have what's left of this night with you. Please."

Mikel buried the tips of his fingers in her hair and pressed his lips to her cheek. "Shh. No need to fear, my one. I won't let them have you."

He didn't tell her what that meant, and she didn't ask.

ૐ

IT WAS A FEW HOURS before the street filled with footsteps and voices. Their torches cast flickering light in the room below, reflecting up the stairs and bouncing off the sandstone walls. Aura started to whimper, and he put a hand over her mouth.

There was a shout below. Someone had found his broken manacle.

"Did you check the room where he sleeps? The roof?"

"He's long gone. See? He broke his bonds."

Aura stiffened, looked up at him in alarm. She mouthed the words, *They'll think you...*

Mikel shook his head. *I want them to think it.*

"Check anyway," one of the voices said.

Footsteps on the stairs. Several men at once. Mikel did not resist them. Someone grabbed Aura and pulled her from him. He felt a physical pain when she left his side, as if an arm had been wrenched off.

"Be careful!" someone yelled. "Bind him tightly. He is dangerous."

His face was shoved into the floor, his hands and feet bound instantly. He was dragged down the stairs and out into the street. The torches formed a circle, and a tall Desert man with a trimmed beard drew a weapon, large and gleaming, the metal curled over itself like a flat claw.

Mikel winced when Tierrof pushed his way in front. Tierrof had warned him.

"You were treated with kindness, slave," Tierrof shouted. "This is how you repay?"

Mikel had nothing to say to that, not until he knew what they'd already assumed and what he had to fill in.

"He attacked my daughter." Norani stepped into the light. Mikel had never seen Aura's father up close, but it was easy to tell who he was. He had the same bones in his face as she. He spoke quietly, calmly. "Killed her protectors in the dark like a cat that hunts and drags off his prey." Norani tipped his head toward the man with the weapon. "Gavriel, do your worst to him. It will not be enough."

There was silence for a moment. Then Aura's voice filled it, thick and hurt. "That isn't what happened, father. I killed them."

Norani laughed, a laugh that bordered on a roar. "You did, did you?"

He raised his voice suddenly. "Perhaps you'd like to tell the priest such falsehoods? You walk a thin line, daughter."

Tierrof held up a hand, then tossed a body into the dirt in front of Mikel. He didn't have to look to see it was Kierstaz. "This one claims *she* did it. Did you ever hear this many preposterous lies in one night?"

Kierstaz broke in, strong and clear, "I did kill them. All five of them. One in the neck with a knife, one in the gut with a—"

"Don't listen to her," Mikel interrupted. "She is a child, and she worships her brother. You cannot believe a word she says."

Tierrof's eyes narrowed. "I don't believe Tev did it." He walked back to Aura and ran a hand down her cheek. "Her dress is torn and her face is bloody, and I swear to Allel if I remove the fabric from her arms, I will find bruises enough to..." He kicked Mikel in the face, as if daring him to deny it. No—Mikel saw it in his eyes—*begging* him to deny it.

"Tierrof—" Aura interrupted.

"Silence, girl!"

"Father, listen to me!"

Norani ran at his own daughter, his face a mask of anger. "You'll say no more." His voice sank to a loud hiss, one Mikel could hear very clearly from the ground. "I am sick enough knowing this slave has touched you. I would kill him this instant with my own knife, but I would never be satisfied without watching him feel a thousand pains."

Aura smacked her father across the face, much the same way she had smacked Mikel. Her voice broke and then went flat, but it was audible. "I tell you, Behret tore my clothes. Behret bruised my arms and hurt my face."

Tierrof blinked and swallowed. He walked back to Mikel and kicked at the dirt near his head. "You would swear this, Aura?" His voice was low, quiet.

"I would swear it."

Tierrof kept his eyes on Mikel as he spoke to her. "In front of Behret's father, a priest? You should fear him more than any of us."

"Yes, I would swear it."

"You know this slave must die, anyway. Killing is for fighters in a ring or for the lions of justice."

Aura choked out, "I know it."

Tierrof waved a hand to the man with the jagged weapon. "Gavriel, if you would concoct a fitting death for my slave…"

Gavriel's mouth twisted. "I would, happily."

Someone dragged Aura off into the shadows. Mikel watched her as long as he could, and when he could not, he felt cold.

Gavriel turned to a man who bore the same tattoo he did. "Bind the slave, cover his face, put him on a horse. Bring the sister." He looked at Norani for a long moment, one eyebrow raised. Then he said, "Bind Aura as well. I will have more questions for her."

ༀ

THEY RODE AT BREAKNECK SPEED for nigh upon an hour, and when they stopped, they were deep in the Desert. Aura held tightly to Gavriel's waist and wished that she could turn back time, somehow undo the events of tonight, start them over and make them happen gently—without blood and threats and beatings.

Gavriel swung down, pulling her with him, and she fixated on his bulging arms for a moment. She wasn't afraid for herself—she knew if he was going to kill her, he would do it quickly—but she was afraid of what his jagged blades might concoct for Mikel and Tev. He was a patient man…far too patient.

The moon illuminated the ground and the dunes about them as if it were day. The landscape had turned to sand and the city was no longer visible, but behind them was a huge stable that looked like it could house a hundred horses. Gavriel drew her toward it. She swung around just enough to see Mikel and Tev dragged from horses by Gavriel's tribesmen, their eyes still covered with fabric. It hurt watching Mikel stand there in the raw night, unable to see her.

Gavriel took her into the tack room inside the stables and slammed the heavy door behind them. "You listen to me and listen well, child. There were a dozen lies told back in front of those men because half of them are loyal to the priest. No matter how much of a livered dragon his son may have been, his father is revered. You know this, and yet you sought to unearth the truth in front of a torn horde. I call that stupid. Are you going to be stupid?"

Aura shook her head quickly.

Gavriel reached for her clothing and touched it gently. "Behret?"

"Yes."

"And his friends?"

"Yes."

He gave a quick nod. "Your little slave girl killed five men three times her size with weapons that weren't even her own."

Aura felt her pulse quicken. "Did you see it?"

"No, I saw only the corpses. I know the players. I know the technique of the girl."

"How could you...?"

He cleared his throat impatiently. "My judgment is trusted because I make it my business to be everywhere at once. To know all and see all."

"Gavriel, will you—"

"There were no witnesses. That means it is your word against that of your slaves. Five Aldadi men died, and someone will want Aldadi blood in return. If not yours, then Tierrof's. Everyone saw how close he was with his slave. Everyone saw him drag his eyes over *you*. He may be my very distant cousin, but he does not deserve to die over this. You, on the other hand..." He looked her in the eyes, and his voice lowered still more. "This is why your father sent you with me. Because he knows how my word is like honey to their ears. I am in good standing and always will be. If I say you have died a bloody death, they will believe me."

Aura sucked in a breath. "Please—"

"No, there will be no petitions. I'm going to spare your life, cousin, in the only way possible. They will scream for your head on the morrow, and it will not end until the girl who was with him that night—who set the slaves on him—has paid. You chose to marry this priest's son, Aura. You chose to be alone with him in a place he could fill with people who would most certainly lie for him. There will be no fair recompense, do you understand this?"

She nodded.

"Good. Because I want you to know never to come back here. Never." He opened the door and led her down to the end of a long hall, down to the end. Horses were prepared. More than a few.

One of Gavriel's men shoved Mikel forward and removed the covering from his eyes none-too-gently. Mikel blinked, and Aura caught his gaze and held it. If this was his last moment alive, she wanted to be the last thing he saw. *I'm sorry, Mikel.*

Gavriel drew a weapon and handed it to Mikel hilt-first.

Aura's breath caught. *What...*

"I've set fighters free before when I felt they had served me long enough. My men will ride with you as far as the northern passes. After that, you must travel to the border of your filthy country alone. Understand I am not setting you free. I am giving you a charge." Gavriel reached for Aura's hand and placed it in Mikel's. "See that she never returns, that she is fed, that she is safe. Swear this and you live."

Aura's arm trembled as she slid her fingers over the scars on his hand. She didn't dare glance up into his eyes for fear someone would yank their hands apart and it would all be a cruel joke.

Mikel gripped her fingers tightly. "I'll not take her."

Aura's mouth went dry. *You must, Mikel.*

Gavriel tipped his head and gave a displeased frown. "You'll not?"

"I am hunted in Serengard. Aura may as well drink the venom of an asp as be found with me."

She dug her fingernails into his skin. *Do not tell Gavriel this.*

"Of course you are hunted. You would not be here if you were not." Gavriel waved a hand. "Funny. Tierrof swore you'd give your last life's blood for her." His forehead darkened, and his eyes wandered to the shadows of figures about them, where Tev was. "I know your sister will."

Mikel ran his thumb over the top of Aura's hand, as if he didn't want to let go. "I *would* give my last life's blood for her. But there is a high price on my head and many eager to take it. I am the last of the Castle Guard if that means anything to you."

"I'm greatly displeased. If you're not useful to me in this way, I'll have to kill you."

Aura's eyes burned, and her teeth dug into her lip. "Don't," she whispered.

Gavriel touched her again, raising her chin with his finger. "You see? You've made Aura cry. You are this close to my blade, Seren."

Mikel tipped his head to the side. His eyes were dark with pain, his voice hoarse. "It would be a lie to swear I can keep her safe. Send her away with someone else you trust."

Gavriel flicked his hand, reached for Tev's wrist and drew her forward. "You fail me, I'll ask her. Are you Castle Guard, girl?"

Mikel cut in. "Yes. There is a bounty for both of us." He gripped Aura's hand especially hard, met her eyes, a message in them. She wished she could hear it. He let go. "We cannot take Aura."

Gavriel threw back his head and let out a long breath, his mouth open in a wide smile. "Ah, you are perfect." He gripped both Aura's and Mikel's hands once more only to nick their skin quickly on a knife. As the blood started to drip, he put their fingers together and leaned toward Mikel. "She's yours, Seren."

{16}
Butterfly

THEY DIDN'T STOP FOR TWO nights and two days, and when they did, it was to fall from their horses into the dust. Gavriel's men began to pitch tents in a semi-circle. Mikel swung Kierstaz down and then reached for Aura, but she'd already hit the ground. He looked at her, wondering how deep her hurt or confusion might go, wishing there was something to say but knowing there wasn't.

She shoved him gently in the chest. "You're going to keel over, white man. Go sleep."

He didn't wait for her to say that twice. He walked into one of the tents and threw himself on the ground. The sun sapped his strength like nothing ever had. They were still hundreds of miles south of the border, but he already couldn't move a muscle.

A dream tugged at the corners of his consciousness, something he wanted to happen but wasn't sure if it already had or if he'd imagined it. A butterfly, warm and kissed by summer, dancing on his nose in a meadow full of flowers. They were soft blue flowers—he'd grown them before. Been there before. Every summer of his life until this past one.

Fabric at the entrance rustled. The dream faded and slipped away, and he saw the blacks of his eyelids again. He wasn't in a meadow in Serengard. It was too warm, even for summer. There was a delicious smell of orchids or moonlight. Or orchids in moonlight. He wasn't sure where he'd even seen an orchid before. They grew in Neroi, and he'd never been that far south for more than a few days. The scent filled his senses until he was driven mad with it, his whole body wanting something, making his soul hurt with desperation. Sensations he had thought dead took hold of him, dreams he thought he would never have: humanity; a wish for peace, not just of the soul, but of the body; a refuge from this endless cycle of duty and violence that had enveloped his life.

"Mikel."

Her.

She was on him, murmuring against his ear, whispering his name like she had a right to him. He opened his eyes, awake all at once.

"What are you doing?"

She smiled, but her voice was breathy, full of nervousness. "I'm yours, Mikel. Remember?"

"Gavriel can't give you away. Not like that."

"No because Gavriel doesn't own me." She leveled her gaze at him— as well as one could from atop him—and the corners of her mouth twitched. "You do."

If he had learned anything, it was that his ways were far more frightful to her people than their own, but the thought that she would accept their bond as final because another man had slit their skin made him feel guilty. "I don't care what he did with a knife. I'm not going to claim you."

Her eyes went wide. "You won't? When I didn't even cost you a herd of cattle?"

"No, I..." He gripped her forearms, his hands three times the size of hers, his shoulders twice that. "In my country, a maiden is wed only after her consent."

"Her consent? Mikel, if you have any doubts..." Aura finished her sentence by rolling her hips into him until he groaned. She reached for his hair. Her fingers tangled in it, fingernails drawing across his scalp while he flexed his jaw for control. One more minute of this and he'd lose his mind.

"It isn't that." Mikel reached up, brushed her skin, touched that stray piece of black hair. "I...I don't think I can promise you anything. I can't give you anything."

"I'm not asking for things. I have nothing, same as you." She put her fingertips up against his face and stroked the skin delicately, softly. "I want you."

Mikel felt a painful roar in his ears. "I might be rejoining a war. I might have to leave you in some little village somewhere and you won't know where I am or when I'm coming back—"

Aura stopped him with a kiss, drowned his words, pushed him past his restraint and deep into some whirlpool that pulled him in and drove him to a feverish place. She ran her tongue along the inside of his mouth: an invitation.

Mikel sat up, lifted her above him. His lips tangled and tugged, hands slid all over her, pulled her against him, felt her wildly. "Aura, I've never... I've..."

She cried out softly, a pleased murmur, and nipped at his ear. "I'm glad."

Mikel flipped her in one fluid movement, flung her down into the sand beneath him. A tremor ran along her body, and for a moment, he was afraid he'd been too insistent, but her eyes were closed in a worshipful sort of revelry. When they opened and looked up at him, he couldn't breathe. He wanted to whisper her name into the air over and over to make it true. Make this more real. Make it last forever.

Aura's tongue flicked across her lips, then lunged up and crushed his with her own. He tasted her gently, let her kiss him just the way she wanted, until she pressed his mouth open and pushed against his shoulders with her hands, and then he couldn't bear the clothing that kept her from him. He kissed the edge of her collarbone with increasing pressure until she pulled the fabric back, untied the knots that held the top of her garb, and guided his hands to her skin.

Euphoria hit him like a wave, and he saw nothing but blankness for a second. He fell onto his side, weak. Aura slid up against him and nestled her head against his chin. Her fingers trailed up his arms to tug on his shirt. She pulled it over his head, cupped his chin again, kissed him deeply, roughly. He mumbled words he didn't even understand, stirred to a point he'd never been—somewhere exhilarating and terrifying all at once.

And he knew this was all he wanted from here on. Aura. Always.

Nothing left between skin and skin, they drove and crushed each other in a fog of mutual wonderment. They bit back silent screams together, danced over sounds with fingertips, and watched each other's eyes go wide and tighten from perfect, happy pain until sleep took them both.

꙰

SOMETIME IN THE NIGHT, AURA wrapped the fabric of her dress around them, but still she shivered when she woke. The tent was just beginning to warm with sun. She trailed a finger down Mikel's cheek to wake him, but his eyelids didn't even flicker.

"Wake up," she whispered against his ear. "The tent will fall down around you in a moment."

His body jerked, but he slept still. It was hard not to notice how very tall and solid he was in the golden light. She'd never seen him sleep.

"Mikel." Aura put a palm on his chest and shook him. "Wake up, my one."

He started, bolted upright, and reached for a weapon, but his hands came up empty. He looked at her. His face broke into a smile that reminded her of childish adoration, and she ducked her head for a moment to keep it from spreading to her own.

"You slept in."

His cheeks were red, either from sunburn or embarrassment. "It's warm in here."

Aura didn't think so. "It will be warmer. The others are up. We must move."

Mikel reached for her arm and pulled her down on top of him. Aura squealed loudly, and he whispered, "Shh. Do you want them all to know what we were doing?"

"They know."

He kissed her. "*Now* they do." His face grew serious. "I don't know what we're riding toward."

She shrugged at him and put a finger to his lips. "It doesn't matter."

"It does. There could be—"

Aura pressed her finger harder. "Hush. Help me take this tent down. And don't look at me like that."

"How should I look at you?"

"Look at me as a man looks at his wife, not as a fighter looks at his master."

"My father always looked at my mother like he wished no one else were around."

Aura pulled the main post of the tent down, drowning him in heavy fabric. "You are hopeless."

The rest of the tents were already packed, the horses finished with their breakfast. Aura hid a smirk from the rest of them as they tried to avoid her gaze, but Mikel looked tired and forlorn enough to curl up and hide in a hole. Was he ashamed about what they'd done, or was it this uncertainty he kept trying to express? Either way, she wished she could wipe the expression from his face.

Aura let him help her up on her horse, balancing against his warm arm more for the niceness of it than the support. He held onto her after she was settled, his head leaned against her leg, and she reached down and ran a hand into his honey-colored hair. It was smooth and silky and made her fingers prickle, as if she'd put them too close to the fire. The feeling tingled up her arm to her shoulder, and she wanted to hold on.

"Is it really so dangerous for you across that border?" she whispered.

He swallowed and looked away. "Likely."

She bit her lip and kicked her horse.

༒

THE FARTHER NORTH THEY RODE, the cooler the air became. It was nearly spring in Serengard, or so Tev told Aura. But if this was spring in the south of their land, what was winter in the north?

Mikel and Tev were tired, their faces as sunburned as any she'd seen. It almost made her laugh, how blistered and red they were. Only white people reacted this quickly to the sun. They stopped for rest and water during the heat of each day—heat that slowly turned to a chill wind the farther north they ventured.

Aura could hardly sleep anymore. She must have, for she was rested in the morning, but her mind was perked up like the ears of a zebra when she hears or smells danger on the wind. Every night she made love to Mikel until she was warm all the way through, then she pressed her bare skin against him and wrapped them both in as much clothing and blankets as she could find.

A hundred miles south of Neroi, she was suddenly afraid. Two days of traveling left and she wasn't sure she could even live a year in that kind of cold. Mikel hardly talked while their horses trotted side by side, but for all his brooding during the day, he freed himself at night. He told stories that made her ripple with delight and ache with sorrow, and even when he grew quiet and whispered about death and betrayal, she could kiss it away and make him laugh.

Thirty miles from the border, the escorts Gavriel assigned to them peeled off and turned south once more, leaving them utterly alone. Tev rode ahead, a determination on her brow that Aura didn't dare interrupt. She waited for Mikel to draw up next to her and flash her a grin.

Her thoughts were on a sober course. She couldn't help thinking about her sisters, her father, her mother. Leaving them was starting to hurt. Strange—she had been ready to die, to abandon them completely, but not to live without them. It made her wonder: *What could they do to him that would be worse than a slave's death?*

She didn't mean to say it out loud, but she did. She said everything to him now.

Mikel's eyes were distant for a long moment. He looked up at the sky, down at the sand. "They could hurt you."

Aura laughed slightly. "You are afraid for me?" By all the snakes, his protests to Gavriel had not been sudden panic. They were real fears. "You were afraid of being responsible for me. You—afraid? When you protected your sister in the midst of a war? I cannot believe it."

"You saw how well my sister defends herself."

Aura flushed. "I will try not to be a burden. But I won't bear a weapon. I won't."

He looked repentant. "It isn't that. It isn't you. I'm afraid that someone will see you and know that I love you and use you to hurt me."

"Gavriel—"

"Gavriel doesn't know a damned thing about my kingdom, Aura."

She turned when he said her name. "You are wrong. Gavriel saw that you have the means and the strength to protect me, even in this ugly land we go to where there are monsters in the open country and siblings kill each other for sport."

He laughed. "Neither of those things are true, and I am only one man."

"One man who has battled thousands."

"Hundreds. And not alone."

She waved a hand. "No matter. I trust in you."

He sucked in a breath and ran a hand around the back of his neck. "You refuse to understand. Trust has nothing to do with it. You think you will be safe with me? Aldad was not your cocoon, Aura—it was your butterfly state. Serengard will be as dark walls about you."

"And what could anyone do to me? I was not even afraid of Behret."

"That is a Dermed lie. You were terrified of him."

Aura felt anger course through her because his words smacked of truth. "I wasn't terrified of death."

"There are things worse than death."

She shifted her shoulders. "I asked what frightened you, not what you think should frighten *me*."

Mikel rode up close beside her and reached for her. "I'm sorry."

Aura pulled her hand away. Her cheeks were streaked with tears, and she hid her eyes so he wouldn't see her confusion.

"Aura, stop."

"Pull me off yourself if you want me to."

"I would, but I'll not be another man dragging you about. You've had enough of that."

Aura reined her horse in and looked at him. He sounded incensed, but from the look on his face, he was more confused than she was. She climbed down and spoke gently. "There is nothing to explain. Take me with you. Pretend I am your slave or sell me to a Seren if you must, but I'll not be left behind."

Mikel swung off and turned and paced, ran fingers through his own hair. "We do not have slaves, Aura." He caught a hold of her by her waist. "Your demands are fair, but my answer cannot be. I could be hung within a week, or I could be leading ten thousand men toward a hundred thousand. It depends on whether there is a force of assassins on the other side of that river or knights of my own."

"I'm not leaving you. I have no tribe but yours. I'm not going back to the coast or wherever you think I should go, Mikel, don't try and make me!"

"Shh. I would never send you away."

"Then why are you saying these things? Why did you try to make me go with someone else?" That had haunted her ever since the words had left his lips. What could he have been thinking? She turned and buried her face in her horse's flank, taking in the salty smell of her sweat and the deep thump of her heartbeat. She knew this horse of Gavriel's, had ridden her a few times—the only one who had not changed this week, the only one she could look at and not see a stranger.

"I didn't want to say those words," he told her quietly, his hands still firm on her waist. "But I want you to stay alive. Safe."

"I am not frightened of anything except being alone. You'd have to kill me to keep me from you, and I know there are other things you would rather do to me."

His hands tightened. "Listen to me, and please stop acting like a child." He caught at her chin, tried to turn her face. "I know how you hate bloodshed. Where we are going, I am quite certain you will see it at my hands. I don't want to make you hate me. And you will hate me."

She shrugged, wiped her face with the back of her hand. "You lie to scare me. The same as my father. I am not afraid of you men and your deep voices."

He kissed her hard, rank with sweat and deep with the wetness of his mouth. Aura stiffened in his tight grasp, gripped his wrists, reacted to the roughness. He drank on her breath, and she gave it, letting him drag a sharp exclamation from between her lips. He bore back down, hands tangling with the wraps on her arms and bringing her body against his chest. When he let her go, he fairly threw her away. She caught the defeat in his eyes.

"I won't hate you," she murmured.

Tev circled her horse back around and yelled at them, "Stop kissing, you children."

{17}
Fоцпð

AURA BURROWED HERSELF IN THE sloping riverbank and hugged her legs tightly. She felt that if the Desert sands covered her over so that no one ever knew where she had gone, she would at least be more at home than she was in this cold place. As soon as she crossed that river, she would be a different person. Someone with strange customs and a strange language. Someone no one would know and no one would like.

She shivered inside her clothing, staring at the river, at the dim lights of the wooden pier across the sand flats. *This is where we have to live.* An empty, ugly place. Even the so-called village looked dead, not alive with fire and sunset. Trees were tall and frightening and brown. There were dark hills beyond. Dark water. Dark wooden structures. The sand was so bland and gray that it felt...dark.

They were going to cross the river tonight. Both Mikel and Tev had grown solemn as soon as they'd seen the village and then immediately had a fight. It was all in the Seren tongue, so Aura did not understand it, but she gathered their next step was dangerous for both of them. She turned to the south, took her knees, and put her face to the ground to pray.

"He is not a mere mortal, you know." Tev interrupted her solitude.

Aura turned and faced her, but the girl was still staring at her brother. He was strapping weapons against his bare skin, not a goose bump on him.

"I am sure a white man needs all the help God can give him," Aura said, tentative.

Tev shrugged, her little frame looking terribly tall. She was at least a foot shorter than Aura, yet Tev dwarfed her in some way. "I've seen him take many wounds and run with cunning a few weeks later. He has led men who owed him nothing into battles of fatal odds. And he is not even the one who inherits the crown. I am." She looked down at Aura, and there was no jealousy. Only fierce devotion. "Many times he should have died, yet he has lived. And you, who by all rights should abhor him and our land, love him."

Aura stood up. "I do."

Tev began to move away as if she were restless. "I know you didn't want me to...interfere. I cost you your family, your life, but I am not sorry."

That gave her a jolt. "No. No, Tev, I am grateful to you." Aura wasn't sure if it was true, but it should be. She ought to be grateful.

Tev shook her head. "It will not be easy for you here." Her voice wavered slightly. "If you are to live in Serengard, you would be better off without my brother and I, but he was never very alive without you." Her eyes were pleading. "If you're going to leave him, please do it now. This is when he expects it. If you wait... His soul would die again if you hurt him. Please do not."

"I couldn't leave him," Aura stammered. "What Gavriel did, he did because he knew me. He knew I...he knew I wanted Mikel." Maybe he hadn't known just that, but Aura had always thought Gavriel had a way of seeing into a person's soul. He knew things.

Tev gulped. "You may want him, but you don't know how bad it can get, the way he is when he loses someone. You won't know him—"

"I love him, Tev. More than myself." It hurt her throat when she said it, and she knew it was true.

Tev ran to Aura and pulled her into arms that were ridiculously powerful for a young girl. Her body shook. Was she weeping? Aura had never seen her cry for anything.

Tev's voice was thick. "Thank you."

ℐ

THE RIVER WAS COLD BUT shallow at the flats. Even in the chill, Mikel felt a certain loosening of the tension about his shoulders, a freedom as he stepped onto Seren soil once more and breathed in the fresh smell of decomposing leaves and briny water. This place meant harshness, it meant running for his life, but it was home. As much as he wanted to hate it for the pain it had caused him, he couldn't.

It wasn't hard to decide where to look. The Flats used to be a place where people hired folk, where they met up with traveling companions and moved on. There was no other port farther up river and no reason to stay. There used to be a square mile of inns and another of markets, but most of them were boarded up and appeared to have been so for a good while. Only the port was busy, as well as the two large ale houses next to it. The light coming from one of them was nearly blinding, the air full of singing and strange, bawdy laughter. It grated on his ears as the sounds of the Desert market never had.

"We'll start with the smallest one," he told Kierstaz in Seren. "If Pier is in this place, he wouldn't draw attention to himself."

Kierstaz pursed her lips. She didn't trust Pier, he knew. Well, she was going to have to.

He slipped inside, the other two behind him. Kierstaz had wrapped her head like a Desert woman in the heat of the day, but Aura's dark skin stood out no matter what she did. Someone grabbed her arm right after she came in and asked Kierstaz, "How much for this one?"

Mikel whirled, furious, but Kierstaz had already bent the man's wrist back until he screamed. Mikel slipped away, let them be a distraction if they would.

There was one Drei here, in a corner where the low, thick tables were surrounded with cushions. They were set up as a revival of the Aldadi custom of eating on the ground, a sort of mix between that and the Seren table. The Drei—so young he must be a boy—stuck out like a sore thumb. Hair chin-length, nose flat at the bridge and pointed at the tip, and jaw slender, with that undeniable rust-colored hair.

Mikel slid in beside him and spoke quietly. "You came with Pier?" The boy flinched. Mikel knew him, didn't he? "Colstadt?"

Colstadt's eyes narrowed. "Am I supposed to recognize you?"

The youth had patched up a wound, hadn't he? Mikel lifted the shirt he wore just enough to reveal the nasty scar he had won the night he'd nearly died. "Tell me you're not the Drei who sewed this?"

Colstadt choked on his drink, but still looked puzzled and shook his head. His words were so quiet they were nearly silent. "Not here. Follow me in a minute. Bring the girls and take this." He handed him a nearly empty purse of coins. "They'll think we've arranged business."

Colstadt disappeared into the back of the building, up a flight of creaky stairs. Mikel tipped his head to Kierstaz to tell her to follow. They passed drunk men, mostly sailors, reeling about with jugs on their thumbs. Some gypsies and traders hawked their wares even through their liquor. There were women everywhere, most of them dark-skinned with bruised lips and averted eyes. Mikel felt rage begin to boil in him. Since when had the Serens made slaves of the Aldadi? Since a year ago? Had they always been this lawless, this cruel, and he simply hadn't known?

His breath grew tight, and he ached to reach back for Aura's hand, but he didn't dare. One glance and he saw her eyes were wide, her fingers gripping Kierstaz's tightly.

The stairs went up for five stories, growing broader and more decorous as they climbed. The last floor had long red rugs, walls of white with gold detail, and lit candles in sconces, though the floors creaked with age.

Colstadt waited at the top of the stairs and led them to a door at the end. The room they entered had glass windows and molding and must have been elaborate at one time, but the walls and floor were scuffed, the furniture bare and simple.

Pier looked up from a book he was in the midst of binding with a heavy needle. He blinked. "You should go, Colstadt."

Colstadt closed the door and left without another word.

"We had near given up hope of you." Pier stood, put out a hand, and touched Mikel on the shoulder, which was as affectionate as Pier got.

A flood of relief burst inside, but Mikel said casually, "Glad you waited."

"Nowhere else to go." Pier shrugged. "Who's the slave girl?"

"That would be Tev."

Pier waved a hand as if Mikel were an idiot. "The *Desert* girl."

"My wife."

That didn't seem to matter to him. "Does she know?"

"Yes."

Pier stalked around the table and bowed once at the waist. "Your servant, my princess."

Aura looked startled. She stared up at Mikel with her already bewildered eyes, and he realized that she had probably never seen Drei. They would look strange at first.

"This is Pier," Mikel murmured in Aldadi. "He was my lieutenant in

Ashlin. He just called you princess."

Aura smiled slightly at him and said, "I am not, but thank you."

Pier groaned. "She doesn't even speak our language? Mikel, where are you going to hide that lovely creature? She will attract every eye in a raiding party. Do you *want* to be found?"

"Shut it, Pier. She can tell you're angry."

"My force is small enough. There are only nine of us left—I had to let twenty scatter northward. Too many, grouped too close together, too suspicious. Hodran has spies out."

"What happened to this port?"

"We are lucky it hasn't spit out every Drei who sets foot in it, but the slave traders don't like to ask questions. Everyone in Dreibourge is either starving to death or being thrown on a spike."

"You said Hodran has spies. Is he still in command of the army?"

"Yes, but now he is also Chamberlain of the Second City, not that he spends any time there. Dreibourge is the conquest of choice, the Fourth City their new utopia." Pier bowed once to Kierstaz at last. "There is still a reward out for your body, dead or alive, my queen, but they have given up overt search. If you want to build a force in the east, now is the time."

Kierstaz's mouth dropped open, but no words came out.

Mikel frowned. "She never said you could call her queen, Pier."

Pier smiled tolerantly, but he kept his eyes locked with Kierstaz's. "You have nothing to say about it, Mikel. You're running off to make babies."

༄

TEV HADN'T A WORD ON her tongue at first. She stared at Pier, but his expression was as matter-of-fact as if they were discussing the need to eat.

"I have something for you," he said, his voice oddly soft.

Tev followed him to the back of the room. He lifted the floorboards and pulled out a set of armor. Not Tev's armor—Kierstaz's. The slight indents on the inside for her breasts were perfectly shaped and sized, her waist the same thickness as her girl body had been. It couldn't be hers, not unless he'd stolen it back from the bastard who'd killed her armor-bearer.

"Where did you get this?" she whispered.

"I made it."

He met her eyes for a second, and every heated word she'd spoken against him ran through her mind. *Pier only cares about his own people.* She had been wrong.

He held it out in his long, slim fingers. "For you."

She picked up the breastplate and held it against herself.

"You have ten loyal men. Reveal yourself, give us your banner, and we can win you more. There is desperation in this hill country. The people who used to hate Orion now hate the Empire ten times greater. A few will fight for you if you say the word. Even some from Neroi will rise." He put a hand on her shoulder and bowed his head. "You are their only hope."

The armor seemed to glisten in her hands. She wanted it. She wanted it badly. Behind her, Mikel's voice mumbled in Aldadi. Aura whispered back, tense and worried, her voice all shaky as if she were shivering.

Tev looked up at Pier. "Who told you who I was?"

He grimaced. "No one. I did not watch you grow from a babe for nothing. You play dangerous games, daughter of the king."

She nodded too many times, swallowing to keep herself under control. "I...don't know if I can, Pier."

His hand was still on her shoulder. "You can."

That wasn't what she meant. If she fought, Mikel would fight, too. He would destroy himself. "And what of your country? You care so much for mine. Can we not slip into Dreibourge and forget all of this?"

"Not Dreibourge." Pier stood suddenly, walked to one side of the room and back again. Mikel and Aura grew silent, their attention on him. "My country is being ruined, destroyed messily with as much desperation and blood as the Council can contrive."

"There is a Council?"

"Kovim has appointed Chamberlains over the cities, and a council that includes the Pitching Boar. The Drei have no food. Now that the Orion treaties have been broken and the farmers are abandoning their lands for the cities, there is no one growing a crop in Serengard. Kovim made trade agreements; the Drei farm Seren land and produce a crop, then sell it to Dreibourge at an extra cost for import. The deal is a good one for those that take it, but it has fractured the solidarity of Dreibourge." Pier showed no emotion, but then, he had always been that way. Tev couldn't tell if he was angry or sad or indifferent. "Kovim has sent his own men into the capital and has begun a hunt for the Generals and any loyal to them. Because he has yet to destroy the power of the Generals, he tortures any man of consequence until he signs an agreement for the land exchange and turns in any neighbors he has who are pureblood Drei. The Drei Generals are still talking war while the Serens are talking annihilation."

Tev couldn't hold her breath in. It came out in a half-cry, heavy. "We can't stay here." She glanced up at Mikel. He looked wretched. She couldn't do this to him. "And there is nothing we can do for Dreibourge."

Pier blinked, as if afraid he'd been misunderstood. "No, my queen. For true. They have lost their own footing."

She nodded, but her chest hurt for them. She and Mikel would abandon Dreibourge just as they had abandoned the border—when it became too much for them. The armor in her hands begged her to strap it on, but she handed it back to Pier. "Refashion it for a boy and shear my head again. I'm not the queen of Serengard. I'm not the queen of anything."

Mikel fell back against the door and let his breath out slowly. Tev heard it and then saw him run a fingertip between Aura's thumb and forefinger.

"We'll find a safe place—any place that won't know us—and we'll stay alive, Pier." She looked up at him, hoped he would understand. "No one wants us anymore."

{18}
Cliffs

PIER HAD CHOSEN AN ABANDONED tower for them to assemble in, ten miles north of the border town. It was grown over with weeds and crumbling at the foundations, but it still had eight stories intact. Mikel held Aura flat against his body.

"It's so cold," she whispered. The wind took her words and drowned them.

Mikel buried his face in her neck and breathed on her. It didn't seem to help. "I'll build you a warm fire tonight."

She nodded, not bothering to speak through her chattering teeth, and he wished he could build said fire in his fingers and carry it with them.

Kierstaz held her armor close until they were inside, and then she handed it to Mikel to fashion. He built a blaze in the hearth, but mere wood took twice as long to heat. He'd been spoiled by Desert ore. Aura huddled next to the flames, her face finally relaxing as the heat seeped into her bones.

Once the metal was hot enough, he took it out and began to refashion it. Colstadt, thankfully, asked no questions. Kierstaz had told him what she needed for her disguise, and he'd obliged her without a word. As soon as he returned, she stripped off her top layers of clothing and slid her dress down to the waist. Colstadt didn't bat an eyelash.

Kierstaz raised her arms and started speaking in a low voice. "The first wrap around must be very tight. My breasts need to be high, tucked under my arms—like this."

Colstadt's answers were quiet, mumbled. Mikel hadn't known she trusted the boy that much, but then, Colstadt had patched a wound of Mikel's the night Kierstaz thought he would die. She was fierce with her friendship.

Aura tipped her head at the two of them. "I can do that for him," she offered in Aldadi. Her voice betrayed how startling it was for her to see a man with his hands on Kierstaz's naked flesh.

"He can do it," Kierstaz said. She mumbled an explanation to Colstadt in Seren.

Colstadt didn't even look up. "I'm best for this. I know bodies better than anyone." He flashed a smile, and Aura nodded, puzzlement on her face because she hadn't understood a word of that.

Then she started to move. Her feet first, legs rolling on the ankles to the rhythm of hammer and anvil.

Mikel glanced at her, distracted by the wish to breathe against her skin, maybe carry her off into a warm room and lie next to her on a hearthstone. "Do you want me to destroy this armor?"

"No." She threw a mischievous smile over her shoulder. "It is warmer to move." The motions of her arms were hynoptizing—something that should be seen only in firelight. And there *was* firelight here.

Colstadt kept his attention on Kierstaz's skin, but his eyelids flickered toward Aura, too.

"Tev," Aura said smoothly. "Before you take that dress off completely, you should dance with me."

Kierstaz blushed up to the roots of her hair. "I have never danced in my life. I mean…not like that. I dance with a sword."

Aura gasped. "Never? You poor soul." She walked over and pulled on her hand. "Dance."

Kierstaz shifted. "There is no music."

"Colstadt can sing."

Colstadt looked like he'd been smacked. He'd somehow understood *those* words. "What? No."

Kierstaz rolled her eyes. "She wants you to sing."

"I don't…" He trailed off.

Aura smiled that warm, carefree smile of hers. It was as if she held some power to compel or intoxicate. Colstadt sang in Drei, something sad and haunting, but with Aura dancing, it felt mysterious and sweet, almost worshipful. Kierstaz kept her dress off, but her eyes closed and she rolled her head gently around on her neck to lilt of the song while Colstadt kept wrapping her in leather.

There was a strange liberty in the air, something Mikel had only felt when under the open sky on his farms. It shouldn't exist here. A mere step away, two nations who'd used to love each other were destroying their bond with slavery and blackmail. Aura was broken. Kierstaz was hunted. Colstadt was forsaken. This should be as dark a corner and as cold a moment as they could find.

But it wasn't. It was warm.

♆

IT WAS NEARLY DAWN WHEN nine horses drew up outside.

Pier came in as he always did, quiet as a fox, a determination in his step. "We shouldn't stay longer than a week. These places are checked often by the army patrols."

Mikel agreed. "We'll leave at dusk tomorrow."

Kierstaz's hair was chopped, and her chest wrapped in leather. She looked like a boy again, curled up against Colstadt for warmth, both of them sleeping soundly. Mikel exhaled hard. As afraid as he'd been of her striking out against the Empire, letting her lead at last would have been a relief. *No rest.*

As they came single-file down the steps to the cellar, every one of Pier's men stared at Aura. There was nothing to do to disguise her. Her eyes were wide and brown and her skin almost as dark. Mikel felt her gravitating toward him, ready to cling to his back as the Drei took the room. He put an arm out to her, caught her hand. She gasped, as if she could not fathom so many olive-skinned men with so many weapons.

"It's all right," Mikel whispered in Aldadi. He kicked himself for forgetting to relay all that Pier had said. She hadn't even known there were more of them. "These men are loyal to me."

Pier stepped up and unsheathed a longsword of Seren steel. "Belonged to Lomius, I believe. I kept it buried."

It wasn't until Mikel took it that he realized he had missed this sword greatly. It fit in his hand, yet it was long and heavy and powerful. He could kill anything—anyone—with it. Aura stepped away from him into a corner.

The Drei each took a knee and raised their arms in salute. It surprised him. They were waiting for a mission, and he had no notion of what to say.

"I have very little to ask. We are outlaws in a land that hates us. We go to seek a desperate survival. As border knights loyal to the Eight Generals, you owe me nothing."

A man stepped forward. He spoke haltingly, a mix between the language of the Drei and the Seren. "You say we owe you nothing, but your knights fight in Dreibourge for our people. We do owe you."

"My knights fight on their own conviction."

"No one would fight at all if you hadn't."

He nodded slightly. *For true...and I feel more guilt over that than pride.* "Pier? You have been scouting this country longer than I. You know what is best."

Pier came forward with a map and placed it in the middle of the floor. "There are the Caps—the best place, in my opinion." He nodded toward Aura. "But she is cold, and this is only the south. The Caps are dangerous in the winters. Cold can kill people of her blood, especially without medicine."

"I won't hold you and your soldiers to me. I can find another place for us."

Pier frowned heavily. "My soldiers have no one else and are loyal to you until the grave. Take what allegiance we offer." He waved a hand and resumed his narrative. "The villages are good but home to gypsies and whisperers. Dragon Country is filling with people from the cities even as it empties of farmers. It is known that people who want to hide from the Empire go there, so bounty hunters are many. The cliffs are the safest choice, but there are savages among those rocks."

Mikel touched his sword. "We can deal with savages better than untrustworthy neighbors."

Pier nodded. "We head north, then east. Find a castle we wish to own and take it."

♋

AURA WOKE TO FIND HERSELF tangled in Mikel. She didn't remember ever going to bed—she'd fallen asleep on the cellar hearth, waiting for him to finish making arrangements. But they must be on an upper level for there was sun coming in the window, and they were wrapped in the skin of some sort of animal she couldn't name.

"When did I come up here?"

Mikel ran his fingers through her hair, stroke after stroke, and it was the most natural thing in the world. "Near sunrise. I carried you up."

"You did?" Aura wished she remembered. If she could have him carry her every night, she would. "It's warm here. Next to you." She slid her hands under his shirt and then remembered why she'd fallen asleep in a corner. "He hates me."

"Who?"

"Pier. He hates me, doesn't he?"

"No. He merely doesn't trust easily."

"Why should he not trust me? I have done nothing."

Mikel smiled slightly. "He has had…many friends turn against him. As have I."

Aura sat up and looked him in the eyes. "You needn't fear that I will turn against you."

He kissed her nose gently. "I have never feared that, nor ever will."

There was the sound of the soft clack of armor in the room above them. Mikel looked guilty. "I don't want to stay like this—running. These knights deserve better."

Aura watched his face. She didn't have anything to say because she didn't know what had happened. "What do they deserve?"

"Somewhere they can stay. Someone." He slid a thumb down her cheek. "Someone of their own who loves them." The longing in his eyes made her sad, even though her heart felt happy. "We'll leave at twilight tonight. But will you slip away with me today…and marry me?"

Aura jumped, confused. "I did marry you."

"Under duress."

She smirked. "How many times do you want to cut my hand, Mikel?"

"I want to marry you the way my parents married."

"If we married the way *my* parents married, there would be a seven-day feast and thirty bonfires."

"I wish I could give you that now." Mikel grinned. "Well, to be entirely accurate, my father gave my mother a bracelet that was two thousand years old in front of ten thousand people of Ashlin, and I can't do that, either."

Again with the longing. Aura kissed him gently. "Are both of your parents dead?" He started, as if someone had hit him, and she was embarrassed. They must be dead. Of course. "You said your mother was, but you didn't say—"

"My father was the King of Serengard. He was among the first to die."

"I didn't know if you made slaves of your dethroned Serens the way we do."

"They took some prisoners, but there is only one king at a time and they wanted his head for a trophy."

Enough of this kind of talk. Aura stood up and pulled on his hands. "You said you were going to marry me. On with it."

They slipped out of the tower after Mikel told Tev and Pier they'd be back in an hour. Hand in hand, they ran through sparse hardwoods until they found a stream. Then they slid down the bank to the edge and walked on the stones and sand for a mile. Mikel kept glancing up the bank and into the thickets. The brush up there looked sinister, so Aura stayed out of it. At last he found what he was looking for and dashed up to it.

"It's early for rose trees to bloom," he called back to her once.

Whatever a rose was. He cut something off a small tree with a knife and ran back to her.

"Yours."

She smiled and held it, puzzled. It was a soft yellow flower, covered with jagged thorns as long as her fingernail. The bloom was pretty, to be sure, but why hold something so sinister?

He found another scrubby tree, one with blooms of a bluish color. He cut one off and ran back to her again.

"What are these for?"

Mikel didn't answer. He knelt in the pebbles beside the stream, laid his sword on the ground at her feet, held out the blue rose, and wrapped his hand around it until it started to bleed. "Aura of Norani, I swear myself and my sword to you. I swear that I will protect you with the skill I was trained with, give you all the love I have and more, and offer my strength of body and mind and heart to draw from if ever you require it. Whatever you need of me is yours." He gestured toward the rose in her hand.

Aura wrapped her own fingers around the yellow flower and let the thorns sink into her skin until it bled like his. She raised her eyebrows at him.

He nodded. "Your turn."

"What do I say?"

"Whatever you wish to say."

She bit her lip. "I give you my body for a possession, my children for a tribe, and every thought I can dream in the night, I share with you. It is...not as pretty as what you said."

His content smile was back. "It is far prettier."

He reached for her hand, and their blood mingled. This part she recognized, only with her tribe it was a deep cut with a dagger. He dipped the cane of the rose in their blood and spliced it onto another tree, wrapping it with muslin to heal the bark.

"Why these flowers? Because they hurt?"

Mikel slid a hand into her hair, tipped her face toward him, and looked at her as if she'd said something that had changed the face of the world. "I don't know, but that could be it. I don't know if love is supposed to hurt, though." His fingers crept around the back of her head. "I hope it never hurts you. I hope that you never have to see me use my sword, either."

She pulled herself up by his shirt and looked into his eyes. "I am stronger than you think."

He dug his fingers against her scalp. Her breath caught in her throat, and it cut, as if she had swallowed a mouthful of sand. She made a sound that came out like the chirp of a bird, not a protest but a question, as his mouth enveloped hers. He nipped at her lips, tasting, pulling. She felt a rush of pain somewhere near her ribs and realized he was pouring into her some kind of hurt—something built up and buried, a tragedy that was not hers and never would be hers. He held onto her, and she tried to understand, to unravel his desperation in a language she knew.

He broke for air, at last. Had it been a moment, a minute, an hour...

"I—"

He interrupted her, his face close against her forehead. His scruff had grown to a rugged shadow, and it rubbed on her nose. "Don't say a word."

But she did. "Stop being afraid, Mikel Orion. I'm here. I'll keep your heart safe."

He closed his eyes, and his body trembled. "I'm not afraid of dying anymore."

{19}
Tгцlч

TEV BURROWED INTO THE WEEDS outside the empty tower used to guard the cliff passes in her father's day and held her knees against her stomach. This was the eighteenth sunset she'd watched in Serengard, and although her fears were nothing, the ache in her chest was heavy with longing.

There was no turning back now. Tomorrow, they entered the cliffs, and still she could not keep herself from wishing they were back at the border or deep in the Desert. A handful of Drei would make no difference. A fortress in the Cliffs of Marek would make no difference. She would still wish for recompense. The blood of her parents and her knights still cried out for justice, and it would continue to cry from the ground, with the voices of thousands of pureblood Drei now added to it.

"All alone?"

Tev snapped her face away from the voice, almost colliding with the trunk of a tree. "Go away."

"I know this isn't what you wanted."

Dermed Colstadt. "I don't want to be bothered."

"But you're crying," he whispered.

"What intuition." She hated to be sharp with him when he had just spent over a year in that Dermed muddy rut waiting for her and Mikel, but she couldn't help it. She never wanted anyone to see her cry.

"Tev." Colstadt knelt next to her and reached for her face.

She flinched away and actually contemplated biting his fingers. "Who do you think you are?"

That did not daunt him. He leaned in and kissed her mouth, firm enough to rivet her but gentle enough that she could feel the pity ooze from him. His soft lips nudged at her, chaste and sweet. A gaping hole opened in her stomach, and she had to shove him away.

"I never figured you for the cruel one," Tev said bitterly.

"I don't mean to be." He looked away for a second and then back to her. "I don't know why you feel you must hide your girlhood from Pier's men. I know them. They would never hurt you or think less of you. There's no disguising Aura, and she's staying."

Tev raised a hand. "You don't know what the Treacher you're talking about."

"Did someone hurt you, Tev?"

"Not in the way you think."

"I know you are unhappy. I know you want something you lost in Aldad or something you lost at the border. And Lomius is taken with some Desert lusciousness. He doesn't deserve your endless loyalty. Neither do I, but I swear I wouldn't trample on it the way he does."

She laughed, dry and bitter. "You don't know Lomius, either. He has always done right by me."

Colstadt's eyes were not convinced. He still bored into her with loathsome sympathy. "Why don't you come away with me? We'll go to the Caps or the hills. You can be a woman again. No one will recognize you, and you can have children..." He blushed suddenly. "If you want them."

Tev let another fit of stupid tears escape with laughter. "Oh, really. We can? Why don't you solve all the land's ailments while you're about it?"

He blushed again. "You're better and stronger than I. I know that. I won't be stifling for you. I'll be anything you want me to be, even if you wish me to merely draw your water and grain your horses and guard your door at night."

She grew sober. People didn't say those things to her. Ever. "You are kind. But I'm far older than you think I am, and some…parts of me…will not go away. I can't be your little village girl. Not now. Or ever."

Colstadt shook his head slowly. "You need me. To make you laugh."

Tev reached for his face, leaned into him, and kissed him hard. He reacted like she'd expected him to: stirred and hungry, gripping her jaw with his slim fingers, his return kiss sloppy and unpracticed and pure. She hated herself for this selfish thing—stealing something innocent from him because it felt good—wondrous, even—to drink him in like a tonic. She reached for his shoulders, pulled him down into the tangled weeds, and rolled him over, her lips locked tightly on his like a jammed key.

Then she shoved herself off of him and pulled away. "There. You know what it will be like now. Horrid."

Colstadt was hardly breathing. He slid his arms behind him and propped his shoulders up to face her. "Am I horrid?"

"No, I am. I don't want to taint you with my goblins."

He half-gasped on air. "Far from it."

Tev shoved him hard in the chest, afraid she would cry again. "Go the Derm away, Colstadt!"

She didn't wait for him to obey. She stalked toward the woods, her armor stiff and annoying once more, then doubled back for the tower once she was out of his sight.

It was dark and dank inside. She found a smooth wall near the top level to sleep against, but she couldn't even sit down, let alone lie on her side and rest. She crouched, rocked, slid her hands up and down the smooth stones. The howling of the wind outside was loud enough that she could've moaned along with it if she'd wanted to, but she couldn't take the loneliness of the sound. She slipped back down to the entrance. One of the Drei whose name she did not know was guarding. Mikel would be haunting the lower levels, where it was warmer for Aura. It wasn't too late yet, was it? He should still be awake. Planning.

Tev slipped down the staircase. There was a corridor and five doors at the bottom. Only one had a light under it. She raised her hand to knock, but already she could hear mumbles and murmuring. Mikel's voice in a soft, deep tone she couldn't remember having heard him use before. Her hand froze. Aura's voice responded, followed by a squeal that had to be of pleasure.

To the Derm with this. Maybe the battlements would be empty.

Tev ran, took the winding staircase two steps at a time until she reached the top. Her breath was shallow and painful, the hole in her stomach hurting wretchedly. The clouds had cleared and the stars were out, a storm tucked away on the eastern horizon like it wanted to avoid them. Good. They didn't want snow. She walked the walls and tried not to shiver in the fierce wind. She almost ran into Pier. He had both hands on the battlement, staring off into the slight glow of the moon.

Pier made a sound in greeting, something that sounded like, "Ah."

Was he disappointed with an interruption? Didn't matter. Tev wasn't going to say a word. She leaned her back against the stone, nearly pressing against his braced arm.

"My queen?" Pier whispered.

She drew in some air and almost choked on it. The urge to whimper or coddle herself was strong, but she drew in another breath and forced it out slowly. There. She *could* breathe if she had to.

Pier reached out a tentative arm and placed it on her shoulder. "May

I do anything for you, my queen?"

She couldn't feel his hand through her armor, and she wished she could. Her head, hands, and legs shook with shivers that felt starved.

"Tev." Pier said her assumed name, tried to catch her eyes. "You are cold. You should go back in."

Tev shook her head and blew air out through her teeth. "No."

He shrugged and did not press her. His eyes scanned the horizon again before they came back to her. "You are the most selfless woman I know, my queen."

Her voice hitched. "Thank you."

He didn't move. "You are holding out."

"What?"

"You will seek the throne again, and when you do, I will be by your side. I wouldn't leave Mikel because I will not leave either of you. I am the sworn bowman of your father, and I always will be."

She shook her head. "I won't seek the throne."

"Perhaps not the throne, but the lives of the people who stole it—"

"No. Vengeance will accomplish nothing."

He smiled slightly. "You fight your own nature, daughter of Petrolai."

That should have made her angry, but it didn't. All this talking was unusual for him. He was giddy, if she were to guess. He must have expected to never see them again. His feelings now were the opposite of hers; he was grateful to have duty, eager to have even more of it. This was what he lived for.

"I am not..." She started the sentence but couldn't finish it. She was not what? Was not vengeful? Was not hungry for justice? Hadn't she just slain a party of Desert men for Aura?

"I have something I should tell you." Pier cleared his throat. "I haven't any experience with Desert science, but before Romianz and Zven and I parted company, we went to an armory a few miles south of Ciar. Romianz placed all of our swords and armor in it. It had been his, as he liked to keep a stash of weapons outside the castle in case they were needed."

Tev wrinkled her brow. Pier wouldn't tell her this unless it was important, but she didn't understand. "Was he hiding something from us?"

"No. No, else I don't think he would have opened the doors. If he'd known what was inside, he'd have known not to show me."

"What was inside?"

"Vials. Vials of blood, preserved in crates of wood shavings and marked in Drei words but Aldadi script. Romianz had never seen the like, and he had no theories. I did, but I held my peace."

Tev felt a prickle run up her spine. "Did Romianz tell you about finding that knight in the bottom of Ciar? About the creeper who was slitting throats?"

"He did. He said he didn't know why anyone would save blood."

"Maybe he…" Tev's eyes widened. "The night we went to Hodran's camp, Mikel was cut with a small, jagged blade, beneath his armor."

Pier nodded. "Yes. If someone in Ciar was looking for you, I think this was their method. I destroyed the vials. But if that was not the only collection and they have his blood, could someone determine that Lomius was not Castle Guard? That he was Orion?"

No, because he was not Orion. Their identity was safe, but she couldn't tell Pier that. "Yes," she answered. "If they had Orion blood to match it to, yes. It is common Desert science, the keeping of blood."

Pier nodded slowly. "If the man who did this was Hodran, he still cannot know *you* are alive."

Tev shook her head. "He could know. I…was foolish when I went after Tofer. I don't think I was nicked, but I could have been. I don't remember."

"You have never been foolish with your sword, my queen." He almost smiled. "You may be quite foolish without it."

Tev had not confided to anyone…well, ever. It was not how she dealt with the heaviness in her heart, but right now, it seemed right. Pier was alone, with no one, as she was. "I killed six Desert men for Aura, and I barely knew her name." Even revealing that much about herself made her breath seem difficult. He didn't answer, so she asked, "Will you tell Mikel? About the blood?"

"He should know, so he understands why I am determined that we stay together, that I and my men protect you both." He looked up at the sky. "I heard what you said to Colstadt. That boy would run through a troop for you, and you turn him down why?" He didn't smile, but his voice was smug.

"Colstadt is just a boy. He doesn't understand."

"He loves you."

Tev drew her hands up around her. Pier didn't understand after all. All she could think was that she wanted someone to spar with her. Mikel or Gavriel or Pem or Ric.

Ric.

Ric would've known what to say. Something gruff and unsentimental. "None of us knows a thing about love, Pier."

part two

Fourth City

War its thousands slays,

Peace, its ten thousands.

— Porteus

{20}
Turning

The Fourth City.

Thirteen years later, in the 5th year of Emperor Vekst.

MIKEL LET THE SUNLIGHT BLIND him for a moment. It hardly mattered that it was reflected off of a blank white wall, that the only glimpse of the sky he got was through a slit in the roof. For a moment, he could close his eyes and imagine the brightness pulsating around him was from heated sand or the fire in a forge. He didn't have to watch where he was going—arms were dragging him up sets of stairs, through hallways and caged doors.

The room they brought him into was massive, spanning the length of a hall and then some. Mikel was dropped on his knees. A part of him wished he could keep his eyes closed forever. Maybe if he stayed in a dream state, Aura might come back to him. He couldn't dream of her in the cell. It was too dark and cold. He dreamed of her in the warmth and away from voices, remembered her bundled in the skin of a fanged cat in the Castle of Marek next to a crackling fire.

Trzl's presence pulled him toward her, toward consciousness and reality. and loneliness. "Glad you could join us."

At first he thought she was speaking to him, but she was facing a girl nearly twenty paces away. The girl's body was slight, betraying her age to be about ten. Guards still held tightly to her wrists. She had bright, wide eyes in a frightened face and features that were stunningly royal.

Not royal, actually. More like his. Castle Guard.

Without preamble, Trzl brought her hand back and hit the child's cheek. The girl cried out and turned away, a look of confusion on her face.

"I am sorry, my dear," Trzl crowed. She bent down and cupped the girl's chin. "There is no help for it. Your mother must see that you are in desperate straits. She must know that I am serious."

The girl raised her face and looked Trzl in the eyes. Her gaze was unwavering, unhurt. Trzl smacked her again. Still, the eyes were clear, without pain.

Mikel's stomach clenched tight. "Who *is* her mother, Trzl?"

Trzl whirled on him and jerked her head up, and a guard brought a whip down on his shoulders. Mikel blinked with a half-smile.

"You will remain silent until all of our guests are here," she told him.

He raised an eyebrow at her. "You touch the girl again, and I won't have anything to say to you or anyone."

"This is not a discussion, Mikel."

The door behind him opened, and Otreya stepped through. Mikel could feel the man's gaze before he could see or hear him. He smelled of sage or some other unpleasantly sweet odor, but even stronger was the prickling of the hairs on the back of Mikel's neck. Ever since they'd first met, there was something within him that knew Otreya as an enemy.

"Well, well." It was all Otreya said, but the words held immeasurable weight.

Trzl gave a half-bow to her grandfather. "Is anyone from the Council coming?"

Otreya waved a hand. "No, no. They've given their approval and are eagerly awaiting our results. Why are there six guards for the warrior?

He is wearing the strongest and heaviest chains a smith can make."

Trzl smiled glibly. "Grandfather, you must know how many times this man has slipped through our fingers."

Otreya raised a hand to the guards. "Chain him to the walls."

Trzl's forehead wrinkled as the men grabbed Mikel's arms again and lifted levers in the wall to reveal heavily anchored rungs made of iron. Her expression seemed to say, *I wish I had known about those.* "Remove his shirt, please. No use having a whip if it does not sting."

The rungs came out a couple feet, leaving enough space between his back and the walls for a whip to have play, but scarcely enough for a serious beating. Strange. Mikel kept his eyes on the floor because he knew it infuriated Trzl. She wanted to look at him, see her beloved prize writhe in the awkwardness of her gaze. He could feel her eyes clawing at his body—wanting to run to him, touch his bare skin—and it made him shiver.

The little girl remained standing in the middle of the room, her hands unbound and her head thrown back. Otreya walked to her with a decided bounce in his step.

"Ahh, Natalya, I am so very glad we have found you, my child. Today will be an excellent day, hmm? There is much to learn!"

Natalya's face clouded.

Otreya put a hand on her forehead and closed his eyes. "Mmhmm. You have the strength of a grown woman, you do. No matter. We'll see beyond that, I hope."

Mikel raised his eyes slowly, just enough to see her. She was young, perfect, tiny. His palms were sweating, and his mind wanted to balk. If they were going to use the girl's pain to draw him out, he would have no recourse but to oblige them. Trzl had not warned him about this any more than she had warned him about Romianz taking the blame for their involvement. Clearly she was more than amenable to all of it—she didn't even look tense.

The doors opened again, and Trzl ran to them. "To the wall as well, Grandfather?"

Otreya nodded once, his beard bobbing up and down. "Ah, it is your show, my dear."

A sly smirk graced her bewitching features. "Not on the wall. The table, please."

The guards pulled someone past Mikel—a Seren woman younger than he was. The skin at her throat was slightly swarthy, but he couldn't see her face, as her dark hair fell over her strong cheekbones. Romianz's daughter? She looked older in this light.

"Pleased you could join us, Riyev." Trzl waited while the woman was strapped to a marble table, her arms stretched from one end to the other, her face settled into a cutout that must have been designed for just such a purpose.

Mikel cleared his throat. "Trzl—"

Trzl strode back to him, used the hilt of her dagger to shove his face up. His hair was too short to fall in his eyes and hide his stubborn aversion from her gaze. She ran a finger along his newly shaven skin.

"That is the last word I want to hear from you, Mikel. You are here to observe." She let his head fall and turned to the room. "Do we all know each other, or shall I make some introductions?"

Riyev raised her face, a maneuver that must have hurt her neck, but still Mikel could not see her eyes. Did she even remember his voice from the dungeons? "What do you want with my daughter, you devil? And where did you find her?"

Trzl didn't move, save to dart her gaze over to one of her minions. A guard pulled out a knife and sliced the woman's dress from shoulder to shoulder, peeling back the fabric. The same whip that had graced Mikel's shoulders came down on hers, causing a bright red welt and a cry that cut through the air and sounded half-earthly, half-angelic.

Trzl spoke evenly. "I know who you are. I know what your family did for the Four Cities. I don't want to hurt you."

Otreya's mouth pulled taut.

Trzl reached for the woman's hair and shoved her face back into the table. "I want you to tell me where your father kept his armory, the names of the spies he sent to maintain contact with Lomius of the Border Wars, and where I can find your brother, Zven, and what he knows. Tell me all that I ask, and your daughter might go free this night."

Riyev didn't answer right away. The cumulative silence in the room was bright and tangible. Her face still in the table, she answered quietly, "My father was loyal up to the last. I have nothing to tell you."

"The loyalty of your family has not escaped me—loyalty only to yourselves and no one else. Now, will you tell me how to contact your brother, or shall I send your daughter to a dungeon where you will never find her?"

"My father had many secrets, I am sure, but they died with him." Riyev laid her head down on the table and looked at the wall. "My brother sends letters. Sporadically, never to the same place. Some make their way to me, some do not."

"If Zven's letters can find you in that country hamlet you were holed up in, surely you can find a way to—"

"His actions are ordered by the Empire, miss." Riyev remained calm, concise. "Should you not know more of his whereabouts than I?"

Trzl raised her head to the guard, and he grabbed Natalya by the arm hard enough that she whimpered. "Do you want your daughter to lose a finger?"

Natalya didn't even wince at the words. Rugged child.

"All of my siblings have been loyal to the Four Cities since the surrender at Berekst. I've raised my child to be just as dedicated, if not more so."

"Truly?" Trzl waved a hand to Otreya. "If I were to take your daughter, give her to one of the officials as a pupil to eventually attain status and stature in our council, you would be most pleased, would you not?"

Riyev met the question with harsh silence. Trzl had talked her way into a corner of sorts. Perhaps she had done it on purpose. This whole room seemed to be set to provoke, one way or another.

Mikel cleared his throat. "I'm afraid you're going at this the hard way, Trzl."

Otreya's eyes flickered to him, almost humored. Mikel knew the man's thoughts were moving faster than a rushing river, but in what direction? He was a manipulator, a man who controlled others whenever he could, and Trzl knew how to do it as well. Mikel could only pray his own mind was strong enough to withstand it for Kierstaz and Malcom's sake.

"And he speaks again," Trzl said. "How am I going about this the hard way?"

"You can see she has no fear for her daughter. If you want her cooperation, a bribe might be more useful."

"Oh, she has no fear for her, does she?" Trzl waved a hand to the guard who held the child. He brought her over. Trzl grabbed Natalya's hand and twisted it so that her palm lay flat against the table. Then she took out her studded dagger—Seren steel that Mikel had seen her use before—and ran the tip along the girl's porcelain skin.

Natalya finally lost her composure and shrieked.

Riyev pulled against the table. "Don't!"

"Give me something, Riyev. A name, a place. Someone your father traded secrets with. Someone who might know how to contact your brother."

"Idelviss." Mikel raised his brooding eyes and met Trzl's. "Idelviss was with him. What did you do with her? Embrace her as a sister? I am sure she knows much more about this matter than Riyev does."

Triumph crossed Trzl's face. "This is what I like to see. Enemies working together to turn on each other. Mikel Orion turning in an innocent Drei pirate. I must confess, I'm impressed."

Riyev's head snapped around. "Mikel Orion?"

Natalya's eyes widened. "Who are you?"

Trzl backhanded Natalya across the face. "Shut it." She glared at Riyev.

Riyev didn't shut it. She turned her head all the way around to look at him. "You know Dermed well that man is not an Orion."

Mikel frowned, confused now more than ever. How many schemes did Trzl have going at once? He thought he knew every possible use for his identity, but apparently he did not. And why did the woman from the cell next to his not remember his voice and his name?

"Yes, he is Mikel Orion." Trzl crossed her arms and leaned in close to Riyev's face. "He has been in my clutches for the past year. Before that, he lived as a vagabond, running from me and my cunning. You would do best to fear me greatly."

Riyev turned her head around once more. Her eyes winced when they met his, then softened. "My God," she whispered.

Her eyes were brown, not golden. She wasn't the woman who'd been in the cell beside his, but she looked like her—almost exactly.

Riyev turned to Trzl. "My father nearly went to the gallows for being the haven knight of the Orion family. If you kill me because of him, I'd take it as an honor and damn you. You want to know whether my daughter is as strong as I? She is. And stronger. No matter where you threaten to send her, she will survive."

Trzl laughed bitterly. "Oh, will she?"

Guards came back through the door on cue, released Riyev's hands from the edges of the table, and dragged her to the door.

"Fifty stripes for her tonight," said Trzl, "and we'll see if she's as cocky in the morning."

The door shut, but instead of silence, there was the sound of

Natalya's footsteps. She'd broken away, and it took Mikel a moment to realize she was running to him. Otreya lunged for her, but she slammed herself into Mikel's leg and wrapped her arms around his waist.

"If you're truly him, you'll save us?"

No one even bothered to peel her off. It was as if they were waiting to hear his reply.

Mikel wished he could put a hand on her head to reassure her because his words were empty. "I can't save people, little one."

Trzl flicked her hair over her shoulder. "I think we've discovered a good deal, haven't we, Grandfather?"

Otreya looked winded, which was strange considering he hadn't done anything. Or had he been in their heads? Was that what this was about? Mikel flushed with anger. Trzl was doing more than necessary to earn the old man's trust, turning herself into a willing servant, turning this search for Malcom into a circus with Romianz's family. It didn't bode well.

Trzl tossed Natalya to a guard and said, "Lock her up. Away from her mother's cell. Away from anyone. But break one of her fingers first, so her mother knows I keep my promises."

Mikel's mouth was gritty. "Trzl."

Trzl did not deign to look at him again. She nodded to another set of guards. "Drop him in my chambers. I have more to question him on."

Otreya kissed Trzl's hand before he left. "Well done, my dear. I will report to the Council."

ೡ

THE CHAMBER WAS LIT BY one candle and had no windows, but at least it was warm.

"You said you trusted me." Trzl's voice—smooth, almost kind—joined him in the dark.

"Not when you break children's hands."

"Why do children always have to love you? Even my own son." That sounded bitter. He could feel her eyes shoot daggers, even before he saw her shadow by the door. "Your head is confused by the herbs my grandfather has given you, Mikel. You would be just as harsh if need be."

"I would never find occasion to hurt children."

"I am sure you were tempted to hurt Malcom now and again. You couldn't help it. He was, after all, the child of your enemy."

"Again, you are wrong. Such malice is your realm, not mine."

Trzl smacked him across the face. "*Stop* contradicting me in private. You do it quite enough in front of the whole Empire."

She crossed in front of him—calm, stately—and washed her hands in a basin. It was too dark to see much, but if there was a wash basin, it was probably her actual bedchamber. He shifted on his knees, causing the chains on his ankles to clank softly.

"Why don't you stand up? I hate having to look down to you."

Mikel narrowed his eyes at her. "As you wish, my empress."

"Oh, please. Emperor Vekst is not old at all." But her eyes twinkled. She liked the sound of it, did she? Of course. Her tone grew soft. "But he may be grooming me."

Mikel gritted his teeth. "Is that what you want?"

Trzl spun away from him. "Well, Otreya and I have similar goals in a sense, but you should be grateful that my questions are very different from what his will be." Her voice was chipper, as if she expected him to forget what had just happened, to forget that Romianz's daughter was getting fifty lashes at this very moment.

"I have no answers for either of you."

"Still sore about my show of force? It was necessary. My grandfather must see that I have been handling things and that you have been properly subdued by the months I've kept you in solitude. He is desperate as ever to have Malcom back, and so far your damned Pier has been no help for us. Do not pretend that you are somehow exempt from my heavy hand. *You* surrendered to *me*, remember?"

The words burned to hear. They sounded true, like she believed the reasoning behind them. Some part of him even wondered if she *was* in control anymore. She would get that look in her eyes... They would turn blue, and she suddenly was her grandfather, opposed to anything he might say, no matter how trivial.

"What excuse did you give for having me sent to your chambers? That must be rather distasteful to the Council."

She smiled tolerantly. "I'm sure they all have different opinions, but Grandfather accepts that I use you for your body."

He shuddered. "I appreciate the restraint you show."

The light caught her eyes, and he saw them flush a little darker. "Having you dragged around in chains does give me a certain pleasure, I must admit."

"I may be as helpless as a newborn lamb on shaky legs, but I will never be your slave."

"No, no." Her lips twisted into a pout. "But I must employ whatever means I have in order to learn your secrets. I know you won't tell them to me."

"You know I haven't any secrets worth knowing." Only a slight lie. "Is that what that was? You truly think Riyev of Romianz knows more than I?"

Trzl shrugged. "She is easier to persuade."

"She likely knows nothing at all. I doubt Malcom would be pleased with your chosen means of protecting him."

"I'm still quite certain she can be useful. You always hated to watch a weaker body suffer for something you could endure, Mikel. You like to save people."

That hit him entirely too close to vital portions of his chest. "You always did want to trample innocents underfoot wherever you went."

"And you want me to accomplish miracles without employing a few distasteful tactics. I hate your rules."

Mikel swallowed. "Trzl, I'm here because you made a promise to me. You told me you would protect my knights and bring Otreya down. As a pawn, I may no longer be useful, but if you tell me what you need me to say..."

"No, that would be too obvious. It is better that you don't know." She leaned toward him, peering at him as she might a new pet. "You should be glad I make time to question you privately, else you would be entirely in the dark."

He knew how true that was. "You'll release that girl, Trzl, and you'll not touch her again or so help me..."

She cupped his head in her hands, tousled his hair gently from one side to the other and around in circles, trailed her thumbs down to cup his jaw—the jaw that she'd shaved herself since she couldn't leave him alone with a razor.

"Do you really think you have anything to bargain with? You already begged me to spare Colstadt's life. Don't think I'm in the sparing mood today." She giggled, and it sounded mad. Then her voice grew sober. "Otreya has located Zven."

Mikel's eyes darted up, but he lowered them immediately. "How?"

"One of Romianz's crew talked. He knew roughly where the communique had come from. You won't be pleased." She looked disgusted. "The Guardian, at the entrance to the Gorges. What would Tev be doing with my boy so far north in Dreibourge? Unless she intends to put as many impediments between Otreya and Malcom as she can? I know you trust your armor-bearer implicitly, but what if she decides she wants a little coin to pocket with her master in prison? I'm afraid for him. I don't see why she would remain faithful to you under the circumstances."

Good thing she didn't know why, else this would be a much more antagonistic discussion.

"Maybe you should have thought of that before you set your plan in motion. You can't have me in two places at once."

"Do not lecture me. Tell me what she could be doing. Do you have friends there?"

"Most likely she was trying to reach the northern coast."

"And rescue you? From my ships?" She laughed again, and jealousy slipped into her voice. "Ah, you should teach your faithful armor-bearer to stay away from me. She is going to get herself nipped sooner or later. Maybe she already has."

"If one of Romianz's crew talked, what were you torturing Riyev for? To make a point? To me or to your grandfather?"

She smiled slightly. "You, Mikel. You have to understand that you have no friends here. None at all." Her eyes told him not to believe the words, but her actions had already ripped a hole through him.

"You didn't have to give her fifty. Twenty would have done."

"Twenty would have barely made her bleed. I was beaten unconscious when I was in *your* castle. Why are we still discussing this?"

"She is not Pier. She didn't do anything to you."

"She defied me in front of witnesses."

Mikel didn't want to feel any of this—the sharp, screaming pain of being Castle Guard, of owing Serengard—but he did. Riyev was as much his responsibility as any of his knights, and here Trzl was rubbing his face in a hot bed of coals.

He cleared his throat. "If Tev is with Zven, they might be coming here. They'll find out that you took me, and they'll come after me."

She looked shocked, and then her face softened. "Why, Mikel. You are sweet to warn me. So very sweet."

"I don't want them to take me back. I want them to stay away." He gave her a quick glare. "Understand?"

She nodded. "Yes, I'll see to it." She reached for him, traced a finger down the edge of his face. "So much for you not compromising. You'll trade tale for tale the same as any other. Oh, mortal Orion." He flinched and turned away. "I'll have Riyev's girl moved."

Mikel looked up sharply. "Where?"

"The cell next to yours. If you want to make her your concern, so be it. I wash my hands of her."

{21}
Дгмог

In the northern portion of the province of Dreibourge.

DREIBOURGE WAS READY. KIERSTAZ COULD feel it—fresh as the first breath of spring. They hadn't yet lost the generation of warriors who'd defended the land against the Seren inquisition, yet they'd had the chance to raise a crop of strong youths. Oppressed, without identity. Blank slates.

Sark and his people were more than effective. They knew every village, every port, every corner in the western hills—which were safe, which they'd best stay clear of, which they could afford to take a risk on. They were more cunning than ruthless. Barely a drop of blood had been shed yet, and their numbers had tripled, now over a thousand. A thousand who knew her name, who could betray her at any moment, yet she was not the slightest bit afraid of that. She was afraid of disappointing them.

Gret, one of the lieutenants, was in the midst of haggling a mine owner out of a mob of horses that he had just been traded for working the pulleys, and Sark himself was in the circle of the campfire making bridles of stag skin. His arms were bare up to the elbows, hands skillfully handling the hot leather while he explained something in soft tones to the boy who fired the kettles.

Kierstaz couldn't help commenting, "Mustn't you boil that longer?"

Sark took long enough to answer that she thought at first he was ignoring her. "Concern yourself not with the mediocre tasks of your company, my queen."

"You concern yourself with mine."

"Only when you wish it."

"A lie."

He didn't smile, but she saw the trace of amusement in his eyes. "I'll grant you that, but only long enough to tell you that you should see to your wardrobe."

"What is wrong with it?"

"You look like the rest of your soldiers."

They were near the first Seren-held castle, at least according to Theo. The tension was building. Kierstaz felt it herself, but more than likely it was because she had to listen to her generals talk strategy all night.

"You gave me this armor," she told him.

He stood and walked toward her slowly, a slight hitch in his step. Probably sore from all the hard riding, but he shouldn't be feeling it. He never felt much of anything.

Sark put a hand out and touched her breastplate. "You should have something more elaborate. You are, after all, a queen."

Kierstaz quirked an eyebrow. "Nice of you to remind me."

He didn't blink. "Rank is important to our people. It must be obvious you are higher than a general, my queen."

"Your wife."

"My queen."

Kierstaz walked away from him, hitching her chin so he would know to follow. She wasn't sure what to do with someone so bland and logical.

Seren men were passionate—savagely moral or immoral as their consciences dictated. Kierstaz had always been more sober and less angry than her brother, less angry than Ric. She knew how to be objective with her passion. But the pureblood Drei always did things that made sense—not one thing was determined according to their hearts—but that also meant they saw no cause to explain. Here, she was out of place, always asking for a reason.

"You are rallying villagers who have not fought for decades. Their world ended when Petrolai Orion fell. They must know that someone of royalty leads this army. Eventually they will need to hear your name spoken, see your crest and your banner."

Kierstaz winced. "You make it sound sentimental."

Sark blinked. "We are not without humanity, my queen."

"I never said... Have you any other advice?"

"Only that you cease this habit of walking away from me soon after you ask for it. It will make your soldiers think you do not value your king's opinion."

She shrugged gently. "I do value it."

"Then wear the armor that signifies your royalty in some way."

"I am sure you would design it?" Kierstaz bit her lip and turned toward her tent, a small, insignificant affair at the most vulnerable corner of camp. "Forgive me if I don't fall into all of the Drei protocols seamlessly. I've been a fugitive for twelve years at least."

"As I am aware, my queen."

"And how are you going to design *Drei* armor in the style of my own monarchy?" She ran a hand the length of her torso. "You forget I was the only Seren woman to ever wear the Orion banner and armor at the same time. If you make Seren armor to fit my shape, I would be far too obvious."

"I'll not. It shall be Drei. I understand why there are no female knights among the Serens. No discipline in your ranks."

Kierstaz sucked her breath in so hard she thought she might faint. "Would you repeat that, please?"

Sark's mouth twitched. "You heard what I said."

"Yes, I did, but I wanted to give you the chance to deny it."

"Are you looking to spar like a couple of lovers? Because I am not in the mood."

Kierstaz would gladly have sparred if he meant that literally. He probably did. "Make whatever you wish for my body. I'll hardly care."

"Your measurements are the same?" He walked to her, reached behind her to the small of her back. His hands slid to her waist, up her front, pressed gently against her breasts. "I'll make the arrangements."

Kierstaz put a hand to her forehead, too confused to know why she had argued at all. She was frustrated with his strength, his calm, the way he eased back into war as if he had never left it. At times she wanted to run away and scream at the sky. She couldn't have grown soft. It wasn't that. But she felt that her hands were tied somehow. That all she could do was make war, not bring peace.

Sark put a hand on her shoulder and squeezed it just slightly as he stepped past her. "Your generals are waiting in your tent for you to inform them of any revisions to your conquests."

"In a moment." Kierstaz swung about and kissed him gently on the shoulder. He looked stunned, then pressed his lips to the hair just above her ear in response.

There. The air was clear.

Crista, one of the lieutenants, stood at the entrance to her tent, waiting for her. The woman was stick-slender, but bulky in the shoulders. Kierstaz could never look like that, no matter how hard she tried. As soon as they stepped in, Theo, the tallest one, and Otto, the oldest, straightened their backs and saluted. Kierstaz did so in return, though it always felt strange. They waited until she walked to her map table before they lowered their arms, and even then, they stood so stiffly that she felt she couldn't breathe until the silence had been broken.

"How many horse soldiers have we at present?"

Sark answered, like the minion he was on this campaign. "Eight hundred, my queen."

"And how many can we have in a week, provided we take every castle between here and Zurik and recruit the locals?"

Sark raised an eyebrow. "I believe we could acquire two thousand, but the number is rough."

"How many do we need to take Zurik?"

"The battlements have not been kept up since Drei rule. They are in disrepair at best. Our horse soldiers may be doing the brunt of the fighting if you choose a direct charge. I believe we will need every one of them."

Kierstaz was a decent strategist, but she had to hear their opinions before she could make sense of things. They knew the ground and the people. "Theo?"

Theo, by far the most imposing and aggressive of her generals, took off a glove and put his finger to her map. "I believe a charge would be the best way, but come in from the south. That way you can have your foot soldiers at the north, and you've twice as many of them."

That estimation sounded high. "Do we have that many?" Kierstaz glanced at Crista.

Crista's mouth opened, but she didn't say anything. She nodded.

Kierstaz clenched her fists. "Can anyone tell me what is going on?"

Theo looked startled, but it was feigned for sure. "My queen, Uvei is here to see you. He brought fresh troops and supplies and…your boy."

"Malcom?"

"Yes, my queen."

Sark's eyes narrowed, but he avoided her gaze.

Kierstaz wanted to find Malcom immediately, run to him and be sure he was flesh and bone, but she said evenly, "And? You were going to inform me when?"

Theo said, "When it became necessary, my queen."

"Because it is not pertinent to taking the tower of Vien," she assessed, "which is our next task and most certainly tantamount to anything I might wish to discuss with Malcom."

"Malcom is not a warrior, my queen."

"I know that, thank you," Kierstaz snapped, but it had no effect on the faces in the room. They didn't seem to care if she was angry or confused. "He will be a warrior soon enough. He's been trained and raised to be one, and he'll ride with me tomorrow. There will be no more discussion on it."

Sark stepped toward her. "With all respect, my queen, he will be in grave danger at the front of the line. And his features are far too Seren. Quite recognizable."

Kierstaz wanted to laugh. "Did you not just tell me I should wear new armor? If Malcom wants to retake Dreibourge at my side, he may draw all the attention he wishes, the world be damned."

"There is a price on his head." Sark's gaze was steely and hard. "Perhaps you should ask him what his intentions are before you assume they are the same as your own."

Kierstaz wished the room was clear so that she could openly disagree with him, but it wasn't. "Understand this, Sark: Malcom is not what you perceive him to be. He is not a son of Hodran and Trzl. He is mine. I raised him more surely than they did. A boy grows more in the years I had him than he does in ten."

A faint smile trailed across his face. "As always, you know best, my queen."

♋

KIERSTAZ LET THE TENT FLAP fall behind Malcom and embraced

him before he had even entered completely.

"Mal, what were you thinking?"

"The physicians said I could go. They said Sark knew best what was to be done with me, and Sark is here." Malcom slid down onto one of the benches. He ran his fingertips along the inside of the canvas tent, only glancing into her eyes now and again. "I didn't want to stay there while you were engaging a kingdom alone."

Kierstaz knew how he felt. She wanted him with her as much as he wanted to be here, but she couldn't watch him as Sark had suggested. And if her lieutenants disagreed... "Then again, this may be the safest place for you."

Malcom rolled his eyes. "I don't want to be safe. I'm not sick anymore. The physicians said I'm well enough to make war if I wish."

"Half of these people don't trust you because you are the blood of Otreya, and I cannot convince them otherwise."

"They'll have to learn themselves that I'm not like him. The mind is stronger than the body."

Kierstaz walked to him and placed a hand on his knee. "It isn't that simple. I am sure both your mother and grandfather believe they have a claim on you, and that belief fuels their actions and the way you are seen by both the Serens and the Drei. It has been this way since you were born."

Malcom picked up her hand and clasped it. "The Drei told me my blood is unusual, that it nearly killed me because it opposed itself."

Kierstaz knew that. "The bastards who set off your ailment would have succeeded in taking you to Otreya if I hadn't killed them, but who knows what Zven may have told your mother? I am making my identity known—all the more reason for you to stay away."

"All the more reason for me to be a soldier. I am strongest with a leader to serve and my sword in my hand." He let go of her fingers and looked in her eyes. His own were worried. "You haven't forgotten Mikel, have you? That we left him in my mother's hands? I don't trust her. Not now."

"I haven't forgotten." Kierstaz swallowed hard. "Everything I am doing—building a force and retaking this land—all of it is necessary. It is my only option, as it stands, and it is also righteous. The Drei need a leader, and I am here."

Malcom nodded, his gaze flickering with impatience. "When may I have my armor made?"

Kierstaz picked at her fingernails to hide a smile. "Immediately. You'll ride next to me."

The tent flap lifted, and Sark stepped in. He wasn't quite as tall as Malcom and his shoulders were narrower, but there was command and maturity in his slender jaw and shallow cheeks. It always gave her a grave start—just how cold and icy his eyes were, how surreal the silky red hair that fell in waves to his neck. Just now, his face was cloudy enough to have brought an entire storm with it.

Kierstaz rose. "Mal, go to the east end of camp. That's where you'll find the forges. Tell them you are my armor-bearer."

Sark smirked. "We don't have armor-bearers in the Drei army."

Kierstaz waited until Malcom had gone before she whirled on him. "Are you enjoying my incompetence?"

"My queen, you are a fine leader."

Her vulnerability with him was a weakness. She wasn't accustomed to confiding her secrets, no matter who knew what she looked like naked. "Well then, won't you explain your mockery? Surely your disagreement with me can be kept civil."

His expression was dead serious. "I would never mock you. I don't understand why Serens mock each other at all."

"Because you have no humor."

"Forgive me, that is a Seren word, and I am not sure I know the meaning."

Now she knew he was mocking. "Would you care to step outside and draw your sword? Perhaps we can understand each other better that way."

"I would prefer that greatly, but I don't think we should." His eyes flickered over her. "I'm afraid any more of that between us would be rather indulgent now that you have secured your followers and are about to declare war."

"Indulgent? How?"

"Our bond has been established. Anything else may feed jealousy among my equals who were a few seconds too late to grasp your family's dirk."

That jarred her. Terribly and deep. "Who? You were the only one who wanted me."

"Want has nothing to do with it. A general never makes a decision based on his own desires, and neither did I." Sark twisted his sword about on his waist with a slim hand. "Drei soldiers are sworn to abstain in times of war, but you're the Orion. You can have anything you wish, even play in the afternoon. I only caution for the sake of morale."

It was hard to remember that not everyone was her enemy. She drew a breath, ran a hand over her face. "Thank you for your honesty."

He nodded once. "My people are very disciplined. Yours, not so much. I intend no insult."

Kierstaz flushed. "How very delicately you put that." She couldn't banish the mention of jealousy from her mind. Her chin tipped back to her shoulder, she whispered, "How can anyone be envious of us?"

Something flickered in his frank gaze—something that might have been hurt. "Does not the very ground you tread inform you of its awe?"

Again with the sarcasm. She could meet that. "I take it you would not wish for half-breed children. Linking our kingdoms by blood would be unwise."

"I haven't said a word about children."

"Sark, the only reason your soldiers do not breed during wartime is because of the risk that a woman soldier would become with child."

"No, it is because it is a sign of lack of discipline, unbecoming of a Drei."

"You think I do not understand because I am a Seren, but I do." More than he knew. More than she could tell him. There wasn't a way to put to words the cold nights in the cliffs. Mikel wrapped up with Aura, their son's tiny coos. Kierstaz in her armor by day, bathing alone, hiding in her room at night, always a step away in case she was needed. Colstadt's wounded gaze across the table. Pier's hope to be her lieutenant slowly dwindling until he gave up on her entirely and treated her as she wanted to be treated: as Tev. As nobody.

"Children are not a consequence to avoid, but a reason to understand discipline wholly and completely." The hand on his sword moved again. "For if one brings a child into the world without first learning how to control themselves, what good have they done in life, and what good will they do such a child? None."

"That has nothing to do with you and I." The sentence stung in the back of her throat. "If you meant to avoid offspring, it was a foolish risk to spend three months in my bed, was it not?"

"No risk at all. That was for your pleasure, not mine." He looked guilty, as if she'd caught him stealing. "I can be disciplined in your bed as well."

He might as well have punched her in the gut. She held up her hand and brushed past him. "Please get out."

"There is more we must discuss."

Kierstaz swung around, her skin starting to boil. "What?"

"Malcom is here for a reason. If you did not observe it, I am not only surprised but disappointed."

The thought chilled her slightly. "What do you mean?"

"The boy spent half of a year in and out of sickness and near death, and the first word on his lips is revenge."

Kierstaz rubbed her palms up and down her shoulders. "Yes, I noticed."

"He is not what you think he is."

He didn't know her very well, did he? She slapped people when they pushed her too far. "I am more to him than the woman who birthed him, you—"

Sark reached for her, and his fingers grazed her arm gently. "Do you know what his blood contains?"

She shook him off. "I only know what your people told me. Nothing more. But I don't care. I don't care at all. I'm not sending him back, and you're not either. I'm not leaving that boy alone again. He's been alone enough."

He caught her arm in an actual grip and held it. "Are you ready to lose him?"

Kierstaz gritted her teeth the way Mikel used to. She'd taken to doing it in his place. "I am not prepared to lose anyone. But I have lost enough in my time that I assure you, you will have no tears from me."

Sark nodded, but he looked past her—through her—as if he knew something she did not.

"If there's something I should know about Malcom—"

His head snapped around, his voice abrupt. "The physicians found that his blood was not entirely human, my queen. Part of him is...polluted, defiled. There's dark wizardry in his family. The superstitions you Serens have adopted about faeries and gremlins are childish stories to explain people with a higher or stronger spiritual ability."

Kierstaz swallowed. "Surely, Sark, those are merely tales—"

"No. No, your progressive ideas have turned them into tales in order to render them impotent. Yet can you explain the way the land responds to the touch of an Orion? That is the strength in blood that you now call gremlin. A foolish word for something so powerful."

Kierstaz trembled. "What are you saying?"

"I am saying that the opposite of gremlins are faeries, my queen. And Malcom has faerie blood in him."

"Are you telling me that Trzl's grandfather truly is a wizard? That he manipulates minds and his granddaughter can do the same?"

"And her son. Yes."

That couldn't be. Malcom had never… "Is this common? How did your people know how to…?"

"It is uncommon, but I have seen it. What I have *not* seen is a blood like Malcom's. He has faerie *and* gremlin blood. The drug he was given induced one to attack the other. That I have never seen, nor have any of the Drei in that castle, and that is everyone under creation who would know. And do not laugh, but I am afraid of such a boy. Even more afraid should he become a man."

Kierstaz shook her head. "I…thought…"

"You did what you should have, bringing him to us. He has been healed as best he can be, but if the Generals sent him to me, it is because they want me to assess him myself. They'll expect me to trade him to Otreya for something of great value—perhaps your brother—or kill him if he is too much of a threat."

No.

He stepped away from her, out of reach of any of her daggers, as if he anticipated her coming fury. "You cannot let him out of your sight, my queen."

Was he warning her against himself? She wanted to shake him. "How can…how can he still be alive with both of their blood? Faeries are not natural. They have always been a cursed thing."

Sark ran his hand around the back of his head. "What can you tell me about his father that I don't already know?"

"He was not an Orion."

"You are sure of this?"

Kierstaz rubbed her shoulders and started to nod, but she had to stop in the middle of it. "He couldn't be."

{22}
Alone

MIKEL KNEW ROMIANZ HAD TWO daughters, but he wasn't sure he had ever given them more than a polite glance and a nod. Something told him Kierstaz would have all of their names and birth places written on her palms. They were her people, after all. A part of the Guard. They were important.

Mikel leaned against the wall and called into the emptiness, "Do you have a sister?"

The cell next to his was dark. Not even a candle flickered. Somewhere, a drop of water hit a dish or maybe only a crevice in the rock.

He plastered his face against the bars and gripped them hard. "Is her name Riyev? Does she look like you?" Thoughts rained through his mind, and he spoke them to the air. "I never met a sister of yours. I never even dined with Romianz's family. How base and brutal is that? I ask the man to give me his honor, his strength, his reputation, the blood of his two young sons... I never so much as asked the names of his other children, if they were healthy, if they...lived."

There was no sound. She'd been there for two weeks, and now she was gone. Or was someone toying with him? In his head? Had it been a figment of his imagination? He could not truly be that lonely…could he?

Mikel lit a candle. "Please tell me you're there," he whispered. He repeated the words, more than a few times. There was no answer. Not a shuffle or a scratch or even another drop of water. He pulled his legs close, hugged them to him, and cried.

{23}
Fealty

MALCOM WATCHED THE SOLDIERS FASHIONING armor, clustered around massive fires contained in frantically built stone forges. He'd never learned a trade, and he'd always wanted to. That he'd managed to survive this long meant Allel had indeed smiled upon him, Uvei had said.

He frowned briefly when he thought of the Creator, of how his mind now saw God as one did a friend. He'd always wanted that as a child. Most children did, he assumed, but grown-ups always had other ideas. It was confusing. Mikel was the only man he knew who made it sound simple—as simple as he'd wanted it to when he was a boy and as simple as he now allowed it to be.

The armor they gave him was strange. Not made of metal at all, it was nearly translucent and light as goram wood. It fitted his chest with near perfection, as if they'd fashioned it for him.

"What is this?"

The Drei who handed it to him narrowed his eyes. "Ancient design from the purebloods. Otto makes it."

"Who's Otto?"

The soldier rolled his eyes. "He's too busy to speak to *you*. Take your armor and get in line for a sword."

Malcom frowned at the sword he was given. It was also light, made from blue steel—Drei steel. Rumor was all of it had been destroyed during the war his parents had waged on Dreibourge. He didn't like to think on that. It made him clench his fists, feel a strange detachment, as if they weren't truly his parents. He'd always felt more protected and loved by Kierstaz, even when she was merely Tev, the washed-up knight. She'd carried his half-dead body across icy mountains to find a cure for him. No one had ever done things like that for him.

Well, his mother had left a life of ease and glamor in a veritable palace to keep him from a horrid father, hadn't she? That had to count for something. Malcom frowned. He should feel more for his mother than this. He knew he should. She had raised him to never believe in anything except freedom and a certain part of him still agreed, but he'd put conditions on it in his adolescent mind. Freedom may be a beautiful thing, but he could hardly believe the people of the earth would ever allow it. Someone would always want to rule others. Best it be an unselfish someone. If indeed such a person existed, she was Kierstaz.

She had never told him of her bloodline. Yet when he'd awakened in a cream-colored room in a Drei castle and they'd informed him she had departed with a force to rescue Mikel and retake her country, it had seemed the most natural thing that little warrior Tev could be a long-forgotten queen—that she always had been.

Malcom took his sword out to the edge of a tent and swung it about in circles, felt it twirl around and watched the tip of it. It was like air in his fingers.

"What are you doing?"

He swung wide, nearly letting the weapon fly. Clumsy of him, but then, the Dermed thing was too light to hold onto. "Fencing."

Sark stood about twenty paces away, but his voice carried. If ever there was an eerie creature, it was the pureblood Drei, and Sark especially so because he had the commanding fearlessness of a saber tooth. "Alone?"

"I always used to while I waited for Mikel to come back from the quarries."

"Ah."

He was quiet, so Malcom continued to swing the sword about.

"You're not much of a swordsman, are you, Malcom?"

Not that he wanted to admit it, but… "No."

"If you ride at the front, I'll expect you to stay out of the way. Kierstaz does not need to be looking over her shoulder to be sure you are breathing."

Malcom swallowed. "I could stay at the back of the lines, sir."

"You could." He smiled slightly. "But I don't think that will be necessary. This tower holds less than three hundred Serens. I expect the skirmish to be light."

Whatever that meant. "Do you need something from me, sir?"

"No." Sark turned on his heel to walk away, then swung back around. "Actually, yes, I do."

Malcom stood up straight. "Yes?"

"I know you have never given Kierstaz cause to doubt you or your loyalty, but I want you to swear to me your fealty for her. I want to hear it and believe it."

Malcom's tongue was dry in his throat. Such an oath should be easy— he could not think of a truer thing—yet the words that came out of his mouth betrayed him. "I've never felt that I needed to swear fealty to her, sir. I've always felt that she had sworn her fealty to me."

Sark blinked, so slight it was hard to catch, and his head drew back. "Thank you. That was all I needed to hear."

Malcom frowned. "I might very well ask the same of you, General

Sark. I have known her far longer. I wake from a haze to find she has married you and made you master of her matters of war. Where does *your* fealty lie?"

Sark's eyes glowed, and Malcom saw they were nearly white-blue. Tev used to say Drei were icy cold. Indeed. "Now I see why she likes you. Quite clever, you are."

"I asked you a question."

"I am loyal to her. Without condition. No matter how strong a force or how frightful their strength is, I will die for her." His face dared Malcom to say the same.

"As would I." But he hadn't anything else to add. He felt, more than anything, that he was protected by her. Followed by her. Trusted by her. There was no way to repay or return that protection and trust. Anything he said would mean nothing because he needed her more than she needed him. "I…don't think she would let me die for her."

Sark's thin cheeks twitched, and he whirled away without another word.

༄

MALCOM WATCHED KIERSTAZ ADJUST THE cuffs on her forearms for the third time. Her reins were loose and easy and she looked as if she'd been born for this, but she showed just the slightest bit of nervousness. Of course she was nervous. He was scared all the way through.

Malcom leaned toward the soldier closest to him and whispered. "How many Serens are…?"

The soldier frowned as if Malcom shouldn't have spoken, but he held up a hand with all but one finger outstretched. Four hundred? In theory, they hadn't been engaged in twelve years. Surely that counted for something.

Since recovering from sickness, Malcom's thoughts would lapse into reciting history, facts, feelings—anything he'd experienced or learned—recounting it in full detail, to be relived and weighed again. At times, the diversions were refreshing, a fine pause in the day for thought. Other times it was as if his mind had an agenda he did not fully understand. Just now it decided to recite the locations of the fortresses of northern and southern Dreibourge, and he had to hush it.

Sark rode up from one of the flanks and saluted to Kierstaz. "They're ready."

Kierstaz looked behind her and raised an eyebrow to Malcom. He tried to smile, but his stomach was quaking. He'd never seen battle. The only violence he'd witnessed was Kierstaz slashing throats a few at a time. This would be different.

She sunk her heels into her horse and let it reach a full stride before turning about to face her army. The snow beneath its hooves churned with layer after layer of ice. Chunks of it sprung up and bit at the ankles of the mount.

"My warriors," she called out loudly. Even with her little voice, Malcom's skin prickled. "As the rightful queen of Serengard, I come not to fight the Drei, but my own people, to drive their rule from this land forever. In return, I ask only for your sanctuary and your loyalty, that you fight beside me to rid Dreibourge of these invaders." Her cheeks grew hot and flushed. "There has always been peace between the Drei and the house of Orion. I signify my faith in you and in that peace by placing my life in your hands. I ask you to place yours in mine."

The air crackled with the sound of ice alone. Not a voice rose nor horse turned. Then they raised their weapons in unison, their faces silent and stony. Skin of olive and tan, hair that was red, brown, and sandy. Not purebloods like the generals and lieutenants, but warrior Drei—the same Drei his mother had wanted obliterated from the earth because they were too independent, too unpredictable, too powerful.

Malcom glanced around him, his dark hair and light skin feeling suddenly obvious. She had just said she was here to fight her own people. They swore their swords to her—Kierstaz Orion, of Petrolai and Teal. The name Orion blazed in his mind like a burning coal, and he winced, felt eyes on him. Sark's.

Now that he thought about it—about the hatred for Drei his mem had tried to instill in him, about the horror she'd unleashed on this people—it seemed ridiculous that General Sark should let him use a sword, should trust him at all. Utterly ridiculous. All he could think was that his loyalty to Kierstaz forced Sark to let Malcom do as he pleased, but that was not likely to be a strong thread.

Malcom blinked. A picture of something flashed in his mind. A burning field. No, *this* field. On fire. He wasn't sure whether it was a ghost of past days or a foretelling of the end of this one, but he realized what was happening in his head. Nightmares. Daydreams. Maybe recollections he didn't know he possessed. Places he must have been when he was younger, before he could chronicle them in his mind.

They had to be something real, didn't they? He refused to believe something was merely happening to him, owning him.

Kierstaz raised her arm in the air and yelled at the top of her lungs, "Forward!"

Malcom squeezed his horse's flanks and eased into the multitude.

{24}
Lies

MIKEL WANTED TO KILL TRZL when they dropped the girl into the cell next to his. Little feet were visible through the grate on the floor next to his bed, and when she sat, he saw her finger was broken, as originally ordered.

The girl curled herself into a corner and looked around with bold, brown eyes. They settled on him, and he met them in sympathy.

"I'm sorry they broke your hand."

The girl slid toward him on her stomach, peering between the bars that separated them. One of her shoulders hitched. "It doesn't hurt all that much." Her face was idyllic—bright, cheerful, childish. "My name is Natalya."

"I know."

"You are Mikel. You're the prince."

He nodded slowly. "Do they let you see your mother, Natalya?"

She shook her head. "Only once." Her arms shifted. Perhaps she didn't want to talk about it. "You are here for a reason, aren't you?"

Mikel smiled. "What makes you say that?"

"I've been wanting to see you, and here you are."

"I was supposed to be dead, little one."

"My uncle said you weren't. He said you were coming back when the warrior stars stopped over Serengard. Mem said it was true."

Romianz's children were far more optimistic than he gave them credit for, it would seem. "Well, mems have been known to tell stories such as that."

Natalya's eyes sobered. "I know when my mem lies, and she was not lying."

"You do, do you?"

The little girl nodded. "Yes."

"Did she lie in that room with the mean lady? When you met me?"

Natalya lifted her chin. "She might lie to *that* lady."

They were interrupted by the clank of metal against iron as the bars to Mikel's cell were lifted. Trzl marched in, a new tiered cape draped across her shoulders and black eye paint on. "Mikel Orion, Emperor Vekst has decided you may leave your cage for a night."

His stomach twisted slightly. Strange. Vekst had wanted nothing to do with him, save an initial interview when he was first brought in. "Why?"

"There is a banquet held at this time every year to honor the victory over Dreibourge. The Emperor thought it would be poetic to have a ghost at the table."

Mikel let his mouth twist into a mocking grin. "Did you tell him this ghost still calculates in the dark?"

"I told him to be aware that you were entirely helpless in my hands, and that you will attend while under a heavy dose of—"

"—opal root?" He filled in for her.

Trzl waved a hand. "Whatever the Desert People use to ease pain. I believe it also delays your comprehension." She had a guard administer the liquid-covered blade this time, right in the arm where she used to do it.

"Such a shame. I'd grown rather fond of you torturing me personally."

Trzl narrowed her eyes at him, turned on her heel, and let the edges of her new cape hit him in the face. Just before the door closed behind them, Mikel glimpsed Natalya's face through the bars of her door, eyes wide.

He was taken to another building, up a set of stairs, and into a small room with a steaming tub in it. Trzl ordered him to wash and then left, not bothering to remove the irons on his hands and feet. Neither of the guards at the door seemed intent on removing them either, so he washed with them on. It took him a moment to realize why the water felt so strange: he hadn't bathed in hot water in over four months. The last time had been when Pier had brought boiling water to sterilize his wound on board Romianz's stolen ship, and he wasn't sure that could be counted. The bathing water sent to his cell was always cold.

A white coat with solid gold buttons down the front was draped over a chair, along with plain tan pants of a material too thin to be useful. The idea of never regaining his own clothes actually made him shiver, but she must want him to wear these, so he pulled them on. Trzl kept his hair cropped short, probably to remind the guards of who he was: Castle Guard, Orion, loyalist. Although, he had his doubts that anyone in this city remembered that far back. The walls themselves were less than fifteen years old, and already it seemed as if these gears had been turning for centuries.

It took twenty minutes of walking to reach the banquet, through several buildings with long, empty hallways. The walls held little to no art or even creative styling—terribly unfitting for council buildings in a capital city. Mikel gulped back a lump or two as they descended some stairs and walked out yet another set of doors into a wide courtyard made of granite brick. It spanned the width of two streets and then some:

white, perfect, merging seamlessly into the wall of a huge building. This must be the hall of the Council of Four, if indeed there was such a thing, but why build it out of Drei stone? Serengard had her own quarries for colored stone in the north and south alike. Far less waste and far less treachery would be employed to build it out of their own materials.

Mikel didn't mean to sound angry, but his voice was close to a growl when he asked the guard next to him, "What is this street made of?"

He received only a shove in return, and then they were mounting granite steps to the entrance. Everything was white, almost hypnotically so. Or maybe it was the medicine hitting his brain. Maybe this *walk* was hitting his brain.

They stopped inside the next set of doors and removed the chain from his hands but left those on his ankles, and when he turned, Trzl was there. Her gown was...white. It wrapped easily around her ample hips and swayed on its way to the floor, and she wasn't even moving. What would it look like when she moved? *Goblins.*

"Let me seat you. How *did* you get that jacket on?"

He looked at it, puzzled. Had one of the guards unlocked his cuffs so he could dress? Or maybe they'd been off of his hands for a while now? Something was wrong with his brain. He couldn't remember. "What did you put in my arm, Trzl?"

She ran a finger along his chin. "No need to worry. I'll be right next to you tonight. Look half-crazy if you can."

He furrowed his brow and fell into step behind her. All of a sudden, there were people there or maybe they had been there all along. White or tan suits, like his. Nothing was colorful—it was all simple, bland. Even the dungeon he'd been in had more variation than this.

Most everyone was shorter than him. His facial scars, thick chest, and broad arms stood out, much as if he were wearing crimson.

Trzl pulled out a seat for him, and he slid into it as quietly as he could. The man who took the chair next to him glanced at him twice, then looked down the table without comment. Emperor Vekst was seated directly across from him. Mikel knew him by the gold medallion pinned on his breast.

Before wine had been poured or food brought, the Emperor placed both elbows on the table and said, "Mikel Orion, how many times have we thought you shredded to a dozen bits? Five or so? And then to find you've been hiding in the cliffs plotting sedition. At last we find your weakness." He grinned and raised a hand, and the bread was brought on cue.

The man next to the Emperor started in, and it took Mikel a moment to decide what he was. A commander of some sort. He knew the bearing, but not the face.

"I always knew this one was a clever one," the commander said. "Never given the responsibility next to Hodran that she was capable of. To you, Trzl." He raised a glass.

Mikel wasn't aware of his eyes blinking, but they must have been for he couldn't get them to stop. He turned slowly to Trzl and tipped his head. She was blushing. From the compliment? "I noticed an utter lack of art on my way here. A shame to have a capital this well-built so devoid of taste."

Trzl picked up her glass of wine. "We don't believe in distracting the mind. It impedes healthy thought to be focused on beauty instead of practicality."

"We. That must include your council and your chamberlains and your army? What of the inhabitants of your cities? Does beauty distract them?" The food in front of him smelled delicious, but his stomach was already roiling. "Why not lock up every person of beauty as well? I am sure they are distracting your more practical citizens. Trzl of the founding council should certainly be kept in a dungeon or perhaps burned alive to rid the world of such a pretty face and fine figure."

Trzl scrunched her nose but didn't make a sound.

Vekst leaned back in his chair, a bemused look on his face. "Well, this specimen is far more agreeable than I anticipated. We must have this kind of entertainment more often. Tell me, do you wish to discuss the citizens of Serengard with me as their unwanted and outcast leader or as a prisoner who knows his days are numbered? There are two ways to speak at this table. Both are acceptable, you'll find. There is no damage you can do. Your ways are old and done with."

Mikel sat back in his chair as well. Like Kovim, Vekst believed his own words thoroughly; that much was evident. "I would discuss the people of Serengard merely as a man, if it pleases you, Emperor."

Vekst speared a piece of meat and held it in front of him. "You, I like." He laughed slightly. "Where did you find him, Trzl? I've always held that knowledge—pure and untainted knowledge—will change a man whether he wishes it or no, but this Orion is quite a different creature entirely."

Vekst was no puppet, and as such, he was likely as immovable as Otreya's other Chamberlains had always been. Except for Hodran. *Well done, Trzl, coaxing me to kill Hodran for you.* Mikel cleared his throat, his mind starting to clear. "Who decides what is beautiful, Emperor?"

Trzl's breath caught jaggedly. Her fingernails dug into his knee. A warning, he supposed. To the Derm with it.

"You claim that if you destroy beauty, everything will be equal, but man cannot destroy what Allel has made beautiful unless he destroy the sky and the ground as well, unless he kills every living bird. You make this land desolate and ugly by your imposing rule and then pretend you have done it on purpose when the truth is that Allel is taking from you because you took from him. One day your people will curse you. They will curse you for stealing every painting from every tavern of Ashlin and burning them on your altar of progress, leaving them nothing but bare dirt and empty thought. What is knowledge without sunshine to illuminate it?"

The placid smile on Vekst's face remained intact, but his eyes hardened considerably. "I am not a destroyer. I am a builder. Kovim tore down that I might build, and Kovim was killed by a marauder that I might may advance us further forward. Who was that marauder?" He tapped his wine glass. "Oh. You."

Mikel smiled slightly. "I bore Kovim no grudge for his ideals, only his rancid execution of them."

"The same could be said of you, could it not?"

That actually hurt, somewhere in his chest. "It could."

Trzl let her fork fall heavily on her plate. Not what she wanted him to say, was it? Well, she put him in this fighter ring.

Vekst took another sip of wine. "I often wonder why the fates of kingdoms could not be settled in tournament, as the Elloyans do. The best of the monarchy against the best of the people, to fight to the death in a ragged game. Oh, I know why—because the pampered Orions have held the monopoly on weapons and technique for thousands of years and there is no way around them but sheer numbers. Still, it would've made one stunning tournament."

Mikel put his elbows on the table. His temples throbbed heavily. He was certain he could make a better argument, but he couldn't find the threads in his head. "The Elloyans fight to the death over anything that pesters them. A hostage they don't want to relinquish, a slave they don't want to sell. If they had kingdoms, Emperor, they would bore of this battlefield of the mind far faster than you do. And they are smart enough with their coin that they would not build their cities out of Drei marble just to brag to future generations that, in the time the Fourth City was built, the Drei were slaves to them. I say the Elloyans are wiser. At least their typical conflict does not encompass children running down well-trained knights—knights who are capable of slaying twenty of them in an instant—"

Trzl's hand came up. "I did not bring you here to talk about the past in such ugly terms, prisoner, and you are monopolizing the conversation. There are other Chamberlains who may wish to speak. It is, after all, a banquet."

Mikel bit back the words he wanted desperately to spew and instead raised an eyebrow at her and shifted his shoulders. "The pheasant is quite good."

Someone at the far end of the table took her cue from Trzl and said, "Do you have anything to say for the woman claiming to be Kierstaz Orion in Dreibourge? Should we ask *her* to a tournament?"

It took him a moment to place the voice. He knew that voice. He knew it. He turned toward that end of the table and caught the delicate face with a hint of olive skin, deep-set frozen eyes, and Seren blonde hair. A face he should have noticed, it was so out of place.

Idelviss.

"I hadn't heard," Mikel answered. His throat hurt like mad. It was one thing to be placed at a table that he knew was rife with enemies. Quite another to have a friend twist a knife in his back. He suddenly ceased to care if Trzl got her full effect out of this or if it accomplished whatever she hoped. He *didn't* care.

Idelviss flung her hair over her shoulder. "They say she looks nothing like her. Couldn't possibly be the real Kierstaz."

My knights carried you from a burning building, he wanted to say. *Brought you through four villages of madness to safety. And this is your thanks? Turn us in one by one?* "I wouldn't know."

"Has scars on her face." She quirked an eyebrow, as if to ask if she should divulge where she'd seen a scarred face before.

Mikel looked at Trzl in question. Her expression was curious, intent. She'd known Idelviss was going to say this in front of all of them. She'd not only known; she'd planned it. She'd put him out here in front of the dogs to see what he would do. Gave him poisons to make him honest. She wanted it to be Dermed real.

Mikel cleared his throat. "I didn't know being Kierstaz was a desirable claim, especially in Dreibourge."

"Oh, it isn't." Vekst had a passive face now, one that was completely inscrutable.

Trzl picked at something on Mikel's shirt. "Are you sure you're not hiding something from us, Mikel? If there is anyone else of your bloodline, we must know or else things will go badly for you."

Mikel shook his head. A head that was pulsing with a new, encroaching darkness. Everything white in the room turned bright yellow, then black. He laughed bitterly and wrapped his fingers around the back of his neck. "This is the first I've heard of such a person."

Trzl did not smile. "Are you sure?"

Vekst shoved his plate away and steepled his fingers in front of him. "His mother escaped the fortress of Orion during the burning of Ashlin. She could have borne another child."

Mikel turned his eyes on Vekst, though he could see little out of them. "My mother died a few days after her escape from the adelweed your valiant rebels had been feeding her. She breathed her last in my arms."

Trzl picked at his shirt again and laughed softly. "Oh, Mikel. You've no need to be bruised about that. *I* dosed her with adelweed. Poor woman wasn't going to live long, anyway."

Mikel stood up, flung his chair to the floor behind him. "You?"

Whether she'd said it for dramatic effect or not, the picture of Trzl in that room, on that day, was enough to make him want to watch somebody bleed for it. He had to get out of here.

Trzl reached for him. He stepped away on instinct.

"Sit back down," she said through bared teeth.

"No. I've had enough of being your little underdog in a ring of jackals."

A dark, heavy frown creased her brow. She flicked her fingers to a guard. "Take him back to the prison and teach him thoroughly what his role here is. The rack, I think. I don't take insurrection from anyone."

{25}
delays

THE NUMBER OF THE SEREN force that held Zurik was unknown, but the spies thought it was somewhere near four thousand. Kierstaz had half that many—Malcom had heard as much from the soldiers who were supposed to be guarding him. It irked him that Kierstaz didn't trust him with his own safety.

Malcom covered his armor in his own clothing and stashed the sword in a cleft rock to the east of camp. He wasn't sure if he would be able to come back for it, but it would be good to have it concealed just the same.

The Seren soldiers at the gate of Zurik didn't question him or the heavy coat he wore with the collar turned up. The fact that none of them even glanced twice was uncanny. Shouldn't they? They were, after all, guarding the gate. Malcom felt as if he'd been given special treatment, trusted where he shouldn't be. Perhaps Mem hadn't put out parchments with his face on them or no one took them seriously or he had grown enough in four years that she hardly knew what he looked like.

Or perhaps he was recognized and the soldiers were waiting until he was deep within the city to snatch him.

He kept an eye out for people looking at him strangely. His father's face—the Seren Commander who had dethroned the Generals, deported workers, beheaded anyone who had given him trouble, and visited the cities of Dreibourge at least twice a year to ensure they hadn't forgotten—would certainly be known here. A shiver hit him every time he imagined his mem at Hodran's side. Most of the time, he couldn't believe it of her. She must have been misled and misinformed, dragged along by the one who controlled her. That was the only logical explanation.

He did not know his way around the city, as he'd never set foot in Zurik before. Kierstaz and Mikel had avoided the guarded and populated areas of Dreibourge, sticking to the fishing hovels on the southern shore. Malcom followed the mud and the gutters until he entered a more crowded part of town with new huts and tall buildings of mud brick with tiny windows. This was where he felt most comfortable. Most of his childhood had been spent in a small village in the east of Serengard, but the past few years had been spent in and out of shantytowns in Dreibourge. He'd learned to speak Drei and understand them. The Serens there were either criminals on the run as he was or bounty hunters. Not soldiers.

Sticking his face into the Drei side of Zurik would not go unnoticed. He had eyes far too brown, a face too solid and a frame too tall to be one of them. The first building he set foot in was a shop of some sort, and he received an arm in the air and the words, "Get out."

Malcom leaned forward and whispered in Drei, "I'm looking for a leader of yours."

The Drei's eyes narrowed, and he reached beneath a board as if to grasp a weapon. "Get out, you well-dressed scum."

This was just the kind of person he was looking for: one who hated Serens profusely. "Please. I'm wanted by the Empire. I simply need a place to—"

"Listen, boy. I have no quarrel with you, but your face will draw the attention of every tax adjuster in the quarter. I can't have you in my shop."

Malcom left. He went around to the back of the building and looked for someone less territorial or at least less terrified. He wasn't sure how he knew to come here—it was merely instinct and a strong one. If he stopped and thought about it, these strange instincts and ideas that came into his head would frighten him senseless, so he didn't do either. He acted.

There was a young woman hanging out a wash. She jumped when she saw him and her eyes narrowed, but she didn't make a sound beyond a curt, "What do you want, gypsy?"

At least she didn't think him a spy. That was better. "I'm not a gypsy. I'm a messenger."

"Messengers of your kind are quite disliked in my house." She tapped a finger against her tiny hip to punctuate the passing of time. "Your message? If the rent is due again, I don't blame you for avoiding my father. He can be quite intimidating."

Her father? Malcom blinked. He'd forgotten that Drei could look as young as him and be nearly thirty years of age. "There's a force of mercenaries from the west headed for the city. They have quarrel with the Serens, not the Drei. If your people were to stay out of the fray—"

"Wait. You should tell my brother this."

"Your brother?"

She bit her lip. "He may have heard of it already."

Must be influential. "That is exactly who I would like to speak to."

"Follow me."

There it was again—a ridiculous, unfounded trust in him. It couldn't be his face, could it? Did he have a trustworthy look about him? Although, he did notice she refused to confide a name.

Thankfully, she led him down the street instead of into the house.

"Where did you get this information? I assure you, if it is not true and you're here to ferret out our leaders, you'll be disappointed. We haven't any leaders, and we are not insurrectionists. We do as we're told." She leaned against a door and knocked on it several times.

Malcom nodded. "Of course."

"My brother would like to know what is happening so that he can help protect the quarter. The Serens tell us nothing." The door opened, and she pulled him inside. "Jens, this is a vagabond Seren who thinks we should disobey our Seren leaders while mercenaries plunder the city."

Jens was by far the tallest Drei Malcom had ever seen. Nearly his equal in height, he had a muscled chest and a neck as thick as his head. His eyes narrowed slightly. "He wants us to remain passive while they burn Zurik?"

Malcom shook his head. "No one wants to burn Zurik. I want you to remain passive while they subdue the Seren force and take the city."

"We are a part of the Seren Empire now. The Four Cities have ruled Dreibourge for your entire life, boy. Why would we do anything but stand with them?"

"Have you heard anything of the fortresses north of here? Have any of your spies?"

Jens' eyes narrowed. "I haven't any spies."

"I wish that you had. If you knew that there had been no word from—"

"I have a simple answer to this," Jens cut in. "You will stay here with us all night. If in the morning the city is under attack from mercenaries, we believe you."

Malcom bit his tongue. "You're not going to warn the Seren forces?"

"If their scouts have not discovered your mercenaries already, they must not exist." But he smiled slightly, and Malcom grasped at that.

"The force that is coming is not Elloyan. They are Drei, and they will likely attack from the north, south, east, and west. There will be no escape, no matter who is warned."

The girl's eyes went wide. "There are no Drei forces in Dreibourge. None of us are allowed to arm ourselves."

"There are now." Malcom peeled off his heavy coat and pulled his smock over his head. The Drei armor nearly glowed in the dim light, the body heat it encased keeping him warm.

Jens' jaw went slack as he stared at it. "Boy, where did you get that?"

The girl narrowed her eyes. "And who *are* you?"

"No one."

ꙮ

THE ATTACK BEGAN SEVERAL HOURS before dawn. Kierstaz sent in the horse soldiers from the north and the west, with Theo leading the charge. She led the second wave from the east herself. The third, with Crista at the front, slipped around her left flank to the south and cut off any escape, but were ordered not to engage unless attacked.

Kierstaz would have been worried that the city might harbor more force than her scouts had anticipated, except she knew one thing that could not be hidden: population. Zurik had held nearly thirteen thousand people before Dreibourge was taken. Now they estimated the same amount, only half were Seren, with the other half of the Drei having been killed during the war or fled to one of the Four Cities where there was food. With the reinforcements brought in yesterday, Kierstaz had nearly eight thousand soldiers all told. The fact that all Drei under the Eight Generals had been trained in war and medicine by the age of twelve meant that only the very young were inexperienced, but even they knew the silent salutes, the raising of weapons in a certain manner that communicated their loyalty to their soil.

There were at least two hundred of the Class of Stealth with her force, and there was Sark at her right hand, who knew how to lead a charge of warrior Drei.

A pang hit her as she watched them quietly move in unison, without a shouted order or months of drilling. They did not dance with their swords as her trainer had taught her—it was as if they *became* their swords. For a brief moment, she feared that all she might accomplish would be to destroy the last of the purebloods, the last of the Generals.

She frowned and wondered if Malcom was among them somewhere. He was supposed to be beside her. Fear for him paralyzed her for a second, but then she had to bury it.

A flare went up, and the soft rumble of hooves shook the ground. First a few hundred, then a few thousand. It was too dark to see them, to know the moment they poured over the hill. Kierstaz closed her eyes and breathed a prayer that they hadn't missed a scout, that no one had warned the city, that none of her soldiers had betrayed her, and when she opened them, Sark was watching her closely.

"You are ready?" he whispered.

She gave a curt nod and focused on the sky again. It felt like hours had passed instead of minutes. "How far is it?"

"A mile."

"We should start moving now."

He did not argue, merely raised his arm in signal, and the entire force moved forward one step. He raised it again, and they advanced on the city, feet so quiet Kierstaz could still hear the lull of the horses' hooves on the next ridge.

The second flare. The horsemen had reached the wall.

"Double quick," Kierstaz hissed.

A third flare. Too soon. The third flare meant victory...or surrender. Kierstaz looked sharply at Sark. "Is that..."

He motioned to the foot soldiers to stand still. "You should ride ahead, my queen. There is a scout on the hill you can confer with."

She did as he said immediately, a knot tightening in her stomach.

From the ridge, she could see the city of Zurik laid out in the valley below, perfect in the darkness, soft yellow and orange lights from torches atop the walls. Light spread just enough to see her entire force of horsemen halted outside the gates.

The gates were open.

"What happened?" she asked the scout when she reached him.

"Surrendered. As soon as they saw us."

"Had we so much as—"

The scout shook his head before her question was out. "Only one volley of arrows had been loosed, my queen."

Across the valley, a bay horse galloped toward her. Either that was Theo or one of his messengers. She urged her horse down the ridge without another word.

It was Theo. When she reached him, he did not rein in but pulled about to ride beside her for the gate of the city. She spared one glance for his face and found it unreadable. Apparently he had nothing to say to her.

Kierstaz dismounted at the gate. There were bodies thrown over the wall, several hundred of them, and she didn't have to move closer to see they'd not died of arrow wounds, but sword. In the entrance stood a young Drei with a knife to the throat of a massive Seren commander.

"He wants to speak to you," Theo said.

Kierstaz walked forward, keeping Theo in her vision to be sure he was behind her. Her sword clanked against her leg, loud in the night air. All she heard besides that was the nicker of a horse and the moan of a half-dead man in the dirt. *Is no one breathing?*

"That's far enough," the young Drei told her.

Kierstaz stopped, her hand on the hilt of her sword. "Do you wish to surrender or no?"

"I wish to negotiate terms."

"If that Seren man is your hostage, you'll find I care nothing for his blood."

"Excellent. All I need is for you to hear his name and rank. Give it, Tuvia."

The Seren cleared his throat. "My name is Tuvia, Commander of Zurik, Lieutenant to Chamberlain Viktor and keeper of his province."

The Drei stabbed Tuvia through the throat, stepped over the body, and walked up to her. "And my name is Jens. I surrender Zurik to you under the condition that you rid us of every Seren pest that dwells within these walls and return it to Drei rule. My people are in control of all of the towers. We only require your assistance to secure the armories and fortress, but half of them should be subdued by the time you take the streets."

The man had a common Drei accent, one Kierstaz was more familiar with. "Am I to understand you wish me to enter the city armed and battle-ready? How will I know your people from those you have taken arms against?"

"It is every Drei against every Seren now." Jens looked her up and down. "If there are any more of your kind in your host, you'd best keep them out of the fray tonight."

"I am the only one." Except for Malcom, but he should be safely back with the scouts.

"And you lead them? Why do you not ride with your own people?"

"I am Kierstaz Orion, and these are my only allies."

His eyes flickered, and he lowered his voice. "Anyone can say they are Kierstaz. She has been thought dead many years."

"My force will speak for me." Kierstaz motioned to Theo. "Send a message to Sark to bring his foot soldiers. Keep half your force outside the city and send half in with him. Jens, please remain with me if your lieutenants are capable of commanding."

He shifted from one foot to the other but said, "I will."

"How long have you held the towers and wall?"

"Nearly an hour."

Kierstaz looked him up and down. Of course the city could have known they were coming. Killing every Seren watch they passed only worked until they were within miles of the city, and then anyone could have glimpsed them and slunk back to the walls. "You were warned?"

"Was he not sent by you?"

The twisty feeling in her stomach settled. She did have a leak but not a traitor. "Who?"

"The Seren boy—black-haired, tall."

Malcom.

Damn.

{26}
Torn

MIKEL'S WRISTS AND ANKLES WERE bloody and blistered by the time he was tossed into his cell, but the throbbing pain of every muscle he owned was what made him want to sleep. He hadn't any knowledge of what the machine had just done to him or if he would ever regain his strength. Maybe Trzl had just destroyed him, shattered his body to make him truly an impotent threat.

He didn't bother to get up and climb on the bed. Even his bones felt as if they'd been torn from him, now useless inside his skin. It had been ages since a rack was used in Ashlin, as they'd all been destroyed under the second Derev. Mikel had only read about them in books. The design that the Four Cities employed was simple and straight-forward—four corners, each with an iron cuff, leather straps, and a gear with a crank on it. Allel knew he would have preferred a beating of any kind over this. A sword wound, even. Those he could handle. His head fell back on the soft soapstone beneath him, and he lost consciousness.

He dreamed of Aura. He hadn't in years. She used to haunt him at night, make him wish he could wake with her warm body next to him, her arms draped around his waist and her hair tangled in his fingers. Sometimes their son was there, little brown hands reaching at the light, tightening around Mikel's thumb. They were a happiness he hadn't deserved nor should have been indulging in at all. He'd been too concussed to talk himself out of it. He had wanted to bury the blood and pain that had come to define him against his will, wanted to again be blameless in the sight of Allel, but he had failed entirely.

First, after they died, there were nightmares. Blood, death, darkness. Things he'd tried to shelter her from. Sometimes she would reach for him or cry out in pain. Then the dreams grew gentler. Sometimes she would lay her head on his shoulder and whisper how much she missed him. Those were even harder. He'd wake in tears, clutching the bedpost and begging her to return.

And then it stopped. After Trzl came to the cliffs, he never saw Aura again. She had abandoned him to sleep in silence. He'd never felt so alone, even with Kierstaz and Malcom. Life was a nightmare without Aura in it, and he lived in terror that one day Trzl would replace her in his dreams as well.

Yet here she was—lovely and real. He could almost smell her, hear her footsteps coming over the sand. She giggled as the sunshine tossed her hair about, and she caught him looking at her. Then the sand turned to dark gray stone, and they were in the cliffs. He held her back, told her not to come, to go back to the Desert and Gavriel, and the words hurt to speak. But she shook her head, smiled, didn't listen. He knew this dream. He'd had it so many times that it had been like a dirge, but right now, the very sight of her warmed him from the inside, healed him, no matter how sad the moment.

He wasn't sure how long he'd been out. Could have been hours, could have been days. When he woke, there was a slim hand on his forehead. He would have smacked it away, but his arm didn't feel like moving.

"Can you hear me?" a cool voice asked. Someone he missed.

Mikel tried to nod. He blinked his eyes, formed a word. "Pier."

The face smiled, eyes crinkling at the corners. "Thought I'd lost you for a moment there."

"How did you..."

"The woman in the cell next to you offered information in exchange for treatment for you."

There was no woman in the other cell. Mikel blinked again. It wasn't Pier. Too young. "Colstadt?"

"I am sorry. I am not a friend of yours. I am a physician from outside these walls."

"Oh."

"You may be bleeding inside. Can you tell me if any one muscle is in more pain than the others?"

Mikel shook his head. That hurt. He twisted it, anyway, until he could see the floor of the cell on the opposite side. The Drei had said it was a woman, so he couldn't mean Natalya. He squinted into the dimness, through the fog in his head. For a moment, he was afraid it was Kierstaz. *No, please, no...*

Sprawled on the floor was a woman with dark hair in a bun. Brown hair. He let his head fall back, ashamed of how relieved he was.

"Will he live?" she asked.

He could tell that it wasn't the first girl they sent down. It must be Riyev. She'd been moved down here, too?

The Drei answered her, "He likely will, unless there is swelling in the next few days. The rack does not kill a man unless he has been torn inside, and I see no signs of that yet. He is fortunate."

"The Wizard knows he cannot die in battle, so they kill him this way."

The Drei looked at her sharply. "You know you cannot say such things. What kind of fool are you?"

Mikel barely made out a slight smile on Riyev's face before his own eyes fluttered closed and hid her from view. He heard her whisper, "The kind of fool who knows this empire will never kill *all* of the Orion sympathizers."

"My people know better than to be obstinate in this city." The Drei picked up a lantern that he must have brought with him. "I'll return in an hour. Watch him, if you like. Send a guard if he faints."

Mikel let his head roll until it felt a little less painful. He couldn't see Riyev's face, but he heard her body press up against the bars.

"You wanted someone else? Someone named Colstadt?"

Mikel gulped in some air. His tongue was dry, but he managed. "He was a Drei pirate, brought here with me...and your father."

"Is it true you helped capture him?"

"I helped capture Stazi." He didn't finish his sentence, but she should know.

"You would never betray Romianz."

"No."

Riyev let out a ragged sigh. "Even though he was quite excellent at betraying you?"

Mikel winced slightly. "I understand the man," he whispered. *And I am jealous that he has children living.*

"And you. You're not here by accident." Her voice lowered as well. "I am sorry they did this to you."

"You are foolishly bold." Listening to her was soothing. He wanted her to keep talking, even if it was about nothing. "It doesn't matter."

"Yes, it does. You are Mikel Orion—the Dark Lady's new prize, even as she is the new prize of Otreya the Wizard. A fate for Romianz, a fate for his daughter, a fate for your Drei—"

"Did you hear something of them? Are they dead?"

He heard her body jolt. "I don't know, but Natalya can check on them."

"How?"

"This prison. There are ways to travel through it if you are small enough. Most of the cells have a hatch somewhere that leads to the ducts beneath and above. It is intentional. We are experiments, yes? Why else are we still alive? They watch us, see if we will turn on each other, form alliances. Some people are in here simply to stir the pot."

"That is..." Mikel shook his head. "I don't believe you."

"You don't have to. None of the Drei here are treated well, and Pier... I know that name. Not well."

"What does that mean?"

Riyev cleared her throat. "I didn't *see* him myself, but he is of the Castle Guard and one of the Knights of Rilch. They have a special section for them. Natalya—she has been treated well. Only a finger broken. Do you know how full these prisons are? I was here once before when I was seventeen years of age because of my father."

Mikel ground his teeth. "Because he was the haven knight? Or because he aided the Knights of Rilch?"

Riyev looked away, her glance growing shy. "Because I was pregnant. Kovim wanted to know who the baby's father was. Her father was already dead, so he kept me until she was born to see what she looked like. They took a little of her blood." She wrapped her arms around herself. "Trzl was there. We called her the Dark Lady in those days. I heard she was back, but I didn't believe it until they told me my father was dead. "

The day she got fifty lashes. He nearly asked to see her back, see the scars, but then he wondered what would possess him to want that. To fuel his anger against Trzl? That would help nothing. "What did they tell you?"

"That he died heroically, serving the Empire." Riyev shrugged. "Yet Trzl had a special ire for anyone of the Castle Guard. Wanted them all hanged or burned. If she heard there was an actual Orion alive? I cannot imagine what lengths she would go to. She and Hodran hunted through every border castle and half of Dreibourge looking for the one called

Lomius. He was a strong knight, and my father defended him. I always knew the Dark Lady had a special hatred for my father. They... Part of why they paid special attention to me is because they thought Natalya could be Lomius' child."

Mikel snorted. "For surely Lomius could not fight a single battle without having the Keeper of Ciar's daughters warm his bed at night."

She blushed so heavily he could see it in the candlelight. "Hodran's imagination always involved fornicating."

Mikel reached again for a bar, grasped it, and pulled himself up to nearly sitting. He must have looked pale because Riyev asked him, "Are you all right?"

He tried to nod, but it was more of a grimace. Her face was closer to him now that he was upright and leaning against the wall, and he could see that her skin was darker than her sister's—or her sister's ghost—her features more like her father's than either of her brothers. "You don't recognize me, do you?"

She looked puzzled. "No, I never met the prince before."

"People don't...know my face," he mumbled.

"But they know your name. Even when you were thought dead, my father hid weapons, maps, and drawings of the layouts of new keeps. A hundred other knights and lieutenants did so as well. They hid what they could from the Empire in hopes an Orion would return someday." She looked wistful for a moment. "It is as if the whole earth has forgotten you. There's been a famine these past three years—too wet for grain, too dry for fruit. Did you ever hear of such a thing?"

"Is that what you told them? Where things were hidden?"

"Told them...?"

"For them to send a Drei down. For me."

"Oh. Oh, no. I made things up, as usual." She smiled.

"Usual?"

Riyev looked at him sharply. "She keeps asking about my brother,

Zven. Apparently, he has betrayed her in some way. I pray sincerely that he did. Our whole family is an unholy mess that Allel will have to judge harshly when the time comes."

Mikel winced. There had never been anything unholy about Tofer. "No one got out of this war without losing one of their virtues, youngling."

"I may have been young, but I'm not anymore." She bit down on her lip. "I fell in love with a soldier, we married in an armory, and I never saw him again. The Drei general he fought under sent me his shirt. Kept his sword, his armor, everything. Said his men needed the weaponry." Her eyes grew dull, her face blank. "Natalya came in her own time."

"At least you *have* a daughter." The words came out before he could stop them, before he realized they sounded bitter.

She glanced up at him again. "Yes. She is lovely, isn't she?"

He tipped his head toward the other side of his cell. "Did they tell you she's in the cell on the other side of mine?"

"Natalya?" Riyev gripped the bars between them suddenly, her eyes wide and hopeful. "Is she sleeping?"

Mikel tried to move, but he fell back against the wall. "I haven't talked to her since I was thrown in here, but she's there. Trzl won't dare take her. She wants my cooperation too badly."

Riyev fell back against the floor. "Thank you. Thank you for whatever you did to keep her near you." Her gaze grew suspicious. "Cooperation? What does she want from you, Orion? Besides to break you into several pieces?"

She had half a dozen reasons for bringing him, and only one or two for keeping him. "Oh, she won't. She was showing off."

Riyev did not look convinced.

He sobered. "I'm not certain what she wants." But he was close to certain. Trzl didn't need him to help her become empress. She wanted him here to make her feel better about herself. Trzl had always had a secret conscience, and permission from the man she'd betrayed and destroyed was about as much compensation as she could hope for.

Well, he wasn't about to give permission.

"I saw what that woman and her lover did to Dreibourge. The things they blamed on Hodran were half of them *her* doings. She'll play games with you until she's broken you, as one breaks a horse." Her voice grew sad. "If she kills you this way, at least promise me something?"

Mikel lifted a hand and braced his neck against it, inching himself away from the light. He wasn't sure he wanted to be so close to her after all. Something ached in his stomach that hadn't been there a few minutes ago. He still wanted to see the scars on her back and seethe. "What?"

"Use me for all I'm worth first. At least let me take the blame for something now and then."

He almost laughed. "I couldn't do that."

The drip of water in a vent filled her lengthy pause. "I'd like to know why not? I know the rules around here better than you do. You're like a poor new dog who's bound to step on all the wrong rugs."

"Because you're young and a mother. I am old and have no one."

"That is goblin vomit." Her eyes pierced through the dark, and he knew she was staring him down. "I tried to kill Otreya once, you know. I would have succeeded if he weren't a freak of nature."

"What? How?"

"I put poison in his glass at a banquet he had invited my father to. He drank the whole thing down with a smile, as if he knew it was poisoned. Then he let a cat lick it and the cat died."

"You shouldn't have done that."

"If it had worked, I would've saved you some trouble."

"And got your family beheaded."

"They were beheaded, anyway."

Mikel looked down. If he'd ever met her before, she'd been an innocent little child he wanted to protect. He cleared his throat. "I never take the blood of my knights in exchange for my own, Riyev. You of all people should know that."

She nodded, looked away in resignation. "I know."

{27}
Scars

KIERSTAZ DROPPED HER SADDLE ON the ground next to Sark's, slid a hand over her horse's back to wipe down the sweat, and did her best to ignore him. It wasn't the sets of eyes at her back that made her do it—it was him. The awkwardness. Three battles had come and gone, and still he had no words.

Not that she wanted him to say anything. What would he say? Nothing. Yet it was hard not to glance up at him when his shoulder rubbed hers or when he swung his saddle off and nearly placed it on the same log as hers or when he brushed her horse after she did as if to fix her mistakes.

"Stop, Sark."

He jumped, as if she'd smacked him. "Something you want to say to me, my queen?"

"Stop touching my horse."

"Touching your horse?" With a furtive look behind him, he leaned in close to her. "For true, I'd do anything you ask, but I don't think that is a reasonable request."

"No?"

"No."

Kierstaz almost wished he would put his arms around her, but of course he didn't. She kept her eyes on her horse's flank. "He's struck out alone entirely, hasn't he?"

"Malcom? I believe so."

"Why wouldn't he tell me where he is going? He always has before."

Sark cleared his throat. "Everyone in the lands cares entirely too much what that boy does with himself. As hunted as he is, you should consider that he may have some persuasions of his own, and he doesn't know how long he'll live."

She whirled on him. "You *let* him get away."

"I did. With you, he is a danger. Alone, he can serve you if he pleases or serve his own purposes. Choices are his own."

"You allowed this without my consent." Kierstaz frowned heavily, but he said nothing. "What if someone catches him and takes him to Otreya? What then?"

"He is man grown, Kierstaz. You cannot protect him forever."

"Did you send him off yourself? Threaten him?" If he had, she was quite certain forgiveness was not in her.

He drew back as if he could not fathom her logic. "No. I could not do so without your approval. He was desperate to prove himself the moment he arrived. You observed it as well only you didn't want to admit it."

Kierstaz trembled with frustration. "Well, you know everything, don't you, Sark?"

"Knowledge is important. But knowledge is not wisdom, nor is wisdom understanding. Pureblood Drei have a gift for healing, but more importantly, a gift for understanding." Sark flicked his hair over his shoulder as if her conversation embarrassed him. As if he shouldn't have to tell her this.

"Understanding?" Sark would probably never get over the presumption that her people were, by nature, weak, and she hated that. It reminded her of the superiority the Seren people had propagated under Altrun and all the ramifications since then. "Your thoughts are full of truth, yet you understand nothing."

Sark stepped in close. "I understand."

She almost smacked him, but he kissed her first—a smooth, gentle kiss on the mouth.

Her stomach settled, calmed, eased into a warm softness. "What was that for?"

"I understand."

Maybe he did. He didn't sleep the same hours at night as she did anymore; he spent it walking the rounds with one of the other generals or aides. He asked what she wanted, what she thought, what she needed, and usually did exactly as she asked, but he didn't kiss her. Like this. Ever. And now that he had, she didn't know what to think.

Kierstaz bit back hard on her tongue. "I'm glad."

Sark followed her across the camp, the reins of both horses dangling in his fingers. She didn't speak, and neither did he.

As soon as the tent flap fell behind her, she pulled off her Drei breastplate and tossed it to the ground. "Sark."

He opened the flap and slipped his slim head inside. "Queen."

"Do you think Malcom was right in what he did?"

He looked surprised. "The risk was foolish, but he was successful."

"I mean that he told them who I was. Do you think I should make my name known everywhere? Would it matter to Dreibourge?"

"It would matter, and it may outweigh the risk. I would not have foreseen it, but Malcom did." Sark furrowed his brow. "You should ask your other Generals."

"But even if they do think our position is advantageous enough..." Kierstaz ran a hand over her face. "Would anyone believe me? You didn't.

My scars..."

"The whole of Dreibourge will hear only your name and your banner. Besides, your face is covered in blood in battle." His voice softened. "I can take care of your scars, Kierstaz. Any pureblood could."

The light in the tent seemed suddenly brighter, better. "You...what?"

"I said, I can heal your scars if you truly want me to."

"Yes." She answered without hesitation. There was no reason to keep them now. "Please."

Sark bit both cheeks. "I will have to reopen the skin. It will take some time, and neither of us should be losing sleep. After we take Vienstrauss. Or after...when you're ready."

Kierstaz nodded. "Whatever you think is best."

"The process will tire you." He looked down and away again. "If there are no other urgent matters—"

"No," she said quietly.

{28}
Return

MALCOM MADE THE FOURTH CITY in two weeks.

He learned to avoid the roads at night and during midday as sentries were more suspicious at those times. The whole of eastern Dreibourge was fluttering with more military activity than the last time he was here. Was it because of Kierstaz? Or were there other reasons why the border was being treated like a Seren weakness of a sudden?

He did have one major disadvantage: his age. Boys that were near fifteen were mostly soldiers themselves. The only reason they could be exempt was if they had an injury, a disease, or a weakness of the mind. He was not good at feigning any of those things. His skin was robust, his face firm, and his eyes bright. He'd been healthy for months before the Drei released him from their fortress. That still irked him occasionally—the fact that they had been insistent on keeping him after he was well, had been suspicious of him because he was Otreya's blood and then had let him go as if there was nothing to be lost or gained by keeping him.

He almost thought it was because they feared him, but Drei did not fear anyone, did they?

Sark didn't fear him—at least, he didn't think so. Sark had been studying him. For what? To see if he was truly well? Somehow he thought not, but he couldn't put his finger on the motive.

None of that had anything to do with his decision to turn himself in to his mother. He had to—much as Kierstaz wanted him to stay away, much as she felt she owed him protection. Most of the bloodshed, most of the hunger, most of the hate was the fault of his family. He couldn't deny that or run from it anymore. He was old enough to know where he stood, and he stood with the Castle Guard. He blamed himself for getting sick on them and having to go back to the cliffs, but his mother was the one he was most angry at. What was she thinking, hauling Mikel off like grain for cattle? With how much she owed him?

The gates to the Fourth City were impossible to approach without first passing through a low wall that was heavily guarded. Malcom wasn't afraid of being stopped. He had a three-week beard, and his face had matured since four years ago. There would be no way for them to know what he looked like, would there? Still, bounty hunters had known his face when he and Mem had been hiding in the village of Klevt, when Hodran or Otreya hadn't seen him since he'd been a babe.

The thought of their names made him shudder. His father was dead, but he knew better than to trust his grandfather or his mother. They all wanted something from him—none of it noble or right, as far as he could tell.

The guard at the gate looked him over with an eyebrow raised. "You have no gate pennant? So you are a visitor."

Malcom nodded. "You could say that."

"Which part of the city are you visiting?"

"The Emperor, sir."

"And just what would the Emperor want with you?"

"I have information regarding a fugitive."

The eyebrow raised higher. "Hmm? And why can you not give this information to me or to my superiors? The Emperor is a busy man."

Malcom crossed his arms. "The information is sensitive."

"Yes, well, everyone's information is sensitive. You can enter the city with this pass." He handed him a small square of paper with a wax seal on it. "One day only, here on business to visit the political quarter, section twelve: information. The name of the inn you are allowed to patronize is at the bottom. If you are here longer than one night, you may be penalized. Don't be found in one of the other quarters or else you will be penalized for that as well. Carrying any goods for trade?"

"No."

"You are free to trade in the market outside the city, but you'll be stripped at the gate and will have your belongings chronicled to be certain that you do not leave with anything that is not yours. Law and order is important to the Emperor."

"I can see that," Malcom answered.

"Be sure to be back here before noon tomorrow so that I can remove you from the list of political visitors. Enjoy your day in the capital." With that, the guard turned away brusquely, repeating the question, "Which part of the city are you visiting?" to a woman with a cart full of hay.

The valley that he walked into was an endless maze of carts and booths set with grains, vegetables, soaps, and strangely enough, animals. Serens had never been skilled at raising or trading animals. They'd relied on Desert People to do that until the trade agreements had been severed. All of that had happened before Malcom was born, but what shocked him was the dark skin of the Desert People interspersed with the Drei and the lack of a Seren face anywhere. The gazes of the traders refused to meet his, even when he walked up to them.

The gates themselves were crowded and heavily guarded. He had to pass through a dark corridor in which his clothing was removed and searched. It was cold in the dark, the spring breeze far from soothing.

Then he was blinking in bright daylight and stumbling through streets that were far too clean for what he was accustomed to. The people who hurried to and fro were clean as well, clad in very little color and wearing no jewelry. For a boy who grew up in gypsy villages, it worried him a little.

And then he was approaching the gates to the political quarter. The guard sent him into an antechamber where he was met by the most beautiful half-Drei woman he had ever seen. She was his mem's age, and she had white-blonde hair that fell past her hips.

"I'm told you have information?"

"Regarding Malcom of Hodran."

Her eyes narrowed just slightly. "What about him? Do you know anything about where he might be?"

Malcom raised his head slowly, letting the light fall into his eyes. There wasn't a flicker of recognition. He took that to mean she had never met his mother or maybe that he did not resemble her. "I am Malcom."

The beautiful Drei nodded, still no surprise on her face. "Your grandfather will be pleased." She took out a tiny blade and nicked his skin, letting the blood she drew drop into a vial. It happened so quickly he barely felt the pain.

"What was that for?"

She shrugged. "The Emperor will want to make sure your blood matches your mother's. To be sure you're not an impostor, you understand. Many people claim they are Malcom. There is a great reward out."

"Oh. Yes. Of course."

The vial sat on the counter for a moment, and then she swept it into her hand and held it with the same bland expression on her face. "Welcome to our city. Your city."

A ripple of elation that shouldn't be there ran through him. "Is my mother here?"

The woman smiled at last. Her ruddy, freckled skin glittered slightly. "She is, but she's otherwise occupied right now."

"I haven't seen her in four years. I want to see her now."

The smile grew a little shallower. She held up the vial as if to make an excuse. "As you wish." The woman disappeared and was gone for nearly an hour. Malcom walked out into the hall, but there were purple-coated soldiers everywhere, so he slid back inside. There were straight, square pieces of furniture around the room, all of them with marble tops. It reminded him of the halls in the First City, when he'd met the Emperor. He'd been frightened out of his mind, but Otreya had been rather kind...until he'd cut open Malcom's hand and let the blood drip down onto a piece of parchment.

Malcom frowned at the recollection and closed his fist around the divot in his skin that the woman had just inflicted. The details were blurry, probably because he didn't want to remember the night, but Gernan had killed Emperor Kovim, grabbed Malcom, and taken him back to Mem. Afterward, Mikel had killed Hodran and nearly twenty of his men in an exchange, but surely he'd been defending himself then. Was that the crime he was incarcerated for now? Or had Mem known he was a prince all along? Even when he was a rugged cliffman with a beard and the title of Lord Marek?

When the Drei returned, she cupped her hand and said, "Come."

Malcom followed her, his steps starting to feel heavy and hollow. His resolve slipped from him, and all he was left with was a frank nervousness. They climbed stairs, entered other buildings, walked halls. Then, suddenly Mem was ahead of him. She stood stock-still, and he could swear she looked angry for a moment. Then she pulled him to her and whispered in his ear, "What are you doing here?"

Malcom pretended to laugh. "A fine question. I heard you were looking for me."

"Indeed, I was." She cupped the shadowy scruff on his face and tucked a clump of his hair behind his ear, but her eyes weren't sparkling. "But I wasn't worried."

The half-Drei woman walked up behind her. "His grandfather would like to see him."

Trzl looked startled, as if someone had snuck up and put a spider on her back. "Yes, well, surely he can bathe and rest up before we parade him before everyone? Spread the word, Idelviss, that he'll be at the weekly banquet. I'll take him to my rooms."

Idelviss' eyes were still glittery and distant as she moved off, and then Malcom got a slithering feeling down his back, as if that spider had actually been placed on *him*.

"Come, dear, I have refreshment in my rooms, and I can get you settled."

Malcom waited until they were walking through an empty hall before he mumbled under his breath, "Why is my grandfather so eager to see me?"

"Many reasons, not the least of which is that he has been searching for you for years. He's not keen on giving up a family line, as you may have guessed." There was a trifle of anger in her voice, and Malcom wanted to encourage it. She hadn't spoken of him much. Now that they were all here, under one roof, it would do him good to know the half of it.

"You never told me much about him."

"You never asked."

Yes, he had. Many times. "Who is Idelviss spreading the word to?"

Trzl glanced up at him quickly and then focused on her feet. "Everyone."

ɔƖ

MALCOM WAS HALFWAY THROUGH DINNER when the door to Mem's rooms swung open and Otreya came through.

"My grandson!"

Mem's face drew a mask over itself, and her eyes went dead. Malcom had never seen her look like that.

Otreya drew Malcom up and embraced him in spite of his mouth full of food. The old man smelled funny, like stale flowers. "How did you escape? How did you make it here? Look at you. You're practically man grown."

Malcom glanced at Mem over Otreya's shoulder, bewildered. She sniffed and looked away.

Otreya drew back and put his hands on Malcom's shoulders. "Can I bring you something? Anything? What would you like to do tomorrow? There's the city to see."

"I..."

"He can see the city later in the week, Grandfather. Tomorrow, he will need to rest and feed himself. Look at him. He's rail-thin."

Malcom pulled away and sat back down. He *was* hungry. There hadn't been much sustenance on the road.

Otreya sat down in the chair across from him. "You must tell us how you escaped."

"Later, Grandfather," Trzl said through her teeth.

"No, no. You were with savages, weren't you?" Otreya's eyes narrowed, as if he hoped Malcom would lie. No, as if he were seeing into his very thoughts. The space between them was heavy and dense. Time seemed to slow.

"Yes," Malcom answered. It was supposed to sound casual, but it came out entirely too cautious. There was something creepy about the old man and not only because he manipulated the rise and fall of kingdoms. There was something worse. Like he would commit murder without flinching. No wonder Mem didn't like him.

"And?" It was Mem who prodded him, her voice tense.

Malcom shifted a bite of dumpling around in his mouth and decided he didn't like the way the conversation was going. Too much like an interrogation. "For whatever reason, they thought they could bring me in for bounty when I was older and you would pay more. But then, cliffmen are very strange ruffians. As old a people as they seem to think themselves, they haven't much knowledge of how the world works."

Otreya looked rather blank. "And have you?"

Malcom snorted as airily as he could. "Have I? Of course. I have spent time in all the backwaters of this country. I know them well now. A half a year without Mem taught me even more."

Mem raised her eyebrows, but a faint smile played on her lips. A half a year. He'd picked the right number of months to fit her story. Excellent.

Mem waved a hand for a servant to take Malcom's empty dish. "We'll have more time to talk about this later."

"No, I'd love to hear more," Malcom said. "I've never met your grandfather, Mem, and I've years of Empire history to fill in. Not that I'm entirely ignorant, but hearing Mem's tales from the first few years of war was never enough."

Otreya's bearded face grew animated with delight. "You see? What an intelligent boy you have, Trzl. I never would have thought you and Hodran could do something so right together, but there he is."

Mem rolled her eyes. "Grandfather, you shoved us toward each other like dogs that must fight."

"And instead you made a child. Entirely not my fault."

"I raised him. If Hodran had, there would have been nothing right about him." The look on Mem's face was hard. She crossed her arms. "I am glad you rid yourself of that bastard."

"Oh, I didn't at all. He went after Malcom. Although, I daresay he had entirely more interest in killing the Castle Guard impostor than in finding his own son. But I knew Mikel's training, and I hoped they would both kill each other for your sake. Alas." Otreya sighed, his face still serenely pleasant.

"You're not killing Mikel yet."

"He is your prisoner, my dear. I am not killing him at all." His eyes wandered to Malcom in a way that was almost steely. "Do you know him, Malcom?"

A question he'd expected since he'd gotten here. It was almost a relief to hear it. "I met him in passing, but Mem wouldn't let me near him. I think he is nearly bewitched by her. Rather a desperate sort, though, to get involved in bounty hunter wars." There. That was easy.

Otreya clapped his hands together. "Bewitched. Why do you use such a word?"

Malcom looked at Mem, and her eyelashes moved, just slightly. It was a gesture he'd seen many times before, but it suddenly meant something else. "Well, she is bewitching."

"Do you think that *you* could be?"

What kind of question was that? Malcom frowned. "Depends. Bewitching to whom?"

{29}
Sedition

COLSTADT'S CELL WAS TIGHT, CRAMPED, and cold. The slats in the ceiling allowed light in but must have somehow been facing north because he never caught a ray of sunlight. The cold was fine with him. He was accustomed to the harshness of the Caps and months wherein the sky did nothing but snow. What he didn't like were the open bars on all four sides that left him without a scrap of privacy.

He had lived in alleys before, dodged in and out of gutters and sheds for corners to sleep in, but that had been different. He'd made his own rules, chosen his own squares of hay. Cages weren't something he took kindly to. Nor whips, and there'd been a lot of those here. Mostly for Pier since he was the one who'd been Mikel's lieutenant since he was blooded as Captain of the Guard. Probably also because Pier had been the one to personally torture Trzl when she'd been a guest in the Castle of Marek.

Old wrongs always did return the favor.

When Gernan became a power-hungry bastard, Colstadt had been the one who'd decided to mutiny, acquired his own ships, and took his own fortress in the north. Pier hadn't a care who he worked for—not since Mikel and Kiertstaz were gone. All he'd wanted was a permanent position as a lieutenant to someone he trusted so he could provide for his family of four children. They were stunning children, too. Half freckled, sharp-nosed Drei and half-almond-eyed, solid-boned cliff Seren. Their skin was neither olive nor tan nor creamy, but a brew of all three.

Strange what kinds of things a person missed in a jail cell, and the things one fixated on. For weeks now, every time Colstadt closed his eyes, he saw those children eating breakfast. And they weren't even his. Allel alone knew what Pier was feeling.

Pier didn't seem to feel much. The man was calloused—always had been—and in some recent cases, he was unbelievably cold. He reminded Colstadt slightly of his own father, with one vital difference: Pier put on a hard shell, but he actually loved someone. Five someones. Probably seven, actually.

Joining up with the Knights of Rilch had been the best thing Colstadt had ever done because he had gained an uninterrupted stream of purpose for ten years. Maybe some of that time had been ill-spent hankering after a broken, silent Kierstaz, but he didn't think so. She may never have admitted it, but a girl so forgotten needs at least one friend, even if he is a worshipful underling who knows his chances are nothing. She'd told him plainly enough once, and from then on, he'd been merely a shoulder.

Shoulders were good, though. She'd confided occasionally. At seventeen and eighteen, many a boy would have shrugged off the trust as an uninteresting history one learns from their tutor. For him, it had been insight into the soul of a girl he was quite certain no one could ever value enough, into ideals he'd wished he'd been taught as a child, into virtues he'd never dreamed could exist in such a pure form—loyalty and devotion, sometimes undeserved and unsought. That alone had been reason enough for him to stoke the fire late at night, wait for her pacing feet to give up on sleep and come out to the hall in search of a midnight laugh.

That was before he knew she was Kierstaz, before he knew she and Mikel were not merely knights, but the supposed last of the Orion family. None of that really mattered to him. He'd always been a drifter.

A voice interrupted his thoughts. "How can anything be funny right now?"

He jumped, startled. It was a young girl's voice. His mind must be playing with him. "Did I say something was funny?"

A little figure stepped up to the bars of his cell and stuck her nose through. "You giggled."

Colstadt raised an eyebrow. He was quite certain he hadn't giggled at anything in years. "No, you're right. Nothing is funny right now. My friend has been gone for two hours, and I wish they would bring him back and patch him up. How did you get here?"

"Through the vents." She pointed to the little slit on his roof, too high for him to reach. "This is the wing for Knight prisoners. It's been empty for a long time."

Colstadt frowned. "And you're here why?"

"I'm looking for my mem." She kicked at the floor. "Have you seen a woman here?"

There had been one, weeks ago. She'd acted suspicious of him and hadn't said much. "Tanya?"

"No. My mem is Riyev. They said...they were moving her."

"Who said?"

"The dark-haired lady."

"What makes you think they would bring her here?"

The girl shrugged. "They're keeping her with the politicals."

"I'm sorry. She hasn't been brought here."

She sank down against the bars. "I'll wait."

"I've been waiting for months. If you can go through these vents, best get back to some sun and some air."

"There's no sun in the prince's cell."

Colstadt jumped off his cot, suddenly alert. "You've seen Mikel?"

"His cell is next to mine."

"Did he send you down here?"

"No, I've come here before. Just not this close to you. I wasn't sure if you were dangerous or not. Lots of Drei are dangerous."

Colstadt winced, wished he could tell her the differences between Serens and Drei could never be that simple. But it might sound as if he was defending himself, and for true, a child could never be too careful in an underground prison.

"Are you...friends with him?"

Her face brightened. "He tried to get Trzl to let me go, which would have been nice, but my mem needs me to stay with her. I can get out whenever I like."

Good to know. Not that he'd trust a child who thought Drei were dangerous, but there might come a time when the last thing he could do for Mikel and Kierstaz was to send a message. A gutter rat who knew all the exits would be helpful in that. They'd talked about the possibilities— he and Pier and Mikel—in hushed tones in the hold of Gernan's warship. If they had abandoned all hope of absolution, they'd sell the gate sequences to the Desert People, let them destroy Otreya's stranglehold with blood and fire, leave a clean earth in their wake.

Let us pray it never comes to that.

Pier would do the deed in an instant if it were handed to him, but Colstadt wasn't sure he would have the strength to initiate slaughter in any way, even if Otreya was mad enough to destroy the world in his own form. He thought Mikel the only one able to make that judgment.

The door at the end of the wing clanged open, so loud it made Colstadt jump. The girl vanished into the shadows, maybe all the way to the vents. He couldn't see.

The contingent was more dense than usual. Colstadt slunk back against the edge of his cell. If they were here to torture him again, they'd have to drag him out.

A heavily accented cliff voice said, "Colstadt."

"Sunn?" He wanted to run to her, but she wasn't alone and she worked for Gernan now. They were enemies, for all intents and purposes.

She walked to the bars and held out a hand. "Come here, if you would."

The air in his lungs constricted so tightly he wasn't sure what to do next. A part of him *was* afraid, he realized—deathly afraid that yet another ally would prove herself to be open to intimidation and the shiny bribe of power.

Colstadt took a step toward her. Then another. He could see her face in the outline of a flickering torch one of the guards held. No, not guards—her men. Cliffmen. He met her at the bars. "What do you want?"

Her hand slipped through and held his, her voice so low he could barely hear it. Something iron was in her hand, clasped against his. A key…two keys. "I am concerned for your safety."

"I am fine," he answered evenly, though his heart was threatening to beat too fast. The iron felt heavy.

"Where is Pier?" The words were light, but her face let him know she was aware of exactly where he was.

"They take him out occasionally. Tell Gernan we are still very vital and angry as a hot bed of coals at his turncoat tail."

Her laugh sounded intentionally hollow, but her dark eyes crinkled at the corners. "Gernan will be happy to hear it. He hates you with a mighty fury." She formed words with her lips before she turned around. *Be careful.*

When they brought Pier back, her sudden appearance and warning held new meaning. His body was pulpy, and he could barely stand.

"They didn't ask me any questions this time, Col." His swollen eyelids dipped and closed. "I think they have whatever they wanted."

{30}
Вапчцет

THEY TOOK RIYEV OUT OF her cell and left it empty, but only for a day. When her body was tossed back in, she made a whimpering sound, dragged herself across the floor, and reached for the grate. "Can I have a candle?"

"Riyev, what have they done to you?"

The body rolled over in the dark. "What did you call me?"

He frowned. "Riyev."

"Are you alone in there?"

"Except for Natalya."

"Natalya." There was alarm in her voice. "Give me a candle. It's dark."

"I'm sorry." He lit one and passed it to her. Riyev had never asked for a candle before.

The image it revealed was unsettling. She was thinner, paler, and there was a bruise on her face. "I am Tanya. Who told you my name was Riyev?"

Her eyes. They were lighter, like the girl he thought he'd imagined. "Riyev was here only yesterday."

Tanya shuddered. "They have her here? Allel help us."

Mikel reached through the bars and caught her fingers. They were bony. "Someone hurt you?"

"Ack. No. Nothing I haven't felt before." Her forehead wrinkled. "Natalya? Why is Natalya...?"

He hadn't meant to, but he caressed her fingers and she didn't pull away. She *was* real. "Is Riyev your sister?"

Tanya nodded. "We are twins, but she is older." There was an empty moment in which she ran her fingers over his hand, around the inside of his palm and back. "Does Natalya know who you are? And Riyev?"

"Trzl told them." Mikel cleared his throat. "I am sorry. I am surely to blame for her involving your family in this."

"Ha." Tanya's voice became desperate, almost panicked. "You are sorry? If it's true, she hasn't been changing out the prisoners in this wing merely to vary who is in the cell next to you. You should be careful. This entire scheme is to get something out of your head or make you suffer for your past. And now that she's dragged Riyev into it and Natalya..."

Mikel squeezed her hand gently. "If it comes to it, I'll do whatever I must to be certain she does not hurt them." *Any more than she already has,* his mind added.

Tanya wiped away a tear with her other hand. "What does that mean? How can you promise anything? They don't even remove the chains from your hands and feet when they toss you in here, the Treachers."

Mikel laughed hollowly. "There are few ways left to make me pay, and she may have found one of them. But I know Trzl in ways that make her vulnerable."

Tanya grew quiet for a long moment. She finally dropped his hand, as if in afterthought. "May I speak to my niece?"

"I'm not sure if she's awake. She sleeps a lot, and she doesn't stay in her cell." He stood and walked to the other side, kneeling down next to the grate. "Natalya?" There was no answer. He went back to Tanya. "She only answers half the time."

She breathed out slowly. "Natalya is better at taking care of herself than either of us. She isn't as young as she looks, you know. She's thirteen. Born just a few months after Dreibourge fell."

"Her father was Castle Guard?"

She narrowed her eyes. "Yes."

"I thought they were all dead."

"He is dead now, too." Tanya cleared her throat and looked away as if to dismiss it. "The Castle Guard went down in their blaze of glory. The Border Guard? Well, we just fizzled into nothing. As you see us now." She ran a finger around the edge of the candle. "Someone wants desperately to be in your thoughts, Mikel Orion. And I don't think it is merely Trzl."

"You don't say?" Her tendency to be dramatic was already wearing on him. "No, just the whole Dermed council and half of the army."

"Mind your speech. There is a little one in the opposite cell."

"She's older than she looks," he snapped back.

"How many substances does he inject you with per day?"

"Who?"

"The physician."

Mikel frowned. "The Drei?"

"No, no. The old man."

"Otreya?"

"Whoever he is. He used to be a Chamberlain or something."

That was an understatement. "He injects me at random, but usually Trzl does it. I don't know what the effects are supposed to be, and I don't ask. Why?"

"Colstadt asked me to check."

Mikel lurched toward the bars and gripped them hard. "Colstadt?

What do you know about him? Is he alive?"

"He's missing some skin, but alive, yes."

"Tanya, if you are withholding anything from me—"

She grabbed the bars herself and slammed her face up close to them, close enough that her skin graced his knuckles. "I *am* withholding from you. I am withholding stories that would make your blood curdle. Do you want to know what happened at the border—what happened to my family—after you left? No, you don't. A person can only take so much guilt, Mikel, and you have more of it than I've ever seen in a person."

Mikel winced away from her, the tension in his body dissipating. "There was only so much I could do."

"There is only so much any one person can do. Those who blame you or hate you have small hearts."

"No." He rolled onto his back and stared up into the dark. "They are right."

Tanya reached for his hand again, but he flinched away. "I am married," she said suddenly, as if this were relevant.

Mikel couldn't help turning to her. "Well, that shouldn't surprise me, should it?"

"No, it shouldn't." She almost smiled. "I am married, and I have three children. My husband is a commander in the Seren army. I am asked often if I will join the Seren underground—those who hate the Empire. My answer is always the same: *I am watched too much, my father is a traitor already, let someone else do it.* And I am never sorry because I would rather create lives than destroy them. It is only now, when I am dragged in here for things I never did, that I feel a twinge of doubt, but if I die tomorrow, would I be happier if I had spent my days killing treacherous men? I think not."

"Your husband is a commander?"

"Yes."

"That makes him my enemy."

"I know. But he is a good man."

Mikel was silent for a long moment. "I'm glad you are happy," he said softly.

"I am happy also that there are souls such as you still living."

He let out a laugh that was more like the sound of the wind being knocked out of him. "And who am I?"

"The day I walked into my father's chamber with fresh linens and nearly stumbled over you—covered in blood and filth and smoke—is burned into my memory. I didn't know you as anyone but Lomius until she said something about you the day she dragged you in. It made sense, then."

"What did?"

"No one is afraid of you because of the battles you fought and won or who you are, Mikel. It's because you're stronger than them. Your heart is stronger." Tanya's fingers twisted in the bars. "They are afraid that a single breath from one of your kind could topple their entire empire. And maybe it can."

Mikel's brow wrinkled. "I'm only Castle Guard, Tanya."

"You are the Captain of the Guard, the voice of justice and truth. Without you, anyone can invent a lie and have it stand. Evidence of that is on every street corner. There are so many lies in this city, one doesn't know where to start."

"I'm not sure that signifies anything. You say one of my kind can topple an empire? Maybe all I do is destroy things. There's nothing honorable in that. What you do—live your life as peaceably as you can, be someone your children can admire—there is honor in that."

Her voice grew soft. "I am sure you would have done the same if you'd been afforded the luxury."

How insightful of her. "Yes. I would have."

🜋

THE WEEKLY BANQUET HAD SEVERAL courses, the first of which took place in a lounge-type room with few decorations and too many chairs. Malcom liked the dim lighting, but that was all he liked. Otreya was there—bright blue eyes twinkling as if they held secrets—as well as Idelviss, the Emperor, and of course, his mother. But when the door swung open and admitted a small horde with Gernan at their head, he stared blankly and hadn't a word to say. He'd known Mem was employing him now—that they were allies, after a fashion. Kierstaz had been angry enough to strangle him when last she'd spoken of him. But Malcom hadn't expected him to be *here* and so soon.

Gernan did not react at first. He said, "Malcom?" His eyes narrowed, and he tipped his head to one side as if ridiculously confused. "Ah, at last! Malcom has been found." He blinked rapidly, his shoulders shifting as if guilt were crawling on him. Well, it was. Malcom had trusted him, but then he'd turned the cliffs into a training ground for Empire soldiers at his first opportunity.

Gernan still looked unsettled as he turned toward the corner where Otreya sat calmly stroking his own beard.

Praying he doesn't put your face together with the night you killed Kovim and rescued me?

"Yes, Malcom is here," Otreya said grandly. "Certainly took him long enough to recognize his destiny. And with Trzl's spy still missing, who are we to thank?"

Gernan grinned instantly. "Thank my soldiers and me for flushing the ruffians out of those hills. I dare say the spy is frightened of us—all valley dwellers are. My cliffmen are worth their weight in fanged cats, and everybody knows it."

A young woman came from behind Gernan and wrapped her arms around his shoulders. Malcom recognized her. An image of her legs wrapped about Gernan's waist, her arms about his neck as he piloted her through a swamp, flashed in Malcom's memory before he remembered her name. Sunn. He had gone with Marek to rescue her from Swamp People. Best day of his life.

Sunn soothed the room like a tonic, made her leader's harsh mountain features and heavy catskin coat look gentle in the stark room. Kierstaz had used to talk about her—they'd been friends. Only after she'd planted a kiss on Gernan's cheek did she turn her open smile on Malcom.

Does Gernan threaten her to be his tame pet, or was that sincere? The feeling Malcom got in his stomach was oddly heavy.

Emperor Vekst said evenly, "Malcom should tell us himself."

The man had a kind face, but guarded eyes. Malcom wasn't sure whom he could trust—if anyone at all—but he was quite certain Vekst was not one of them. Vekst should feel threatened by Malcom's very presence. If he didn't, he was a fool.

Malcom took a tankard of something off of a platter and raised it to his lips. Wine. "I was taken prisoner by some washed-up knights. They didn't take kindly to my mother seducing their leader into a false alliance only to drag him to the Empire."

Mem leveled her eyes on Malcom, and he was aware that one wrong word could ruin them both. He sipped the wine a little to look mature, mindful of how quickly it could put him on his back.

Gernan had the gall to ask, "How did you escape their clutches?"

Malcom gestured with his tankard. "None of those knights are as good as they think they are. They have mead in the mountains too, you know." He wished he had some smoke to blow out to make his story seem more eloquent. The room was riveted by his words. He could feel it. "Sometimes I thought they were planning to exchange me for that prince, but as you can see..." He shrugged.

"And now they have nothing. Excellent." Otreya rubbed his fingertips together and raised his eyebrows at Malcom, as if he expected a comment.

"No need to worry about any of those renegades, my emperor." Gernan crossed his arms. "I thought you said he was being brought up?"

Mem's head jerked up, and her eyes narrowed. "Who? Orion?"

Otreya put a hand on her arm, and his eyes twinkled. "I thought it would be a fine time for him to see we have Malcom. He should be elated that there will be no more need of him here, should he not?"

"Certainly." Mem's face cleared. "I still have need of him, Grandfather, for other things."

Otreya looked most pleased. "Let us eat dinner first, shall we?"

Gernan's hand rested on the hilt of his sword. "I have business to attend to after dinner. If you'll let me see Orion—"

Mem shrugged. "And what do you need to know from him that cannot wait until after dinner?"

"Locations of—" Gernan hesitated.

"He hasn't exactly been cooperative, Gernan."

"Well, have either of the Drei been cooperative?"

"Less so."

Gernan quirked his mouth. "Then Orion has been cooperative."

Mem ground her teeth. "Yes. When you say it that way, I'm surprised I've kept them breathing this long. See to Colstadt and Pier's execution before you leave the city, won't you, Gernan?"

Malcom looked to Gernan with a hard glare. Gernan's eyes flickered slightly, but he ducked away.

Otreya sighed. "Please, please. Enough arrangements, Trzl. I give you a decision hall for that."

"Grandfather, Gernan has just arrived, I have much to confer with him about..."

"You may sit next to him at table."

Malcom had the sudden urge to slap the old man. Who did he think he was? Mem was saving Otreya's precious Empire from being chipped away at, and her relationship with Gernan was a part of that. She had as much right to order this unsavory banquet as Otreya did.

Maybe she wasn't only hiding me from Hodran. Maybe she was hiding me from her own grandfather.

Malcom met his Mem's gaze in sympathy, but her eyes were hard. Focused. He blinked, looked away. What had she just said? See to Colstadt and Pier's execution? Hadn't Colstadt nearly died for her once?

No, Malcom had no sympathy for her. He didn't even know her.

He let the rest of the evening pass without involving himself in much until Mikel was there—in chains, winded and pale—flanked by four guards. He didn't spare a glance for anyone in the room save Malcom. There was an infinite amount of pain in that glance, as if Malcom had personally stabbed him in the back. Well, he hadn't meant to, but he wasn't going to be the desperate, protected little child forever, succumbing to every poison his grandfather could conjure. He wasn't going to be the avenged; it was time the tasks shifted hands.

Malcom strode across the room and bowed in slight mockery. "To a valiant renegade, who guards his prisoners well. I hope they've been treating you with as much respect as you treated me."

Mikel bowed his own head just enough to acknowledge that he'd been spoken to. "Not as much, but one cannot have everything."

"Well, be seated won't you?"

Malcom could feel the occupants of the room staring at him in surprise. He pulled out the chair at the head of the table and motioned for Mikel to sit on his left side and Vekst at his right. He raised his glass before he was certain there was any liquor in it. "To our past leaders and to our future. May we always be as close as we are at this table tonight."

⁊ℓ

MIKEL STAYED OUT OF TROUBLE by drinking seven glasses of liquor and not saying a word. Gernan was nervous—the fingers on his right hand thrummed out a pattern on the table and his eyes stayed away from anyone but Sunn's. If he had a guilty conscience, good—but it didn't seem that way.

Trzl herself looked rather pale. Because of Malcom? Mikel didn't blame her.

There was a moment when everything stopped moving, and he looked into his drink and wondered what had been dropped into it this time. Then he glanced up at the table, and his eyes focused on Gernan.

Gernan's face had tightened, concentrated. Mikel had trained him from a boy—he knew that look. Gernan was about to raise a weapon.

There. A tiny dagger.

Every muscle in Mikel's body tensed, and he was ready to steal a sword, use his chains as a weapon, whatever was necessary.

Gernan did not raise it. He twisted it under his arm and drove it nonchalantly toward Otreya's heart with an arm flexed to its full power.

But Otreya stopped the dagger with his hand, eyes gone steely, his face smiling. He had raised his arm so fast he must have known it was coming. The blade went straight through the center of his palm, but he didn't look to be in any pain. He was hardly even bleeding.

He laughed. "Trzl, where do you find these savages?"

Gernan's hard black stare met Otreya's. "You are sitting too close to me." He pulled the knife out and stabbed it into his food, blood and all.

Otreya perused the table, a slight smile on his face. He met Mikel's gaze and raised an eyebrow as if to say, *You see?*

A ripple of ice ran down his spine. Mikel glanced at Malcom. Had he even noticed the exchange? Or was he under Otreya's spell now, too?

And the one question that wouldn't stop echoing in his head: *How the Derm did he get away from Kierstaz?*

Malcom was Trzl's son. He could be just like her—a player, a deceiver, a mess—but Mikel knew he wasn't. The boy wasn't made of that mettle. He had his own.

Malcom glanced up from cutting a piece of a beef, eyes no longer wide and clear. They were thinking, calculating. Damned if he wasn't here to rescue Mikel.

Mikel shook his head at him slightly. *Wrong move.*

Malcom furrowed his brow and raised an eyebrow. *I think not.*

Mikel ground his teeth. *Damn.*

{31}
Confrontation

MIKEL WAS SENT TO TRZL'S rooms after dinner instead of the rack, but tonight he wasn't sure which was worse. As soon as the door was latched behind him, Trzl reached for the chains about his wrists and unlocked them.

"Did they hurt you too much?" Her eyes were clear again, concerned. Her arm slid up to his shoulder.

Mikel stiffened but didn't pull away. Her fingertips felt too good. "No, I didn't feel a thing." He swallowed hard, his mind still in a heavy fog from the wine he'd consumed at dinner.

"I would have come to see you after the...but I am not that kind of counselor."

Mikel pretended to laugh. "Is that what you are now?"

She shrugged. "That is what Grandfather is, and I serve the same purpose. I keep threats away from the Emperor. I make alliances in his name. I do all things that may keep the Emperor happy."

"Did my turn at the rack made him happy?"

She shuddered. "Oh, sweetness. I didn't do it to impress him. I did it to strike fear in the rest of their hearts. None of them want to be my enemy now."

"I am sure that is quite valuable."

"It is. I'm going to need their loyalty."

"And Malcom's?"

Her face sobered. "I don't know about Malcom."

"That's why you're keeping me alive after I've served my purpose, isn't it? To ensure Malcom does as you wish." His throat tightened. "I'm yours to command." He didn't mean it. He felt as if he'd been forced to say it.

Trzl slid back onto her heels and reeled away from him. She walked to a corner of the room and poured herself a drink, then downed it in a gulp. "I'm keeping you alive, Mikel, because I would be quite alone without you. I may pretend otherwise, but it is true. Even Gernan failed me tonight. You saw. I don't know why Malcom came back, but I think it had something to do with you. He follows you now." She stared at him, but she wasn't looking at him. "I don't know much of anything anymore."

For the first time in ages, he truly believed she meant what she said. "That sounds very hopeful, Trzl. That sounds just fine."

She gulped down another drink. "Are you still sore from...?"

He shifted, not entirely certain he should tell her. "Why—more things to try on me? Do you want me still lucid?"

"Lie down." She clasped his hand and pulled him up to sit on a long, bench-like cushion that was piled with pillows. He didn't recognize the styling from any land or people. It was plain, like everything. She pushed him down and started to disassemble his shirt.

He stiffened and tried to sit up. "Trzl, don't—"

She shoved him back down. "Not to worry. There were no substances in your glass tonight."

He looked away to hide the redness climbing his cheeks. "Why don't you leave me be and go dote on your son?"

"Because Otreya wanted time with him." She swallowed hard. Her fingertips slid across his chest, touching the skin and wincing when he flinched. "Where is it not healed?"

Mikel shook his head. "I don't know. I just know it still hurts."

"Did the Drei that I sent to you not know his medicine?"

"He wasn't Pier." He was annoyed with her. Not angry, just terribly disenchanted. She may have tried to move against Otreya tonight, but she hadn't tired very hard. Whether he was going to pull away or let her push this as far as she wanted didn't even seem an option. He wanted to leave, and she kept him here. She would use anyone to get what she wanted, even compel, the same way Otreya did. Did it matter if she had ideals of freedom that drove her? Not if she was going to grind people into pulp beneath her heels.

She reached up under his shirt again, around his ribs, to trace the scars on his back. Aura used to do that. For a split second, Mikel closed his eyes and imagined it was her, and then he felt dirty and smacked her hands away.

Trzl drew back. "I'm sorry I had them hurt you." There were tears running down her cheeks. He could feel them against his face. "If I could fix all of this... But I will. I will. When I am empress—"

"I pray that you'll never be empress," he spewed out.

Her back went rigid. She pulled away from him, but she wasn't hurt or angry. Her eyes glazed over. "But I will be. Even Vekst will bow to me. He was once a tailor. He is not so proud a man that he will not swear allegiance to the right usurper."

Mikel stared at the floor. "Is that what I am? A proud man since I've always been a prince?"

She shrugged her shoulders and looked at him blankly, as if he should know without her saying.

"Yet I have always done what I could to help you when my conscience allowed."

Trzl climbed onto him and kissed his jaw. "Yes, you have. Forget I spoke of it." Her mouth trailed back to his ear, down to his collarbone, and her hands tiptoed to his sternum. She dug her fingernails into his skin with one hand and gently stroked his cheek with the other. "Forget everything I have said and done, Mikel, and be with me."

He tightened his hands on her waist, but he didn't say anything. His side hurt from the inside, oddly clenched and angry. He wanted to throw her off—against the wall, away from him—but half of him was afraid throwing her anywhere would be catastrophic. He lay there and waited for her to tire of touching him, but she didn't. Her tongue plunged into his mouth before he even knew what she was doing, and she was kissing him—hot, hungry, the way Trzl always kissed. He let her, and the throbbing ache in his side grew to a dull, heavy pain.

"Trzl, stop."

Her words came fast and desperate. "You're lonely, Mikel, I know you're lonely."

He gripped her arms. "You'll gain nothing." But even as he said it, he knew his own weakness for her. He knew he couldn't fight her all night.

She bit at his lips in an almost feral way, made a deep, heavy moan when he didn't return her fervor. "Mmm, but I already have."

His hands were sure to leave marks on her arms, yet he couldn't let go. "You're making a fool of yourself."

"You're the fool. You can't be alone forever."

Mikel gritted his teeth so hard he thought he'd break something. "I can try."

She drew back and smacked him. More like the Trzl he knew. The Trzl that made him want to kiss her.

He grabbed her hand. "Don't test me. Not like this."

"You owe me better." Her eyes were hysterical, entitlement and want mingling with a dead emptiness that would have made him shiver if he'd stopped to think about it.

"I owe you nothing. I've given you everything I have, Trzl, and still you want more. I tell you true, I have nothing left."

"You do. You pretend your heart is dead, but it is alive. I know you want to love me."

"If it is alive, it is not yours. I love you, Trzl, but mostly in the way one mourns a lost soul."

She hit him again, a flat palm against the chest. "Damn you, I'm not that Treacher anymore. You've been denying yourself. Every time you're near me, you can hardly keep from running your eyes over me and sometimes your hands. If I have to tie you down, I will."

Mikel let go of her. "I've often thought that you were coerced or seduced into half the things you did, but that isn't true, is it? You have always been yourself. And you're even more yourself now. The more you're around him, the more your true colors show."

Her eyes grew stormy. "Otreya is not—"

Mikel put a finger to her mouth to stop her protests. "You've become the monster of the revolution again in a few short months." Her skin shuddered beneath his fingertips, and he slid them slowly down up to her chin and cupped it. "I'll help you, as I've sworn, but I'm not going to spend my nights with you as long as I've a choice."

Trzl shook with rage. "Someday you will. Someday you'll be drunk or sick or something and you'll want me as you used to."

"Allel help me if I'm ever that rotten."

"You have to stay, Mikel. I need you."

He closed his eyes, fighting the urge to clamp a hand over her mouth. "Please don't take this any further."

"I need you to help me with Vekst and with Neroi full of Desert People and the Chamberlains splintering... There is no way I can do this without you."

"What?"

"I said you have to stay."

"No, after that. You said Neroi was full of Desert People."

She sat up, shrugged. "Didn't I tell you? Oh, I could have sworn. Weren't you afraid of that, years ago?"

"Afraid of…?"

"They've always been possible buyers for the gate sequences, haven't they? Well, they don't need it now." She laughed a little too loudly. "Serens are hungry enough that Vekst gave the Desert People the southeastern tip for pasture if they'd sell meat to the Four Cities. The Chamberlain of Neroi was furious and threatened to incite a rebellion against Vekst, but Otreya had him disappear and appointed a new chamberlain who knows how to handle the situation. The Four Cities were starving, Mikel."

Mikel pushed her body away and tried to stand. "Because you progressives are all fools."

Trzl shoved him back down. "Don't start with your superstition, Mikel. I know you think this is all because there is no Orion on the throne, but even your blood will not save us. I know better. I know your success at feeding this mob is due to your training. A shame all those books were burned, else I could be your equal and not need you at all."

"You burned the Books of the Lands right next to the Books of the Peoples and the Books of Derev and the Books of Elohai…no surprise you need the Aldadi to save you. They, at least, have some faith. Some strength."

Trzl laughed, devious again. "Oh, the Aldadi won't *save* us. They are integrating into our society quite smoothly, and once they've taught us all their tricks, we'll know how to duplicate it on a broader front. They can walk in straight lines and live in brick buildings the same as the rest of us, but like the Drei, they will only have certain privileges. Can't let them get out of hand."

Mikel's mouth went dry. He threw her to the floor so quickly that she landed on her back, no time to put her arms behind her. "You break the spirit of a single Aldadi, and I'll shred the skin off your bones."

She stood up, her hair tousled. "Oh, you're back to making threats, Lord Marek. Forgive me, I did not know you held the dark-skinned folk in high esteem. They've always been insolent jackasses. Most of the trouble with slave trade has been—"

"If you say another damned word—"

"You object to everything, Mikel. I daresay if you asked your father how to run an empire, his methods would be far more selfish than mine."

"You didn't know my father."

"Everyone knew him, and he was a vile man. We are in luck your sister died before she could become just like him."

"And what am I?"

"You're different, Mikel." She put a hand in his hair and twirled it. It was getting longer. He wished she would cut it.

"Put me back in my cell now, please."

"If you want to sleep there, you may, but from now on, you'll be assisting me daily. I don't want to hear any excuses."

Mikel's fists clenched tight, his knuckles white. "Just put me back."

৯৬

MIKEL LET OUT A STRANGLED yell when the cell door slammed behind him. Anger coursed through him like lightning, something he couldn't control nor banish. He slammed his shoulder into the wall, yelled at it, swore at it. Something in him had cracked, gaping open like a wound. He'd never wanted to hurt her so badly before—never wanted to be hurt *by* her so badly, to let her have her way if only so he could rest. He was sick of keeping his walls up, of fighting her and throwing her off of him.

One of the twins' voices broke through the fog of his mind, and he rejected it immediately. He pressed his palms above his head, against the corner wall. "Leave me be."

Her voice was soft, tentative. "Are you hurt?"

"No, damn you."

"What did she do?" Not Tanya this time. Riyev.

Mikel flexed his arms against the walls. "You don't want to talk to me right now."

"I do."

There was no way he was going near that grate. "I should spare Natalya's ears."

"Natalya is not here. She went to the streets tonight."

Good. "Did you ever hate someone enough you wanted to see them bleed? She likes to see me bleed, but I'd love to watch the terror on her face if I ever put her through the same paces."

Riyev was silent for a moment.

"What? Didn't think I had that in me? For true, I'm as savage as they say I am."

"You aren't what they say you are."

He wished to Allel he could have a smooth glass of arabica, calm this fury with a cup of morning. "Aren't I?"

"It's she who is poison for you."

He swallowed once. "I used to have a higher tolerance for it."

The heavy grate fell to the floor with a ringing clatter. Riyev came through the opening, legs first.

Mikel backed against the wall, fingers steepled over his head. "No. No. Back on your side."

She stood up and put her hands against his face.

He shoved her hard. "Get out."

Her forehead pressed against his lips in defiance of his words. "I won't."

A half-loud, half-whispered protest came from deep in his throat. "I don't need your comfort."

Her voice was low, but it didn't meet his in gravity. "Maybe I need yours."

Mikel hated that lightness of hers right now. Did she not sense his dark rage? How close he was to breaking? "Not mine. Do you know what I just did? Almost did?"

"No, what did you almost do?"

He shoved her body into the wall. The skin at her neck was soft and smooth. He held his face against it, his eyes closed, breathing. She didn't run. She didn't move. Nothing. He kissed her skin, as lightly as he could, but his body was pulsing with too much angst and instead he kissed her over a dozen times, damnably insistent. He wanted her, and he didn't even know her. He wanted freedom and forgetfulness for a moment.

Her hand slid up and caught his, fingers entwining with his white knuckles. "It's all right," she whispered.

No, it wasn't. He did not use people. Not this way. His voice was hoarse. "I told you not to come in here."

"And I don't care what you said. If you need me, I'm here."

He reached for the hair that fell in her face and leaned in, close to her ear. "You are not beholden to me. Not as your prince or as your father's friend or as... You're not."

"I don't want to be beholden. I want to give you something."

"I'm quite sure you shouldn't."

"And why not? The worst that comes of it is another child." She paused, and the air was dense, heavy. "I would not be sorry for that."

Mikel stepped away from her, but she followed, her dress rustling softly. "I've only ever loved one woman."

Riyev's face shot up as if she'd been startled. "What was her name?" She'd untied the laces at the front of her dress. He couldn't see them, but he hadn't missed the movement.

His head throbbed madly. *You're not going to do this.* "Aura."

He damned himself for telling her. Damned himself for pulling the dress roughly over her head, feeling her hips as he followed the fabric down. It had been too long. He hardly remembered what this felt like. In his mind, it was all one running image: *Aura Aura Aura Aura.*

And he *didn't* want to talk about her. He wanted to see her. Feel her. Hear her. Find her in his dreams again.

He fell backward, onto the bench, and Riyev followed. His hands slid up her waist and dug into her shoulders, coaxing her mouth down to meet his in a tangle of soft lips and hard foreheads. She climbed onto him, wrapped her legs around him, and leaned down to kiss him—to tug on his lips and dip back down for another.

As Trzl would have. Gladly.

"I can't do this," he mumbled roughly.

"You can," she whispered back.

He pinned her flat on her back on the slim bench. Riyev caught a handful of his shirt in each fist and yanked his chest down onto her. It felt like she'd torn something inside of him, ripped it out harshly and brutally.

She slid a hand up his cheekbone, then drew back when his hot tears soaked her fingertips. "What is it?"

He turned his face away, slid slowly off of her, and hit the floor on his knees. His reply was a broken mumble. "I miss her."

{32}
Blind

"I THINK THEY MIGHT KILL her."

Colstadt woke up and gripped one of the bars, then nearly jumped. Natalya was standing right in front of him. "Who?"

She motioned to the next cell. "My mem. I heard them say they were going to bring her down here." She wasn't crying, but her lip trembled. "The dark woman said, '*Think she might say something to the Drei?* That means they are bringing her here. If they don't kill her first, they're planning to kill her soon."

Colstadt pulled her into his arms. "Shh. That's the most foolish thing I've ever heard."

She curled up against his chest and the tears came, but she didn't whine or ask for sympathy.

Colstadt fingered the keys in his hands. "If you need me to...I can look for her."

Pier pulled himself up to the edge of his own cage. "Don't sell an arm and a leg when you're already a carcass, Colstadt."

The door to the wing clanged open, and Trzl came through, shoving a woman by the shoulder. She looked perfectly fine, except for a limp. Colstadt pulled Natalya back into the shadows as the torches came closer.

"Colstadt." Trzl always cooed his name. It made him shiver, but today it made him rigid and alert as well. "Come here."

He tucked Natalya down against his bed and prayed the shadows kept her concealed for a moment longer. "Yes, Chamberlain?"

Trzl waved a hand at his formality. "I'm giving you a companion. Her tongue is loose enough, but before I decide if I'm done with her, I thought I'd see if you could use her for your own ends. You and Pier, as I know, have your own little dreams of glory. Perhaps she has some information for you." She unlocked his cell, tossed the woman in and relocked it. "Well, enjoy the night." She turned on her heel.

That made about as much sense as Trzl ever made.

Natalya let out a muffled sound and ran to her mother. Way too soon.

Trzl turned around. Her footsteps sprinted back to him. "What did I hear from you, Colstadt?"

Colstadt shifted. "The massive rats that live in here, no doubt."

Her voice was icy. "I doubt that." She stormed off again.

The woman looked up from stroking Natalya's head and said in a voice strangely pleasant and singsong, "I am Riyev. I apologize for the horrible introduction." There was a slight tremor there, though. She, too, was afraid of Drei.

Colstadt raised an eyebrow, but he was rather speechless.

Riyev stood up and turned around as if assessing the place, although it must have been impossible to see clearly in the aftermath of the bright torches. "I've been here before. The Knights wing?"

Colstadt frowned. "There is such a thing?"

"Of course." She ran her hand along the bars. "It's the hardest to break out of."

"Well, that's reassuring," Pier drawled sarcastically.

Riyev peered over at him. "Oh, right. You're here. The one she especially hates. Well, I'm dying tomorrow if I don't break out, and I'm going to push on every wall of this place until I do."

Colstadt slid the keys inside his shirt and bit back his own retort. "And why are you here the night before you die? Forgive me for my distrust, but I don't understand."

Riyev rolled her head. "She's angry. There are rumors of a Kierstaz Orion trying to claim the throne in Dreibourge, yet Trzl cannot get Mikel Orion to join with her so that she can make an opposing claim. At least, I think that's what she's trying to get him to do. I wouldn't know. He didn't tell me."

Kierstaz trying to claim the throne? Colstadt's heart beat a little faster in spite of himself. "Trzl let you see Mikel?"

Riyev shrugged. "She tortured us together. I am Romianz's daughter. It served her purpose."

A snakelike feeling crept down Colstadt's spine. Romianz. The man had been a traitor to his own Guard. It didn't speak well for his daughter.

"Join with her?" Pier let out a cackling laugh. "He wouldn't even take her willing body as collateral when he had her in his very own dungeon. She must truly be mad if she thinks he will ally with her now because she smacks him around with a chain."

Riyev gulped so loudly Colstadt could hear it. "I don't... What do you mean by that?" She sounded timid.

Even in the dark, Pier's stone blue eyes were glinting. "Mikel and Trzl have a sordid history together."

"I know *that*. I... What you said about dungeons."

"Frightened of him, are you?" Pier had every right to be surly with how much physical pain he was in, but Colstadt was truly about to yell at him to shut it.

"No." Riyev raised her chin. "No, I'm mortified at myself."

Pier outright laughed. "For true? Do tell us more. We lonely souls have nothing to entertain us."

She shook her head emphatically.

"Shut it, Pier," Colstadt snapped.

"Oh, look who's sensitive. Haven't been down here long enough to lose your manners, Colstadt? I'm impressed, and I thought I knew you as well as I know my own son."

That jarred Colstadt for a moment. *For true?*

"I can get out of here," Natalya broke in. Her foot tapped the floor in a slow, impatient rhythm. "But I'm not leaving until you get my mem out."

Something still wasn't right. Colstadt ground his teeth. "Who said we were dying tomorrow?"

Riyev stared at him for a moment. "Trzl did. She told Lord Marek to kill all of us before he left, and he leaves tomorrow."

Lord Marek...Gernan. That would coincide with Sunn's warning. "Lord Marek won't kill us."

Riyev clicked her tongue. "Oh? In case you hadn't noticed, no one holds life very dear in this city."

"No, I hadn't noticed. We've been kept needlessly alive for months."

"Uh-huh." The little square of light from above was enough that he could see Riyev was a few years older than him, but light could play all kinds of trickery and he wasn't certain her features were anything like those of Tofer or Zven. She looked like...Tanya, who had been here days ago and had not shared nearly so much about herself. "Have it your way," she said. "Natalya, have you a way out of here yet?"

The door to the wing unlocked yet again.

Colstadt shoved Riyev farther back into the cell. He heard a soft whooshing sound and knew Natalya had already secreted herself in the ventilation tunnel, but Riyev wouldn't fit. Colstadt had tried, and he was far skinnier than her.

A force of cliffmen entered with torches, armed with their traditional curved blades and jagged knives, but they wore new uniforms of soft leather that looked green in this light.

Damn. They worked for the emperor now.

The keys turned in each lock. Pier was dragged out first, then Colstadt.

"There's supposed to be a woman here as well," a voice called. "Find her."

And Riyev.

Colstadt breathed a momentary prayer for Natalya, that she'd stay the Dermed away from them.

They were pushed along the corridor, through tunnels that led to staircases, down into the lower levels. Then they were in a stable. The cliffmen tightened woven sacks over their heads and tossed them onto horses. They rode through streets cobbled with new stone, the sounds made by the horses' hooves fresh and sharp, not dulled by hundreds of years of wear.

They entered another building—this one with a dirt floor—and the sounds became muted again. When the sacks were removed, he blinked in the dim light for a few moments. The faces in the room were passive and unfamiliar.

Until Sunn stepped out and gave a curt nod to the men standing closest to him. "Unhorse them."

One of the cliffmen grasped Riyev's arms and jerked her off of her horse, causing her to yelp. Colstadt slid down without assistance. He glanced at Pier, but the man was doubled over on his horse, eyes shut. Had he fainted?

Sunn tipped her head. "Sorry about the rough ride. This way."

Someone carried Pier up the flight of stairs and into a large, central room that had no windows. He wasn't conscious. Colstadt went straight to him as soon as the cliffman set him down on a bed. Riyev looked at Colstadt with wide eyes, but at least she didn't ask any questions. Pier was torn up pretty bad—Colstadt hadn't been able to see well in the cell.

The woman on the bed next to him sat up and whispered, "Hello, Colstadt."

He jumped, spun around. His chest tightened when he saw her. "Idelviss."

She raised her eyebrows. "Thought you'd be happy to see another Drei here."

Colstadt looked to Sunn. "Why is she here?" A harmless enough question, but one that came with a world of weight, considering they'd shared a ship's hold with the woman.

Sunn stuck her chin in the air. "An ally I don't approve of, but she's here nonetheless."

Ally. He doubted that. *Pier, hurry up and mend.*

"You'll have to stay here and not set a foot outside," Sunn continued. "Stay away from the rooms with windows. You're supposed to be dead. These are my quarters and those of my soldiers, but Gernan will come here occasionally. If he does, you're on your own. I work for him now." Sunn didn't stay to catch Colstadt's gaze.

He caught at her arm, his voice low. "May I send a personal letter?"

She stared at him as if he'd asked her to provide him an army. "Do I want to know to whom?"

"No."

Her brow furrowed. "Do not involve yourself any further in this, Colstadt. It would be foolish."

He lied. "No, nothing of the sort."

Sunn raised a hand to a young cliffman with hair as long as hers. "Talla will take it. I never heard anything of it." She swung back around and sprinted to the stairs as if he were a plague to flee.

Colstadt raised his voice to her as she left. "Sunn?"

"Hmm?"

"Thank you."

"Don't thank me. The city is shut up like a tomb since the news of

Kierstaz came in." She smiled slightly. "I just thought you might like to see the sky before you die."

ꙮ

VIENSTRAUSS SENT A RUNNER: SURRENDER of the entire city if Kierstaz entered in peace.

Sark shifted as soon as he read the communique. Kierstaz could tell he had misgivings, but he said nothing at first. "Do you think this is Malcom's doing? Is he alone in there?"

Sark checked the clasps on his gloves, even though he'd already done so a few moments ago. "No, I think this is Zurik's doing."

She blinked and looked away. "I don't like that they claim a victory is mine when only half of it was."

He shrugged. "You should take what you can."

"Damn, Sark, I am asking your advice."

His forehead wrinkled, and he squared his shoulders. "I don't like it. Means you will have to take several thousand prisoners, and we've nowhere to keep them. I've never liked the idea of prisoners."

"What did you do with them?"

"Our warfare is simple. If they stay inside our borders, they die. If they retreat, they live."

"You are not being helpful."

A sigh slipped through his teeth. "You want to send them back?"

"It is the only way."

"Your judgment to make, my queen."

Kierstaz tilted her neck, her back sore from so much time in the saddle. "If birds have flown at all, the Four Cities have heard of me by now."

Sark nodded. "We disarm them, keep the leaders in whatever prisons they have here, send back the foot soldiers. It has risks involved, some that I don't appreciate in the slightest. These soldiers won't be going home. They'll be re-stationed at the border, which means you'll have to fight them eventually. I'd rather you pack them on Elloyan ships bound for Allel-knows-where."

Kierstaz flinched, but she felt strangely calm and detached. "Make the arrangements. Sell as many as you can to the Elloyans and lock up the rest in the city. I don't want to spare the men to guard them, but there's no help for it."

Sark's eyes sparkled slightly. He was pleased, was he? "I'll speak to Otto about it. We'll need a sufficient force to escort them to a port, but it shouldn't take more than a week."

Kierstaz nodded. "I'll accept the surrender." She rolled up the parchment and put it in the crux of her arm before she spurred her horse and rode to meet the city guardian. She half-expected Malcom to be on the leader's coattails, and when he wasn't, a stirring uneasiness claimed her. Sark's words about his blood haunted her. Malcom had never been hers, but he was more hers than anyone else's. *Where are you, Mal?*

When the gates opened, she marched her horsemen through first, then her foot soldiers, and lastly the few hundred who had joined them at Zurik. Drei armies traveled light. They had no physicians because all were trained in medicine, no women and children because all were warriors, and no trebuchets or machines because speed was their greatest weapon. Every warrior had a horse; the only difference was that some rode them in battle and some did not. No food besides a saddlebag per person was necessary because they knew how to glean from the land. Although, Kierstaz had to admit, the land was quite lean now. She didn't know where they were getting their food, but no one had complained.

After they took the battlements and her soldiers were spread out along the walls, she started to breathe again. The city was not hard-won. Lindt or Dorscht would likely make up for that, but Vienstrauss was the westernmost hub and that made it an unparalleled key piece. With

Vienstrauss in the west and Zurik in the north, she held a third of Dreibourge—probably a third of the population, as well. If she marched on Dorscht now, they would likely meet with a prepared force. But march they would. Dreibourge would be hers.

Would be Sark's, she reminded herself. She had promised him power over her military for an eternity, anything he wished that was hers, and then admitted to him that she was not seeking to reclaim Serengard. She would be queen of Dreibourge, but it would belong to him. Surely restoring the rule of the Eight Generals would be the first wish he would name, and she would grant it. Then...maybe then she would have the kind of leverage that would make Trzl fear her. Enough to make her surrender Mikel.

The armory and its surrounding buildings appeared to have been the headquarters of the Seren military here. They hadn't bothered to replace Drei buildings with their own, and so they held a quaint bit of personality. Kierstaz stabled her horse and then walked in the massive front doors, her lieutenants and generals on her heels. Her soldiers had been efficient—there wasn't a Seren in sight.

She turned to Gret. "Bring me Sark and Theo and Crista as soon as they report here and keep me apprised of the city. If we run into any resistance..." She did not finish.

"Of course, my queen."

"Has Malcom been seen?"

Gret looked startled. "No. Was he not with us?"

Kierstaz bit her lip. "No." She went up to the roof immediately and surveyed the city. Eight towers, a hundred or so staircases leading to twisting, narrow battlements that dead-ended at strange places and started again a few feet later. A slow smile of wonder claimed her face. Every city and fortress had its own layout, its own secrets and quirks. This one was already screaming uniqueness. Too bad she could not stay and discover its secrets.

When she came back down to the meeting room, Sark had his feet up on the long table and a tumbler of clear liquid in his hand. It made Kierstaz start. She'd never seen him that relaxed.

"Are you celebrating?" she asked dryly.

He didn't blink. "I don't celebrate."

"That's what I thought."

"Where is Malcom?" He took a sip, not breaking from her gaze.

"I don't know. I thought he would be here. I thought he was the reason they surrendered the city."

"You know where he's gone."

Kierstaz swallowed. "I pray that he hasn't."

His blue eyes narrowed intensely. "Do you truly believe his own mother would hurt him?"

"I don't believe she would *want* him hurt, no."

"And I would never want you to break a promise."

Had he just meant more in a sentence than his words conveyed? She was proud of him. "Are you afraid I am vulnerable where he is concerned? Malcom has never tried to manipulate me. Not once."

He shook his head. "That is not what I fear. If he succeeds in his wish, you may find yourself prematurely in Serengard, attempting to salvage his intended rescue of your brother."

The silence that settled over them both made her want to throw something.

"Are you afraid I will abandon Dreibourge? Truly, Sark? I believed you had more faith in me than..." She couldn't even finish the words.

"I know how much you love your brother."

Kierstaz drew a dagger from her waistband and stabbed it into the map table to keep herself from flinging it against the marble wall. "I love him, yes. I love Malcom, too. But I swore myself to Dreibourge. I don't swear anything I cannot uphold."

He smiled faintly. "We all do, oh Castle Guard descendant with the name of a queen."

She looked at him as coldly as she could, trying to be impassive, dry, logical. It was hard to do when he was so damn sweaty and quite possibly right. "That lie was not my choice."

"I mention it only so that you will remember that there is nothing to be gained by charging into Serengard before your stage has been set."

"I don't plan to take Serengard at all. You know that."

He picked up her dagger from the table and handed it back to her. "Don't fool yourself, my love." His gaze grew heavy and sober. Not a muscle in his body twitched, but he stared at her with something that was dark enough to tug on her.

"What did you just call me?"

He didn't answer, and his eyes didn't waver. He stood up, slid his chair in, and walked to her.

"What?" she said again.

He walked past her, stopped, and caught her hand. "You heard my words," he said, his voice husky.

She kissed him, reaching up behind his head and pulled him down to her. His shoulders relaxed slightly, his eyes closed. Time stopped and silence stole the moment, freezing their hands in place and their lips against one another's. Their breath was calm, silent.

Then his fingers tangled in her hair. He tugged her toward him and nudged open her lips, wider and deeper. They pushed and pulled each other halfway to the floor, bent and curled their bodies, him following her until her back was arched, shoulders drawn in. An invitation.

He reached for her neck with his hands instead of his mouth, sliding them down and unclasping her armor, slipping it from her body and then doing the same at her hips.

"We are at war," Sark mumbled. He kissed her cheekbones, her throat, her eyebrows.

"Not today."

{33}
Inheritance

MALCOM TRIED NOT TO STARE at the perfection of the Fourth City as Otreya showed him the streets. Knowing that his mother helped design this…this…gigantic clock, where everything that moved had a purpose and always in perfect time… It was surreal. It wasn't what he'd expected, given Mem's stories. When she'd said there were workhouses and tenement houses packed to the gills, he'd thought for sure there would be dirt and mud and grime. But there wasn't. It looked like it was swept by hand every day.

Of course, there weren't many horses, either. Otreya said there were plenty of stables in the countryside when one needed to rent a horse. That would cut down on the grime, wouldn't it?

"All of the streets have marble edging," Otreya told him proudly. "The marketplaces were built at the same time as the city, so there is nothing that must be rearranged daily."

Malcom frowned. "What about the market stalls outside the gate? Aren't they part of the market?"

"Ah, no. That is where the importers bargain with sellers inside the city. You must have a permit to sell in the city."

"But I thought the importers outside needed permission to be there as well?"

"They do. It is all very complex but necessary to keep not only the city, but the entire Empire from having troubles with commodities."

Malcom thought that sounded arrogant, but he didn't want to pretend to know more about it than Otreya. "I am sure."

Otreya's eyelids flickered, and his gaze bored into Malcom's, causing him to want to look away. "It is much less complicated than the Orion method of keeping order. They believed trade agreements were enough to hold things together, that personal honor on the part of the farmers and the tradesmen would solve all other disputes. It made for a tangle of ugly disagreements that could never be resolved."

"You avoid much of that with this system?"

Otreya shrugged. "Never had one complaint. Serens appreciate order, they appreciate cleanliness, but they also appreciate not having to wonder where their next meal will come from. We are enough of a power that the Drei and Aldadi now wish they could be us, and that puts us in the position to profit the most from their attempts."

Malcom didn't know much about the Aldadi, but he had lived in Dreibourge long enough. "I don't think the Drei wish to be Seren."

Otreya quirked an eyebrow. "No?"

Maybe he shouldn't have said that. "No. Something in their...attitude."

"Ah." The old man was silent for a moment, long enough that Malcom could feel the waves of questioning between them. "Well, it is excellent that you seek to understand them. You will make a fine official someday."

"Official?" Not that it surprised him, but he was tired of the silence.

Otreya waved an arm. "You are the son of two of the first Chamberlains. You did not think you would get away with the role of celebrated child, did you? I am old and tired, and you and your mem will wish to do things." His head bobbed up and down excitedly.

"For true, I'm not sure what I would be capable of doing."

Otreya's gaze grew distant again, and Malcom had the distinct feeling he was being examined whole as a physician would do. "You? Capable? Ah, but Malcom, you are capable of so much. Even you do not yet know the extent of your power."

"But what kind of power could I wield? You use words such as this all the time, and it confuses me. What can you call power?"

"Power." Otreya stopped walking. He stood in the middle of the road with people passing, his white hair fanning out behind him and making the sunken hollows in his cheeks dark with color.

Malcom faced his grandfather squarely, but he was watching the expressions in the faces around him: alarm, admiration, fear...but mostly a dull blankness, as if Otreya were a commonplace piece of furniture. Yet there was nothing common about the man, from the long white beard to the intimidating midnight blue robe he insisted on wearing in every room and in all company.

And then there was one glance from a little boy with blond hair that was pure hatred. Malcom's eyes followed him, wondering what would make a child hate Otreya. He knew what made his mother hate him, but a youngling?

"Malcom, have you been listening to me?" Otreya sounded stern.

"Yes." Malcom closed his eyes for a second and recounted the senseless drivel. "Your power is in your knowledge, and your knowledge is something you pass down to your descendants, and I will inherit even more than you did. Something the ruling Orions never had...something about a woman named Izannah?" He could sort through things in his mind with ridiculous ease, as if he were waking up without a headache for the first time after having been ill for weeks. It made him wonder if he'd been sick for his entire life or if the pureblood Drei had given him faerie potions.

Otreya started walking again. "Yes, Izannah. You see, the king before Izannah, Altrun, was willing to admit that the knowledge in our family had value, but he thirsted after absolute sovereignty and it ruined him." He turned to his right, and there was a statue there—a Seren king with his head in his hands and a crown at his feet. Malcom didn't recognize the features, but the face tugged at him as if he should know it.

Otreya faced the statue and continued. "But Izannah undid every good he had done and even sought to hunt down those that supported him and purge them. The Orions were as savage and self-centered as any cliff lord or Desert multan, and their pride was their ruin."

You know nothing of cliff lords, grandfather. Malcom tried not to be distracted by the story and focused on the words that had alarmed him. "You said there was knowledge in our family that had value. What knowledge?"

"Your mother hasn't taught you?" Otreya took Malcom's arm and walked hurriedly, his voice growing excited. "Ah, I suppose she was quite torn about it, and who can blame her? Hodran was so very hard on her. The man was a dullard. And now to be so unhealthily tied to a son of the Castle Guard... Well, she is longsuffering."

"To...whom?"

"Mikel Orion."

Malcom was thoroughly bewildered. "How is she tied to him? And what would she teach me?"

"The Castle Guard has always passed judgment on the Seren people. It is their function. They are bred for it. Ever since the first Derev chose the families that would be the Guard, they have been a plague nearly as strong as the blood of Orion. Derev Orion was not a fighter, and neither were any of his offspring. That is why he chose families that were strong in warrior traits. They fight tenaciously, and they influence where they have no right to. Mikel—Lomius, Marek, whatever you call him—is a weight on Trzl. I wanted to prevent her from meeting any of the Guard. I even kept her away from Ashlin, the city where they were stationed, but it happened beneath my nose. Once a connection has been made, it is hard even for *me* to sever it. Some small part of her nature wants to please him, as so many common folk before her. I wish I could have bred her from pure blood, but even a wizard must mate with someone.

"But all of that will work itself into nothing. When she is ready, we will pull her away from her plaything and finally eliminate their kind from influence. Then there will be nothing to chain either of you. We will be free again. I will have fixed *everything.*"

Nothing to chain either of you. Malcom shuddered. *Allel, don't let him know about Kierstaz. Please don't let him know.*

Otreya cleared his throat. "You do understand that if you speak of this to anyone, they will think you are talking gibberish. I have no reason to hide or pretend anything with you, my grandson, but your friends may not be as wise as you."

Malcom smiled to reassure him. "I haven't any friends, remember?"

They took a wide set of steps into a lower level of the city. The crowds grew thinner and the sunlight a little dimmer.

"*Are* you a...a wizard?" Malcom asked it under his breath, a little shakily. As soon as he'd learned his parentage, there had always been theories—none of them pleasant.

"Ha! No. A wizard conjures things. I am no conjurer."

He seemed content to leave it at that, but Malcom was not. "*What* are we then? I have nightmares with things in them I shouldn't know. People do as I ask—even if I don't ask, they do as I *will*—and there is nothing to explain it."

"You see why your mother tries to invent a lord to hold her in check? She and I can manipulate spiritual power. We can take thought and feeling and transform it into our own thought and feeling and return it to its keeper. So can you. But you are a different specimen altogether,

Malcom. You can do all of those things...but you have the charm to influence more than one mere mortal at a time. You can influence multitudes without even trying." His voice grew low, and he glanced furtively around him. "Never before has there been a person with your abilities combined."

"You searched for me for all those years, put a bounty on my head...because I was special?"

Otreya's beard bobbed as he nodded. "Yes, yes. And because I missed Trzl, of course."

"Ah." Malcom did not even ask from whom he'd acquired his charm because he knew the answer. He knew because it was the reason Kierstaz's eyes had flickered in pain when he'd flirted with a girl, told a crass joke, grinned for no reason.

He would ask her, "*What did I do?*"

"*Nothing. Nothing.*" She would shake her head and smile, but it was always a sad one. "*You just... You look like your father.*"

What he didn't know—and what Otreya seemed to dodge around no matter how many times he asked it—was how these powers had anything to do with the right to be lords of the world, to grind other nations under their thumb because it suited them. Why use such power and influence? If, as he said, King Altrun was ruined by a thirst for absolute sovereignty, how was Otreya's cause any better? Did he not seek the same control?

Malcom felt suddenly released from a duty, as if he owed the world nothing now. He smiled evenly and lied outright. "Well, I am glad you missed her, and I am glad you found me."

{34}
Heal

THEY'D TAKEN FEW CASUALTIES AT Dorscht. Under two hundred. Kierstaz would say Allel loved her, but instead she was still angry over the fact that one of the dead had been a boy younger than Malcom. The Seren force inside the walls of Dorscht hadn't been amenable to their terms, not quick to surrender even after they'd lost half their force to a swift flanking maneuver. Her Drei had taken them down most thoroughly. Their entire wall force was dead to a man.

As soon as the surrender was made, she rode back out to camp, restless. Something didn't feel right about the victory. It came at too small a cost. Dreibourge had fallen body by body to the Serens; now, even when they resisted, it fell city by city to her. *My dead body must be worth a half a kingdom to Otreya by now.* The thought twisted in her belly as Theo charged toward her.

"I want anyone under fifteen out of my army," she told him. "Dreibourge cannot spare their young."

He kept his face passive as he bent his head toward her and

whispered, "But they want to fight, my queen."

"Doesn't matter. I want them out."

"Their strength is as much as a grown man's. Our people are not like yours."

"So Sark tells me daily." Kierstaz had to step around a woman with a severed arm. A glance into her eyes told her that the woman was handling this war better than she was.

"At least discuss it with your lieutenants, my queen."

"You are my lieutenant." Kierstaz whirled on him. "I am an excellent fighter, Theo, but do I look like a general to you?"

He quirked an eyebrow. "Do you want me to answer that honestly?"

"You look as much a general as anyone else," Sark interrupted.

Kierstaz could have laughed, but she looked back at the gates instead. Gates they had just decimated with war. "I leave the tactical decisions to you and yours for a reason, my king."

Theo rolled his eyes. "And by that, I take it you wish me to inform the rest of your decision?"

She missed Mikel. If Mikel were here, he could read her gestures and turn it into a new battle plan, one that satisfied both of them. "I do."

Theo saluted quickly and left.

Sark cleared his throat. "You are tense. Would you care to have bathing water heated?"

"I don't want a bath. I want my face cut open."

He stepped up beside her and walked backward so he could see her eyes. "Now?"

"Now."

He smiled, just slightly, but he looked nervous. "As you command, my queen."

Kierstaz stepped inside her tent and stood still for a moment. No matter how warm the bricks around the fire pit were, she still felt a chill here. It was too cold for her Ashlin breeding. Slowly, she removed her bloody armor and wiped her sword several times on a wet strip of velvet. Everything in her tent was of the highest quality, outfitted for an Orion with rights to the throne right down to the calfskin beneath her feet, yet it did not feel decorated or indulgent. The contents were practical, imperial.

The tight leggings beneath her greaves were wet from the snow she'd trudged through, but she didn't remove them. The rest of her soldiers would be wearing theirs for some hours yet until they could get back to warm fires at which to dry them. Her helmet slipped off into her hand, and she set it on the ground, then reached up to touch her carefully braided hair and found it damp. From sweat, probably.

Sark's hands slipped over hers. Light as air, his fingertips danced over the bumps and valleys of her braids, down to the complicated tangle at the nape of her neck.

"I hate to cut you."

Kierstaz turned to look him in the eyes. They were icy and unreadable, as always.

His hand was still in midair, near her chin. "This will hurt."

"It hurt the first time."

"Much more than that."

"I don't mind."

He nodded and took out a small, blue knife of Drei steel, pulled out a stone, and sharpened it several times without breaking her gaze. "You never do." He tucked the knife inside his palm and examined each scar with his fingertips. His touch made her flinch, not from pain but from the warmth in her stomach that slowly crept toward her face.

"Why did you want to wait to do this?"

He did not answer, just kept feeling her skin. Kierstaz ground her fingernails into her palms as hard as she could, but he didn't stop. His fingers slid briefly down her neck to the horizontal slash on her collarbone, and she had to close her eyes.

"This one, too?" he whispered, as if he knew why Mikel had put it there.

"Yes."

His touch turned instantly to a sharp, searing pain that caused her to start. She couldn't see it, but she felt warm blood begin to run down her throat, and she knew he had cut her. It throbbed heavily, and he placed his hand over it like a cage. His eyes closed and his lips moved, his brow heavy, creasing as if power was leaving him. She wasn't sure she should watch, but it was hard to look away. Especially when he bared his teeth for a split second...as if he were in pain. He, who never felt anything.

Her skin burned like he'd poured hot liquor in it. She bit the inside of her lip as another wave hit her. At last he let go, but the pain stayed, turning dull and almost roiling her stomach.

His eyes opened, calm and nearly vulnerable. He didn't say anything, just slid the backs of his fingers down her cheek—the one with the deep, twisted, purple scar that ran the length of it. That one would hurt the most, she imagined. Before she could formulate the full thought, he'd slit it open and pressed his entire hand flat against it.

Kierstaz held in a moan that wanted desperately to free itself from her lips. The pain spread to her temples, burning and freezing at the same time, as if her mind were on fire. Sark was saying audible words, but she couldn't decipher them as they weren't of the Drei tongue. They were something different—deeper, heavier, and more moving than his language. He sounded angry, as if he cursed the air about her.

"Sark." His name slipped from her lips in a soft gasp. She hadn't meant to say anything.

He gripped the other side of her head with his free hand, still holding the knife, and pressed. She didn't mean to whimper, but something hurt, something in her chest, in her racing heart. Memories were being drawn up—things she couldn't tangibly name, but she could feel them. Her entire consciousness could feel them, oozing out through the blood that slipped from her skin. She could hardly breathe. Maybe he could breathe for her.

Please breathe for me, Sark.

He didn't. He let go of her and drew back. "Another?" His lip was swollen, as if he'd bitten down on it too hard.

Kierstaz didn't hesitate. "Yes."

He glanced over her face from left to right again, then cut more. Too many little slashes to pay heed to. She let the feeling wash over her and tear at her insides until she couldn't catch her breath at all, and it felt glorious, as if he was taking everything that hurt and haunted her into himself and causing it to dissipate in the cold air. Her legs went weak, and she fell against him. Still, he kept his fingers cupped over her bleeding skin, his lips moving, his eyes closed. She lost consciousness at some point, though she wasn't sure when or what urged it. Her thoughts became a mesh of images and sounds and ripples of feeling.

Nights full of screams. Her skin was singed, her mind burning with the memory of flaming buildings and scorched bodies. She hadn't dreamed of these things in ages. They hadn't haunted her and she hadn't known they'd meant anything at all to her, but as they dredged up and through her, she felt the rage again—raw, burning rage. At the time, there had been nothing she could do to stop the slaughter and heal the pain, so she had buried it, pretended it wasn't real. But it was real. It was embedded in her, like a huge spear in her stomach, impossible to remove. Sark's fingertips reached for it—through her cheekbones, down past her bulwarks and shields and battlements to where her darkest wounds still held themselves sacred—and she felt him trying to unseat the power she gave them. Power that was kept in the open, bleeding scars, her protection from having to be herself. Her soul screamed at him not to come close, not to expose her—but he didn't hear her, and she had no defense in her delirium. She had given him permission, and he used it.

When she woke, it was to heavy nausea and cool water against her face. She was on her own sleeping mat, her sword next to her. The first thing she wanted to do was vomit, but her stomach was strangely settled. Sark knelt next to her, a wet cloth held to her face and her collarbone. He'd opened her underarmor and soaked up the blood that must have been dousing her shirt.

Kierstaz felt like she should ask a question, but there was nothing to say. He looked pale, she thought.

Sark leaned down and placed a light kiss on her forehead.

{35}
Turned

MANAGING TO BE ALONE WITH Mem proved difficult. It was over a week before Malcom was able to get rid of both Otreya and the numerous other shadows that followed him about as if he were already some kind of lieutenant who needed training. Or watching?

Not that he hadn't expected this. Honestly, he hadn't expected to have a chance to see Mikel at all, let alone tell his Mem outright, "I want a private audience with your prisoner."

She raised her eyebrows in surprise, but it wasn't genuine. "Which one?" Her breath hitched up at the end.

"Mikel, of course. I know you have him."

She shrugged and looked away. "Not now."

"Why not? Idelviss says you bring him here all the time to talk about Allel knows what."

"You've been speaking with Idelviss?"

"She pushes herself into every conversation I have. With anyone."

Mem rolled her eyes and shuddered. "I don't trust her."

Malcom didn't either. "But do you really bring him here? People won't talk about one more questioning, will they?"

"She is not people. She is half-Drei, and she has worked with Otreya for years." Mem crossed her arms. "I don't think you should meet with him. You're too young to understand what is happening."

"Fine. I'll go around you. I have my own rooms, all the guards listen to me, and Otreya trusts me—"

"No!" Mem stepped in front of him. "No, I concede. Have him come here. Better this way." Her hands were interwoven with each other, but he still saw them shaking. She stepped close to him. "You mustn't say anything that I am not welcome to hear, understand? I will be nearby. I will listen."

That would make conversation rather strained, but Malcom said, "Fine."

Mikel had always looked about the age of Mem—still young enough to be a decent knight and tough enough to beat a young man at fists—but when the guards brought him up and dropped him on the floor, he looked old, worn.

Malcom couldn't keep his anger hidden. "What have you been doing to him?" he hissed under his breath.

Mem shrugged. "Prisoners cannot be pampered, Malcom." She glared down at Mikel. "I thought you said you were going to make my boy as a roughling? You haven't, else he shouldn't care that you have a few new scratches."

Mikel peered up at her but said nothing. The only part of him that seemed alert and alive was his eyes. They had something in them... Defiance. How could he be defiant? Malcom could, but Mikel hadn't a scrap of footing here.

Malcom extended his hand and helped him to stand. "I'll see to it that you're not a prisoner for long."

Mikel quirked a smile. "Don't go drawing swords, Mal. I've no complaints with the arrangement."

That was as odd as anything Malcom had heard since he'd come to the Fourth City. What was it about this place that made people lose their minds? He wished his mother was far away. He drew Mikel into the corner and lowered his voice to a whisper. "Has word of Kierstaz reached you?"

Mikel didn't move a muscle. "I heard of her, yes."

"Some say she is of your blood. Some say she is not. Regardless, she has taken Vienstrauss and sold its inhabitants to the Elloyans."

A hint of dreaminess crossed Mikel's face. "Well, I am sure that caused a stir."

Malcom caught the jealous glares Mem cast his way. She wanted something from Mikel, and he wasn't giving it. There had always been something between his mother and Mikel that Malcom never understood, and he still didn't. What if Otreya was right about that?

Malcom swung open the doors to the portico and jerked his head for Mikel to follow, chains and all. Mem's mouth dropped open behind him, but he closed the doors quickly before she could protest. He had a moment before she opened a window and could hear their words on the wind—at least, he hoped so.

"Otreya does not let on, but I think Vekst is afraid that Kierstaz will have everything she needs to retake Serengard," he said quietly, under his breath.

"How do you know he is afraid?" Mikel was distracted, watching the people in the streets several blocks away in the Workmen's Quarter.

"Otreya spends most of the day drilling me on mystic things, but Vekst only asks me about my time with the cliffmen. If I was a prisoner, if I was tortured, if I'd ever been to Dreibourge, if there was a slight woman there with freckles... He wouldn't bother if he wasn't nervous." And there was something else that made him think that—a tangible feeling. Malcom frowned to himself. These sudden instincts he had about people were starting to worry him.

As if on cue, Mikel said, "Can you...compel him? Or anyone?"

"Control thoughts? No." He studied Mikel. "You knew about that, too? Why am I the last to learn of my own heritage?" He ground his teeth.

Mikel shook his head. "Maybe we all wanted you to have a chance to be a boy."

Malcom knew Mem would have a window open by now, maybe even a few lackeys lurking on the roof. If she could force people to do her will, could she make them spy for her? Could Otreya? The thought made his skin prickle.

He picked at the stone railing, waiting for Mikel to speak again, but he didn't. "My mind has been different ever since the Drei cured me—"

"The Drei cured you? Who?"

Malcom shook his head rapidly to tell him that he couldn't say it aloud. "They said my blood was fighting with itself, but whatever they did cured me of that. I don't understand it all, but I am different." Malcom let out a loud breath and then mouthed the words, "*I don't think I have anything of my mother left in me.*"

Mikel's head snapped to the side quickly. "I never thought you did."

There was something else Malcom wanted to tell him, but he wasn't sure if he should speak it. "Otreya said something to me that I'm not sure I believe." He glanced behind him, feeling his mother's gaze from somewhere. "He said that even a progressive society cannot maintain the balance of the land, that the very tales of Orion blood that he has spent his life refuting are actually true, and that only the commanders should know this to keep the common folk from worrying. I thought maybe he was testing me. He does that—watches for reactions. Maybe he was trying to determine whether I was loyal to you or not?" He was trying to ask a question, but Mikel didn't seem to get it.

"That wizard has always confounded me."

Malcom rolled his tongue over his teeth. "He said the lands around the Fourth City stayed luscious during the Border Wars, that a wheat crop has begun to sprout since I returned, that Orion blood in the capital was the only thing that could turn the infertility around, and that...he knew I was coming here because the birds proclaimed it. He could pass for a mad man."

Mikel looked less puzzled and more alarmed.

"But did he mean you? Does he believe in your lineage in spite of his claims? Or..."

Mikel drew his hand into a first. "He is saying someone of Orion blood is in this city? Or is he testing you to see if you know?"

"But are you or aren't you? He says you aren't."

Mikel shook his head rapidly. "No. He knows I am not."

The door behind them opened. Mem's face was equally white, only hers was flushed with anger. "Enough. I want to talk to Mikel now. You may speak again later."

ℶ

MIKEL WAITED CALMLY WHILE THE guards took him to Trzl's windowless room. As soon as the door closed behind them, Trzl tossed him to the floor. He landed on his shoulder with a dull thud. The darkness was comfortable, like a blanket, but it was pierced instantly by the lighting of a candle.

"You knew, Mikel Orion. You knew, and you hid it from me."

Mikel looked up at her slowly. "Knew what?"

"Kierstaz. All those years Hodran searched for her, she was by your side. You let me think I could trust Tev. I gave her my *son*."

His arms should have been trembling, but even his stomach was calm. He cleared his throat. "Tell me. How does it feel to be fooled?"

She backhanded him across the mouth. "Zurik and Vienstrauss fell to a force of Drei weeks ago. I only now get the messengers, traitors from the Drei forces, because her goblins killed every Seren in the cities. And now there is rumor that Dorscht is under siege."

Mikel felt a smile tugging at the corners of his mouth. "Again...how does it feel?"

Trzl grabbed him by the hair. "You are so very Dermed lucky I stepped between Vekst and the city spikes for your head. There is one more thing I need you for, and then Allel help you because you will die, Mikel. The same way your Drei died, damn them—alone and in secret."

His mouth went dry. "You...killed them?"

The snarl in her voice turned to a snicker. "The kindest way I knew how. I had Gernan do it. Oh, don't look at me like that. If I hadn't, they'd have been tortured publicly when the news of the uprising in Dreibourge is unveiled to the city. We'll have to tell the people, eventually, and lock up every Drei in Serengard to keep them from rioting as well."

"You're sick, Trzl."

"Me? Sick? No, Mikel, it is you who have always turned a blind eye. You think you can rescue everyone. Well, you can't. You can't save Pier or Colstadt or Malcom or Kierstaz. Or me."

"At least I have given you every opportunity."

"I don't want you to change me, Mikel! I don't want you to shame me and guilt me into being better than I am! I don't!" Her voice had risen far too loud. She must have realized it, for she gulped heavily and lowered it to a hiss once more. "Vekst wants to have you dealt with quietly. He's going to kill you by the full moon if you don't escape first. I tell you because if you know a way to do that, you should. I gave you a promise: that you'd live. I can't keep that promise. And now that I've told you this, consider any debt I owe you nullified."

Mikel should have felt rage breaking through his very skin, but he didn't. He felt numb. "I came here to help you, to destroy a man who uses the world as his own private game. I was willing to die for you so that you could accomplish this."

"Consider it accomplished. I've learned that he is not as dangerous as I thought. I can influence him just as much as he can influence me. I am strong now." Trzl paused, almost smiled. "I thank you for that. You let me cut my teeth on you not once, but three times. I wouldn't be here without that." She knelt down and lifted his chin. Her lips graced his. He stiffened, and she laughed again. "Oh, Mikel. Do you know why I really had to kill your Drei? Because you love them." She spewed the words, and their vehemence struck him right in the gut. "If I could kill everything you love, I would, but you have thoroughly thwarted such a thing by loving my son. And he is the only person *I* love."

There was a lump in his throat that threatened to choke him. "I...didn't want to change you, Trzl. I wanted you to...understand. To be kinder. More forgiving."

She laughed raggedly. "Yes. To change me. I do care about Serengard but not in the way that you do, and I *hate* how you make me feel guilty for not being as perfect as you. The way I cannot rid myself of your...your righteousness. Even when I've known your wrongness and your hypocrisy, you are always superior in some way, always enviable."

"Trzl, you have no reason to envy me now." He held up his wrists, worn raw from chains. "I have nothing. If you wanted to destroy me, you have done it."

"No!" she fairly shouted at him. "No, I haven't. Your sister is alive. She lived at your side for how many Dermed years? She is just like you, and she is free, not here in my hands. I can't change you, I can't change her, and that is the only way I could destroy you both. You have forgiven too many who've wronged you—even me—and I cannot do the same. I hate them all. I hate you. Why, why do you love Malcom? Why can't you hate him? Then we could be amicable enemies."

Mikel cleared his throat. "Have we ever been anything but amicable enemies? We have never been friends. Even when I thought I wanted you, Trzl, I never trusted you."

"Then you lied."

He smiled thinly. "You knew someday I would stop swallowing your falehoods and turn them on you. Someone had to."

Trzl shook her head repeatedly, sank to her knees in front of him, and brought her face up inches from his. "You know what I don't understand? How I can control anyone in the kingdom but you. You...escape me."

He didn't feel that way. He felt trapped by her. Enticed, ensnared, bewitched. Never able to give up on her, never able to let her go. He whispered, raw and bare, "I want you to be free."

She jumped, winced, tipped her head to the side. A tear ran out of her eye. "Oh, Mikel. You sweet baby. I was never going to be free of this...whatever it is...that you hate. It's who I am. Admit that you hate me."

Mikel narrowed his eyes. "It doesn't have to be."

"It is. Haven't I proven my ruthlessness to you? What more do you want? Your sister torn limb from limb on my rack? Because I will do that when I find her. I will do that and more."

"No. You won't." He didn't believe it. Even now with her blank, black eyes staring him in the face, he didn't believe it. "You're not yourself. Otreya is influencing you. He's hurting you. Remember why you came back? Do you? Or was that all a ruse?" He could swear it wasn't. He'd seen truth in her eyes the night she'd told him her purpose. Seen her bare ruthlessness and known she would do it.

She threw back her head and laughed. "I remember, but if you recall, I had conditions. I wanted Malcom kept away. He's here now, so I have another plan. One that will be appealing to all—yourself included."

"It won't be."

"Malcom will be emperor."

He stopped his retort. That was actually quite brilliant of her. "Malcom?"

"Yes. He is Otreya's great-grandson. Hodran's son. *My* son. Who can boast better qualifications? His grandfather loves him, and therefore so will the rest of the Council."

Mikel was quiet for a whole minute, long enough for her to pace the length of the room in loud footfalls. "Just how do you think you will bring this about?"

"It will not be hard."

"Malcom could be a just ruler if you allowed him to use his own mind and stayed out of his ears."

"And have you in them instead? You think you will use my son as your shield? I won't let you confuse him any more than he already is. His destiny is to replace Vekst. He will do it without your help."

Mikel lowered his voice to nearly nothing. "So Malcom is going to be your new puppet? Please tell me you care for him more than this."

She shrugged, her eyes blank and looking straight through him. "At least he won't be *your* puppet. I don't see as it is any of your concern."

Mikel's hair fell in his face. He looked up at her through it, hoped the open disgust in his eyes was none too prevalent. "For true, I'll not bow to you nor aid your reign in any way, but I'll do whatever I must for Malcom. You know he'll be easy prey in Otreya's hands, as has every emperor before him. I should think your own son—"

Trzl shrugged again. "Otreya is dangerous, but I daresay I have more influence over Malcom than he does and I can do far more good in such a position. You have too many inhibitions, Mikel. He won't be keeping you as an advisor."

He looked at her there, cutthroat and hard, terribly capable and without a vulnerable place—at least that he could name. In a way, he'd helped bring her to this. Whenever she'd needed him, he'd been there. Ready. Willing. He hated himself for it now, but looking back, he wouldn't have done differently—he wouldn't have refused. He gave up on kingdoms, not on people.

She shifted her shoulders. "I'm sorry that your plans went awry.

Really, you should have foreseen my determination." Halfway to the door, she paused and turned to him. "Malcom's rise will be soon. I'll send the guards for you."

A cold ripple ran down his spine. "Is that the one last thing you need me for?"

"It is. Otreya wants you there."

{36}
LOST

EMPEROR.

THE GUARDS DIDN'T EVEN have to touch Mikel on the way back to his cell. He went willingly, the word reverberating in his head, as loud as the clank of the lock falling in place behind him.

Malcom would make an excellent emperor. He would. Trzl, in her usual mad scramble for control, may have stumbled on something that could save the wretched Four Cities in spite of herself.

But what did *save* mean anymore? At the price of what? Was there even a scrap of sentiment left in the hearts of the Seren people? Or were they pleased with this…mindless structure?

If Otreya would be pleased with the idea, something was wrong with it—deeply wrong at its very core—and yet, who was Mikel to judge? Was Trzl right? Did he cast a shadow of blame and guilt over her that truly should have been his? He was the one who was supposed to have held the kingdom together. He and Kierstaz, the perceived last Orions. Yet, without the blood of Derev Orion, they had always been doomed to lose.

All they had done was try to stem the tide of mayhem that had been coming for nearly a century.

The fact that Pier and Colstadt—that any one of his knights—had survived this long was pure providence. The realization hit him, and strangely enough, he wasn't angry. He wasn't hurt. He wanted revenge, but not on Trzl. He wanted revenge on cruelty, on the eagerness to kill innocence, on the ideas that could drive humanity to be nothing but dust, make them not care about the person next to them enough to realize that they, too, were human. He wanted to crush such ideals with everything he had, but he didn't want to go to war for it. He didn't want to go to war again for anything. Ever.

He'd had this fire before, during sleepless nights in the Castle of Marek, wishing into a jug of mead that he could blame someone for the death of his wife and son when, truly, there was no one to blame but himself. If they'd stayed in the valleys, she might have been healthier, might not have wasted away into nothing because there was not enough sunshine and not enough fresh food, might, might, might... Too many things they hadn't realized until she was pregnant with their second child and their first grew sick. Too many things he should have foreseen and planned for.

Six years of perfection. Enough to make every hurt and pain he'd ever felt fade into nothing, but why had he had to survive it? And was it worth it for her? To die so young? To watch her child die?

As soon as Pier had realized how weak she was, Mikel had taken her and their son and headed south. She'd fought him the entire way, told him it was foolish to return to Aldad. It still sickened him to think of her protests: that she would be fine, she would get better, that they should all stay safely tucked away in the cliffs. The guilt that had crept into him, knowing that he should have made sure she was safe in the Desert all along, that she should never have come north, that she should have chosen Gavriel's blade.

Serengard could go to the Treacher. This land had never needed him. It had spit him out over and over—as it had the night they'd tried to cross the border near Neroi, a border that must have been fortified nearly twenty times since the last time they'd come through.

Too many soldiers and only him and Pier to protect Aura and their little boy. When the Seren soldier had slit his son's throat, calling him a "worthless half-breed," Mikel lost his mind. He'd killed almost all of them, but the one had gotten close enough to stab Aura through the throat. As the light went out of her eyes, he'd cut the bastard who'd done it in half. It still burned him that the last sight she'd beheld had been the very image he'd never wanted her to see: blood slinging through the air at the will of his sword, bodies broken at his hand.

He and Pier had buried his son above the sands of the river, but Mikel had carried Aura to the northernmost city in Aldad. He'd stayed with her body until Gavriel came and claimed it for her tribe.

He should have known he could never have what he so desperately wanted. He should never have been so brazen. From then on, he could only protect his knights, make sure they had lives, because his was gone, buried with Aura.

To the Treacher with the rest of it.

The only part that had remained constant was what he wanted to protect: truth, innocence, and his family. Three things he meant to keep alive, and he'd failed all of them. More than failed—he'd watched them burned brilliantly and slammed into the ground. He was getting damned tired of it. If Malcom was going to be emperor...

Mikel sat up. He hadn't meant to sleep, but maybe he was? It was hard to tell in the dark. What had he been thinking about before he sank into a well of anguish?

Malcom. If he was capable of curbing the broiling tensions between the Seren and the Drei and the Aldadi, Mikel would have faith in him, but Malcom loved his mother and his mother was a madwoman right now. Yet who could blame the boy for loving his mother? Mikel had loved his own mem fiercely enough to make war for six months to avenge her death. Little good it did. His parents died for nothing. They hadn't even been royal.

Neither was Mikel. So how could Otreya think that he was? Was Kierstaz missing some vital piece of history in her tale?

He wanted to talk to someone. Anyone.

"Tanya?"

He heard nothing from her cell, not even a breath.

"Riyev?"

He rolled over on his cot and stared at the blackness. Then he lit a candle. The light didn't help. It made him lonelier.

Pier and Colstadt had just died for no one. For nothing. Why was he still living? He didn't want to be. He'd been ready to die since Aura was killed. No reason to be here and no reason to fear death. She'd saved him, and as soon as she was gone, he'd lost himself. He'd begged Allel to take him from this world, cursed the blessing of the Captain of the Guard to never die in battle. Every time he came close, someone held his bloodied face and told him he'd be fine. Someone patched him up, healed him. Pier, usually. Damn Pier.

How could Otreya be mad enough to think any Orion blood still lived in this godforsaken place? Could he know? Could he have followed a line of illegitimate offspring long enough to have an heir ready and waiting? How old *was* the man? No one even knew Otreya's bloodline. All they knew was that he could be a wizard—a conjurer or a sorcerer—which meant he could have mystical blood in him.

Mystical blood is the opponent of Orion blood, the Books of Derev said. *Mystical blood seeks to oppress, Orion blood to liberate.*

But the last Orion king, Altrun, had children who'd gone mad, hadn't he? They could have broken the fidelity law that was supposed to keep the bloodline traceable, but who had killed all of the Orions? According to tradition, the only person who could kill an Orion—besides an Orion—was the same person who protected the Orions: the Castle Guard. Mikel had lived long enough now to believe in the balances Derev had declared; the mere fact that he was still breathing was enough to convince him of that.

Only an Orion can kill one of mystical blood.

Only one of the Guard can kill an Orion.

Only a Kymsai can kill one of the Guard.

The second two applied to any blood, as anyone under Allel's sun could be appointed Castle Guard and anyone could choose to be Kymsai. That gave power to the common person—power over the Orions, but not power over mystical blood. If the Orions were gone, was there anyone who could stop mystical blood?

Only one of mystical blood can kill a Kymsai.

That was why the Orions had done their best to keep wizards and sorcerers out of Serengard. Without the Kymsai, the country was dead—Mikel knew that firsthand. But he had always thought these writings of Derev's were merely a failsafe. It had been hundreds of years since any of mystical blood had been evident. Most had thought them a legend, a superstition, and called them faeries.

If Otreya truly was mystical and he knew of a live Orion, he should be frightened to death, shouldn't he? Or was that his entire plan? Destroy the Orion family until there was only one left, one who didn't know the laws of Derev, one who had no Guard, one he could influence...

But could he ever influence his opposite?

Malcom's words came back to him: *I don't think I have anything left of my mother in me.* Was mystical blood a curse that a Drei could cure? Was that yet another reason why Serengard had always needed the Drei?

Mikel's mind hurt.

Malcom's blood had had an imbalance, and so had Trzl's when she was a girl—she'd told him as much. Didn't that mean they were both mystical? If Malcom were Orion, that would mean Hodran would have to be Orion, and he couldn't have been. Hodran had been Kymsai. Hadn't he?

Trzl had once said to him, *"Grandfather does not care what I do, so long as I eventually succumb to my fate and marry the Corsai of Neroi."*

Otreya had wanted Trzl to marry Hodran. He'd wanted her to have a child. He'd wanted that child brought back to him when Trzl ran off. And why would he let Mikel, the Captain of the Guard, make it all the way to the Third City with Malcom only to send an ill-equipped Kymsai after him?

He wanted Hodran dead. Once he saw Malcom was alive and well, he was done with his father.

Mikel felt slightly sick, and no less confused than he had been before. There was no way to say who was whose blood. Not unless they had a blood-keeper. But...hadn't Pier found blood vials stored somewhere?

Idelviss' taunt could mean something entirely different: *"They say she looks nothing like her. Couldn't possibly be the real Kierstaz. Has scars on her face."*

Otreya probably held those cards as well. He held everything. Secrets. He would run this Empire on them for another age, and he'd train Trzl to do the same, and she would train Malcom.

Mikel knelt down next to the grate. "Natalya? Natalya, please be here." He held the bars until his knuckles were white. "Please."

She slid across the floor, scuffling like a small dog. "What is it?"

"Allel bless you." Mikel reached through the bars and held her hands.

"They took my mem. I don't think she's alive anymore."

"Who did?"

"The Dark Lady had her taken away while I was hidden in the wall."

"You need to get out of these dungeons, Natalya. They're going to kill me next, and after that..."

"But you're the prince!" Her eyes were wide and angry and insistent.

"You're supposed to stop this."

"I meant to." No promises left. "I thought I could control the Dark Lady at least a little, but I can't. I'm sorry." He wanted to beat his fist into the wall at how wrongly this had all gone. If only Malcom hadn't come, if only Trzl hadn't brought in Romianz's daughters, he could have torn this building inside out without fear of his actions harming one more person he loved. That had been the plan: If Trzl had failed to kill Otreya, if she'd failed to take down the Council, Mikel would kill them all himself in one move. They'd find a way to kill him back, of course—probably Gernan would do it with a dagger at dinner—but it would be finished. Colstadt and Pier would have been casualties, anyway. He highly doubted mere Castle Guard blood could kill a mystical—Otreya had shown no fear in the face of Petrolai, and he'd laughed outright with Mikel in the room—but that wouldn't have kept him from trying.

But why the Derm did Malcom have to be here? Why did *Natalya* have to be here? "Listen. You need to leave the city, but can you do one last thing? For me and for your mem?"

Natalya shrugged as if to say she didn't care, but he heard her drag in a breath.

"Can you find someone at the border near the Second City?"

"I could. I have been there before. But this city is locked down since they heard of the Drei uprising. I will need a pass from my uncle."

"Will he give you one?"

She bit her lip. "Not unless I have a very convincing story."

Dermed. "Do you know who Lord Marek is?"

Her eyes went wide and round. "The cliffman who works for the Dark Lady?"

"Tell your uncle you're working for him as a scout. Marek is a pirate and a renegade, and nothing he does is subject to the laws of the Cities. Whatever you do, do not tell anyone your real purpose. Once you get out, procure a fast horse and ride east. Find a group of Desert People near the

Second City and ask them to send word to a multan named Gavriel."

Natalya was trembling now. "I...I don't trust Desert People, you know."

"No one expects you to trust them, little one, but you needn't fear them." They were the only people he knew were intent enough. Maybe he should have sold the gate sequences to them four years ago. Maybe the strength in Aldadi blood could better take on the mystical.

"What if they sell me for a slave?"

"If they do, it will be better than staying here." Mikel ran a hand over the tattoo on his back—the symbol of Ladin's tribe. He peeled back his shirt. "Memorize this symbol. Draw it for them. Tell them you are friends with a man named Tierrof and you want to see Gavriel. They will protect you if you show them this. Tierrof speaks Seren, and he will know my name."

"Friends of Tierrof. Must speak to Gavriel. What do I tell him?"

"Tell him if he still wants to purge the Four Cities, I will hand him the Fourth."

ୠ

LINDT FOUGHT HARDER THAN ANY fortress or city yet. Theo foretold that they would. His scouts had caught a troop of reinforcements headed south and engaged them, depleting Kierstaz and Sark's force. When the city fell, it left Kierstaz with one hundred dead and over four hundred wounded, but her soldiers knew how to mend themselves and hold the battlements by now.

Sark propped his legs up on a table and raised a tankard full of water. "To your reign, Queen Kierstaz."

He hadn't changed from his battle garments. Dried sweat and blood still ran down his neck, arms, fingers. Kierstaz thought he had never looked mightier.

"The southern ports and fortresses will send a surrender."

Kierstaz smirked. "How do you know?"

"I know that the Serens care little about protecting them. And I know Theo and his breed."

She laughed. "Well, I am glad I have you as my strategist, king."

He tipped his head. "You know I am no king. A General I will always be."

"I'm going to entrust you with this country. All of it." She waited a moment before she glanced into his eyes. They had spoken of this before, but she wasn't certain he had believed her. "I was never meant to rule Dreibourge."

"I know that, but I wasn't sure *you* knew that." His eyes crinkled. "You were surely meant to conquer it, though."

"I am most serious. I hope you will return the Eight Generals to power and hold the borders."

He cleared his throat. "And how could we repay this debt to Ashlin's Guard whom we did not even support in battle?"

"Repay is not the word."

"You are shrewd indeed."

"I am not bargaining with you, Sark."

His eyes lingered on her throat, where her jagged scar used to be. "No. We were through bargaining a long time ago."

"I won't expect anything in return. I haven't done this myself."

"You have. Our people would not have united again without a queen. Their faith needed to be rekindled in someone besides themselves—in an Orion. Faith is a fragile thing." There was a touch of wistfulness in his expression. Kierstaz quirked an eyebrow as he wrapped an arm around the back of his chair. The liquid in his cup rolled around, his gaze focused on it. "A letter came for you."

Kierstaz tensed. "When?"

"Just before you came in. I did not open it."

"From whom? Theo? Crista?" He didn't reply, and she caught her breath. "Malcom?"

Sark shook his head. "I don't know. The rider was Seren but had the long hair and sharp eyes of the cliffs. We locked him up. I wanted to ask you something before you open it."

"What?"

He let a leg fall from the table and used it to lean further back, his stare focused on the floor and not her face. "Before you'd taken a single city, you were certain that because my bloodline is strong and pure, I would not want to weaken it with yours. But why would you weaken yours with mine?"

"Mine is only Castle Guard. You know that," Kierstaz whispered. He didn't blink or reply. She gulped, the necessity of reading the letter pulling her away from him. "I... How could you ask that now? You have already decided you do not want children."

"No." He took a quick swig of water. "No, I decided no such thing. That decision has always been yours, my queen."

"So we are back to the title."

"Only in this matter."

Why must he speak of this now? "Are you asking me for permission?"

"I am. I have always told you that I would cost you nothing. That anything between us was yours to take and not mine." He glanced up at her—quick, piercing. "I don't want this alliance to be yours anymore. I want it to be ours."

Kierstaz closed her eyes. She hadn't realized how badly she wanted this admission from him. *Sweet faeries, Sark. How could you...* She sucked in a heavy breath. "You needn't have held back from me. Ever."

Sark let his other leg fall off of the table. He leaned forward on his elbows and held his chin with a hand. "I crave... I envy... I want children with your courage. You are little and mortal and you think your strength is only in making war, but you are strong in much greater things. There is beauty in you, and I desire it. I would not have you be a Drei. You are as Seren as exists on this earth, with more passion than I will ever be capable of. I want you that way. I want you, all of you. I want to stay yours."

Kierstaz's hands shook. "You will. You have me." Her voice came out half-broken, half-laugh, and she couldn't decide which was true just now. "You *did* say that eloquently."

"I've been told decent thought can be a casualty when a Drei keeps the company of a Seren." A faint smile played on his lips. "Confessions are not my strength, but I try to speak truth."

"I'm grateful that you are not pretentious."

"No need to be grateful. I would not change you, and I've not changed myself."

Kierstaz wanted to kiss him, but she whispered, "Give me the letter please."

It bore the official seal of the Fourth City, and her heart slammed against her ribs as soon as she saw it. She held it out as if it would bite her. "Open it."

Sark read it in a moment, and his brow wrinkled in confusion. "The penmanship is common Drei, and the language is the same. It says, *If the rumors are true, you are better equipped to topple this edifice than I from a dungeon in the Fourth. He's still alive. Right about now would be nice, little dog.*" He looked up at her. "Who would send this?"

Kierstaz grabbed the paper. The handwriting was fluid, but not flowery. Warmth and fear flooded her in one rush.

Sark whispered, "Who wrote this?"

Confused tears poured down her cheeks, and she wanted to damn them for running. "It's from Colstadt."

"Who?"

"He's...an old friend. A very old friend."

{37}
deception

COLSTADT DIDN'T HAVE LONG BEFORE Gernan did come. A scant nine days, and he stormed in late at night, claiming he needed a picked force to go after an escaped prisoner. Colstadt shrank back into the shadows, but Pier couldn't hide very well.

Sunn must have been immediately behind Gernan because he took two steps up the stairs and she was there. "My lord, a word with you?"

"In a moment, yes." His eyes rested on Pier. Colstadt. His face turned ashen, then red with anger. "Sunn!" he yelled. His voice was a scale lower than Colstadt's, and when he yelled, the rest of them formed into straight lines with weapons drawn. "What in all the dark purple flames of the Derm are those two Drei doing here? And don't tell me you know nothing."

Colstadt glanced at Sunn. He hated that she'd had to stick her neck out. She'd been on the verge of doing it once before when he was locked in the hold of a ship, and he'd asked her not to.

Now could be infinitely worse—how much worse was evident by the way Gernan slowly reached for Riyev's hand, picked it up, pulled her toward the wall. "Maybe this one will tell me?"

Sunn stepped toward Gernan. "Your fickle partner made a bad call. I amended it for her."

"My partner may make many a bad call, but didn't *I* tell you to see they were dealt with?"

"You did. As long as I've been in your employ, such a command means many things, but most of all, it means to use my own good judgment."

Gernan backhanded Sunn across the face gently, but it still left a red mark. Sunn grabbed his long hair and pulled like the savage girl she was. He grabbed hers, brought her face up inches from his own. "Don't you ever go behind my back again, or I'll skin you as I would a cat."

Sunn spit on his cheek. "If you wanted your friends dead, you should have done it your own damn self."

"They're not my friends, damn you. And neither are you."

"I'm the only friend you have if you hadn't noticed. Trzl doesn't care a whit whether you're here or not, so long as she gets her Dermed kingdom in the end."

Gernan's brow crinkled. "Do not try to make me doubt an alliance that has served me well. Aren't you dressed in stag skin? Kept in good health? You have rooms to yourself."

"Which you frequently barge into."

He waved a hand. "It matters not. We eat better than we ever have. We own half the ships on the sea. You command a thousand warriors and two ships yourself. What more do you thirst for?"

"I want you to use your blackguard head, Gernan." Sunn shoved him in the chest and walked away from him. "We came to kill the wizard and slice out the hill country for ourselves, or have you forgotten?"

Gernan turned on his heel and paced the room. "Everything does not happen in the space of a heartbeat. You are this close to having your throat slit clear across, Sunn, so help me—"

Colstadt stood up. Both of them stared at him. "Forgive me, but whether my life is to be short or long, Sunn speaks true. Trzl is unsteady as a broken scale."

Gernan walked up and stuck a finger in his face. His broad shoulders loomed over Colstadt's small form. "You. You have always been a tiny bane on my glory. I wish I had killed you when we found ourselves in battle."

Colstadt held his black gaze. "Why didn't you?"

He flinched, a slight raise of the lip that turned into a sneer. "I don't stab in the back. I fight to the face. You were already wounded."

He didn't think he could take me. "I'm not wounded now."

Gernan didn't answer. No one moved. The silence in the room grew heavy and palpable, until a soft, whispery laugh broke it.

"We're all such an agreeable lot here," Pier cut in. "We forget there is one in our midst we can trust to betray every one of us, no matter our dislike for the other."

All heads turned at once. Pier held a sharp knife against Idelviss's throat. Weak though he might be, his grip was strong enough to hold her. She didn't move.

Gernan's jaw shifted, but he said nothing.

"She is in your barracks because she is Otreya's little mole," Pier said. "Wouldn't be a problem, except I thought I heard you let something slip about killing him and slicing out a piece of a kingdom. Grounds enough for you to hang."

Gernan stared hard at Pier. "Put the knife down."

Pier's eyes were stone, as always. "Not until we decide what to do with her."

"She is valuable to Otreya. If she disappears, suspicion falls on all of us."

Pier smiled slyly. "Precisely my point. Your mind is sharper than I give you credit for, Gernan."

Gernan growled. "I'll kill you myself in a moment."

"No, you'd be more likely to let Colstadt and I walk out of here with Riyev. And Sunn, if she wishes." Pier was bargaining with nothing, but Gernan didn't seem to realize that.

Sunn shook her head. "No. You will both be caught and hanged in a moment, and I am loyal to Gernan."

Gernan smirked. "I'm not an idiot, Pier. You're going to kill Idelviss, anyway, and you don't want out of this room. What do you really want?"

"Oh, no, I won't kill her. She has too much information in her little head, haven't you, sweets? Secrets about the troops, the spies, the briberies." He tilted the blade up and down so that the light glinted off of it. "Don't pretend you're not curious, Gernan. You're salivating."

He blushed. "I..."

"Give me a day with her, and I'll have her singing."

"And then you kill her? And then I kill you?"

Pier nodded. "Colstadt and Riyev may slink out of here if they wish."

Gernan paced a few steps, hands folded behind his muscular frame, long black hair waving with each step. "I do not think Trzl cares much about this Riyev, but I do not know about Colstadt."

"Well, what difference is it to you if Colstadt is thought to have escaped when you have my corpse to make excuses with?"

Colstadt's mouth went dry. *None of that, Pier,* he whispered in his head, but he didn't dare say it aloud. Pier knew how to twist words and impulses far better than he did.

"You know Trzl doesn't care about Colstadt." Pier's voice sank to a deep whisper. "I was the one she tortured, the one she wanted to punish. If he slips away now, it won't matter. She's bored with him."

Gernan narrowed his eyes. "Yes, you have a bargain, but they can't leave until tomorrow. I expect you to deal with this half-Drei snitch by then. I'll have you shackled to the floor. No daring escapes."

Pier grinned. "Excellent."

Colstadt hadn't the words to protest. He queried with his brow at Pier, but he received only a distant smile in return.

It could be Pier loved more than seven people. Could be he loved eight.

ℒ

"THE MORNING IS LOVELY, IS it not?"

Malcom turned at Otreya's voice and forced a pleasant smile on his features. "Indeed."

But it wasn't a lovely morning. He hadn't slept well, and there was fog in the air. He gripped the railing of Mem's porch as the nightmare flashed in his head again. He'd dreamt he was in a long hall lined with golden statues and no windows. The architecture was like nothing he'd ever seen—something old, he guessed. There was an altar at the end of the room. Throughout the dream he'd wanted to see what was on the altar, but he'd been too afraid to go near it. He awakened several times, but whenever he closed his eyes, it was there again.

"Ah, how I've looked forward to this day."

Malcom quirked an eyebrow, but he kept his face out toward the city. "Why?"

Otreya looked surprised. "Did your mem not tell you? Well, we're to perform a ceremony that will change the fabric of the Empire. Mind you, it doesn't mean much in terms of perception. No one will treat you any different. But it will mean everything eventually."

Malcom didn't have time to ask what that meant before they were interrupted by the arrival of Mem. She swept in with the swish of a dress that was far more elaborate than what she usually wore. "Ah, Grandfather, what are you doing unannounced in my rooms again?"

"Your rooms are also Malcom's rooms. Which should change after today."

Mem rolled her eyes. "He is not emperor *yet.*"

Malcom stiffened. "Emperor? Who said anything about—"

Otreya raised a hand. "Now, now, no need to be alarmed. Look, Trzl, you've shocked the boy. You should have told him sooner."

Mem shrugged. "He's still a boy. I don't see the need to hurry things."

"A Castle Guard rogue burns Dreibourge, and you see no reason to put Malcom in power?" Otreya's eyes narrowed. "You always were short-sighted, my dear."

"As if you are any better. Malcom has no practical experience, and Vekst has. And *I* have more experience with war than either of them."

Were they fighting? It almost sounded like Mem was angry that she was not Otreya's first choice. Malcom took a step back from both of them. "You know what puzzles me? Why does Vekst not mind that you make free with his title? He should, shouldn't he?"

Otreya laughed. "Why should he? He is the Emperor for a reason, Malcom. That reason is that he cares more for the good of the empire than he does for himself. He knows, as I do, that you will make the perfect emperor. Your mother and your grandfather orchestrated the rebellion that led to this impressive society, these beautiful cities full of people doing their part to make a perfect machine work."

Malcom frowned. "I don't understand why you need me, then." He felt as if he was missing something—that the air was supposed to be dense with compulsion, that his mind was supposed to intrinsically understand something Otreya communicated beneath the stream of consciousness— but it wasn't there. Whatever hold Otreya had over his daughter, it was as if Malcom was immune.

Otreya and Mem looked at each other, and an uneasy glance passed between them. Otreya said, "Malcom, your...your inheritance is...unique."

"How?"

"Does it matter? You should know in your heart already. It is why you are such a conflicted soul and why you have wandered far."

"I want to *know.*"

Otreya quirked an eyebrow. "Your blood is Orion." He paused, studied Malcom's face.

Malcom felt…nothing. It wasn't a revelation. It was an admission. "How?"

"Hodran was a bastard, but he was one of them. Luckily, the man didn't even know it. Your blood is as pure Orion as it gets, except that half of you is my blood. And *that* is what makes you powerful. My blood. The Orion was only necessary in order to complete the circle, to save these people from themselves. They'll accept you because you are an emperor, not because of your lineage, but your lineage will make this country flourish. It is how I planned it all along."

Mem rolled her eyes and sniffed noisily. "You bred him? You pushed me toward Hodran so that we would produce a child for *you*? Good goblins."

She didn't actually seem all that upset. She should be angrier. Malcom was. Mem simply pursed her lips and looked away. But then, maybe she had always known it and had just been waiting for him to admit it. Her grandfather had always used her.

Malcom took another step back. "I don't want to be emperor."

Otreya took a step toward him. "I've known you only a short while, Malcom, and even I can see there is brilliance in you. Please don't think less of yourself because your life has been tumultuous. You of all people are qualified to be here. You are qualified to lead this city, this nation, and all the lands."

Malcom shifted, looked at Mem again. She nodded, her eyes clear and eager.

"What if I don't want to?"

Mem smiled, a smile that reached her eyes, and put her hand on his shoulder. "But you will."

Otreya rubbed his palms together. "Now. Are you ready, my boy?"

Malcom felt trapped, but he was determined not to show it. He squared his shoulders and looked at Otreya head-on. "I want to talk to the prisoner first."

A grimace crossed Otreya's face before he could turn it placid. He glared past Malcom to Mem, as if this was her fault. "Why?"

"Because I need to ask him some questions about the Castle Guard. If I'm going to be emperor, I need to understand my enemies as well."

Otreya looked impressed. "Not to worry. He'll be there." His voice took on a tinny, mocking tone. "Your very own Captain of the Guard."

Mem entwined her fingers with Malcom's and tipped her head toward the door. "Come with me, son."

He didn't argue. She rarely used such an endearment, and it made him wonder if perhaps she was in danger now, if she was becoming expendable. The thought made his stomach twist.

They walked down to the main floor through halls that echoed with their footsteps, Otreya trailing behind. The sounds were eerie, like the clacking of the gypsy fires at a melee. The room they entered was below ground, with only a small shaft of light from outside and the rest lit with candles. Otreya led him to the far end and had him stand on a platform. There were about thirty guards posted around, standing silently, and the whole Council of Four. The air still smelled of marble dust, as if it had never been swept or even used.

The doors opened and the draft nearly blew out the many small flames, but each one recovered. The strangeness tugged at Malcom. Two guards and one prisoner entered, and then the doors closed again.

Mikel. Malcom met his eyes. They weren't calm or defiant this time. They were incensed.

A heavy stone chest that Malcom could swear he'd seen before was brought out and set on the ground next to the platform. Malcom glanced up at Otreya in surprise. Otreya just smiled. The lid was slid off of it, and the contents were visible. Scrolls. Now he remembered.

Hundreds of scrolls. Flickering torchlight. His hand cut open. Blood dripping down onto the parchment.

He knew what would happen next. Someone would have a knife.

Mem, on his right, held out a large dagger and her hand raised for Malcom to give her his palm. The man to his left—Malcom didn't know his name—proffered a heavy pendant. Malcom had worn it once before, but he wasn't sure he was ready for the weight of that thing. It had hurt last time. Hurt like the Derm.

He drew in a breath and let the man place it around his neck, but it wasn't heavy at all. Had it changed, or had he?

Mem cut Malcom's hand across the palm, and his blood dripped down onto the scrolls, mingled with the blood of countless others. The pendant on his neck started to pull at him, but it didn't hurt. It was light, solid. Like it wanted him to keep it, wanted him to do this. The faces and candlelight in the room disappeared for a moment. He closed his eyes and felt a strange kinship with the scrolls his blood had just been poured upon, then opened them and saw that his hand still dripped. It didn't hurt. Nothing hurt at all.

He took a breath, and it was the most natural breath he'd ever taken. Otreya's gaze was glistening with tears, and he wore a smile too wide for his face. *That's what this was. In the crypt. He'd been testing me. Testing my blood.*

Otreya raised his palms. "According to the manner set out by the first Derev Orion, Malcom Orion the First has had his blood shed on the commandments of his ancestors, with the approval of the Castle Guard, and has taken his rightful place as the Orion king of Serengard."

Malcom's eyes darted to Mikel's again. They were burning and blustery—the opposite of Otreya's gleeful, insane happiness.

Mem reached over and squeezed his shoulder. "You are the most powerful man on earth, Malcom."

{38}
ᶁгащ

COLSTADT HAD NEVER SEEN PIER like this before, though he'd heard tales. Kierstaz said he'd beaten Trzl with a whip until she'd passed out. Colstadt hadn't believed it, but now he did. The reality of it was making his blood curdle.

Pier had taken Idelviss into a small room near the staircase and tied her to a chair. He'd covered the windows, asked for a lone candle to light the area, and set to work.

That was thirteen hours ago. Now she was bloody and he was frightful and the tales she was telling were disturbingly strange. Sunn and Gernan stayed in the room to watch, and even they were pale. Whether he intended to or not, Pier had made certain that Gernan would have no regrets about killing him. None at all.

"You're quite lovely, even with your skin hacked up," Pier crooned. "At this point, you can still be healed of most of these disfigurements, so let us talk like civilized folk, yes?"

Idelviss stared at him, her eyes dilated.

"Ah, so you're afraid to be forthcoming, are you? That I can understand. I'm not the kind to trust people myself. Ask Colstadt here."

His eyes glinted, and Colstadt clenched his jaw.

"That's all right. You're part-Drei, so you're a tough little thing. A few more broken fingers will be fine. Get us past certain hurdles and walls of yours and into the light."

"You are part-Drei as well," Idelviss hissed softly. She'd been saying things like this for the past hour. "You have their special stomach for blood."

Pier smiled slowly. "I do indeed, as you have. Many a border guard woke with his throat slit at your hand. I'm being forgiving in taking my time."

"Don't pretend you're not hardened like a stone, Drei. All of us are. Otreya doesn't make me a Chamberlain because he knows Drei cannot be loyal to principle. Only to themselves."

"And he is a principled man, is he?"

"Once you embrace the truth of it, the ice blood in your veins is actually quite nice." She leaned forward, but her eyes focused on Colstadt. A ripple ran down his spine. "You, olive-skinned boy. You have it in you, too. You thirst for this. The cliffmen are twice your size, but you know in the quiet and the dark you could take their lives without blinking. You know you are superior. You long to prove it to yourself, to be flush with that power."

Pier stepped deftly between her and Colstadt. "Col's been blooded. If you care to exchange body counts…"

"Don't pretend you care. You are an empty tomb as I. Admit that you would like to skin every Seren to the bone and reclaim the freedom of your people. You've been enslaved too long." Idelviss craned her neck to see Colstadt again. "You look like you could be pureblood. If you've killed, then you know. It is in our blood to make war—to be dominant. That is why my father doesn't trust me, and why you should."

Pier tipped his head. "Your father?"

"Trzl is not his granddaughter," Idelviss spewed. "She is his daughter, and so am I. If he dies, all of his power falls to me, but if I am already dead, all of that power falls to Trzl instead, you see? You don't want me dead if you're planning to kill the wizard. Not unless you think you can kill Trzl, too." She looked smug, not afraid. Strange. "You don't want me dead."

"See, you could fib your way through this, or you could be honest and it would hurt a lot less." Pier slid a knife into her forearm and gave her a neat vertical cut that came dangerously close to her wrist.

Colstadt wanted to throw up.

Idelviss moaned through her teeth, but after a few moments of bending over double in the chair, she sat up again. "I am not lying. I have nothing to lose except my life. Don't kill him and don't kill me. Trzl is your enemy. Kill her."

"Are you jealous?" Pier looked puzzled, but he was smiling. "You're jealous. Och. Makes things more difficult for both of us, making up tales that Otreya can pass on his powers."

"He can! His powers are learned, but wizards can transfer that power if they share blood."

"That is preposterous. Ah, well. I need to break your toes, I see."

"No! Otreya tried crossing his blood with a pureblood Drei to see if his powers would be replicated in me, but they weren't. Drei strength overshadowed his. That is why he was so afraid of the Drei race. That is why he sought to conquer them all."

Pier grinned evilly, but Colstadt saw a glint of belief in his eye. "And if you inherit his powers, they will be inert? You shouldn't tell me things that you want me to hear. It makes me quite certain I will have to burn every inch of your skin off of you before we are finished."

Colstadt turned to face the wall, convinced the world had gone mad. That Pier had gone mad. And that surely Gernan had as well if he thought it perfectly fine to be yet another manifestation of Trzl. He pulled back the curtain just a sliver, enough to watch the eastern skyline as he had every day since he'd been out of the dungeons.

There it was. A rider with a banner. *A teal banner.* His heart pounded madly in his chest. "Just kill her, Pier."

Gernan ran to the window and grabbed Colstadt's arm. "What did you say?"

"I said, kill her. She's a liability." Colstadt pulled back the curtain an inch further so that Gernan could see, but he frowned in puzzlement. "The banner. In the west, toward the border."

"Where?"

Colstadt grabbed Gernan's sword out of his sheath and cut him on the cheek in one swift motion, but he couldn't reach the keys to unchain Pier. Sunn drew her own weapon as he sprinted toward the staircase.

"Sunn!" Colstadt called. She met his eyes, and he knew her answer before he asked. "Choose your side now."

There was no hesitance. "Yours," she answered calmly.

Gernan flinched, his voice deep and angry. "You'll regret this, imbecile."

"Unchain Pier," Colstadt demanded.

Gernan growled. "I think not."

Colstadt glanced at Idelviss. She was dead. Pier must have stabbed her immediately.

Pier held the dagger in his hand in front of him. His voice was quiet, serene. "Who is out there?"

Colstadt tried to hold in his elation at speaking her name, but it flew from him in full force. "Kierstaz." It sounded like the first bird of spring.

Pier blinked, smiled. "Don't worry about me, then."

Gernan had two knives in his hands, no doubt from somewhere inside his armor. "Neither one of you can take me." He took a step toward them. "You'll have to run, bastards, and you won't get far."

Probably not. Colstadt's leg hadn't healed well. He hadn't told anyone, but it hurt to walk, much less run.

Sunn swallowed hard. "I'm sorry that it has to be this way, Gernan." She threw a knife that hit him in the right thigh. Gernan cried out, pulled it out of his skin, and hurled the knife toward Sunn, missing wildly. He threw another, missed again. He had only one now, in his left hand, and he ran toward Colstadt with it raised.

Pier lashed out at just the right time, caught Gernan in the shins with the chain that held his ankles. Gernan went down, the dagger in his hand coming far too close to Pier's wrist.

Colstadt ran back into the room, but Pier waved him off. "Get out of here." His knife was busy slashing at Gernan's armor, his hands wrapping chain about his neck. "I can look after myself, youngling."

Colstadt caught his eyes for one moment. Pier gave him a nod.

Sunn was already down the stairs. Colstadt sprinted after her.

{39}
Besieged

THE ROOM WAS SEALED, BUT Mikel pressed himself against the door to be the first one out. His presence fulfilled one last requirement of the ceremony—the Guard must be there. Well, he was. Malcom's Captain of the Guard was here.

Otreya used the secret ceremony of the Orion family down to the slight shaft of filtered light falling on the original Books of Derev written in Derev's own hand, the blood of Malcom mingling with that of millennia of kings. And he was wearing Kierstaz's teal stone, the pendant of the heir to the throne.

To top off the elaborate display, Otreya himself placed a crown on Malcom's head. Petrolai's crown. It must have clattered off in the square of Ashlin just before they impaled his head on a spike fourteen years ago. Mikel wished he had a spike for Otreya, but then he laughed bitterly at himself. Could he ever kill anyone that way? Probably not.

When the door opened, Mikel fell through it, staggered as fast as he could up to the ground floor and fresh air. No one seemed to notice him or care, save Otreya. Every time he glanced behind him, the man was there, surrounded by guards, focused intently in Mikel's direction.

Mikel squared his shoulders and tried to steady his heart. They were both coming up those stairs in a few moments, and he had to be composed. Blank and empty.

Trzl was the one who met him first, a shallow smile on her face. She grabbed his arm and said through her teeth, "You did well not to raise a word. Otreya would have stabbed you."

"You could have warned me."

"Otreya wanted to see your mettle."

"What does he care? You're killing me after this."

"Not yet."

"Can I speak to Malcom? I am, after all, his Captain of the Guard." He tried to give her a humorous smile, but she could surely read through it.

"I'm sorry. You can't." She walked away.

Malcom passed, entirely surrounded by a group of guards. The crown on his head had disappeared. He glanced over his shoulder, and there was understanding in his eyes. He knew what had just happened. What it meant to them both.

Otreya came up behind him. "Bravely done," he cooed.

Mikel felt himself begin to sweat again. "I hadn't a choice."

"Oh, but you did. I wonder, do you care so much for your own neck? Would you protect it again if I told you why you are still living?" There was a glisten in his eyes that told Mikel he probably did not wonder anything. He was far too many layers of pretend.

"No." Mikel answered flatly. He turned and followed the stream of guards into an open hall, the chains at his ankles clacking softly. He was glad to wear them. He wouldn't want to be free in this city. To be free would be to condone its methods. Better to be a prisoner. Better to be persecuted.

"Mikel Orion," Otreya said loudly, his voice carrying in the massive room. "You should join us on the roof. We have matters to discuss."

Mikel looked back at him. Were Trzl and Otreya getting that cocky? They didn't care. They didn't Dermed care. How could he not be a threat—this close to Malcom, this privy to their plots?

Finally going to attempt to kill me. Again.

Mikel leveled his eyes at Otreya. "Yes. I'll be happy to join you."

The roof was vast. The guards who shadowed him slipped back down the stairs, and he was alone with Otreya. Not exactly what he'd had in mind. The sky was heavy with clouds, but it was still beautiful. Being killed under the sky wasn't the worst thing, was it? But who was doing the killing? Otreya himself?

"You've been a real troublesome pest, Mikel of the Castle Guard, did you know?" Otreya leaned against a rail and took out a tiny piece of jewelry. He flipped it in his hand several times to mark the seconds.

"I gathered," Mikel answered stiffly. Inside, he started to calculate. The height of this building was substantial. Being dumped over the side would instantly kill a mortal. Could it kill a man of Otreya's resilience? But surely that was what Otreya wanted him to think of, else why would they be up here alone?

"But somehow, you've managed to serve my purpose at the same time. Trzl has come back to me, at last having triumphed over her old enemies, the Knights of Rilch. Your draw was strong, yet she overcame it."

Whatever that was supposed to mean. Mikel snorted. "I never had any power over her."

"Ah. Of course you would think that." He grinned, tossed the jewelry into the air, let it fall back again. "Do you know what this is?"

"I can't see it."

"It is the Orion marriage band. I took it off your father's dead finger."

Mikel flexed his jaw to hide the hollow feeling that shot through his chest.

Otreya put up a finger and pulled out another ring, as if this were a game of charades. "Ah! And another. The prince's royal seal. Found it after the bodies were burned down in the square. You see, even *I* am sentimental." He tossed both rings back and forth. "Do you know why I was not surprised to learn that you'd lived?"

"The Captain of the Guard cannot die in battle."

"He is clever. I wondered when you would start to realize that superstition holds truth. You didn't seem a likely student when I first met you. Far too certain that the world could be explained in a few short sentences, weren't you?"

Mikel shrugged. "There is still right and wrong, and right and wrong have always been rather simple."

"Says the shackled man. There is always right and wrong when a person feels he has been treated unfairly, but put him in a place of power... The only right is his own mind. There is no wrong." He smiled again, opened his hand toward the stairs as the sound of footsteps approached.

Mikel glanced back. Malcom topped the stairs, with Trzl behind him. He couldn't read Malcom's face at all, but it wasn't elated. It was calm. Accepting. *Dermed.*

"I have something for you, Mal," Otreya said. "The royal seal, given to the Captain of the Guard for the passing of judgments. It is time to destroy it. To place the passing of judgments in the hands of the king, where they belong. As Altrun intended from the first."

Malcom's brow wrinkled in confusion. "I thought you said Altrun was wrong."

Otreya smiled until his eyes crinkled. "Only because he hadn't the clemency and wisdom that you have in you already, Malcom Orion."

Another set of footsteps approached, but Mikel didn't dare tear his eyes from Malcom's face.

"What position is he losing now?" a heavily accented voice asked coolly. Gernan. "Whatever it is, I'll take it, as I usually do."

Mikel didn't turn to look at him, but he sensed his nervousness and smelled a little blood on him. That calm facade of his was trembling. *Who nicked you, Gernan?*

"Don't concern yourself with it, Gernan," Trzl said drily. "The Castle Guard has always been a bane."

Otreya only smiled. "Oh, but we did need their presence for the ceremony to be a success. A shame they are such sticklers against reproducing when we need them to."

Mikel's eyes flickered to Trzl for a moment. She shifted, her face a mask of unreadable emotion, but he could tell embarrassment was in there somewhere. She ignored him, but no one else spoke and the minute grew long.

"I could have had him if I'd wanted him," she said finally. "Surely a bounty on his sister will pay off. And there's always the girl."

"The girl whom you misplaced." Otreya glared at Trzl. "You have failed me in this, Trzl. Quite thoroughly."

She winced. Her eyes glanced toward Mikel's, and she threw her hair back. "I will find her."

Otreya let out a long, heavy sigh. "Of course you are forgiven. Besides, your son can easily redeem you."

Gernan drew his sword from his sheath, slow enough to let the full effect of it drag out. Mikel glanced at him out of the corner of his eye. He looked guilty, like he was hiding something. There were cuts and slashes on his face, blood pulsed from a wound in his leg, and he held his sword in his left hand. "Ahem," he said loudly.

Trzl nodded. "Yes, Gernan is here for a reason. You're late, though, Gernan."

"I was delayed."

"By what? Who've you been fighting with?"

"No one important. I took care of them." Gernan's chin jutted toward Mikel. "Poetic, isn't it, Marek?"

Mikel laughed raggedly. "Quite. Not exactly the way I'd imagined it."

"I did warn you."

"Yes, in many ways." Mikel didn't give Otreya the satisfaction of another glance. The old man couldn't have known how successfully he was stabbing Mikel in the gut. Dying on the sword of a young man he'd taught to fight was going to hurt enough, but doing it in front of Malcom was truly cruel. Trzl knew that. Trzl of all people should have had the mercy to sentence him to a real execution.

Gernan rolled his head around on his neck, shook out his shoulders. The sword in his hand glittered, but his voice was dry and almost pained. "Well, at least arm the man, won't you? I'm not going to stab him through without a fair fight."

Otreya glared heavily at Gernan, his gaze focused. "No, he is not to be armed."

Trzl frowned. "A duel is not a battle, Grandfather. At least let them sport it out."

Otreya addressed her without breaking his gaze from Gernan's. "Not a risk we need to take, I'm afraid. On with it."

Gernan shook his head slowly, his eyes starting to glaze over. He looked back to Trzl. "I answer to her."

Otreya looked at Trzl himself, a dark glare between them. "On his knees," he fairly bellowed.

Trzl put her fingers to Mikel's shoulder. Her touch sent a shiver down his neck, his spine, to his toes. He wished she would do it herself—run him through, as she had run his heart through years ago. If he could only hate her enough to turn and strangle her right now, he would, but he couldn't make himself do it. Not in front of Gernan, whom he'd always tried to impress mercy upon, and not in front of Malcom, who'd always given him grace.

Did that make him more selfish? That he valued his own integrity more than he valued the good it would do to have Trzl dead and gone? Had that made his father more selfish when he'd left the decision of whether to kill Otreya to his son, who'd let him go for the love of a girl?

You're right, Trzl. I care about Serengard very differently than you do. I care what they see. I care that their hearts are not empty. I care that they know strength and forgiveness and that they know it in the depths of their own souls.

Malcom stepped in front of Gernan, his arm raised as if to call a silence. It startled Mikel just how tall he was, how broad his shoulders were, that flush of assurance on his cheeks. "A moment, please? Am I not king, and is he not my Captain of the Guard? Who authorized this execution?"

Otreya laughed nervously. "Come, come, Malcom. We're done with him. Didn't he hold you captive against your will, sell you to bounty hunters and the like? He is Castle Guard. He stands between you and glory, and he is a renegade and a marauder." His eyes snapped wildly, and Mikel realized with a sick twist that Otreya wanted Malcom here for another purpose: to blood him.

A single ripple of victory ran through him. *Too late, you bastard. Kierstaz already did.* Mikel almost smiled. He threw his chin out and looked at them defiantly. *I'll be free soon, Aura. We won't have to dream apart anymore.*

Gernan swung his sword with a half-grin on his face, his eyes dead, as if this were a joke. Mikel almost wanted it—anticipated the slick blood pouring out of him, the last breath leaving him. *Do it, Gernan.*

Otreya clucked his tongue. "Make him hurry it up, Trzl."

Malcom lunged forward and grabbed the sword from Gernan, swung it wide, catching at the leather cuffs on Gernan's armor. The air, already thick and heavy with fog, seemed to steam up and then freeze over. All four of them stopped thinking and breathing and stared at Malcom.

He held the sword with a sure grip and the stance of a man, not a boy. Then he turned it on Otreya. "That is the last order you give my mem. She answers to me, not to you. You have never caused her anything but pain."

Otreya's brow darkened. "I raised her. I protected her. I groomed her. She is *my* creature."

"She isn't." Malcom took a step toward him, flicked the tip of the sword up and then down as a threat. "None of us are yours. Not her, not Gernan, not Mikel. You can go back to the Derm where you came from."

Otreya laughed a rather hideous laugh, but it was shaky. "Put the sword down, Malcom."

Malcom stared down the eyes that had cowed so many and took one step closer. "No."

Trzl put out a hand to Malcom. "My son, put it down."

Otreya took a step toward Trzl as if she would shield him. Maybe she would. His bright blue eyes were still fixated on Malcom's. "I know the two bloods that battle within you, boy. I know the Orion will try to assert itself at times, but I know whose blood is more potent because I've seen the impotence of Hodran and the strength of Trzl. I know which part of you is stronger. Although, perhaps I was unfair to invite you to an execution." He laughed again, nervously. "I may have taken that a little far. Forgive me."

Malcom shook his head slowly. "I don't forgive you."

Mikel drew a sharp breath in. *Don't fight him over me, Mal. Not worth it.*

Otreya shrugged, his fearful look dissipating. "Oh, well then." He grabbed Trzl and held a slim dagger against her throat. Her eyes grew wide. She grunted softly, but didn't struggle.

"No!" Gernan was the one who shouted it. Mikel didn't say a word.

Otreya hissed through his teeth. "Your mother can die, if you wish. Only be assured you'll not be able to handle the rush of power that will overcome you when *I* die. It's one or the other, my boy."

"You won't do it," Malcom said, but his voice was shaking.

"Oh, yes, I will." Otreya's eyes glowed hot, his words spewing from his mouth in a ragged lack of control. "Trzl was only a small part of my plan. She never guessed that she was the conduit of so much. You inherit all of it, Malcom, don't you see? Ages of planning. Hundreds of things you don't know yet, but you shall be privy to. So put the sword down."

Malcom swallowed hard. The fingers that held the sword started to move, to slip.

Mikel grabbed Malcom's wrist and wrenched the sword out of his hand, and without another moment's hesitation, he shoved it under Trzl's arm and into the side of Otreya's chest, knocking him to the marble stones of the roof. Trzl fell with them, the dagger still tight in Otreya's hand, wrapped around her neck.

"You can't kill me, Mikel of Petrolai," Otreya hissed.

The wound didn't even bleed, and he struggled to free himself. Mikel held him down, but the man was insanely powerful for how old he should be. Trzl didn't move, the dagger tight across her neck, a few drops of blood starting to drip down the blade as it pressed into her flesh. She looked up at Mikel, unblinking, as though she were dead already.

He held the sword down with all his might. There had been a slight chance that there was a drop or two of Orion in his blood, but it must not be. Either that or the Books of Derev were figurative after all. Otreya could have been using them as fodder for his own tales, the better to manipulate Malcom. But Malcom wasn't going to watch his mother bleed out at the hand of his grandfather, not if Mikel had any choice in the matter. He held Otreya down, waited for his own strength to wear out, for Gernan to stab him in the back or hit him over the head with the hilt of another sword. He would let go when he had to and not before.

Suddenly, Otreya's eyes went wide with terror. Mikel felt a heavy shove in his shoulder, and Malcom pried the dagger out of the old man's fingers.

By all the faeries.

Malcom wrapped his hand around the hilt and plunged it into Otreya's neck. Blood spurted everywhere, but Mikel didn't turn his face away. He watched the light go out, the breath slip away, the consciousness leave him. Otreya's eyes turned purple and white and red, and then went blank. It felt like a lifetime. Malcom breathed next to him, so fast and loud that it sounded like he was going to faint. When the body stopped moving, Mikel stayed there, focused on his face. Malcom didn't move either.

The first to speak was Trzl. "Well, that's over." She was already standing behind them. Mikel hadn't even seen her move. She let out a soft cry. "What happened to Gernan?"

"He tried to stop me," Malcom answered. He sounded numb.

Mikel stood, staring at the empty carcass that had been Otreya for a minute longer before he pulled the sword out.

Trzl chattered on behind him. "He isn't dead, is he?"

Mikel wondered if he needed to slap her out of shock. "Yes, he is dead."

"No. Gernan."

Malcom still sounded detached, but he said, "I only threw a brick at him."

Mikel took the dagger out of the body's neck and wiped it on his clothes, handed it hilt-first to Malcom. A chunk of marble lay next to Gernan's massive frame—a chunk Malcom must've wielded. *Well done, Mal.* Mikel tucked the sword under his arm, picked up the marble, and smashed it against his ankle shackles at their weakest point.

"What are you doing?" Trzl's voice was steely and hard.

He smashed it three more times, and his legs were free. He picked up the sword again, walked to Gernan, and took the rest of his weapons.

Trzl raised her tone to shrill. "*What* are you *doing?*"

He went to the edge of the roof, found a jagged, protruding piece of marble, and slammed his wrist cuffs against it until they also broke. He glanced out to the east, then looked away as Trzl followed his gaze.

Banners. Aldadi tribal banners. A full flank against the eastern gate, swinging all the way around to block the south as well, nearly a thousand men. Waiting for a signal.

Well done, Natalya.

On the opposite hill, one lone banner caught the wind and made him swallow and wince. There were no troops, only the teal pennant. Someone was flying the banner of Orion. *Kierstaz?*

Without another word, he headed for the stairs, the weapons gripped tightly in his free hands.

{40}
Ветгач

COLSTADT FOLLOWED SUNN THROUGH ALLEYS and down dark passageways entirely devoid of the type of life he would expect to see in them. Of kittens, mice, and snot-faced children, there was not a one. The place was entirely too neat and orderly. A place for everything and no place for anyone.

"You are certain you know the way?" he mumbled to Sunn.

"You are certain you know the sequences?"

His leg hurt damnably. He bit his lip to keep from moaning. "I learned them on the ship, but my memory has always been..."

Sunn turned to give him a frustrated stare. "I'm not fighting my way up a tower only to have you forget how to figure."

"I'm not a Desert scientist, Sunn, but I know my numbers."

She shuddered. "This way."

Colstadt flashed a smile at her, though he hardly felt like smiling. "I'll be forever indebted to you."

"The Treacher you will, if I'm not impaled on a shiny city sword. I hate this place. I hate what we had to do to Gernan."

Colstadt knew this wasn't the time, but he couldn't help it. "What *we* had to do to Gernan? What of what he did to *us?*"

Sunn shrugged and shoved open a door in the inner wall that led to a staircase. She turned suddenly and whispered, "Stay behind me and pretend you're a servant. That damned nose and your eyelashes and your hair and…all of…this. Drei aren't allowed up here."

Colstadt scrunched his flat-bridged, pointed nose. "Then I hate this place, too."

She shoved on his chest. "Be silent."

They met soldiers as soon as they broke into the sunshine. Sunn tipped her chin and walked straight past them. The soldiers glanced at her uniform, looked at her face, and turned their eyes down. Afraid of cliff people, apparently. But one of them stepped up and stopped her.

"What are you doing with a Drei up here? Can't you see we're about to be invaded by them?"

Sunn squared her shoulders. "I've been sent up here to keep an eye on the situation. This Drei is my advisor, a traitor from their camp."

"Then why is he armed?"

"To protect himself from fools like you. Out of my way, please, I'm here on Emperor's orders."

The soldier let her pass, mumbling something about rules and improper documentation. They kept walking, following the inner curve of the wall until they reached the steps to a tower. Nearly twenty soldiers guarded the entrance, and there were sure to be more inside.

Sunn didn't waste any time with formalities. She drew her sword and held it out with one hand. "Which one of you wants to open this gate for me?"

Hands went to sword hilts.

She struck out first. Colstadt unsheathed the sword he'd stolen from Gernan, a heavy, cumbersome blade he wasn't accustomed to. Didn't matter—he was still excellent with it. But they couldn't kill them all fast enough, not in broad daylight. An alarm was raised, and more swarmed toward them.

96

MIKEL HADN'T HELD A WEAPON this bloody in a good while. The knives he used right away, saving only one, tucked into his belt. The sword, though not Seren steel, was balanced well. It nearly sang as it sliced through bodies he couldn't look at, couldn't count. Anyone who was in his way.

Allel forgive me.

The irony hit him as he stole a horse from the guard building: this time, the rebellion was his. This time, he'd started the bloodshed.

The gate was heavily guarded. There had to be more than thirty. He knew he could handle thirty. He'd done it before and survived. He stood in the middle of the main street and demanded, "Where are the sequences entered?"

Someone stepped toward him. "Who do you think you are?" He gestured to the blood on his clothes. "You wounded?"

Mikel kept his left and right flanks in his vision and glanced back to be sure no one had come up behind him. "I'm the Captain of the Guard."

"Like the Treacher you are."

Mikel fought them until reinforcements came, and then he fought the reinforcements. He hadn't any armor, which made him vulnerable, but it also made him quicker. He'd gone months with shackles on his hands, and they were ready to be free. He made it to the gate tower twice, only to have to fight men coming up behind him, drop more wounded and dead into the street. They weren't well trained. None of them.

Or perhaps they were and he was just stronger than he'd thought. He'd always been too good of a fighter—too good for what he wished he could be: a farmer, a husband, a father. Perhaps, as Kierstaz said, that came from being the grandson of King Rendl, the greatest Captain of the Guard to ever live, or perhaps it came from killing men every year of his life.

He was bleeding from too many gashes to count by the time he made the top of the gate tower on the outer wall, and his right leg was cut so badly he could barely hobble on it.

There was a massive oak door in front of him, locked with a heavy iron bar. Mikel slammed his body against it, and it gave. He hadn't thought he was that heavy. Maybe it was adrenaline. Maybe nothing in his way was actually strong. His left arm was dangling uselessly at his side. Damn left arm.

The sequence was entered in levers—four sets of four. He closed his eyes and pictured the numbers Pier had whispered to him and Colstadt on the ship. When he opened them, Trzl stood behind him. In her hand was a long dagger, one he'd seen her use before. He'd known she'd follow him. To what purpose, he wasn't sure.

"What do you think you are doing?" she rasped out. Her eyes were wild, her hair tumbling from her tight bun.

He would have laughed if his body hadn't hurt so damn much. "These gates are only raised to let armies in and out, are they not?"

"You wouldn't dare." She stepped up close to him and held the weapon against his ribs. "I'm not a soldier. This is not battle—at least, not yet. And my dagger is poisoned."

Mikel shook his head at her. "You really think that will stop me?"

She laughed. "Do you have an army, Mikel? One you haven't told me about? Oh, is it Kierstaz? She's here, you know. I was just given word." She drew back with a jolt, as if the idea had just now occurred to her. "You didn't...*you* didn't send for her, did you? You said you didn't want her here." Her eyes dilated wildly. "But you can tell her all is well now. It is our city—*ours*—to do as we please with. I'm going to make everything worth it. You'll see." She put a hand to his cheek and smiled.

"I've seen you make it worth it." He grabbed her arm and pulled, gently enough not to hurt her but hard enough to throw her out of his path. "I'm giving you the chance to surrender. You should, you know. They may not look like much, but Desert science is a frightful thing when it is applied to war."

She looked out of the tower, and he heard her swear under her breath. "What are *those* banners? Some new allies of your deceitful sister?"

"Aldadi. I wasn't always as alone as I am now." He gestured to the tattoo, still visible in spite of the blood on his shirt. "This mark has meant nothing to your eyes, true? You should have bothered to learn a little more culture."

Her voice hardened. "You did this? To me? How could you turn on me in this way?"

Mikel ignored her and pulled the first lever, the second, the third. "Forgive me, but you've never been what I call trustworthy."

"If you are going to destroy Malcom's reign, I would rather you kill me, too."

"That is the most pitiful thing I have ever heard you say." The fourth lever. Again starting at the first, second, third. Each in a different slot at a different time. It took concentration, and he barely noticed the dagger at his back or the blood pulsing from his arm. And his leg.

"Mikel." Trzl's voice grew cold. "Mikel, turn around."

He did not spare a glance. "I'm not going to give you the satisfaction of fighting you, Trzl. Not today. I'm too Dermed tired."

She ran at him, and he caught the wrist that held the dagger with his right hand. The last set of sequences. He moved the levers with his bloody left arm, though it barely obeyed him.

There was a heavy rumble as the tumblers set off a chain reaction deep in the guts of the mechanism. The gate creaked. It was going to open. Trzl screamed at him.

"*No!* Don't!" She struggled against him, her breath coming in shallow gasps. "Those tumblers will take an hour to bring that gate up. It will take an hour to close it again. Don't you know that is our most defensible..."

"I know, Trzl. I know. You told me about them."

Trzl shoved her dagger straight through his stomach. His body crumpled, the last of his strength gone in an instant. He grunted once, put a hand to the wound. It gushed blood far too fast. Faster than he'd ever bled. It didn't hurt, though.

"Mikel." Trzl knelt next to him. Her went eyes wide with horror and hysteria. "I... Don't die. I don't want you to die!"

He didn't have any breath to answer her. For a moment, he winced with regret. Kierstaz would never get to hold her trophy of a throne in front of him and tell him how well she'd fought for it, how well she'd won.

You'll be fine, Kiers.

"I'm sorry." Trzl started to cry. She picked up his shoulders and held his head in her lap, stroking his hair. "I'm so sorry. I don't know why I did that. Please don't die. I need you, Mikel."

Mikel's vision was gone or maybe just cloudy, but he still had the strength to whisper, "It's all right. You meant to since the day we met."

♊

MALCOM LEFT OTREYA'S BODY ALONE on the roof as soon as Mem ran down the stairs, but she left so quickly he wasn't even sure where she'd gone. He knew where Mikel went. He left a trail of bodies in his wake—soldiers who'd been in the wrong place at the wrong time. Malcom walked among them, checked their wounds, and called for physicians. He was still a little shaky. He ran back up to the roof, slapped Gernan's cheeks until he was awake, and hauled down flights of stairs to the main floor. He wasn't sure what would happen when someone discovered Otreya's body. Maybe panic. Maybe nothing. But he didn't want Gernan blamed for it.

He helped him out onto the steps of the Council building. "You all right?"

Gernan grinned sheepishly. "Most of me."

Mem drew a horse up to the front step and tossed a body to the marble street. A crowd of soldiers gathered about her so quickly that Malcom didn't have a chance of reaching her, but he ran and pushed on the crowd anyway.

Her voice rose up above the clamor with a shrill order, "Find me Vekst. Someone, find the Emperor for me!"

She didn't have to look far. Vekst was there, charging toward her with his brows drawn together. "What is the meaning of this?"

Mem stared into his eyes. "You must go to the east gate and ensure that it closes. I have set the reverse tumblers in motion, but you must enforce my orders. The army is in disarray and needs your leadership."

Vekst mounted a horse and left without a word of question. He must have been trained to do her bidding.

Mem raised an arm to another orderly. "Where is Otreya's inner guard? Why must I do everything myself? Find me the leader of the elite force or I'll—" Her eyes fell when she saw Malcom. "Mal, I need you to—"

They were interrupted by a detachment of soldiers reining in at the entrance to the quarter, one of them charging up to the steps. "The west gate is open, counselor. There is heavy fighting in the tower, but we cannot secure it to get the gate closed again."

Mem hit the man hard. Malcom flinched. "Damn you imbeciles! How can it be open? Have you sent reinforcements?"

He shrugged. "Of course. Not so many bodies can fit in the tower at once, counselor. We don't even know who is in there. They barricaded—"

"The eastern gate is of more importance."

The soldier blinked. "Begging your pardon, Chamberlain, but where is the Emperor? He has been informed that there is a larger force of Drei moving in from the south, has he not? Why are not all of the troops at full armor and on duty?"

"Oh, Treacher." Mem's face went white. "*More* Drei? Whose banner do they fly?"

He shrugged. "A teal one?"

"The Orion." Mem barred her teeth and grabbed Malcom's arm. "You see to this." She lowered her voice. "You know how. Use the power of your mind and get it done. Arm the gates with every soldier we have. I am going to the Emperor at the east gate. Let them know I'll be sending him to the west, so that as soon as our troops break into the tower, the man with the recognized authority can reverse the tumblers."

None of that made sense to Malcom. "Mem, I don't know how to run an army."

Mem laughed, and her eyes looked wild, flushed madly with the same distracting twinkle Otreya used to wear. "It isn't hard at all. Use your influence." She mounted a horse and kicked it toward a square now churning with soldiers.

Where are the commoners? Malcom suddenly asked himself. *Why would they stay in their homes, even as the world is falling down on them?*

Gernan cleared his throat behind him. "If she wanted that tower open, she should have sent my people. We wouldn't botch such a thing so horribly."

Malcom turned to look at him. "You are not reliable for anything right now, especially with that knot on your head."

"Not even the fact that I know who is in that tower? Your mem gave those sequences to Pier when we were in the Castle of Marek, Malcom. Not difficult to surmise who would be using them. Apparently, she forgot about me and the fact that I have one thousand men here, awaiting any command."

Malcom frowned. Was Mikel opening the gate? Or would…

His eyes finally focused on the body that no one had bothered to move from the street. His stomach clenched. Not the leap of anticipation, but a tight, sick feeling. He ran to it.

It was Mikel, every limb torn badly from swordplay, his face almost sleepy and serene. He wasn't dead, though, was he? Malcom had seen him recover from something like this before. Seen it with his very own eyes. He knelt down and listened for breath. A heartbeat. Anything.

Gernan peeled back Mikel's clothes and looked at the wounds. "I don't understand," he mumbled.

"He's alive, isn't he?" Malcom asked. He couldn't swallow. It made it hard to breathe, hard to speak.

Gernan's eyes were confused. He kept feeling for a pulse, looking at the wounds. "He…by the Derm."

Malcom finally filled his lungs, but they burned. "Is he dead?"

"I don't know. Without a Drei…" Gernan shrugged, but his black eyes were drawn. Dull.

"He's dead," Malcom pronounced. He must be.

Gernan nodded. "Yes." He stood up, adjusted his armor. "Well, I will need a sword if I'm going to be of any help to you."

"Steal one. Take a horse."

"What? And go where?"

"Take a horse and take Mikel. Ride out the west gate." He looked up, met Gernan's eyes significantly. "She'll want his body."

Gernan looked as if he'd been struck. "So she will," he whispered.

{41}
Requiem

KIERSTAZ KNEW THE BORDER WELL enough to slip through overnight. Sentries were felled easily, guard stations cleaned out. Quickly, quietly, as the Drei did everything. Theo's force got through first, enough to meet the gray dawn with a banner on the western hill, three miles from the city.

Kierstaz wished she had eyes inside the walls. If they headed down this hill, they would be going in entirely blind—not an excellent choice given the massiveness of the city and the impressive size of the Seren army that was believed to be held inside and on every rampart.

Her Generals said to show her hand and show it heavy, but she didn't want to storm the walls, even if she could be assured victory. Wouldn't that ensure the death of Mikel, Colstadt, Pier...possibly Malcom? And no certain outcome other than war with the Four Cities? She owed her warriors better than that. Far better.

Sark insisted that, without Malcom, she had nothing to negotiate with besides the formidability of her force. So she stayed on the hill, her banner in sight, waiting for nightfall and possibly for a sign.

I'm here, Colstadt. What are you thinking?

The sign came mid-morning when Crista burst into her tent. "The gate is open."

Sark, who'd fallen asleep when they camped, swung off his mat and grabbed a weapon. "Storm it," he said before they'd even stepped outside.

Kierstaz narrowed her eyes at the open gate, three miles away across sloping ground littered with carts and small buildings. Nothing too difficult. But the ground dipped about a half mile away from the walls. Anything could be in that dip.

"How do we know it's not a trap? Otreya and Trzl command that city as surely as anyone else does. It could mean anything."

"Doesn't matter. We may never be afforded another chance."

"They could be drawing us in."

"That could be your brother."

Kierstaz put a hand to her forehead. She knew that. But she didn't want to destroy her one chance to save him. She had to play this right. "Ready a force of five hundred," she said softly.

Sark left her side instantly to make preparations.

Kierstaz mounted a horse and rode out to the edge of the hill to stare at the gate. She wanted to go in so badly, her heart hurt with the need. *So close.*

Then a small detachment of soldiers rode out. Not Seren soldiers. They looked different. Kierstaz squinted at them. As they gained a few miles—across the dip in the earth, up over the rise again—she urged her horse and rode a few paces closer. Still, she couldn't see anything. Another few paces.

Slender eyes, wide brows, and sand-colored skin. Cliffmen. A shudder ran through her. The only reason cliffmen would be here was if they worked for Gernan. For Trzl. They had a body draped across a horse. Mikel? He was the right height, and his hair was blond. Did they come to offer terms? What had they been doing to him?

For a moment, she didn't want to know. She wanted him here in her arms, right now—alive, safe, speaking to her. She kicked her horse to double-speed. Sark came up behind her. He didn't say a word, just waved an arm to her lieutenants, also on horseback, and they shadowed her.

It was Gernan himself. He rode toward her until he was only a few hundred paces away. He raised a hand to say he came in peace, but before Kierstaz could return the gesture, he tossed Mikel to the ground. The body didn't flop or land gently. It was stiff.

Kierstaz trembled with rage, a scream in her throat. "Gernan! You Treacher!" she shrieked at the top of her lungs. "I will kill you!"

Gernan turned his horse around and spurred it. Kierstaz galloped down into the dip after him but reined in when she reached Mikel's body. Sark galloped past her, his arm out to tell her to stay. Another horse whipped past her. Theo. They would have Gernan before he was in range of the walls.

Christa dismounted next to her and tore Mikel's shirt off his body. She let out a soft gasp.

His skin was rent so badly in places that Kierstaz could see down to the bone. She cupped his face in her hands and whispered against his cheek. "No, no. Come back, little brother..."

"How could he sustain such wounds?"

"Is his heart beating?" She knew the answer. His skin was already cold.

Christa gave Kierstaz a blank stare. "He hasn't any blood left in his body, my queen."

Kierstaz went cold. Her arms wouldn't respond anymore, not even enough to pull Mikel up against her. She laid her head down on his collarbone and still the cold spread. She didn't feel rage or hatred or pain anymore. Just cold.

Christa gripped her wrist, but it tingled like an icicle. "My queen, how did he do this?"

Kierstaz stared into the soft grass. It crinkled with frost. "He was the Captain of the Guard. He wasn't ever supposed to die."

♄

MIKEL'S BREATH GREW SHALLOW ENOUGH that he didn't bother to try. A blush of warmth filled him from the inside out. He'd always thought dying would be cold. Most things were cold for Serens.

No, it *was* warm. A breeze picked up and took him away from the frigid stones of the east gate tower of the Fourth City. He lost sight of Trzl, and relief like he hadn't known in a long time flooded him. He shouldn't be happy. He shouldn't be pleased. But he was—he was pleased through and through. He slipped into unconsciousness.

There was a dark, miry thickness about him for a moment, air he couldn't breathe in. There were voices here, people he knew. Malcom? Gernan? They were far away. He had a moment of wishful reaching, of wanting to tell them things. Malcom, you are mighty and wise. Gernan, don't play the fool.

He woke to sunshine on his face. Sand on his bare feet. He knew both were there before he even opened his eyes. His fingers brushed little stones on the Desert floor. Jasper? Opal? Pearls? Was this a dream? He didn't dare open his eyes.

But it was so warm. Even if it was a dream, even if it would hurt him to feel the beauty of this place and wish he could keep it, he had to open his eyes. He wore only a plain white wrap with a bare chest, much like he'd been working a forge. The scars on his arms were gone, and there was no longer a hole through his stomach.

"I've missed you, my one," Aura's voice said—full, warm. The breeze in his hair was actually her fingertips.

He wanted to speak, but he couldn't right away. He stared at her, hoped to Allel she was real and that he wouldn't wake. In the distance was a city. Not Perena—it was too small for that—but it was tall and sandy, with banners atop Seren moats, a combination that wasn't earthly.

"Am I dreaming?" he rasped softly.

"No." Aura trailed a finger down his face. He'd never felt that in his dreams before. Ever. Mikel closed his eyes and tried to hold the sensation inside of him, but when he opened them again, she was still there. Still smiling. Still holding his head in her lap.

He swallowed tightly. "This is real?"

She nodded. "Real."

"Where have you been?"

Her face broke into that clear, thorough smile that only Aura had. "No, my one. Where have *you* been?"

Acknowledgments

I literally cannot thank my editor, Becca Weston, enough. Without her, my books would be footnotes instead of masterpieces. Darci Cole, your story brain is the cream to Serengard's coffee. Thank you for your patience with me, for pulling this novel through so many shades of weird, for being there.

My second line editor, Brianna Shrum, you're incredible, and I look up to you in a hundred ways. Brett Jonas! Girl, reading the manuscript three times with your eye for detail? I am so, so lucky to have you on my side. Hugs forever.

Coley, Elisabeth Garland, E.M. Castellan: your hearts keep me grounded. Seriously. <3 Amanda Aszman, H.E. Griffin, Jenny Perinovic, the best CPs and beta readers a writer could ask for, and priceless friends besides. xoxo!

Gina Denny, Megan Eccles, and Lauren Garafalo, thank you for critiquing the blurb until it shined. Hafsah Laziaf, for the cover reveal and just being a wonderful shoulder. Asma Laziaf of IceyBooks.com, Mara Valderran, Kathi L. Schwengel, M. Andrew Patterson, you're wonderful for reviewing my words.

Shauna, Faith, Esther, Katie, and Crystal, for propping me up. Always.

My little boys: thanks for letting Mama write in the middle of your days. Love you to the moon and back! My husband: thank you for the art, the dinners, the babysitting, the story tuning, the belief in me. For everything.

Everyone who bought *Coldness of Marek* and *Knights of Rilch* reviewed it, blogged about it, sent me those beautiful emails that made me melt, you are the bomb.

The Mystical

ALLEL (ah-**lell**) — the Creator God, a singular being who created man and gave him free will and dominion over the earth

CREEPER (**cree**-per) — a creature of Seren lore thought to inhabit only warm places and drink the blood of humans

DERM, THE (**dur**m) — common word for a deep pit where evil beings are believed to be encaged

DERMED (**dur**-med) — sophisticated swear, referring to something kept in the Derm or deserving of the Derm

FAERIE (**fay**-ree) — a nearly human being believed to inhabit the northern reaches, capable of seducing humans to act against their will, and interfering with the spiritual realm

GREMLIN (**grem**-lynn) — a nearly human being believed to inhabit the southern reaches, capable of manipulating the seas, and interfering with the physical realm

GOBLIN (**gob**-lynn) — a small evil spirit being believed to live in the Derm, allowed to come up to earth and dwell wherever evil is present, capable of manipulating the minds of humans

TREACHER, THE (**tre**-cher) — the most powerful evil being, sometimes believed to be a fallen faerie, opposed to humanity and intent that they should fail.

THE EARTHLY

ADELWEED (**ae**-del-weed) – Seren swamp flower used for poisoning mortally wounded animals or vicious predators

ALDAD (**all**-dawd) – the Desert lands of the Aldadi, kept by their tribes since ancient days

ASHLIN (**aj**-lin) – the first city of Serengard, built in the days of the first Derev Orion

BEREKST (ba-**rek**-st) – Seren port city built in the days of Marek Orion

CAPS, THE (caps) – glacial mountains in the far north, tapering into cliffs in the east

CIAR (see-**arr**) – border castle built in the days of Marek Orion

DERC (dirk) – border castle built in the days of Tame Orion

DORSCHT (door-sht) – Drei trade city, the youngest and wildest

DREIBOURGE (**drye**-borg) – the land of the Drei, ruled by the Eight Generals enstated by the great Drei warrior Hugo in ancient days

ELLOYA (el-**loh**-yah) – an uncharted chain of islands believed to be the land of the Elloyan pirates and traders who have ruled the seas since ancient days

GUARDIAN, THE – Drei fortress at the entrance to the Gorges

GORGES, THE — a treacherous mountain range kept by the purebred Drei as a refuge since ancient times

LINDT (lint) — Drei trade city, built when the first treaty with the Serens was signed

MAREK, CLIFFS OF (**mair**-ick) — uncharted multi-leveled cliffs that have existed since ancient days

NEROI (ni-**roy**) — Seren city by the southern border, a major port of trade since the days of the second Derev Orion

NERVYET (nerv-**yet**) — Seren Kymsai city in the north of Serengard

OPAL ROOT — used in Desert science to disorient prey

PERENA (per-**ee**-na) — city in the west of Aldad, known for its many priests

SERENGARD (**sair**-in-gard) — the land of the Seren, ruled by the line of Orion since Derev Orion in ancient days

VIENSTRAUSS (**veen**-strowss) — Drei city, built by purebloods in the days of the pirate wars

ZURIK (tz**oo**-reek) — Drei city, commonly called the oldest city

The Human

ALDADI (all-**dawd**-ee) – ancient word meaning "keeper of the desert"

ALTRUN (al-**trun**) – Seren name meaning "steadfast". An Orion, second son of Calum, father of Izannah.

AURA (**arr**-ah) – Aldadi name meaning "of northern light"

BEHRET (bay-**rhett**) – Aldadi name meaning "fortuitous"

CALUM (**cal**-um) – ancient name meaning "dweller in the light". An Orion, son of Tame, father of Altrun.

COLSTADT (k**ohl**-stat) – Drei name meaning "great leveler"

CORSAI (core-**sye**) – appointed by Tame Orion to organize tributes and uphold trade within the cities. An expansion of the Kymsai.

CRISTA (kr**iss**-tah) – Drei name meaning "anointed"

DEHLI (**dell**-ee) – Aldadi name meaning "full of flowers"

DEREV (**dair**-ev) – the name of the first Orion, or righteous king of Serengard

DREI (**dray**) – ancient word meaning "keeper of the trees"

ELLOYAN (el-**oh**-yen) – ancient word meaning "keeper of the seas"

GAVRIEL (**gahv**-ree-ell) – ancient name meaning "messenger"

GERNAN (gur-**non**) – cliff name meaning "horseman"

GRET (grett) – Drei name meaning "powerful"

HODRAN (**hoe**-drin) – Seren name meaning "brought up in peace"

IDELVISS (i-**dell**-viss) – Drei name meaning "pleasant"

IZANNAH (iz-**ahn**-na) – Seren name meaning "bringer of dark"

JENS (yenz) – Drei name, meaning "prophet of good"

KARAMOV (**kar**-a-mov) —Seren name meaning "owner of all". An Orion, son of Marek, father of the third Derev. Another Karamov led in the Border Wars

KIERSTAZ (**kee**r-stahz) – Seren name meaning "spoken for"

KOVIM (koe-**veem**) – ancient name meaning "torn from cloth". First Emperor of the Four Cities.

KYMSAI (kim-**sye**) – appointed by the first Derev Orion to keep the lands, to ensure a fair crop every year, and enforce the law that every man plant a field. Once Serengard became rich and plentiful, Tame Orion added the Corsai to oversee the cities.

LADIN (la-**deen**) – Aldadi name meaning "rebellious one"

LIA (**lee**-ah) – Aldadi name meaning "favored child"

LOMIUS (**lo**-mee-uss) – Seren name meaning "of the sea"

MAREK (**mair**-ik) – ancient word meaning "warrior"

MIKEL (mi-**kell**) – Seren name meaning "protector"

NATALYA (nah-**tahl**-yah) – Seren name meaning "dangerous"

NERRI (nerr-ee) – Aldadi name meaning "morning star"

NERSAI (ner-**sye**) – a slang term originated in the days of Izannah Orion, referring to any owner of land who adheres to the tradition of the first Derev Orion to plant a field every year and pay tribute

NORANI (nor-**ahn**-nee) – Aldadi name meaning "desperate fighter"

ORION (oh-**rye**-an) – ancient word meaning "chosen"

OTREYA (**oh**-tree-yah) – ancient name derived from the faerie lord of ancient lore, thought to be the first faerie that fell

OTTO (aw-toe) – Drei name meaning "loyal unto death"

PETROLAI (**pet**-ro-lye) — Seren name meaning "doppelganger"

PIER (pee-**air**) — Drei name meaning "born to betray"

RIC (rick) — Seren name derived from the ancient word "Rilch"

RILCH (**rill**k) — ancient word meaning "fruitless revenge" or "ill-fated vengeance"

RIYEV (**ree**-ev) — Seren name meaning "girl of the river"

ROMIANZ (**row**-mee-aunz) — Seren name meaning "loyal and ardent"

SARK (sark) — Drei name meaning "ransomed"

SEREN (**sair**-in) — ancient word meaning "keeper of the fields"

SERTETH (ser-teth) — Aldadi name meaning "snake charmer"

SUNN (sun) — cliff name meaning "strength of the stag"

TAME (**tay**-may) — Seren name meaning "valiant". An Orion, son of the second Derev, father of Calum

TANYA (**tahn**-ya) — Seren name meaning "soldier"

TEV (tev) — Seren word meaning "mean little dog"

THEO (thee-oh) — Drei name meaning "keeper of the streams"

TIERROF (**teer**-off) — Aldadi name meaning "gentle"

TOFER (**toe**-fur) — Seren name meaning "brilliant"

TRZL (**turr**-zull) — Seren name derived from the ancient word "Trz" meaning "daughter of faeries"

ULRIK (**ull**-rick) — Drei name meaning "broken-hearted"

UVEI (**oo**-vey) — Drei name meaning "music of the valley"

VEKST (veckst) — Seren name meaning "of the whale". Second Emperor of the Four Cities

ZVEN (tsven) — Seren name meaning "thunder"

Limited Edition Trading Cards

based upon the Serengard Series

four characters released with each novel

find them on **rachelolaughlin.com**

turn the page for an excerpt from

SERENGARD: BOOK FOUR

BLOOD
of
ASHLIN

the final sequel to

COLDNESS OF MAREK,

KNIGHTS OF RILCH,

and RISE OF ORION

Coming October 2015

IRINA SCREAMED WHEN SHE SAW him—dressed in hard black leather, taller than most men, with arms that could rend a lion. She knew who he was. He'd been down here before, talking in buttery tones to the serving maids, but now he had his sword drawn and his gloved hand grabbed Irina by the front of her dress, pulling her out into the narrow hall.

Baskets and casks tumbled. He ignored them, yanked on her chin, shoved her face from side to side, inspecting her features with calfskin gloves.

"Don't—" Irina started, but the words stuck in her throat.

He mumbled to himself—something that sounded like "*not here*"—and then yanked on her arm, pulled her out into the main kitchen, and threw her against a cold oven. His gloved finger traced her collarbone, pulled the fabric away from her shoulder as if in a fury, but his frown lightened as he cupped the bone.

"Perfect shoulders," he whispered.

Irina turned her face away, eyes closed tightly. She was afraid she would be sick. "No."

He tore off the top two buttons and slid his hands into her dress for half an instant. Irina panicked. She twisted her body away, flung herself as hard as she could, but still she barely moved an inch. He held her in too many places. Protests came out as whimpers. Her lips formed the words, "*Please don't hurt me,*" but she couldn't speak them.

Another voice cut through the fog in her head. "Rendl, you're scaring her."

She knew that voice.

Hands slid inside her waistband, down to her hips, pulling them toward his armor-encased body. "Let her be scared. She should be."

Thumbs graced her pelvic bones, then he grabbed her arm with both hands and yanked until her body recoiled against his. He wrenched on her dress and ripped it off of her in one tear, leaving her in her underclothes.

Irina screamed again, but he stifled it with his glove. She wished she had grabbed a knife in the pantry. He hadn't touched her hands and forearms— she could have secreted it in her sleeve. She dug in her heels against the stones and threw her weight away from him.

Rendl rolled his eyes, yanked her into him again, and tossed her over his shoulder. "Get rid of the rest of them," he snarled to someone. "Permanently."

His shoulder was so hard it pressed into her lungs and up into her ribcage. Irina tried to fight with him, to grab his hair and ears and twist, but he didn't seem to notice. He carried her up flights of stairs and toward the royal wing of the castle, the one section into which a kitchen urchin like her never set foot.

Andre was behind them. Irina tried to capture his eyes, but he averted them, kept walking, face ashen. He nodded at her slightly, as if to tell her not to fear, but why was he doing nothing? Was his rank so much lesser that he was unable to help her?

Maybe the bloodshed in the castle spread to the Guard. Maybe Rendl won and he's choosing his prizes, one by one. Maybe I'm the fourth. The seventh. The nineteenth. But there was no reason why he would choose her. She heard that he liked to mess with experienced women with tall, shapely bodies. Irina was a child still and far too pale and willowy to be his type.

She wished Andre was not silent. Irina knew his fiancé, Miana, and she knew Miana would never marry a man who harmed children. But tonight, he looked like a bystander. Certainly not an ally.

The rooms Rendl hauled her through were empty—tousled, wrecked, full of broken furniture and clothing, but utterly devoid of life. He kicked open the door to a room where the slight pink of sunset was reflected on the walls and tossed Irina onto a bed so hard that it hurt her ribs.

She started to beg him, words she didn't even understand herself. The only one that recurred was, "Don't."

"Shut up," Rendl snarled.

Andre finally said something else. "Rendl, easy."

Rendl did not heed him. He grabbed her shift at the collar and started to tear it with both hands. One wrench. Two. His grip was so powerful it ripped the cloth all the way down the front to the hem, and it was gone. He met her eyes then, and it was like looking at death.

"Don't ever wear anything like this again. Burn your nasty rags. And forget you ever lived in that hovel of a kitchen."

Andre finally grabbed his brother by the arm and shoved him out of the way. Impressive because Andre was much smaller. "Damn you, Rendl. You're hurting her."

She wasn't as scared of Andre. He didn't glance at her naked body; instead, he handed her the torn undershift to hold in front of herself. Rendl pulled things out of the closet and tossed them on the floor, on the chair, on Andre. Irina took the chance to climb farther onto the bed, all the way up to the headboard, and curl into a ball beneath her ripped shift.

And then she saw it. There was blood everywhere—inky stains on satin sheets, a murky smell that made her throat close up. She tried to stand up so she wasn't sitting in it, put her head up on the wall, but there was blood there, too. She couldn't breathe, and she was out of screams.

Rendl threw a red silk gown at her. "Put it on. And stop crying. Don't be a baby."

Was she crying? She felt sick, like she was part of some game of his. How she managed it, she didn't know, but she raised her chin at him and said, "I won't."

It was the first thing she'd said that hadn't been a request. For a moment, she wanted to take it back, afraid he might unsheathe a dagger and stab her—or, worse, take her to the dungeons and use some of the torture devices.

"I...won't." It was less sure the second time, but she leveled her eyes at him. *I'd rather rot in the Derm than do your bidding, bastard.*

Rendl's eyes physically hurt her skin—more than his hands had. She didn't want to be looked at that way again. Ever.

Andre caught her hand and held it gently between his fingers. She didn't resist. He pulled her into his arms slowly, picked her up like she was a baby.

Rendl snorted. "Don't coddle her."

"She's a child, Rendl."

"A child with hips and breasts. You're a princess now, girl. Your name is Izannah. You own Serengard, you own this palace, you own me. These are your things, and this is your room." Rendl paused.

At last Irina looked at his face—truly looked—and saw that he was worn. Exhausted. There was anger in him...and sadness. He was shoving it onto her to get it off of himself.

He gestured. "And that, Izannah, is your blood."

About the Author

Rachel O'Laughlin grew up writing adventure stories on an archaic laptop that only ran one program, couldn't connect to the Internet, and died every few days—which provided a nice excuse to use a typewriter in the middle of an epic murder scene. After high school, she pushed novels to the backburner for immersion in the arts, tours with her band, and a hands-on education in sustainable living. At last, she admitted to herself that she missed her first love and returned to fiction full time. She lives in New England with her husband and two kids, listens to The Fray, and drinks too many lattes. *Rise of Orion* is her third novel. Find her online at **rachelolaughlin.com**.

Author photo by Dan Tare.